Ultimately, we know deeply that the other side of every fear
is freedom
Mary Ferguson

The heart wants what it wants

Emily Dickinson

Introduction
August, 1986

CHAPTER ONE

August 12, 1986

I can't believe what I just did. In a way, I was more like me than I've ever been, except when I'm playing the piano, but...wow, I can't make myself write it in my own diary.

He couldn't stop staring at me, he's the most perfectly gorgeous man I've seen in my life, and I've watched him play football for the Edmonton Eskimos since last year (which shouldn't matter). Still, Cecile Alexander is not supposed to be the kind of girl who meets a guy at a party, goes back to his apartment, and has sex with him. My parents will freak if they find out. That's an understatement. And they definitely don't need any more stress, right now.

The whole thing was like a dream. A Midsummer Night's Dream—I couldn't form a conscious, intelligent thought, and I felt like I was on drugs. I guess. I could hear a voice in my brain screaming, "Slow down!", but when Devonte kissed me it was like two parts of my personality were in hand to hand combat, and the part that tried to hold me back got pushed into a pit.

It's not like I attacked him, or anything. I mean, he had to undress me, because seeing him naked was...I don't know how to say it. I froze for what felt like forever, staring at my very first live penis, trying to get over how much it looked like a thick, one-eyed snake. Then Devonte stood behind me and started touching me, so I closed my eyes and imagined I was Apollonia in that scene in *Purple Rain*, where she's in Prince's bedroom and she lets him put his hand between her legs. In front of a movie camera! I felt embarrassed for her every time I saw that scene, but I get it now, because Devonte made me feel so good, I don't think it would have mattered who was watching. Even God.

I'm so weird, though, because even when he was giving me an orgasm, I was listening to myself making high-pitched shrieks and him breathing low and hard and thinking, what interesting counterpoint. Who thinks that? Even if they are musicians.

I came right there, standing in his living room. Then he picked me up like I was a baby, carried me into his bedroom, and put me on the softest sheets ever. I wasn't dumb enough to forget about the condom, but I didn't even need to ask. I can still see the way he smiled at me as he was putting it on. Kind of like he'd just won the lottery, and he couldn't believe his luck, which made me smile back the same way.

I thought he was going to crush me, because he was so big and muscular and...omg, he was perfect. So perfect I can't even put it in words. And strong. He held himself just far enough away that I could breathe, but close enough that I could still feel the heat coming off his skin. He smelled like Drakkar Noir, and I wanted to eat him, even though I thought that was a really gross idea when I read it in a book.

I wasn't sure I could pull it off, and besides, he really seemed to want to be inside me. No big surprise, but I still got scared and tightened up. I started wondering how he was going to fit, and then I started thinking that maybe I shouldn't be doing this, because there has to be a reason fornication is a sin. But I told myself it was too late to stop now, and besides, the part of me that had overpowered my home training wanted him inside me, too. So I took in a deep breath, let it go, closed my eyes and tried to relax. I cried out a bit when he pushed into me, because it hurt. It hurt even more when he did it again, so I said, "Devonte," about an octave above my usual range.

He said, "Yeah," like he could barely catch his breath, and I said, "I've never done this before."

He stopped for a second and his eyes got really big, like he was afraid, and he asked me how old I was. A little late, under the circumstances. Anyway, when I told him I was 17, he let out a sigh of relief, and asked me if I wanted to stop. Then he shut his eyes and his mouth twisted a bit, like it hurt him, too, and I thought, I may burn in Hell for this, but how can I stop in the middle of one of life's greatest discoveries, instructed by an expert, with a voice like a french horn and a chocolate-dipped body sculpted by Michelangelo? And he needs me. ME! Right now.

My throat went so dry I could barely get the words out, but I still managed to say, "Don't stop." He kissed my neck, and then he started pushing again, slowly, then faster and faster, pausing every once in a while to ask if I was okay. I was about to ask him the same thing, because his voice kept getting higher and tighter, but just then he stopped moving, with his eyes squeezed tightly and his breath coming in gasps. When he opened his eyes, he smiled at me again. Then he held me close. We were both really slippery, but I didn't care.

I wanted to ask him if he minded being second-string, but somehow I managed to realize how insulting that sounded before I said it. To be honest, I'm impressed he's good enough to play pro football in the first place, but since I've stopped being absolutely sure I'm good enough to be a famous pianist, I wanted to find out how it feels to settle. It was more than that, actually. I wanted to know how he feels about everything, and I wanted him to know how I feel about everything. I wanted to find out if it was finally safe to open up completely with someone. But I just lay there instead, liking how warm he felt beside me, not wanting to mess everything up by talking too much.

Then again, I couldn't have stayed long enough to find out his deepest secrets anyway, since Teresa and Edwin had followed me and Devonte to his building, and were kind enough to save my life by waiting downstairs. Dream or no dream, I wasn't out of it enough to think I could explain to my parents why I'd come home in a cab. Or worse, with a random guy. Or worst of all, with a guy my dad might recognize watching football on Sunday afternoon. The point is, I thought I was pushing it just hanging around for half an hour to absorb the afterglow. As it turned out, I was wrong, because when I knocked on the window of Edwin's car, he and Teresa were about as close as you can get to what I'd done with Devonte, with your clothes on.

Maybe they were too embarrassed, but I'm glad they didn't ask questions, since I didn't want to answer them. I just wanted to lose myself in the memory. And imagine the looks I'll get from the kids at school when they see me with Devonte Jones.

August 25, 1986

If I could be good enough to qualify as a piece of shit, at least I could get flushed down the toilet.

I can't watch football with my dad anymore, because I keep remembering when I was 15, and he said that if he ever found out I'd had premarital sex, he'd be so disappointed, he'd cry. I've never seen him cry, except when we buried Calvin.

I can't believe it's only been a month. I don't miss him, really—I'm sad he died, but I'm glad I don't have to deal with him anymore. Not missing him is the worst part, in a way. Maybe it will hit me later on.

I probably had sex with Devonte because life is short, and I didn't want to die a virgin. That's a lie. It kills me, though, thinking how much it would hurt my dad to find out. Even if I still don't believe what I do with my body should be as painful as losing a son.

I can't look my mom in the eye, either, now that I'm neither pure nor unstained, or whatever that Scripture says. I'm just glad Betsy doesn't seem to need a role model, because I keep thinking what a crappy excuse for an older sister I am, setting such a bad example. And for what? A guy who definitely doesn't know my last name, and probably doesn't even remember my first name. Come to think of it, I only know his last name because I saw it on his jersey. I'm such a fucking moron.

What did I expect? We danced a lot, and smiled a lot, but we barely talked to each other. Then again, aren't you supposed to be able to connect to someone without saying a word? I know he felt it. How could he seem so into me, and not call me? Maybe because I didn't know what I was doing. But I would have learned. He could have taught me. Didn't he like me at all? Why act so sweet, then? Maybe he just takes pride in his work, and I was one of hundreds of satisfied customers.

I was going to show him off at high school? Like that would ever happen. I mean, why would a grown man who can have any woman he wants choose a nerdy, teenaged beanpole? So what, he thought I was beautiful. I bet every woman he's ever laid is beautiful. I also bet none of them are misfit losers who play classical music and can never figure out when to speak, and when to shut up.

I keep hearing songs in my head: "Mona Lisa," "Where is Love," "Alone Again, Naturally." I don't want to be a cold and lonely work of art. I don't want to ask where there's someone who I can mean something to. I don't want to always be alone. Maybe I should have given Isaac another chance. Then again, we were 14, he isn't very bright, and I never liked him that much. I never seem to like anybody who really likes me that much. I know it's pathetic to worry about this stuff, at my age.

Maybe it isn't, though. Maybe I should start preparing myself for the inevitable. Practice six hours a day instead of four, because I'll need to be even better than I thought, if I'm going to have to look after myself for the rest of my life.

I'm so sorry, God. I'm so sorry, Mom and Dad. If I ever meet another guy who wants me like that, I'll make him wait until we're married. Or at least until I know he loves me.

I'm going to stop thinking about how Devonte looked at me, and what a great kisser he was, and how it felt when he touched me. And I definitely won't think about touching him, or having him inside me, or how incredible it felt to give him the orgasm he needed. The problem is, the more I think about not thinking about it, the more I think about it. And smile.

I'm going to burn in Hell.

CHAPTER TWO

"Hey Langston," said Mr. Zappatore, poking his head into the kitchen, "Marcus is here."

Langston continued to rinse a pot he'd just finished scraping. He often wished that the osso buco at Gino's tasted less delicious, because the cleanup was never much fun.

"What does he want?" he yelled over the sound of the water.

"Dunno. I told him you were off in fifteen minutes, and he said he'd wait."

"Is that okay?"

Langston turned off the tap and faced his boss. He'd been working at Gino's for a year and a half now, since the summer before twelfth grade, and he didn't want to do anything to jeopardize their almost familial relationship. Langston had tried his best not to make a stereotypical comparison, but he couldn't help it—when angry, Mr. Zappatore's weathered face reminded him of a much older Sonny Corleone. Which wasn't a stereotype, come to think of it, because despite his prominent role in *The Godfather*, Langston had never thought James Caan looked Italian.

Thankfully, just then Mr. Zappatore looked more like Brian Piccolo.

"Every member of the Andrews family is welcome at Gino's," he said, with a smile. "Especially when they buy something."

Langston chuckled, and continued to clean, his grin fading as soon as Mr. Zappatore disappeared through the door.

Something was up. Langston's family might be welcome at the restaurant, but if they came down to the Little Italy section of Toronto, he never knew about it, because they never stopped in to see how he was doing. His menial job was anathema to them. Or more accurately, it was anathema to Grandma Felicia, which meant that anyone else's acceptance of the situation had to be covert.

Or conditional. Langston's eldest sister, Zora, had actually stood up for him when they'd gathered at Grandma Felicia's for Canada Day. Probably because her husband, Bernie, had stood up for Langston first—even though Bernie had dealt with Grandma Felicia for years, having met Zora in Sunday school, somehow he didn't know better.

When Langston arrived at his house in Scarborough that July 1 at four in the afternoon, eager for a Canada Day barbeque, everyone else had already eaten.

"What happened?" he said, glancing at the plates of leftovers sitting on the dining room table, and then at Marcus, who had opened the door.

Marcus motioned with his head towards the kitchen. Langston ventured inside. His grandmother was taking an apple pie out of the oven, bending her knees with difficulty, leaning away just enough to keep the thin strand of pearls that dangled from her neck from touching the pastry—as usual, she was overdressed, in a mid-calf pink shift whose only concession to the casual menu was a lack of sleeves. She placed the pie on the table, next to an identical pie and a plate of homemade gingerbread, gazed at the golden crust admiringly, then pulled off her oven mitts, her arms jiggling as she did.

"Get the pie cutter for me, darling," she said without looking at Langston, her Jamaican accent still as strong as it had been when she left the island generations ago.

He sat across from her, thinking about the countless pies that had been served with this very tool as he passed it across the red and white vinyl tablecloth.

"Thanks," said Grandma Felicia, expertly dividing the pies into equal portions.

There was a silence as she maneuvered her short, chubby frame onto a step stool. Langston jumped up to assist, but she waved him off, retrieving glass dessert plates from the cupboard. Langston sat down again, debated, then decided he was just resentful enough to risk a possible verbal beating.

"You ate?"

"We left you something."

Langston watched her putting portions of pie onto the plates. When she finally looked at him, he spoke.

"I thought I told you my schedule."

"You did."

"So..."

There's no point to this, Langston realized. He stood up, and was about to go back into the dining room to get his dinner when Bernie and Zora came in, laughing. Even after two children under the age of four and eleven years together, six of them as husband and wife, they still seemed to enjoy each other. Twenty-one hadn't seemed too young to marry when Langston was thirteen, but now that he'd turned nineteen, he couldn't imagine it, despite their positive example.

"Hey, man," said Bernie, clasping Langston's hand firmly. "You made it."

He was a wiry man with ebony skin, a few shades darker and five inches shorter than Langston at not quite 5'7", but he had large hands and feet, as Langston had overheard Zora telling one of her friends with a knowing laugh.

"Seems I'm a bit late," Langston couldn't resist saying.

"But you're just in time for dessert," said Zora, choosing a piece of gingerbread, then taking a bite.

Grandma Felicia glanced at her. "Do you need that?"

Zora took another bite. "Yes, Grandma," she said, "because I want to be what you always call yourself. 'Stout but stylish'."

Zora kissed her grandmother's cheek, smiling. Langston tried not to smile, too. When puberty came for Zora, at the age of twelve, her petite frame filled out into an hourglass, much to her grandmother's dismay. A big part of the reason Grandma Felicia liked Bernie was that he managed to keep his eyes off Zora's chest, at least in her grandmother's presence.

"Am *I* allowed to get fat?" he asked playfully, reaching for a dish of pie. "'Cause if I'm not, it would help if you'd stop cooking so well."

Grandma Felicia grinned, making a clucking sound.

"I didn't want to be in time for dessert," said Langston, "I wanted to be in time for dinner."

"Well, if you didn't spend so much time scrubbing some white man's toilets, you would have been here," Grandma Felicia fired back.

Pointless, Langston reminded himself, his stomach clenching.

"A job is a great way to learn responsibility," said Bernie mildly. "Plus, he'll graduate with money in the bank, which is a good thing."

"We've done enough cleaning up after white people," Grandma Felicia countered, her hands on her hips. "Slavery ended a long time ago."

"He's going to college!" said Zora. "This isn't a career, it's just a job. And what kind of job is he going to get with no experience?"

"There are lots of other jobs," said Grandma Felicia, her voice rising. "And now that he has experience, he could get one of them. If he wants to scrub floors, he can do that around here."

"Not the way you like them done," said Langston, as evenly as he could. "Besides, I'm not a janitor."

"You're a dishwasher and a busboy, most of the time, but you also clean the bathroom. Don't try to deny it."

"How do you know? You never come down there."

"I know because you told me."

Langston considered explaining that he loved the smell of Italian food (any food, really), and that he wasn't just sweeping and scrubbing, he was learning, just as he had learned some of his grandmother's secrets before she started chasing him out of the kitchen—despite her feisty attitude about racial equality, she firmly believed that food preparation should be left to women.

It was impossible to change her mind, and besides, anything he said would probably be seen as an attack. He couldn't be disrespectful to his grandmother. She had raised him, Marcus and Zora, and was still raising his little sister, Maya, though at fifteen she was nearing the finish line. The alternative would have been foster care. The fact that she wanted the best for them was a blessing. A mixed blessing, at times, but still a blessing.

"It's temporary, Grandma," he said quietly. "You know that."

"We all know that," said Bernie.

"That's right," Zora added. "He's going to quit the day he graduates."

Everyone looked in Langston's direction. "Right," he said. "Anyway, I'm hungry."

He was always hungry. Grandma Felicia spent a lot of time scrutinizing Zora's weight, but until junior high school, Langston had been the chubby one. He'd discovered exercise that year, or rather, he'd decided he disliked it less than being fat.

Eventually, he fell in love with letting his legs carry him wherever he decided to go—around the track after school, through his neighborhood, over the ice in the winter. He took up hockey relatively late, adding just enough weight training to avoid getting his new, slimmer self killed when guys from the other teams smashed him into the boards. He was the only black kid on the team, and a popular target; if he'd had doubts that the two things were related, they disappeared the first time some asshole whispered, "Nigger!" at the point of impact. Which only made him more determined to play, much to Grandma Felicia's delight. She made it clear that she didn't enjoy hockey, but went to all of his games anyway, just to see her grandson refuse to be intimidated.

#

As he emptied the sink at Gino's, Langston asked himself why he could absorb physical punishment and verbal abuse over and over at the rink, and yet his brother could upset him just by deciding to show up at his job. He couldn't find an answer.

Langston dried his hands and took off the dark green apron he always wore in the kitchen, grateful, as always, that his fade was short enough that he'd been spared a hairnet. He took a deep breath, then nodded a goodbye to Vince, the dapper maitre d', and Mario, the genial head cook, and pushed open the black double doors that led to the dining room.

It was nearly 11 p.m. on a Thursday night and the restaurant had already closed, leaving Marcus and Mr. Zappatore alone in the dining room. When Langston came in, Marcus picked up the white plastic to-go bag that had been sitting in front of him, and stood. Mr. Zappatore shook his hand, smiling again, and headed for the kitchen, waving to Langston as he did.

"Goodnight, Mr. Zappatore," said Langston. Then, he turned to face Marcus, watching his brother extract a small box from the bag, open it, and pull out a cannoli.

"You want one?"

Langston shook his head.

Marcus took a bite, and Langston held the door. They walked past a row of Gino's College Avenue competitors while Langston waited for Marcus to finish eating, then Langston said, "What's up?"

"I have something really important to tell you."

"Such as?"

"Danita and I are getting married."

Langston stopped walking, laughing with relief. Then he grabbed his brother's hand, pulling him in for a soul handshake and patting him on the back. Marcus broke into a broad grin.

"When?" Langston asked.

"We're working that out."

"When did you ask her?"

"Yesterday. I figured I should come down here and tell you, to make sure you heard it from me."

Langston frowned. "Meaning?"

"It's the sort of thing you should tell your family yourself. Gino's is the only place I'm sure I'll find you. Don't be mad."

Marcus started walking again. Langston hesitated, then caught up to him.

"Were you trying to make me mad?"

"No. Look, you're never home, especially now that

school's started again. You work, you work out, and you study. I mean, West Indians are supposed to be industrious, but..."

They turned left at the corner, heading past the depressingly generic brick and clapboard houses that lined Manning Street as they approached Bloor Avenue.

"I don't want to rely on Grandma Felicia anymore," said Langston. "She's done enough."

Marcus nodded. "Zora thinks you're trying to move out."

Langston's head turned suddenly. "Why?"

"She thinks you're tired."

"How could anybody get tired of living with Grandma?"

Marcus laughed. "You could always move to Edmonton and stay with Aunt June."

"If I liked freezing my ass off every winter."

Marcus shook his head. "We all get to leave, you know."

"Yeah, when we get married. I'd need a girlfriend first."

"Don't you and Glenda have a pact, or something?"

"Nope."

"Waste of a perfectly good woman, if you ask me."

Langston smiled. "I prefer her as a best friend," he said.

"That's what your wife is supposed to be."

Langston stopped again. "I'm nineteen, Marcus, and since my name's not Bernie, I'm not planning to get married when I turn twenty-one. Besides, I'm not in love with her. Should I go on?"

"Nope."

They were about to pass the pub on the corner of Bloor,

still bustling even late at night on a weekday, when Langston asked, "Can I buy you a drink?"

Marcus looked at him as if he'd just suggested they strip naked and rob a bank.

"To celebrate your engagement," Langston continued. "And wipe that look off your face—I'm legal now."

"You drink, though. Really?"

Langston rolled his eyes. "Every day, and all day on weekends. No, Marcus, I'm not sliding down the slippery slope. I just have a beer or something every once in a while, on special occasions. Is that okay, or does Al-Anon forbid it?"

Marcus smiled slowly. "You should really try it before you criticize it. Nar-Anon, I mean."

Langston moved away from him, just enough to let a couple who were so wrapped up in each other that they'd become oblivious to their surroundings pass between them.

"Who needs to try it with you and Zora around? I can pick it up by osmosis."

For a minute, the street noise seemed louder, and the distance between them much larger. Then, Langston sighed.

"I'm sorry, Marcus."

His brother turned toward him again. "It's okay. Hey listen, I'd love a drink."

"You don't have to..."

"I know. Neither do you."

"What do you mean?"

Marcus held his eyes. "You don't have to feel guilty about

wanting to move out."

Langston stared at the ground. "I don't." Then he looked up. "Do me a favor, though? Don't tell her? Grandma Felicia, I mean."

Marcus laughed. "I promise."

CHAPTER THREE

September 9, 1987

Survived the welcome picnic, but just barely.

Why is it so hard to just be somebody else? I mean, nobody at Juilliard knows me. Not that anybody really knows anybody, but whatever—it should have been easy. All I had to do was smile at people and make small talk. Whatever that is.

I sort of spoke to Allen from Philly, the guy at the registration table. First friendly black person I've met in New York. Then again, we're a dime a dozen, so why would it be like Edmonton, where we all feel like fellow soldiers in the war against irrelevance? Still, I hoped moving here would be like diving into a warm, welcoming pool of negritude. Wrong.

Allen asked where I was from, and I said Canada, and he asked me to be more specific, because it's a big country. Then he laughed at me. Or maybe it was with me? He did take my hand and look me dead in the eye when he gave me my brochures. I blushed (as usual), and of course the beige skin did nothing to cover it up—couldn't I have been born chocolate, like Betsy? Or with a clue how to deal with other humans, like Betsy?

Then again, I can learn, right? Or fake it? Like I fake being confident when I walk to the piano. Of course, I get caught up in the music when I sit down and start to play. Humans are trickier, because you never know what's coming next.

Allen probably wasn't flirting anyway—he seemed just as

enthusiastic about the next person in line. I think. He's kind of loud all the time, so it's hard to tell.

He's very cute—sleepy eyes and a chiseled jaw. And big. He could be a...football player. Which doesn't matter, because I'm done sharing my body with random men. Aside from the spiritual side of things, it seems like a smart move, in an AIDS epidemic.

There were all these other people I could have talked to after that, but I didn't know how to start. Everybody seemed to know each other, and I couldn't think of a good way to approach anyone. Not even Mr. Balog, which is ridiculous, since I'm going to start lessons with him in a few days. Then again, when I spotted him, he was in the middle of a conversation and I'd just put a whole meatball in my mouth, which made it hard to speak. I was really hungry, because Aunt Mimi isn't a very good cook (I may finally be forced to learn), but I'm lucky I didn't choke to death. Note to self: you're not a snake.

I can't believe I'm studying with Ambrus Balog. He was always a name on my music books: edited by _____. Or a name on my favorite recording of Brahms First Concerto. And now I'm studying with him. I can't believe it! I just wrote that.

He's so elegant. Really old, but very dapper, and his suit looked expensive. Plus, he has all of his hair. I hope he knows how to teach. I hear some of the people around here can play and sing, but they aren't great teachers. Fingers crossed.

Well, fingers crossed about New York, too. I can only imagine how many prayers Mom and Dad are saying, trying to protect me from the crackheads. I wasn't even sure they'd let me come here, but Juilliard is Juilliard, after all. Still, I know they're nervous about it. Mom warned me not to look people in the eye so many times, it became a joke. I wanted to ask if she thought New Yorkers were like dogs, and would see it as a sign of aggression, but I restrained myself. Just barely, though. And then there was the thing Dad said about standing back from the edge of the subway platform, because sometimes people get pushed onto the tracks. That freaked me out. Then again, if I ever end up on the tracks, getting anywhere near the gigantic rats I've seen down there would kill me before the train did.

Hopefully, now that I'm here I can stop having those nightmares about a big white guy in a black ski mask committing mass genocide with a machine gun. Then again, maybe I need to find a way to cope with being awake first. My heart was pounding just as hard, standing on the patio at Lincoln Center trying to figure out what to do after my plate was empty, as it does when I wake up from the piles of bloody, twitching bodies in my dream.

I ended up off to the side watching everybody, thinking about how there are a lot of big stars on the faculty. Then I started thinking that a lot of the students are little stars, and then I thought about the Mozart variations on "Twinkle, Twinkle, Little Star" I learned when I was in high school. For about ten seconds, I wondered if maybe I was a little star, too. Nope, because "pride goeth before destruction, and a haughty spirit before a fall." Right as usual, Mom.

I'm not here because I'm haughty. I'm living in Ed Koch's

messed up, amazing city because I'm a piano fanatic. I love music with all of my being, and I am grateful and so very blessed that I can play the piano, because I can bring life to the glorious visions of great geniuses. I want to be a transcendent artist because I want to be able to do music justice all of the time. I want it to flow through me, like it does sometimes when I can get my brain to be quiet, when I go to a place where I don't exist, because I am nothing more than an empty channel, filled with music.

That's my story, and I'm sticking to it.

I'm just a little bit out there. But probably not compared to the rest of Juilliard. Well, actually, I'm out of step with them too, because my mind is a weed-infested swamp. Then again, there are trees in a swamp with roots so deep, they can survive a hurricane.

I almost talked myself into asking Allen more about himself, but I was feeling too awkward, so I decided to check out Lincoln Center plaza instead. Sitting by the fountain in the middle and listening to the water calmed me down a lot, just by being repetitive and—watery. After a while, I looked up at Avery Fisher and The Met and wondered how tall they are. They're so beautiful, with all of that glass and stone, and the chandeliers in the opera house are such amazing works of art that I didn't even notice all of the tourists around me. It was like I was all by myself, which was fine, because crowds always feel like quicksand, to me, pulling me down.

New York is big, and kind of scary. So is Juilliard, but I'll be okay here.

I have no choice.

CHAPTER FOUR

Langston's height and athletic body refused to cure his awkwardness with high school females, so after a while he didn't bother to approach them, figuring he'd try again, with a fresh crop of women, in college. By senior year, his seeming disinterest had spawned rumors. If anyone asked about his sexual orientation, he always said, "I'm straight. Why do you ask?" No one ever answered him, of course.

His failure to grasp the narrow parameters of acceptable masculine behavior cemented the misunderstanding. It always struck him as ridiculous that real men weren't supposed to notice if other men were handsome, or watch foreign films or get enthusiastic about fine cuisine. At least, not in high school.

He blamed Grandma Felicia, since he and his three siblings had been taken from his parents and relocated to her two-story, red brick house in Scarborough when he was six. Maya, who was two at the time, seemed to have no memory of the Andrews' chaos, growing up completely immersed in excellent, home-cooked food; trips to art exhibitions, especially when his grandmother's paintings were being shown; plays (for many years, Langston's favorite was A Raisin in the Sun); and fine literature (he developed an early fondness for Dickens). Langston couldn't remember his former life either, although Marcus and Zora, who swore by both twelve-step meetings and therapy, kept trying to convince him he was repressing a lot.

"They need to mind their own damn business," Grandma Felicia frequently said, her Jamaican accent exaggerated for emphasis. Langston agreed. If his brain was working that hard to forget something, there had to be a good reason.

Grandma Felicia also inspired the qualities that sealed Langston's outsider status—honesty and integrity, characteristics so foreign to the boys he grew up with that by high school he could barely hold conversations with them, and so antithetical to what attracted teenage girls that he resigned himself to the role of sidekick. This meant he could have deep conversations with girls who otherwise wouldn't give him the time of day, in exchange for the tacit agreement that he not even think about touching any of them. Frustrating, but better than nothing. At least the fantasy women in his head when he masturbated seemed a bit closer to reality.

In the midst of that, he'd found Glenda, who had moved to Toronto with her family in 9th grade. They sat across from each other in science class, but they didn't acknowledge each other until they were thrown together by their science teacher, who decided that, since his desk was next to hers, Langston was the perfect frog dissection partner for Glenda.

He was picking up the scalpel when she said, "Who died and left you in charge?"

"Uh...nobody," he said, holding the tool out to her.

"Oh, so now you're trying to stab me?"

His eyes were wide with alarm. "I'm sorry...I didn't..."

"I'm kidding," she assured him, with a wide grin. "I

mean, I'll help, but....yuck! I don't mean to be girly about this, or anything, but can you imagine going to a pond and seeing that thing? Gross! Close your mouth, by the way. I'm not *that* weird."

They'd sought each other out ever since. And yet, somehow the idea of taking their relationship to another level had never come up. Langston was glad. He didn't want to lose her friendship, and, more importantly, he'd never found her attractive. He couldn't figure out why. She was short and her figure was boyish, but that wasn't necessarily a turn off, for him. Ditto her exotic blend of black and Asian features, which came from having a Chinese Jamaican mother (Glenda's eyes were somewhat like his, though, in her case, there was an obvious reason). Maybe it was her skin, typically a bright red moonscape of acne. Although after a while, he didn't even notice.

Despite the odds, Langston managed to lose his virginity before he graduated, through no fault of his own. It didn't make sense that Anthea Tanner, a girl who had seemed to notice he was alive only once (the day he'd accidentally backed into her in the hallway at school), was suddenly flirting with him, asking for his number, seeking him out after class. It was a dream come true, though, to be the companion of such a popular girl, and even better to imagine that she was brushing against him deliberately, perhaps even disregarding the usual assumption that his penis was completely incapable of being stimulated by female proximity.

The day she seduced him, he had gone to her place to watch TV and work on their calculus assignment. There had never been a hint of ulterior motives before, so when he sat on the couch and she put her head in his lap, he assumed she saw him as an extension of the furniture until she turned her face away from the screen, unfastened his jeans and centered on his crotch.

His initial shock gave way immediately, submerged by the physical awakenings her mouth expertly drew from his groin. He still wasn't sure what she was up to, though. Even with his lack of experience, the whole thing struck him as impersonal.

She straddled him, but there were no kisses, and while she let him touch her back, she never took off her shirt. At the time, he'd wrongly assumed it was because someone might come home, and doing more than just lifting her skirt and dropping her underwear would have made it impossible to cover up what had just happened.

Despite his misgivings, he felt grateful. Anthea had large, brown, almond-shaped eyes and voluptuous lips, and even though he wasn't allowed to touch them, her 36D's right there in front of him were almost exactly what he'd seen in several wet dreams (minus the fabric). She eventually let him kiss her neck, then her cheek, and he thought she might allow him her lips, but she stopped him with, "My parents are gonna be home soon," an announcement so frightening he didn't pursue the issue.

At the door, he held her hands and looked into her eyes, which were opaque, although her smile held something that could have been confused for affection.

"Thank you," he said, and her grin changed to a smirk.

"You're welcome. See ya, Langston."

He leaned in to kiss her, and she hugged him instead.

"Not in front of the neighbors," she whispered, releasing him.

He glanced back at her as he walked away. Was she shaking her head? What did that mean?

It meant she was about to call her girlfriends out of the den, where they'd hid and watched Anthea win a bet. That they were going to laugh together at Langston's facial expressions, even as they expressed pity at his cluelessness. That they would start calling him "Two-Minute Andrews" in honor of the quick release Anthea provoked.

Once the sexual encounter became common knowledge, an invisible wall was lowered, and Langston's male counterparts wanted to talk to him. Apparently, his membership in the elite club of those who had been physically intimate with Anthea immediately vaulted him up the social totem pole, regardless of the reasons behind the seduction.

His new status was no remedy for his shame. He couldn't speak to or even look at Anthea's friends, who mocked his coital facial expressions whenever he accidentally exchanged glances with them. He wished he had the nerve to speak to Anthea herself. Then again, he wasn't sure the words to convey his emotions even existed.

When he walked down the hallway, he couldn't tell who knew the story, and if so, how much of a description of his inadequacy had gone into the telling. So he spent the end of his senior year with his head down, speaking to no one except Glenda.

Two days before graduation, which was three weeks after Anthea had humiliated him, Glenda stopped by Langston's house unexpectedly, inviting herself in and leading him to his room. She closed the door, sat on his bed, and said, "Okay, Andrews, what's wrong with you?"

"What do you mean?"

"I mean, what's wrong with you. It's English."

"Nothing's wrong with me."

Glenda folded her legs beneath her. "You see, that would work with somebody who doesn't know you, but unfortunately I'm not one of those people. Aren't you happy you made it with what's-her-name?"

Langston was momentarily at a loss for words. He'd done his best to convince himself the only thing that mattered was losing his virginity to the prom queen. He didn't want to discuss the rest of it, not even with his best friend.

"I'll tell you your problem," Glenda said. "You thought that shallow bitch liked you. Didn't you?"

She was gazing at him with an intensity he hadn't seen before, and the edge in her voice was making him nervous.

He cleared his throat. "Maybe," he said. When she didn't respond, he continued, looking away. "I guess I figured she wouldn't have been so nice to me unless...but she let people watch and she told everybody I was...it's...it's embarrassing."

When he looked at her again, Glenda's face was softer.

"There's good money in porn, you know," she said, and Langston, caught completely off-guard, laughed uncontrollably, until he found himself crying. What the hell is wrong with you, he thought, hoping the tears seemed to be the result of the joke.

"None of these people," said Glenda, hugging him tightly, "will matter in a year, or even a month. High school is the high point of their lives, but you? You're just beginning. Fuck them— well, not literally this time..."

CHAPTER FIVE

September 16, 1987

I can't believe the pianos on the fourth floor! Yeah, they're Steinways, but some of those instruments are lousy. I know they get used a lot, but wow, isn't this supposed to be The Juilliard School? I'm sure all those instruments came with benches, so why do half the practice rooms have boxes to sit on? It's ridiculous. Sucks that people try to hold onto rooms with good pianos when they know they won't be back for two hours, but I get it. Good thing Aunt Mimi has a grand. Although I can't run home to practice in the middle of the day. I might have to start evicting people if they don't get back to their room in 15 minutes. The rules are on my side, after all.

I am the only black pianist! What's that about? Then again, all of the black instrumentalists come in ones or twos. There are quite a few black dancers and singers, though. Stereotype, anyone? Not that opera and ballet conform to the caricature, and I should also mention the actors. It's kind of a pressure situation for me, though, like I'm representing the right of my race to play the piano at this school. Whatever—that's stupid.

I'm starting to feel like my terror of dying a horrible, violent death here might have been unnecessary. I mean, if I'm in the wrong place at the wrong time, anything can happen, but there's no point worrying about it, right? If I die, I die. I could get killed anywhere. I like the city, so far—the excitement, the cool clothes, the energy. It feels like something interesting is going on, round the clock. I even like the smell of hot dogs and roasted nuts from the street vendors. And all the famous people play here. Of course, a lot of great musicians came to Edmonton, too. But if you can afford it, you can see and do anything in New York. Not that I can afford it, mind you.

Mom told me not to trust anybody, and not to look around too much, or everyone would know I'm new in town and take advantage of me. I really think she's wrong (for once). People don't stare at things that would draw attention in most places, like drag queens or couples arguing loudly on the street. But even though the sure indication that you're a tourist is craning your neck to look up at the tall buildings, I don't get the sense that all New Yorkers are just waiting for a sign so they can pounce. Maybe I haven't been in the right neighborhoods for that sort of thing. Come to think of it, those would be the wrong neighborhoods, wouldn't they? Whatever.

I think my classes are going to be pretty easy. Which doesn't mean they won't be stressful. Piano Lit with Mr. Dubal is definitely going to be both. I don't know what to make of him. He obviously knows a lot, but it's also like he's putting us on. I mean, does he really expect us to play every piece ever written by Liszt? And seriously, pound for pound, Brahms is better than Beethoven? Who cares?

I guess he wants us to think (which is dangerous, in my case!). Whatever. I like the old recordings he plays. I don't even know who most of those pianists are. Everybody else seems to, though. Guess I should have been listening to some Josef Hoffman with my Prince

Rogers Nelson.

Here's the plan: I'll just sit in the back and keep quiet and hope he doesn't call on me. Whenever he asks someone to play, he makes him or her wait for a good ten minutes while he explains how difficult the piece is to pull off. Nobody else seems to get nervous after all of that preamble, but I'd probably screw up the first measure.

One thing I hate about Juilliard is that people come around to listen when you're practicing. I see them, sometimes, out of the corner of my eye. Usually Asian kids, and they lurk near the window but not right in front of it, so you can tell they don't want to be seen. Scoping the competition, I suppose, but it's unnerving, because I can't play any of my pieces very well yet, because they're all new. And that Scriabin etude is killing me. I love it, though. Definitely worth the trouble.

They need to get a life. And I need to practice more at Aunt Mimi's.

#

For the first ten days of school, Cecile avoided the cafeteria, and even more than that, the student lounge; not knowing where to sit was an unwelcome throwback to freshman year of high school. The lounge, in particular, had clear sections: the dancers marked their territory by stretching on the light green carpet; the drama majors rarely seemed to venture out of their corner of the building, but when they did, the ones determined to use their theatrical intensity to own every room made the other corners less than appealing, too.

There were also the ethnic cliques. Cecile qualified for entrance in the tiny black subgroup, but everyone seemed to already know each other, and even though they always smiled when she passed them in the hall, she didn't feel comfortable intruding. One of them was familiar—Allen from Philadelphia, the guy she'd met at the welcome picnic—but he spent most of his free time in deep conversation with a girl who, based on the way they looked at each other, seemed a tad more than friendly.

Hiding in the practice room between classes felt like focusing on school, but in mid-September the windowless starkness of close, white walls, black pianos, and musty, navy blue velvet drapes became too much. As luck would have it, the first time Cecile felt compelled to take a break, the cafeteria was almost deserted. She bought a bottle of water, sat in one of the gray metal and plastic chairs at an empty table by the window, and took a long, cold drink, gazing down at Broadway.

Usually, Cecile didn't mind being alone. That day, she could feel herself nearing the abyss. The part of her descent related to the misfit inner Cecile who refused to go away, no matter how much her brain tried to kill, or at least ignore her, felt familiar, but this time, there was something more involved. A formless nightmare had startled her awake at five in the morning, prevented her from falling back asleep, and ever since, memories of her older brother's funeral had refused to stop playing in her mind.

She hadn't expected to mourn Calvin for as long as a year, but here she was, missing him, despite repeatedly wishing him dead. Her mind traveled back to the helpless terror he'd inspired every time she'd seen him high, the gut-level fury when her parents had catered to him, the shattering anxiety that her brother would cause their divorce when she sometimes overheard them fighting late at night, after she and Betsy were supposed to be asleep. She couldn't stand to listen to the recordings of Calvin's singing her mother had given her to take to New York, but on this day, Cecile couldn't escape memories of his voice, belting like Stevie Wonder or caressing each word as tenderly as Peabo Bryson, spinning phrases like Nat King Cole or riffing like Jackie Wilson, his tone an unlikely combination of liquid gold and sandpaper, his guitar a perfect extension of his body. She never looked at the pictures of him she'd brought with her, but on this day, his impish smile hovered around her no matter what she did, making focused practice impossible.

Sometimes, she could pull back from the edge of the pit, but others, depression became a black hole she had no power to resist. She always survived, going through the motions of life until the sun came out again, or soothing the pain by playing with a deeper level of expression, if the gnawing in her heart didn't hurt so much that she couldn't feel anything else.

She was halfway through with her drink when a voice startled her.

"You're a pianist, right?"

She looked up to see Allen, sexy as ever with his full lashes, sleepy eyes, and square chin.

Cecile's upper lip started quivering as she tried to smile at him. "Yes. You're a singer?"

"Guilty." He laughed. He always spoke as if he were on a stage, with every word well-supported by his diaphragm.

Allen pulled out a chair and sat across from her. "So I finally caught up with you."

Cecile studied his face, trying to tell if he was flirting or not. Didn't matter, now that she'd seen him with that other girl. He was cute, but she had no interest in being his side piece of ass.

"Meaning?" she asked, her nervousness dissipating along with her sadness.

"That you're always hiding somewhere. Some of us were trying to figure out why you don't want to hang around with the black folks. Then it occurred to me that you don't hang out with anybody. Except your piano."

Cecile's ears started burning. "I wasn't sure how to interrupt you guys," she replied, willing herself to resist a strong urge to look down.

Allen brought both of his hands down on the table with a resounding slap, making her jump. "I knew you were shy," he said triumphantly. "I told Tonya that just because you're a pretty, yellow woman with long hair doesn't mean you have an attitude. I mean, you were born with light skin. That doesn't mean you think you're better than everyone. Especially now. I mean, it's the 80's, not the 20's."

Cecile frowned. "Do people really believe that?"

Allen looked wide awake, which was saying a lot. "Wha-at? Where you been? No, wait...that wasn't a serious question, right? Oh, wait, I get it. You mean do people believe that about *you*, even though they don't know you. Right?"

"Well, that too," said Cecile irritably, setting her bottle of water on the table. "Look, where I grew up, there weren't enough black people to start dividing into groups for stupid reasons."

"Slavery really messed us up, didn't it?" He chuckled. "So, which of your parents is white?"

Cecile wrinkled her nose in disgust. "Neither, and wow, that's a hell of a question to ask someone you don't even know."

"Why? It's nothing to be embarrassed about. We all got white blood somewhere, pretty much. Or Indian, or whatever."

She paused, looking away. He had a point, but the question still felt offensive, somehow, or too personal. Like he knew why she didn't fit in, as a black person, but wanted confirmation. I'm probably too sensitive, she thought.

"My dad's mom was from New Orleans," she said. "Grandma could pass for white, but my grandpa was a dark-skinned Jamaican. They ended up in New York, so my grandpa wouldn't get lynched. That's where my dad was born and raised. I'm obviously not as light as

Grandma, but I'm still sort of a throwback, because my sister isn't this color, and neither is my dad."

"See?" said Allen, folding his arms across his expansive chest. "That was interesting, not embarrassing. Where did you grow up? You told me Canada, but I forgot the rest."

"Alberta. Near Edmonton. By the way, who's Tonya? Is she your girlfriend?"

"She's interviewing for the position..." He uncrossed his arms and leaned towards her— "...but I'm still taking applications."

Cecile rolled her eyes, picking up her bottle again. "Does that line actually work?"

He leaned back, unfazed, and grinned. "Depends. Hey, do you have a minute to read through an aria with me?"

Cecile glanced out the window, watching the movements of the tiny people and toy cars and trucks below her. Couldn't hurt, might be entertaining. Especially since there was no way she could ever take Allen seriously again, a sure cure for her natural introversion. She grinned back at him. "Okay."

"Great." His chair squeaked against the floor as he pushed back from the table. He waited for her to finish her water, and then stood, leading the way out into the hall, carpeted in the same unremarkable green as the student lounge.

Cecile wondered about the old Juilliard. She'd heard it was a much more ornate building somewhere in Harlem, now the Manhattan School of Music. Then again, the current Juilliard suited her fine. In fact, Paul Recital Hall, with its burnished wood, qualified as lovely, and the rest of the school was well-appointed, too. Just not very interesting, like most modern office buildings. She'd never cared much about fancy surroundings, anyway.

"Listen," said Allen, as they waited for the elevator to the fourth floor, "I know pianists need to practice, and this is none of my business, of course, but...you do know it's okay to hang out once in a while, right? I mean, you're in New York. You could stare at four walls anywhere."

Cecile glanced at him. "Are you offering to show me around?"

"I'd love to," he said, with a smile that implied his apartment would be the first, and possibly only, stop.

"So find out when Tonya is free, and we'll all go together."

He chuckled. "It ain't over till it's over, you know. Nothing wrong with being single and mingling a bit."

A high-pitched ding announced the arrival of the elevator. Cecile stood back to let the occupants and their instruments out, then followed Allen inside and pushed the button for the fourth floor.

"I don't believe in fighting with another woman for a man," she said, eyes up to watch the numbers change as the elevator ascended. "So if you want to read through some music, great. But if this is a job interview, I think you should forget it."

Allen shook his head. "I hear you, Ms. Cecile. But you can still sit at my table anytime. Got it?"

She smiled at him. "Thanks."

#

Later, after dinner with Aunt Mimi—tuna casserole made with noodles and cheddar, overcooked to the point that the cheese had formed a black, acrid crust—Cecile went upstairs, closed the door to her room, lay on her bed, and started thinking about Calvin again. She tried to imagine how her parents were feeling, considered calling them, and decided against it. After all, what was there to say? She knew she had no words of comfort to offer if her call upset them more than they were already. Then again, maybe they had found "a peace that passed all understanding;" if that was the case, she had even less reason to call, because she'd either have to lie about how far from peaceful she felt herself, or absorb a testimony that would probably make her feel worse.

I haven't called Teresa since I've been here, Cecile thought suddenly. She'd vowed not to waste too much money on long distance calls, but this one felt like a necessity.

"Hello?"

"Hey, Terri, it's Cecile."

"I was just thinking about you!"

"You were?"

"Seriously. I was going to ask you how you were feeling today, but I wasn't sure I should."

Cecile's stomach twisted into a knot. "Wow," she said, laying back against her pillow. "That's exactly why I haven't called my mom and dad."

"Seriously? You should, you know."

A splinter of guilt flew from Cecile's gut to her chest, threatening to lodge in her throat. She pushed it down by reminding herself how little her parents had done to protect her from Calvin's random spasms of violence. "Maybe later," she said, trying to hide her irritation.

"I hope so. None of my business, of course."

"Correct."

The awkward pause that followed lasted for a moment, which was how long it took Cecile to remember that she was paying for the call.

"Don't you want to know about New York?" she asked, choosing a tone of voice meant to convey that she was unoffended, but ending up sounding overly eager, like an actor on a kid's TV show.

To her relief, Teresa responded, "Of course."

"There are black people here, Teresa. Lots of them. But they aren't very friendly. Especially if you order fast food—oh my God! I don't even understand that level of hostility. I mean, is it my fault that you have a job at McDonald's? It's like they hate you for ordering something, then they make you wait, just because they can, and then they dare you to have an attitude. Not that anyone can have an attitude as big and bad as theirs."

"Well, that sucks. Especially for you, since you're not exactly the friendliest person in the world, either."

"I'm friendly!" Cecile protested, sitting up.

"No, you're not. I don't mean that you hate people, just that you won't speak unless you're spoken to, especially with men. Don't try to argue."

"I didn't come here to talk to people. I came to..."

"...become a great pianist, because that's all that matters to you. Bullshit."

Cecile chuckled, glad that Teresa couldn't see her cheeks flushing, deciding whether to be dishonest or to change the subject. Then again, a half-truth wasn't really a lie...

"There's already a guy who's interested in me. So there."

"Good work."

"I didn't do anything."

"I knew that. Who is he?"

So Cecile described Allen, leaving out the part about his shadow, Tonya, and the fact that Cecile had already decided he, like most human males, wasn't her type.

"Sounds interesting," said Teresa approvingly. "So he likes classical music, but does he like foreign films?"

"Probably." *Not.*

"Too bad you turned down the Toronto Conservatory, because I'd have definitely given you my friend Langston's number. You two would be perfect."

"Because?"

"It's hard to explain."

"Try."

Cecile bent her knees. When Teresa moved to Cecile's home town, she, her sister Karen, Cecile and Betsy were the only black kids on their block. Karen was in eleventh grade and Betsy was in elementary school, but Teresa and Cecile, who were also the only black kids in 8th grade, hung around pretty much by default.

Their friendship was based on more than just the color of their skin, though. Both were excellent students who loved football, Prince, and their second-hand Island heritage—Teresa's family was from Barbados; Cecile's mom was Bermudian, her dad, half-Jamaican. Both had plotted their escape to a place where bloodlines that went back to Africa were the norm, not the exception, although only Cecile had followed through, at least so far. Still, Cecile sometimes felt like Teresa and Betsy were laughing at, rather than with her, that her cluelessness in the practical matters of life—especially male/female relationships— was amusing because they found her ridiculous, rather than endearing.

"It's nothing bad," said Teresa defensively. "You and Langston are just both really shy. And you're into things most people don't enjoy, like foreign films or talking about current events. He's actually a very cute, sweet guy."

"Who lives in Toronto."

"Right. Never mind. So how do you like New York, otherwise?"

Cecile told her about the rats, the tall buildings, and the smells—garbage and pretzels and car exhaust—and the sounds—street musicians, blaring horns, and the deafening echoes of the trains in the subway. She said she was still a bit scared, but it was going away. That she'd hoped not to be in such a small minority at her school, but that she was determined not to let down her race by screwing up.

"Um...believe me, most of the race doesn't know you're at Juilliard," said Teresa.

"And they don't care. Yeah, I know, but I care. And I know that the other people there are waiting to see if I'm any good, and that they're not expecting much because I'm black."

Teresa snorted. "That's ridiculous. I mean, you wouldn't even be at Juilliard if you weren't any good, would you?"

"I guess not." It was the same rebuttal Cecile had been giving to herself. Somehow, it held more weight coming from Teresa. Since she couldn't explain herself in a way that felt logical, Cecile said, "Anyway, how's Edwin?"

"*Lawdamussy*, that man! Him too much boderation, y'see?"

Cecile laughed. "You'll marry him."

"Nope."

"Mark my words."

"But I can't stand him, half the time. Then again, the sex is amazing. Every time I smell him, I want to—"

"*Way* too much information, Teresa!"

"You're such a prude."

"Whatever. Can we move on?"

"You could learn something from me, you know. You might want a few skills for the next time."

Cecile's face was on fire. "Can you please stop? I'll figure it out when I have to."

"Okay, okay." Teresa paused, then said, "I need to go somewhere with more black men."

"Then why are you going to U of A?"

"Money. Actually, there are black men there. Most of them are

African, though, so you know they have no respect for women."

Cecile frowned. "Are you saying that on the whole continent of Africa, there isn't a man who respects women?"

"Well, since I haven't been to Africa and met every single man, of course not. But I've met enough of them here, and if they're representative, I don't want to meet any more."

"How many have you met?"

"Four or five."

"Hardly a scientific sample."

"That's why I'm planning to be a lawyer, not a scientist."

"You should move back to Toronto," said Cecile, grinning.

"You're right. Hey, Cecile? I have to go. Class has barely started, and already I've got an English paper due in two days. I'm supposed to analyze some crap written by a poet I can't even begin to understand. What's the point of poetry if it only means something to the person who wrote it?"

Cecile grinned. "Gives English professors an excuse to pretend they know a lot?"

"Probably. Well, talk to you soon. Okay?"

"Okay. 'Bye. Or maybe I'll write you a letter."

"That would be nice, but I won't write you back. I do enough writing for school."

"You were always really good at it in high school."

"But see, that's the thing. Just because you're good at something doesn't mean you enjoy it."

"I guess I'm just lucky."

"Yep."

"Well, have fun with your paper."

"Thanks." Teresa paused a moment, then asked, "Hey, are you sure you're okay? I mean about Calvin."

Cecile paused. The call had accomplished its goal—making her forget—until that moment.

"Yes. Thanks for asking, though, Terri. I mean it."

"Of course. So you're going to call your parents?"

"Yep," said Cecile brightly.

But when she did, all she said was, "I just thought I'd say hello."

"Hello," her mother said, drawing out the last syllable, a smile in her voice.

"Everybody okay?"

"Yes. And you?"

"I'm fine."

"I'm glad to hear that, precious."

There was a short silence, and then Cecile said, "Okay, well, I guess I'll get ready for bed. Tell Dad and Betsy I said hi."

"I will."

Her mother's cheerful tone reminded Cecile of playing a major chord and hitting a wrong note in the middle, but she was grateful to be spared a conversation about her brother.

Lying under her covers that night, though, she kept hearing Calvin's voice singing "Man in the Mirror," the song he knew irritated her the most, even though she had voluntarily listened to Michael Jackson's version at least a million times. She didn't understand how Calvin could sing those words, look in the mirror and change nothing. Why seeing how much it upset his family when he crashed—lying in his room for days, barely getting up to go to the bathroom—didn't inspire him to do better. Why he threw away his gift, why music wasn't enough to save him. Cecile and Calvin played together, sometimes, working out the tunes by ear, harmonizing effortlessly, both of them blessed with perfect pitch, and in those moments, Cecile loved him, felt that maybe she could reach him. But when he put away his guitar, he'd slip out of the house, meet one of his shady "friends," and return, transformed into his cocaine-fueled alter ego, an aggressive, cocky, motormouthed asshole who radiated dissonance to anyone nearby.

It was the cokehead Calvin who appeared in her dream that night. When she woke up, she couldn't remember what he'd said, only that she'd tried to hug him, and he'd pushed her away.

Her frustration followed her all the way to school, its grip finally loosening in her practice room, washed away by Bach, Scriabin, Chopin and Beethoven.

CHAPTER SIX

"We're going to Machu Picchu, Langston."

"I just told you I can't afford it, Glenda."

"And I just told you I'll pay for it!"

Langston pulled the phone away from his ear. He'd never noticed how shrill his friend sounded when she got excited until she'd started calling him from British Columbia. "How?"

He sat on his bed and stared at a small, brownish bird perched in the asymmetrical pine tree outside the window of his room. Which wasn't going to be his room much longer, unless he blew the money for his hypothetical new apartment on a trip to Machu Picchu.

"My dad is a doctor, remember?" said Glenda, more calmly.

"So he's going to pay for his only child and a guy to go to Peru by themselves?"

"You're not a guy, though."

"Excuse me?"

"You know what I mean. He likes you, we've been friends forever, and he knows I miss you."

"Nobody forced you to go to UBC."

"Vancouver is beautiful! You should visit."

"I can't afford it, Glenda. That's my point."

"Okay, you're starting to annoy me."

"It's mutual. Why can't you ask someone else to go?"

"Because I don't want to spend a week hiking up a mountain with anybody else. First of all, I don't know any other jocks..."

"What?" Langston started laughing. "Wow, you're really desperate."

"Yes, I am. Please, Andrews? Please?"

"You're begging me?" Langston's mouth fell open. "Wow. Okay, I'll go. Then again, maybe I shouldn't, since the Glenda I know was obviously abducted by aliens."

"You won't regret this!" she replied triumphantly. "I'm back in Toronto as soon as exams are over in the Spring. We can go in May. I'll tell my dad. Or maybe we should go to New Orleans. What do you think about New Orleans?"

"Now you're talking. I hear the food there is incredible. I wish you could see my face right now, Glenda, because you'd say, you think I'm crazy, right? And I'd say, yes."

She laughed. "This is news?"

He smiled, picturing her in her dorm room, undoubtedly smaller but probably more elaborate than his bedroom, which was a pretty low bar. He had a bed, a nightstand, a cheap, plastic phone, a small closet, and a dresser, with a multicolored braided rug on the floor. Nothing on the walls, except a painting Grandma Felicia had done of him sitting in a chair in the living room when he was ten. He was sure Glenda had posters, and carefully chosen linens, and meaningful knickknacks. My new place will be more personalized, he thought. Although the only things he really wanted to buy were cookbooks.

"You do realize," he said, "that you can't arrive half an hour after departure time and expect to get on the plane."

Glenda kissed her teeth. "I'm on time when it's important."

"You are? When was the last time I asked you to go to a movie? When you were still in Toronto, I mean. I'll answer that. A long time ago."

"I don't need to see every preview, like you do."

"Or the first fifteen minutes of the film either, apparently."

"Anyway..."

"Anyway," Langston said, using his free hand to rub his calf, still sore from yesterday's run, "how do you know your dad will be okay with this?"

"The truth?"

"Yes."

She hesitated. "Don't be mad. You promise?"

He frowned. "Maybe."

"I told him you were gay."

Langston stood, nearly knocking the phone off his nightstand. "What?"

"He didn't believe I could have a best friend who was a guy, so I told him..."

"I can't believe you did that!"

"What difference does it make?"

"You have to ask?"

"You know I could never be cruel to you, Andrews," said Glenda. She sounded hurt.

Langston walked over to the window, trailing the phone's cord behind him, trying to imagine Glenda doing something to him maliciously. And failing.

"What are you going to tell him," he said, "when I get married?"

"I'll worry about that when you meet someone worthy."

He smiled. "Perfect."

"Anyway, gotta go. You've run up my phone bill enough with your futile arguments."

"Let me know when you've booked the tickets."

"Of course."

"Bye, Glenda."

As he placed his phone back on the nightstand, Langston

remembered Marcus' suggestion about making a pact with her to get married if neither of them found someone by a certain age. Maybe his brother was right—she was an extraordinarily good woman. Just a little bossy. Like Grandma Felicia.

Never.

CHAPTER SEVEN

The day after Allen invited her to sit at his table, Cecile tentatively approached the cafeteria at lunchtime. Her heart accelerated to match the crescendo of voices and laughter as she neared the entrance, but she still managed to force herself to stand up straight and keep her eyes off the floor. You're so pathetic, she thought, as she spotted Allen, Tonya, and three other familiar faces whose names she'd never learned.

There was one spot left at their table. She suddenly felt that joining them would be an imposition, and tried to turn around before they saw her...too late. Allen waved her over, all but silencing the room by calling her name with a volume only a soon-to-be professional opera singer could muster. She smiled and made her way towards him, blushing, as usual, as all heads turned to watch her.

"Cecile," he said, as she pulled out the remaining chair, "have you met Tonya, Chelsea, James, and Nelson?"

Cecile cleared her throat. "Not yet. Well, actually, yes. Just now."

She sat down and looked from face to face, starting on the other side of the table. First was Allen, and next to him, Tonya, dark-skinned, with straight, black hair, slanting eyes, high cheekbones, and a long nose that made Cecile suspect Native American ancestry. Chelsea, who was plump, with kinky reddish hair, freckles, green eyes, and an engaging, gap-toothed grin, was seated directly across from Cecile. Two chairs away on the same side of the table as Cecile sat James— tall, thin, and regal, with a neatly trimmed beard and mustache and skin the color of mahogany. Nelson, whose chair was next to Cecile's, had bronze skin, wavy hair, a broad nose, full lips, and a perpetual twinkle in his eyes.

They all smiled at her, even Tonya. Cecile relaxed. Everything was going to be okay.

"I hear you're a fantastic pianist," said Nelson, shifting over a bit to give Cecile more room.

"Really?" she responded, equally surprised by the comment and his British accent. "I don't think I've played anything I know since I got here."

"Then you must really be amazing," Nelson continued.

Don't blush, don't blush...

"Allen said you played the heck out of Il mio tesoro," said James, whom Cecile immediately assumed to be a bass.

"It's Mozart," said Cecile dismissively.

"Yeah, but the ending is tricky, if you're reading," said Allen.

Cecile shrugged. "It's just arpeggios. If you'd have given me Stravinsky, or something, I would have screwed up."

"Hey, are you signed up for chamber music?" said Chelsea, sounding a bit like Minnie Mouse.

"Not this semester."

Chelsea looked at Nelson. "Are you thinking what I'm thinking?" she said.

"Definitely," he replied, turning toward Cecile. "Chelsea is a cellist and I play violin. I was hoping they'd let in a black pianist so we could finally have an all-black trio. And since Mozart is too easy for you—"

"I didn't mean—"

"It's okay," Nelson said with a grin. "Anyway, we'd love to work with you, if you're interested."

Cecile smiled, glancing at Allen gratefully. "That sounds like fun."

"Told you hiding in your practice room was bad policy," he said. "So by the way, everyone, Cecile hasn't done a damn thing but practice since she's been here—"

"I met my Aunt and some of her neighbors..."

Allen yawned theatrically, and the others at the table laughed. "So anyway, girlfriend needs to see the city. What are y'all doing Saturday?"

"Y'all?" said Tonya. "Hanging around me doesn't give you license to use y'all, baby."

"Oh, that's right. If you were born anywhere but Georgia, you can't use y'all. Am I right, Ms. Dixie Peach?"

Tonya pushed him playfully, rolling her eyes.

"I can hang out for a while on Saturday," said James. "I think Olivia is busy, though, so I might be solo."

Cecile mentally crossed him off her list of possibilities.

"10 o'clock, Strawberry Fields?" said Nelson.

"What's Strawberry Fields?" asked Cecile.

"72nd Street entrance to Central Park," said Chelsea. "There's a mosaic there that says, 'Imagine.' It's in memory of John Lennon, donated by Yoko Ono. He lived at the Dakota, which is a big, expensive, creepy-looking apartment building right near there. The spot is named after the Beatles' song."

"Oh." Cecile remembered the shock of hearing about Lennon's death, in her father's car on the way home from a piano lesson. He was the first major figure who had been murdered in her lifetime, or at least, the first one who had resonated, because the news had made the world a scary place where living happily ever after was only guaranteed in fairy tales.

Everyone consented to sightseeing, so that Saturday morning

Cecile said a cheerful goodbye to Aunt Mimi, who was excited that Cecile had made some friends, and took the train to 72nd street. When she arrived at Strawberry Fields, James, Nelson, and Chelsea were already there, all dressed in acid wash jeans. Cecile, who was wearing a belted tunic and stirrup pants, resolved to get some, and soon.

"I guess Allen didn't start putting on his makeup early enough," said James, and Nelson and Chelsea snickered.

"You have the most beautiful speaking voice," Cecile couldn't help observing. "Are you a singer?"

James smiled broadly. "Bass-baritone."

"If you'd said anything else, I would have been shocked. Where are you from?"

"New York."

"That's convenient."

"Yes and no. Sometimes it's nice to get away from the family, you know?"

Their eyes locked for a moment, then Cecile nodded. "I do."

"There they are," said Nelson, and Cecile followed his line of vision to spot Tonya and Allen, who were crossing Central Park West.

"Boy, she keeps him on a short leash," Chelsea remarked. "Do you ever see them separately anymore? I mean, are they living together, or something?"

"There are people who don't need a lot of space, Chelsea," said Nelson, with an edge. Then he smiled, but Chelsea didn't reciprocate.

Chamber music could be interesting, thought Cecile.

"Tour starts now," Allen announced as he reached them. "James is the guide."

James raised his eyebrows. "Sure, Allen. I know everything there is to know about mid-town Manhattan. They teach you all about that stuff uptown."

"Oh, is it that separated?" Cecile asked. "I'd love to see Harlem, too."

James smiled at her. "Another time."

"Look out, Olivia," said Chelsea, not quite under her breath. Cecile turned toward her, frowning, and resolved to keep quiet for the rest of the day. Or only talk to Tonya and Chelsea.

"Hey," said Allen, "can't a beautiful woman speak to a man without trying to seduce him? What is up with you females!" His laugh practically shook the ground. "So she looks a lot like Olivia! That's not her fault. James, lead on, brother."

As it turned out, James knew a lot about Central Park. Cecile was glad she'd brought a camera, but sorry she hadn't brought more film. Starting with the black and white Imagine mosaic, she took picture after picture of her companions standing beside the towering trees, the wooden pagodas on the lake at Wagner Cove, the horse-drawn carriages at Cherry Hill, the ornate black cast iron of the Bow Bridge, Bethesda terrace with its angel statue and fountains, and Alice in Wonderland, rendered in bronze in the midst of the Mad Tea Party.

"You didn't take any pictures of yourself," Chelsea observed as they were about to emerge onto Fifth Avenue.

"I don't really like being photographed," said Cecile.

"That's insane," said Allen, reaching for her camera. "Give me that."

"Girl, you look like a model," said James. "What's wrong with you?"

Don't blush, don't blush...

"I never know what to do in pictures," Cecile protested, as Allen raised the camera.

"Okay, we'll jump in with you," said Tonya, motioning to Chelsea. The two of them squeezed against Cecile on either side, their heads just reaching her shoulders. After the first picture, Tonya folded her arms in front and leaned back, like a wannabe gangster rapper, and Chelsea mirrored her, so Cecile folded her arms too, striking a power pose that made the men in the group double over with laughter.

"There you go," said Allen. "Okay, our turn."

He handed the camera to Tonya, who waited for a group of people to pass, then pointed the camera and counted to three, snapping the picture just as Nelson pretended to grab Cecile's breast.

"No you didn't!" howled Chelsea, cracking up.

"Show some respect," said James pointedly. "Okay, we need another one. Without the niggerishness, please."

"I object," said Nelson, his British accent extra-clipped, "to the use of that hateful word."

"Oh, puh-leez!" James responded. "My ancestors' blood was spilled by people who called them that word. If I want to reclaim it, I'm damn well gonna reclaim it."

"How dare you criticize him, you Limey bastard," said Allen, and everyone smiled except Nelson.

"It's ugly," he said, "and unnecessary. It's not a term of affection, it's a term of derision, and I would be very grateful if you'd avoid using it in my presence."

James raised his eyebrows. "If it upsets you that much, I will abide by your wishes." He bowed, and Nelson's face relaxed.

"Aren't we supposed to be taking a picture?" Chelsea said, in her high, nasal whine.

"Damn right, Chelsea," said Tonya. "No more political shit, please, we're having fun here, y'all. Now pose!"

As Tonya counted to three, Allen, James and Nelson started dancing in unison, like the Pips.

"Can't take you fools anywhere," she said, handing Cecile her camera.

"Lunch?" said Chelsea.

"Then the Guggenheim," James insisted. "There's an exhibit of photographs by Hank Willis Thomas."

"Ooh—who the hell is that?" said Allen, and everyone laughed. Cecile was grateful he'd asked, because she had no idea, either.

"There will be black people in them."

"Sounds good to me," said Nelson.

Cecile glanced at her watch. 12:35 p.m. She'd hoped to get in six hours of practice, starting with Scriabin Op. 42#5—which she'd played through just enough to realize it was going to kick her butt—and ending with the Bach C sharp minor Prelude and Fugue from book one of the Well-Tempered Clavier. Both were new, and she had a lot of work to do before her lesson on Tuesday...

Chelsea interrupted Cecile's runaway train of thought by slipping her arm through Cecile's as they crossed Fifth Avenue. Cecile flinched, then pasted on a smile, trying to pretend she was comfortable with the space invasion.

"New York is a cool city, isn't it?" said Chelsea.

"Definitely. I bet it will take me years to even scratch the surface."

"It would take you years just to tour the art galleries, actually. Is this your first time living away from home?"

"Except for summer camp in Aspen."

They stepped from the street to the sidewalk across from the park. "Oh, you went to Aspen? I did Tanglewood. Closer to home. Did you like it?"

"I did. I'd been in the Rockies before, but never in a place with so many rich people. I think every other person had a Porsche."

Chelsea laughed. "The best part about going away," she said, "is new experiences. If you're open to them." She held Cecile's eyes for a moment.

"Then again," Cecile replied, gently pulling away, "who has time for every experience?"

She glanced at Nelson, who was talking to James a few steps ahead of them, and wondered if...no, Chelsea had definitely been coming on to her. He'll figure it out, Cecile thought, creeped out, flattered, and slightly turned on, all at the same time.

Their lunch destination turned out to be an old-fashioned diner, complete with red vinyl and aluminum stools, a long, white formica counter, and oversized pies stored in a large, glass cabinet. Tonya and Allen sat across from each other in a booth near the back, and as Cecile watched Nelson and James sliding in next to Allen, she realized there was no way to avoid crowding beside Chelsea. She took a deep breath, reminding herself that there was no reason to be nervous, managing to keep her ears beige rather than red until her knees brushed James as she sat down. She glanced up to see him smiling at her, immediately focusing elsewhere, just in time to see Chelsea rolling her eyes.

Yup, I'm very straight, thought Cecile. Can't blame you for trying, though.

An hour later, Cecile glanced at her watch again, watching in near-despair as Tonya continued to toy with her food. *Relax...*

"You graduate in May, right?" Nelson asked Allen.

"That's the plan."

"Juilliard will never be the same," said James sarcastically, then he smiled.

"What then?" Nelson continued.

"Lots of auditions."

"Any particular places in mind?"

"I've always wanted to go to Europe."

"Europe?" squealed Tonya, looking up suddenly from her salad.

"Europe," said Allen, in a voice so soft, Cecile hardly recognized it. "I told you that."

"I thought you said you were going to audition in Santa Fe and Houston, too."

"Sure." He smiled, not quite convincingly.

"They don't hire black tenors in Houston, baby," said Chelsea.

"They do when they're better than everybody else," said James.

"That's so much bullshit," said Nelson. "Why should black people in this country need to be better than everybody else to get a chance?"

"Is it that much different in England?" asked Cecile.

"I think it is. I'm not saying we don't notice differences—well, it's more about class than race over there."

"And there's SO much black aristocracy in Britain!" Allen remarked.

"How is it in Canada?" James asked Cecile.

"How is what? I don't know much about how they cast operas."

"Then how is it being a black pianist?"

All eyes turned, but Cecile didn't mind anymore. "I was definitely the only one, but I gained respect because I played my instrument well."

"Why aren't there any black classical pianists?" asked Tonya. "I mean, we play every other kind of piano."

"There have to be some," said Nelson.

"Name three," said Allen.

"Phillipa Schuyler, Natalie Hinderas, and Andre Watts," said James.

"I've heard of Watts," said Nelson.

"We've all heard of Watts," said Chelsea dismissively. "Hey, when was the last time any of you performed a piece by a black composer?"

"I do them all the time," said Allen. "Hall Johnson, H.T. Burleigh..."

"That isn't a spiritual, I mean," said Chelsea.

"There's a piece by Dorothy Rudd Moore we should do," James said. "You, me and Cecile. It's called *From the Dark Tower*. She wrote it for her husband, Kermit Moore, and Hilda Harris, I think. Poetry by Countee Cullen."

"Wow," said Allen. "You are a walking black history encyclopedia, aren't you?"

"No, I'm a sitting black history encyclopedia." James grinned, and Cecile laughed, then looked down. Nobody else had done more than smile. Then again, nobody else seemed to be fighting hard not to stare at him. And how was it that nobody else got shivers from the sound of his voice? Even if she was gay, Chelsea had to feel something, hearing all that warm, deep, soul-stroking resonance. *Damned Olivia...*

"Did your teacher actually give you pieces by black composers?" Tonya asked him. "I mean, besides spirituals."

James shook his head. "I got curious, so I went to the Schomburg and did some research. Do you know Wayne Sanders and Ben Matthews? Then again, why would you? They run Opera Ebony. I'll introduce you."

Tonya grinned. "Thanks!"

"And I'll introduce Allen," James went on, winking at her. "Maybe that will keep him in America."

"Maybe, maybe not. Besides, there's already a black opera company in Philly, if that's what I want."

"By the way you said that, I'm guessing that it isn't," said

Nelson.

"I want to be like Watts," said Allen. "And Price, and Anderson, and Estes. I want to sing famous operas on famous stages with famous conductors—the stuff I went to Juilliard to learn. After that, maybe I'll do some stuff by black composers."

James sat up very straight. "The thing is, if we don't do music by black composers, who will?"

Allen laughed loudly enough to cause a passing waitress to nearly drop her tray. "You will. Life is short, my brother. I intend to spend it doing the things that really move me."

"How do you know music by black composers can't move you?" James said with an edge, leaning forward. "Are you implying that because they're black, they're somehow inferior?"

Allen put up both hands. "I'm not trying to upset you, James. Sing what you like, and so will I. Freedom of speech. And like I already said, I sing spirituals. Not good enough for you?"

James leaned back, with a thin smile. "Doesn't matter, does it?"

"Look, I appreciate your activism," Allen went on calmly, "but it's hard enough to be a classical musician, never mind a black classical musician, never mind a black classical musician who specializes in music by black composers. It's like being a microscopic speck in a tiny niche in a miniscule corner in an abandoned building."

"Impressive," said Chelsea. "*Work* that metaphor, Mr. Washington!"

"I never said you had to specialize," James retorted. "Then again, why not? Natalie Hinderas decided to focus on piano music by black composers, and that's probably why we know who she is today."

"Actually, that's why you know who she is," said Allen, smiling.

Cecile watched James' jaw clench and unclench, let her eyes

trace the contours, deliberately keeping her focus away from his lips. She wanted to support him, but she wasn't sure how—there were so many pieces by dead white men she had been yearning all of her life to learn, and she couldn't think of a single piece by a black composer. Canadian composer, yes, but black Americans had never been on the rather extensive list of repertoire priorities for her or her teachers.

Something came to her: "Do you know where I can get the Hinderas recording you mentioned?"

James relaxed his face into something close to a smile, and gazed at her with soft eyes. "I'll tape it for you," he said.

"Thanks."

"So Tonya," said Allen, back in jovial mode, "You done, woman? James says we've got to absorb some cultured blackness, and we ain't got all day."

James shot him a warning, and Allen smiled and said, "I appreciate your passion, brother. You are a far better man than I."

James grinned, his eyes still angry. "I know."

"Can we be friends anyway? I need someone to show me the error of my ways."

James chuckled, shaking his head. "That's a lifelong mission, man."

"Great, y'all are friends for life," said Tonya. "Can we get out of here? And don't you dare say I kept you waiting, 'cause I'm the only person who won't have indigestion in about half an hour."

Cecile slid out of the booth, glancing at her watch again as the others followed her lead. It looked like this outing was going to take up most of the day. You'll make it up tomorrow, said a little voice in her head. Let go and enjoy yourself. She stepped outside the diner, glanced back at the path through the park, a long and winding road full of unexpected pleasures, and knew the voice was right.

All the way home on the subway, Cecile alternated between basking in the glow of a whole day spent with her new friends, especially James, and a sense of dread about her approaching piano lesson. The glow won—she ate a hasty dinner, tried to practice afterward, then gave up when it became clear that the need to call Teresa and tell her stories was a lot stronger than the prospect of disappointing Mr. Balog.

Teresa listened in silence, then said, "Wow. So is that the first time you've been hit on by a lesbian?"

"No, actually, it happens every day. You?"

Teresa chuckled. "I think you should have asked her what new experiences she had in mind, so you could tell me about it. I mean, if you're going not going to do anything constructive all day, you may as well make it worth your while."

Cecile frowned, stretching out her legs and crossing her ankles, her head sinking a bit deeper into her pillow. "Something you'd like to share, Teresa? I won't judge."

"Nope. Just suggesting a way to get a little action while you figure out how to make a move on James."

"I can't make a move on James. He's got a girlfriend."

"So?"

"So I wouldn't respect him if I could make a move on him while he has a girlfriend."

"Chuh!" Teresa kissed her teeth. "What's the point of your life, Cecile? Seriously. Oh right—you want to be a famous pianist, and that's it. No sex, just music. I forgot."

Cecile decided not to be offended. "First of all, there's an AIDS epidemic going on. Second, I'm not desperate, so I don't need to sleep with a woman, or steal somebody else's man. Why can't I just be me, without a man? Isn't that okay?"

"Sure it is. But why would you want to do without? I can't even imagine it."

"You don't need a man to have sex."

"I can't believe you said that."

"It's true."

"It's also true that it's way better with a man. Don't deny it."

"Depends who he is," Cecile replied, grinning.

Teresa laughed. "That's true, too."

Cecile rolled onto her side, her smile fading. "The men I like are always taken, and the ones who like me are boring. I don't understand why it always has to be this way. Is it me?"

"Of course not. Well...maybe a bit. But you'll figure it out."

This time, Cecile couldn't help being offended. "What do you mean, maybe a bit?"

"Why ask the question if you don't want an answer?"

"What do you mean, maybe a bit?"

Teresa hesitated. "You don't know how to play the game, Cecile. You never flirt with anybody, and when guys try to talk to you, you're way too—reserved. I really wish I could introduce you to Langston. He never learned to play the game, either. You guys would be...actually, neither one of you would make a move, so never mind. Listen, forget what I said. You'll meet somebody. In the meantime, you're going to be a great musician, and that's way more important, isn't it?"

"I agree," said Cecile untruthfully, wondering why being a great musician wasn't enough, and why she'd lied.

CHAPTER EIGHT

Maybe I do spend too much time studying, thought Langston, putting his cheek on top of his French textbook and shutting his eyes. As he sat in an out-of-the-way corner in the Glendon College library, he tried to forget that Yonge Street waited just a block away, ready and willing to distract someone who had no interest whatsoever in an education degree. He'd had the first of his two annual conversations with Teresa, marking her birthday, the night before, but he'd cut things so short that he barely had an idea how she'd celebrated, never mind what she'd been up to in the last twelve months. I like French, he reminded himself. Still, he wasn't sure how he'd survive the rest of the year if he already felt burned out in mid-September.

One day at a time, sweet Jesus, he thought, smiling at the thought of his grandmother's favorite tune. He could almost hear her singing in her clear, full alto voice, only slightly frayed by the passage of time.

He lifted his head, opened his eyes, and nearly had a heart attack.

"Hi there."

A tall brunette with a medium build, olive skin, and a small mole just above her upper lip, like a less attractive Cindy Crawford, was smiling down at him. She was standing in front of a gray metal cart full of books, and had been about to shelve one of them when he opened his eyes. She pushed the book into place, then turned, crossing her arms.

"I forget your name," she said.

I'm awake, thought Langston, who had never seen her in his

life. "Have we met?"

"No, but I've seen you around Gino's once or twice."

Langston sat up. "Oh, are you a regular customer?"

She shook her head, grinning. "I mean, I eat there, but I never pay for anything. I'm Marietta Zappatore."

She extended her hand, and Langston took it, wondering why she didn't look familiar. Probably because she never had a reason to go into the kitchen, and when he ventured into the dining room, he was focused on wiping down tables, not scoping for chicks.

"I'm Langston Andrews," he said.

"Nice to meet you. So are you learning a lot?" she asked, glancing at his textbook.

"Definitely. You've heard of sleep-teaching?"

"Oh, is that how it's done?"

"Nope." Langston chuckled, leaning back against his chair. "You work here?"

"Sometimes. It's work study, so I don't get a lot of hours."

"Too awkward to be in the family business? Your dad has been talking about needing more help in the kitchen."

She ran her fingers through her shiny, dark brown hair, gazing off to the side. "Oh, working at Gino's is pretty much inevitable. That's why I'm getting an accounting degree, so I can help out."

"You sound so excited."

She laughed, chose a book from the cart, examined the spine, then bent to put it on the bottom shelf. "It's guaranteed employment." She stood again, turning towards him. "What's your major? French?"

"Sort of. I'm going to teach secondary school, French immersion."

She nodded. "Teaching's a noble profession."

"I suppose so."

"You sound so excited."

He grinned. "I didn't want to be a doctor, a lawyer, or an engineer. My grandmother was a teacher, though, which made this acceptable. That said, I'll probably have to get a Ph.D to satisfy her."

"Have to?" Marietta ran her hand through her hair again. "That's a lot of years in school to fulfill an expectation."

"*C'est la vie.*"

She hugged herself, rubbing her arms, which were bare even though the weather had started to become cool.

"Are you cold?"

"Not for long. I left my sweater in my bag behind the desk. You're sweet to ask."

She smiled at him again. Was that a flirtatious look in her eye? Langston's freshman year had been marginally more successful than high school, when it came to female companionship, but he still hadn't learned how to move things to the next level unless he was led there. Either way, she was his boss's daughter, which made her intentions irrelevant.

She cocked her head. "When are you working next?"

"Uh...tomorrow."

"Maybe I'll come by and say hello."

Was there a correct answer? He couldn't think of one.

"My dad says you're a pretty cultured guy," she continued. "Maybe you'd like to go to the Royal Ontario Museum? I never meet guys who like to do that sort of thing. I think history is so interesting! I could spend hours there."

Langston felt himself dropping his guard, despite the voice in his head that was screaming a warning.

"I love the museum," he said.

"So we'll go tonight. They're open late on Fridays. Meet me at the front doors at 6:30?"

He studied her face, trying to decide if she was as warm as she seemed—the last thing he needed was another bad experience. Her brown eyes were wide, like a child's, almost innocent. Almost. Close enough.

"Okay."

"Great! Glad I'm finally meeting you, Langston."

"I'd say the same, Marietta, but I didn't know you were alive."

She laughed heartily, then looked him straight in the eyes and said, "You will now."

Langston's heart did a back flip, then sank into his stomach.

"Well, I'd better get some studying in," he said, his words unnaturally fast. "See you later."

"I'll be there."

She smiled at him again, and pushed her cart around the corner and down the next row of shelves.

Langston glanced at her, found himself surveying her rear view. *Not bad.*

Idiot, he thought. There is no possible way this can turn out well. But as he glanced at her again, just as she disappeared from view, he couldn't help smiling.

CHAPTER NINE

Cecile liked to get French fries at the McDonald's on the corner of 72nd and Broadway before boarding the uptown train to Aunt Mimi's brownstone for the evening's practice session. On the 22nd of September, she turned away from the counter, taking a bright red carton full of salty, crisp deliciousness out of a to-go bag while searching in vain for an empty chair. The fries were so fresh they almost burned her fingers, which was quite a feat, since years of practice had turned the tips to leather. She could have eaten in the street as she walked to the train station, but that particular day she needed a moment to relax before facing the prospect of being crammed into a tube with a multitude of random strangers. To her relief, just as she considered her other options, a booth cleared. She quickly settled into the hard plastic seat, grateful to have the tiny table to herself—

"Mind if I join you?"

She heard a baritone voice so resonant that for a moment she expected Blair Underwood. Wrong, but close enough. On that warm autumn day, she looked up to see a tall, chestnut Adonis wearing a black t-shirt that accentuated his toned upper body, without being conspicuously tight. Her eyes surveyed him involuntarily.

"No, that's fine," she said.

He had a tray full of food, all for himself. Cecile glanced at it and smiled.

"What?" he said, grinning back.

"Hungry?" The experience felt so unreal that she wasn't even nervous.

"Okay, I'm a glutton. I admit it."

"I didn't say that."

"You could have."

"Well, you seem to be burning up all the calories somehow."

"I try."

He took a bite of his quarter pounder with cheese, chewed, swallowed, and said, "I'd be a fool to sit here with a beautiful woman and not at least ask her name."

Cecile smiled. "I'm Cecile."

"That's pretty. I'm Teddy."

She had taken another handful of fries, which she chewed and swallowed with gusto even though they nearly burned her mouth, when something occurred to her.

"Your name is Teddy? Not Theodore or something?"

He grinned. "Okay, it's Theodore. Just don't call me that in public again, cool?"

"Cool."

He took a long drink of his milkshake, then asked, "Where are you from?"

"What, I don't sound like a New Yawker?"

Teddy laughed. "Nope."

"Guess." Cecile smiled at him flirtatiously, then got to work on another mouthful of fries.

"Midwest."

She shook her head, swallowing.

"California."

"Nope."

"Give me a hint."

"Maybe there's a world outside the US of A."

"You're kidding."

"Well, you'll never guess, with that attitude."

"I'm kidding. Okay, you're Canadian."

"Bulls-eye."

He took another large bite of his quarter pounder, waited until his mouth was empty and asked, "What brings you to New Yawk?"

She decided that naming her famous school right away sounded like showing off. "Getting an education."

"Where?"

"Juilliard."

Teddy's eyebrows shot up. "Wow. What do you do?"

"I'm a pianist."

"I would have guessed a singer."

Cecile rolled her eyes, before she could stop herself, and was relieved to see Teddy grinning.

"Did I say something wrong?"

"No, not really. I'm just tired of people assuming I'm a singer. I get it, because black female classical pianists are rare..."

"I thought you were a singer," Teddy interrupted, "because you carry yourself like a queen. I could imagine you owning the stage, so I thought singer, or maybe dancer." He held her eyes for a moment, then finished off his first burger and leaned back. "How did you fall in love with playing the piano?"

She liked the way he'd asked the question, as if he understood that being a musician was a compulsion. I should have thanked him for the compliment, she realized. Too late, as always. Remarks about her poised appearance weren't new, even if they didn't make sense to her. Then again, nobody else knew what was going on in her head, most of the time, and besides, regal bearing wasn't exactly an approachable trait.

Cecile swallowed her last few fries, determined not to get nervous, then realized that she still wasn't blushing and relaxed.

"My mom is a part-time church musician, so we had a piano from before I was born. Mom says I started trying to play when I was about three. I couldn't sit on the bench without someone lifting me, so I'd figure out melodies standing up. She finally started teaching me something when I turned four, but I picked it up so quickly that my parents decided I needed to be taught by someone more professional."

"Four? Wow," he said, as if her story were the most awe-inspiring thing he'd ever heard.

"It's not that unusual for pianists and violinists," Cecile said quickly.

"Is it unusual to be good enough to get into Juilliard?"

She glanced away, cursing the inevitable warmth in her cheeks as they reddened. "I guess so."

Teddy chuckled. "You guess so? Okay, let me clear it up,

then. It's unusual." He waited a beat, then leaned forward slightly, adding, "I bet that's not the only unusual thing about you, though."

He had just put some french fries in his mouth when Cecile responded, "Are you calling me an oddball?"

Teddy's hand came up in the nick of time, caught the piece of barely-chewed food that flew from his mouth at the sudden force of his laughter, then stayed there to cover his cough as he narrowly avoided choking.

Cecile jumped out of her seat, instinctively touching his shoulder as she asked, "Are you okay?"

When he finally managed to recover enough to nod, she reluctantly pulled away, unable to stop watching him even as she slid back into her seat. He drank some of his milkshake, then gazed at Cecile, who was relieved to see that his eyes were sparkling with amusement.

"This shit is too damn thick," he said. "They should serve it with a spoon."

"Are you really okay?"

"Never felt better in my life."

His smile made her uneasy, but only for a moment. The air between them felt electric—the cliché was true. She thought of Devonte, tried to remember if she had felt the same way, and realized she had. Devonte didn't know anything about me, she thought, and didn't care to find out. Teddy is different...or maybe he isn't. I may never see him again, either. Especially if I don't keep this conversation going...

"Are you in school?" she asked.

He nodded, chewing and swallowing. "You know, Cecile, there's a lesson here somewhere. I mean, children are starving in Africa, and I'm filling my face with so much junk food I can barely hold a conversation."

She laughed. "I'll wait."

"I have a better idea. Why don't you keep talking until I'm done? You can say anything. Doesn't have to even make sense, as long as I can listen to your voice."

This time, her whole body flushed with warmth. Her eyes landed on the people in the booth next to them, a trio of teenaged Latinas with a little boy in tow, speaking animated Spanglish loudly enough that the only reason she could possibly have been hearing them for the first time had to be Teddy's power to draw her in. When she gazed at him again, his face seemed not just handsome, but impossibly so. She found herself staring at his eyelashes, so long and thick that she had to restrain herself from touching them. She tried not to imagine them tickling her, like butterflies, while he explored her with his tongue, maybe tracing a line down her center, from her neck to her...

"That was strange," he went on. "I'm sorry."

"No, I'm sorry," she said, blinking away the vision. "I just...I don't do small talk very well. Maybe you figured that out already."

Teddy shook his head, taking another bite, and chewing it hastily. "I like big talk better anyway," he said. Then he took one last sip of his shake, and leaned back again. "So, about your question. Yes, I'm in school. I'll cut to the chase and tell you I'm studying Administration, Leadership and Technology at NYU, because I want to work to empower the black community, because it's important and I was raised to give back. I'm the head of the African American Student Union, which is kind of a pain in the ass, but it's important, too, and besides, it makes my mommy and daddy proud. I've been volunteering since I was little, so I see the problems up close, and they're big, and sometimes the people we're trying to help are their own worst enemies, but I know that making a difference takes work, and somebody's got to do it, so why not me? I don't think I'm Martin Luther King, or anything—kind of good, since I'd like to live past 40, if I can—but maybe I can help one or two people, and maybe they'll help one or two people. Or maybe those two people's changed lives will be enough to move things forward a bit. I don't know. Well, yes, I do. I believe that."

Cecile listened, mesmerized not just by his face but by his passion.

"I don't know what to say," she finally managed. "What I do seems so trivial."

Teddy held her eyes. "No, it's not. Was Marian Anderson trivial? How about Paul Robeson?"

"I'm not Marian Anderson, though."

"You don't have to be. You're showing people that we can do anything. Even if it's a few people, that's enough. Maybe those few people's changed opinions will move things forward a bit, too."

He smiled slowly, and Cecile smiled back, unable to look away until she felt someone brushing against her back and turned to see an overweight white lady with a cane.

"Oh, I'm sorry, honey," she said, her voice high and fearful. "These tables are so close together."

"It's okay," Cecile responded warmly. Ordinarily, she would have been irritated by the woman's tone, which seemed to come from the assumption that young black people were dangerous, but on this day, even if Cecile had been scalded by spilled coffee, she probably would have smiled it off.

Fairy tales can come true, it can happen to you...

A small voice was saying something softly, underneath the swelling strings inside her, then louder, then loudly enough to cut through: *it's getting late.* Cecile glanced at her watch, then back at Teddy, eyes wide: "I'm so sorry," she said, alarmed, "I have to go."

"I knew that would happen eventually. Does this mean I'm never going to see you again?"

She looked into his eyes and had trouble looking away. "You can always come to Juilliard and track me down."

He laughed. "Do I seem like a stalker?"

"No."

"Although if that's what it takes…"

"I wouldn't want to get you arrested."

"So you'd file a complaint?"

She grinned. "Probably not."

She gave him her phone number, and he walked her to the

subway. They were going in opposite directions. Her train arrived first, and as she pulled out of the station she looked at Teddy, still on the platform. Saw him watching her until she disappeared from sight, a smile on his face to match the one she couldn't wipe from her lips all the way home.

CHAPTER TEN

If Mr. Zappatore knew his busboy had gone on a date with his daughter, he never let on. Langston wasn't sure whether Marietta hadn't told him, or Mr. Zappatore was waiting for Langston to confess, but he decided to keep quiet, especially since nothing scandalous had happened.

Marietta had insisted on looking at the dinosaurs, early mammals, birds, and bats, and Langston had insisted on looking at everything African and Native Canadian. An impossible task in two hours, so they'd ended up practically sprinting through the museum, which made the whole experience a game.

"You're so predictable," said Marietta teasingly, as they and a few other stragglers left at closing time. "Africa? Don't you know anything about Africa yet?"

"That was for your benefit." He grinned, opening the door and letting her step through first.

She rolled her eyes. "Presumptuous, aren't we?"

"You know I could have found that remark offensive, right?"

Marietta stopped. "Why?"

"Because I'm black, in case you didn't notice. And don't tell me you didn't notice, because that's a lie."

She put her hands on her hips. "Of course I noticed. That's why I made the joke. You couldn't tell I was joking?"

Langston folded his arms. "I assumed you were joking."

"So what's the problem? I didn't say anything bad about

Africa. I just said it was predictable that you picked out those particular collections."

"Well, I have to know about the whole continent, since my ancestors were stripped of their specific identity. That takes a while."

Her eyes grew wide. "Wow. Did I mention I was joking?" she said, running her hand through her hair.

Langston grinned. "Relax. And by the way, I'm surprised you didn't want to see the Roman collection."

"We're Sicilian," she deadpanned. Then she smiled, and started walking again.

Like the Corleones, thought Langston, in spite of himself.

It was that thought that kept haunting him the next day, at work. Maybe Mr. Zappatore was waiting for his shift to end, and then...

You watch too many movies, Langston, he chided himself. Besides, what had they done? Nothing. They'd looked at the exhibits, made conversation, then she'd asked if he'd like to get together again, he'd said yes, and she'd given him her number. He'd offered her a drink or some dessert, but she'd said she needed to go home. Despite her boldness in the library, she hadn't even tried to touch him, which was good, because as he'd walked up to the doors of the Royal Ontario Museum and seen Marietta waiting for him, he'd felt self-conscious. To have a white girl kissing him on the street would have been too much for him.

She didn't say anything to anyone, he thought, wiping down the table in a booth near the front door of Gino's, then running the cloth over the dark green vinyl seats. She won't. And neither will I.

Langston knew how his grandmother would react if she found out he'd even gone on a friendly date with a white girl. At least, he thought he did. No one in his family had ever tried it, at least not to his knowledge. Grandma Felicia had made it very clear that black women, who came in every shade, were the most beautiful on Earth, and that black men who even looked at white women had serious mental problems. She did admit a measure of admiration for Jack Johnson, the first black heavyweight champion of the world, but she saw his tendency to date and marry white women in the early part of the century, when doing so was downright dangerous, as more about defiance than anything else.

I bet Marcus has dated a white woman, Langston thought, getting to work on another table...his lip curled back in disgust, and he barely controlled an impulse to throw the damp cloth across the room. What the fuck am I doing? Hanging around with a girl I can't even fully see as a human, because of her skin color.

He rubbed his shoulder, felt the muscles relax a bit. It wasn't true. He saw her as a human. A human whose company he enjoyed enough to call her, maybe hang out with her some more. Why not? To stay endlessly available for a hypothetical black woman he might never meet?

He'd dated two black women in freshman year. Thanks to his indoctrination from Grandma Felicia, their skin color had been a prerequisite, but not the only thing he'd thought they had in common. Darleen was a petite, flirtatious French major who loved to cook. She dumped him because he didn't try to seduce her fast enough. He moved faster with Venitia, whose wickedly hilarious sarcasm he attributed to her high heels; after all, it was hard to be sweet all the time if your feet hurt. Langston found out he was part of a triangle when he saw her kissing another guy the day after she'd told Langston they were through.

He'd felt disappointed about being back in the same old high school world again, but only for a little while. When I meet the right person, he told himself, I'll know. I won't have to think about whether or not I'm going too fast or too slow, or anything else.

He walked back into the kitchen, rinsed the cloth, and hung it up to dry, wondering if Marietta Zappatore was the right girl. If she was, would he have to guts to acknowledge it to the world? Would she?

He glanced at Mario, who was seasoning some tomato sauce at one of the stoves, and was suddenly bothered that the only black person working in the restaurant was the busboy. True, nobody had forced him to apply for the job. And nobody treated him poorly. But—

"Hey Mario," said Langston.

The head cook glanced over at him. "Yeah?"

"Need some help?"

"Nah," he said, turning his eyes back towards the sauce, "but I'll let you know when I'm done with this pot."

"No, I mean, some help in the kitchen."

Bob, the other cook, looked up, frowning.

"Maybe with preparation," Langston went on, undaunted. "Chopping, peeling, stuff like that. I've heard Mr. Zappatore talk about hiring somebody."

Mario shook his head. "Where is this coming from, Langston?"

Langston shrugged.

Mario stirred the pot for a while, tasted the contents, then said, "Ask Mr. Zappatore."

"I will," said Langston glancing at Bob, whose eyes, already overshadowed by brows so heavy they looked like a caricature, were narrowed to the point of disappearance. "Thanks."

CHAPTER ELEVEN

Cecile cursed her decision to finish her practice session with the Bach Prelude and Fugue in C sharp minor—really smart, she thought, picking a meditative prelude and an slow five-voice fugue when I'm completely freaked out over a first date. She was glad the piano bench was hard enough to provide a much-needed dose of reality to balance the swirl of erotic fantasies in her mind.

Teddy was meeting her in the lobby at 6. She kept her eye on the clock, determined to arrive downstairs at 6:05, not a moment earlier, but not a moment later, either. At 5:50, she closed her music. Teddy, 1; Johann Sebastian, 0.

The cacophony in the hallway on the fourth floor of Juilliard didn't bother her, except today, when the voices in her head were so loud that another layer of noise was too much to stand. Halfway to the elevator, she decided to take the stairs. For the quiet, and because she needed to do something to distract from her nerves. After all, the time she'd spent obsessing about her date would have been wasted if she tripped, fell and broke her neck.

Two flights down, she grasped the ridiculousness of her overblown anticipation and smiled. By the time she emerged from the stairwell, it occurred to her that Teddy had just as much reason to be excited as she did, a thought that finally cleared her mind.

She had just given Nora, the elderly Irish lady who had been a fixture behind the massive wooden desk by the entrance since time immemorial, and Joe, the middle-aged Italian security guard who was almost as much a part of the furniture, a cheerful wish for a wonderful evening, when she heard, "Cecile."

The deep richness of Teddy's voice melted her inner cool

immediately—

Breathe. It's just a date.

She'd needed both her barely teenaged sister and Teresa to remind her of the obvious, the night before when she'd called for advice on what to wear and ended up babbling about her insecurities. Why were such things obvious even to Betsy?

It's just a date, you idiot!

She smiled. Her upper lip was quivering, just like it usually did when she posed for photographs, but she somehow found her voice: "Hi."

They talked and laughed all through dinner at Captain Nemo's, a seafood place on West 72nd street, then walked past the Dakota (so massive and brooding Count Dracula should have been its main tenant), through Strawberry Fields and into Central Park. The sky was already orange and mauve, and the trees were towering above, blocking what was left of the sunlight.

Cecile looked up at Teddy and said, "Um...is it safe to be here after dark?"

He smiled playfully. "Would I bring you somewhere dangerous?"

"I don't know. Would you?"

He stopped walking. "I'd protect you, Cecile."

"So you can stop a bullet?"

He took her hand and led her to one of the benches by the side of the path. She'd expected to sit, but instead found herself draped across his lap, laughing so hard at the surprise of being literally swept off her feet that she could barely catch her breath.

"Of course I can," said Teddy. "But I do other things better."

He kissed her, and she felt herself dissolve into him, her soul seeping through her skin wherever they touched. He tasted like wine and after-dinner mints, and his kiss felt like the missing piece of the puzzle that had been her future, until they'd met. No one else in the world existed anymore; another cliché, true. It had to be, because shy Cecile was locked in the most intimate of embraces in full view of any number of passers-by, and she didn't care.

He stopped. "We should go."

She opened her eyes, and Teddy stood, still holding her, then set her on her feet. He put his arm around her, and was guiding her firmly back onto the lamp-lit path when she saw rats, as big as chihuahuas, scampering across the field behind the benches where they'd just been intertwined.

 She screamed and bolted. He caught up to her just as she reached Strawberry Fields again, pulling her close and laughing.

"Are you okay?"

"Were those rats? Oh my God..."

"They're as afraid of you as you are of them."

She pulled away abruptly. "Bullshit, Teddy. I've heard about the rats in New York."

He tried to keep a straight face, but couldn't.

"I'm sorry. I just...I really wanted to kiss you, and I couldn't wait."

She looked into his eyes, glowing from within, and knew that if he'd asked her to follow him back into the park, rats or no rats, she would have.

#

September 25, 1987

Who'd have guessed McDonald's was the place to me et a brilliant, spontaneous, gorgeous man with a great sense of humor who cares about humanity? Teddy wants to change the world, but he's still like a little boy, in some ways. I never thought I'd find anyone at all, and God sent me someone absolutely perfect. He does work in mysterious ways.

I could get my emotions out of my head if I could play them on the piano, but it's the middle of the night, so I guess I'm out of luck. Or in luck. *If they asked me, I could write a book...*no, I couldn't. But I could light up a city. I have that much energy when I think about the way his tongue felt in my mouth. I could melt an iceberg, because he makes me that hot...

I should stop thinking about this, but I can't, just like with Devonte. I guess that makes sense, because I want it to be like it was with Devonte, except I want Teddy to call me the next day. Which would make it better than it was with Devonte, of course.

I'm not supposed to want that, unless we're married. I wonder if that's really true, though? The part of First Corinthians where Paul mentioned the body being a temple talks about prostitutes. Maybe it's okay if nobody's getting paid. Or maybe Paul was just saying his own thing. After all, Teresa has been doing it with Edwin for years, and nothing bad has happened to either of them. Maybe it all gets worked out at Judgment Day?

I don't know. I just know I'm scared of the way I'm feeling right now. But isn't God supposed to love you no matter what? Then again, there were a whole lot of people who got punished in the Bible, even the ones He really loved. Then again, I don't remember anybody getting zapped for just having sex before marriage without it being adultery or gang rape. Then again, I'm hardly an expert.

When the time comes, I'll trust my gut.

CHAPTER TWELVE

Langston's undercover search for a new apartment ended the last day of September, in a brown brick low-rise building on Eglinton West. His main criteria were price and proximity to school, his job, and public transportation, the first of which ruled out most of the places he wanted to live. He could have kept looking, but his friendship, or whatever it was, with Marietta gave him focus. There was never a mention of going to her house, or bringing her to his, but it seemed time to do one or the other. Having his own apartment was the only solution he could think of.

Not that their relationship had a schedule, which was fine with him. And given his reservations, knowing there were limits to their contact felt reassuring, rather than frustrating, even though he couldn't help thinking how ridiculous it was that he couldn't introduce his new friend to his family. Actually, he could have done it, if he'd had the guts. Either way, living in a place where his decisions would be free from backlash had become a consuming passion, so if that place was far from fancy, so be it.

The apartment itself wasn't bad, and the neighborhood was okay with him, too, with Jamaicans all over the place, and hole-in-the wall restaurants that smelled like home. His main concern was the bad things he'd heard about the crime rate in Oakwood-Vaughan, which he took with a grain of salt, because he'd heard bad things about the crime rate in Scarborough, too, and pretty much every neighborhood, ever, where working class black people lived. It was true that the streets in his new neighborhood were far from quiet on a Friday night, but he could deal with that. Being robbed at gunpoint, however, was a different story.

I've got nothing worth stealing, he reminded himself, scanning the street for signs of Marcus. Langston kept telling himself that he didn't need anyone's permission or approval, but he couldn't fool himself into believing a thumbs down from his brother wouldn't hurt.

Two minutes later, Marcus appeared, walking with a limp.

"What happened?" Langston asked, as soon as he was in earshot.

"I was painting the porch at Grandma's and I fell."

"Are you okay?"

"Probably. And no, I didn't tell her where I was going."

Langston smiled. "That obvious?"

Marcus grabbed his ankle, leaning against the building as he pulled his foot up behind him to stretch out his thigh. "You're going to have to tell her, you know," he said, grimacing. He released his foot and rubbed the sore spot. "She'll send the police after you otherwise."

"I'm going to tell her."

"Before or after you move?"

"Before. Why am I so afraid of a little old lady?"

Marcus laughed. "I don't know. What's she gonna do to you?"

"Make me feel like dirt."

"Which you'll survive. Ready to go in?"

Langston nodded, pulling out what had become his key, just that afternoon. His hands shook as he'd signed the lease, but once it was over, he'd felt proud of himself, like he had when he got the job at Gino's, also without telling Grandma Felicia first. So yes, he thought, opening the door, I will survive this.

There was no lobby, just a tiny room with silver rectangular mailboxes on one wall, decorated with last names of tenants at the top and buzzers at the bottom. Langston pushed his key into the inner door's lock, then led Marcus up the dusty stairs to the second floor. The hallway was covered in thin, dark blue carpet, worn in spots, but the walls, which were white, had been recently painted. Langston opened the door at the end of the hall, and stepped back to let Marcus look around.

The tour lasted a few minutes, since the apartment consisted of a bedroom, a bathroom, and a small kitchen that opened onto the living and dining area. Marcus glanced out the windows, covered in cheap, white plastic blinds, and faced Langston again.

"Are you sure?"

"Yeah."

"What about furniture?"

"I'm going to Ikea soon."

Marcus shook his head. Then he smiled, extended his hand and said, in a Jamaican accent, *"Langston, yuh a bad bwai, y'see?"*

Langston laughed. "Thanks. Where'd you learn that? It almost sounds authentic."

"Friends in low places."

"Low? Wow, Grandma really got to you. I wish I spoke patois."

"Living here, you will. And by the way, they're not low because they speak patois. They're low because...well, they're low. Former friends, of course."

"Do I know these people?"

"Of course not. Let's just say I didn't bring everybody I've ever hung out with to the house."

Langston considered for a moment, then leaned against the wall. "Hey Marcus..." He studied his brother's face, then his own fingernails, debating.

"Yes?"

There was a long pause.

"Are you in trouble?" Marcus finally said.

Langston looked up. "No. Well, not really."

Marcus started to lower himself to the ground, then winced, leaning against the wall beside Langston instead. "You'd better tell me what's going on," he said. "Quickly, though? I'm meeting Danita in an hour."

Langston sighed. "I'm seeing Mr. Zappatore's daughter."

Marcus straightened up. "*Yuh mad?*"

"Because she's white, or because she's my boss's daughter?"

"You're moving to Little Jamaica, surrounded by black

women, and you're dating a white girl? *But Raatid...*okay, I'm done. What happened? I mean, how long has this been going on?"

"A few weeks."

Until that moment, it hadn't occurred to Langston that bringing Marietta to his new place would mean walking a gauntlet of disapproving stares. So in a way, Grandma Felicia will follow me wherever I go, he thought.

"I could break up with her," he went on. "Actually, I can't, because there's nothing official."

Marcus gazed out the window for a moment, then faced him. "Do you really like her?"

"What do you mean?"

Marcus chuckled. "It's not a trick question, Langston."

He studied his fingernails again. "I'm not in love with her, or anything. I don't think, anyway."

"You'd know, trust me."

Langston looked at Marcus for the first time since he'd mentioned Marietta. "I'm not, then. But I do like being around her."

"So she's a stand-in for Glenda?"

"Not exactly."

"Are you screwing her?"

"Hell, no. Where would that happen? Mr. Zappatore's house or Grandma Felicia's?"

"A motel." Marcus smiled slyly. "Hey, how many times have you actually had sex?"

Langston stood up straight. "What does that have to do with this?"

His brother shrugged. "Think you'll do her, one of these days?"

"Wow, Marcus, thanks for everything." Langston pulled his keys out of his pocket, ready to leave.

"Listen, I'm trying to help you, but I have no idea what's going on. I mean, are you friends? More than friends? Is she target practice? What? Because if you're going to hang out with Mr. Zappatore's daughter, you'd better know why you're doing it. Whose idea was it, anyway?"

Langston hesitated. "Hers."

"And Mr. Zappatore doesn't know?"

"No."

Marcus nodded, rubbing his thigh again. After a while, he said, "May I give you a word of advice?"

Langston hesitated. "Yeah."

"If you want to get laid, get laid, Langston. It's not that hard. You don't have to hang around some white girl who's too ashamed of you to tell her family—"

"I get to know women because I think they're people. I know it's crazy, but I still haven't figured out why it's wrong. Besides, I'm too ashamed to tell *my* family, so maybe she should get the hell away from me, too."

"Same thing," said Marcus, looking at his watch. "Well, gotta go."

He was reaching for the doorknob when Langston said,

"I'm sorry."

"Me too."

Marcus stepped into the hallway, waited for Langston to lock the apartment, then started towards the stairs, his limp a bit less pronounced than it had been earlier.

"Marcus."

He turned. "Yes?"

"Do you like engineering?"

"Sure."

"But wasn't it Grandma Felicia's idea?"

"I wanted to be able to eat, and I didn't have anything else in mind. Why?"

Langston searched for the right words, but they refused to come to him. "Nothing," he said. "Thanks, man."

"I didn't do anything, but you're welcome anyway. Let me know when you're moving, okay? I'll help you."

"I know. I appreciate that."

Marcus started walking again, and Langston fell in beside him. When they reached the street, they went in opposite directions, Marcus toward the subway and Langston toward one of the many shops selling Jamaican meat patties. A car blaring reggae drove by just as they separated. Marcus smiled, and started to do a little dance, cut short by his leg injury. Langston smiled back, held up his hand, and then turned away, picking up speed.

Why do I even talk to my family? Then again, he thought, why should they understand me any better than the rest of the world?

It didn't matter anymore. He put his hand in his pocket, patting the key that was his ticket to the freedom to truly be himself.

CHAPTER THIRTEEN

October 22, 1987

I really felt like I was ready to make love to Teddy tonight, but I guess God had other ideas. It was pretty interesting meeting Teddy's mom, though.

I don't think she hates me anymore. Maybe she didn't hate me at first, either, maybe she was just surprised to run into me on my way to her son's bedroom. So much for his parents never being home.

It's a good thing I read the newspaper, because Mrs. White asked me so many tough questions, I felt like I was on *Meet the Press*. Actually, I'm impressed I could respond at all, because it took me a while to stop imagining the movie scene that was supposed to happen when Teddy and I made love. Oh well—everybody gets an upset stomach now and then. Didn't seem to stop his mom from making conversation. Too much conversation.

They must have a lot of money. Aunt Mimi's brownstone is nice enough, but she doesn't have an art collection. And some of those were originals! Romare Bearden, I've heard of, and I remember seeing a Synthia St. James somewhere. If I ever get rich, I'm going to buy something by each of them—a painting of women from her, and musicians from him. In the meantime, maybe I'll just buy a print off the street. I love the bright colors.

Then again, if Teddy and I get married, maybe his parents will give us one of them.

I wish we'd decided to come to my house. It was okay to see Sugar Hill, and everything, but we would have had plenty of time to celebrate our one month anniversary (as if that makes sense!) at my place.

Maybe I'm supposed to wait?

October 24, 1987

I played my emotions on the piano, and it felt incredible. I haven't touched Petrarch Sonnet 104 since I auditioned in February, but I remembered every note.

Teddy, darling...you were everything I'd hoped for. I still can't believe we made love in your living room. What would your parents have said if they'd walked in? And that couch is black leather. Even with a towel under us, it was completely insane! But oh my god, Teddy, I've never felt that way in my life. I had to concentrate at first, because I was so scared we'd get caught, and then you told me to close my eyes and you made me forget everything except you.

You were so gentle, and then you weren't, but everything you did was exactly what I needed, Teddy, and I thank you. How could you know my body so perfectly? Even the way your eyelashes brushed against me—I never told you about that. It's as if you know everything about me, like we were the same soul in a past life. And I don't even believe in past lives.

I can feel every cell in my body vibrating when you're near me. Not just when you're touching me, when you're looking at me, or even talking to me on the phone. It doesn't make sense.

Does it need to make sense, though? I should stop trying to analyze it, and accept that some things are mysterious. Like music. I know you can break down sound waves and pitch frequencies, but you still can't explain it. Every time I translate something from a page, it's like breathing life into something dead.

Like you breathed life into me, Teddy.

I have to laugh, because I can just imagine Betsy rolling her eyes if she ever reads this. I can imagine myself rolling my eyes if I ever read this, and someone else had written it.

But maybe not, because now I know words like this can be true.

#

Cecile met Teddy's father at a fundraiser for David Dinkins' prospective run for mayor, two days after they made love for the first time. All of the other women at the fundraiser had chosen knee to cocktail-length dresses except Cecile. Walking in, she looked down at the tight, midnight blue mini that Teddy had picked out for the occasion and felt conspicuous, though her self-consciousness lessened with each admiring comment.

"So you're Cecile," said Mr. White with a grin. "Teddy wasn't lying."

Teddy grinned, too. "You should hear her play the piano."

The man standing next to Teddy's father, an entrepreneur whose name Cecile instantly forgot, said, "You're a musician?"

"She's studying at Juilliard," said Teddy proudly.

This was the standard introduction, and it was already starting to get old. Maybe she would start introducing Teddy as an NYU student who was head of the black student union. Probably not. Instead, she'd just mention his name and let his credentials come up in conversation, or not at all, because Teddy was more than his alma mater.

The room was full of New York City's black elite: doctors, lawyers, judges, media moguls, each one dripping with money. Was the prestigious school the reason Teddy thought she belonged at his side? Or maybe it was that she had the kind of long legs that accentuated a short skirt. Then, suddenly, he looked at her with so much love and admiration, as he leaned very close and whispered, "I want to tear you apart," that all of her reservations evaporated.

"Let's see if anyone's in the men's room," he went on, still whispering.

Cecile's mouth fell open in shock. She glanced across the room at Teddy's mother, laughing with Percy Sutton and his wife. Mr. Sutton winked at her, and her cheeks flamed.

She wasn't sure Teddy was serious until he grabbed her hand and pulled her into the restroom, having made sure it was empty. As he lifted her onto the sink and pulled off her underwear, she felt herself disappear into a place in the garden of her mind she'd never been before, but wanted to visit again, and soon. Because in that place, the swamp gave way to a humid rain forest, full of the heady aromas of hibiscus and bougainvillea. Dragons, serpents, and giant spiders lurked there too, fierce and powerful, but in that moment, she knew she could slay all of them, if she had to.

Afterward, Cecile and Teddy returned to the gilded ballroom hand in hand. The only clue that they'd done more than take a stroll was their flushed skin and the look in their eyes, which, thankfully, no one seemed to link to passionate, slightly illicit sex.

Teddy was The One. He has to be, thought Cecile, or I'm a slut. No, just a sinner. Like everyone else.

She couldn't stop smiling, and every time she thought about what they'd done, the adrenaline rush hung a thick drape over the all-seeing eye of God. She hoped He understood.

CHAPTER FOURTEEN

Langston chose the day after Thanksgiving to tell Grandma Felicia he was moving. He slid next to her as she sat on the couch in the living room watching TV, wearing one of the shapeless printed house dresses she put on in private. She didn't acknowledge him, but he hadn't expected her to, because her favorite soap opera was on. For her sake, he hoped Jesus didn't come back during The Young and the Restless, because Langston could imagine his grandmother voluntarily missing out on a trip to heaven so she could find out what happened to Victor and Nicki.

Five minutes later, the theme song began to play. Grandma Felicia picked up the remote, and the screen went dark.

"What do you need, darling?" she said in her lilting Jamaican accent, angling her body so she could look him in the eye.

Langston tried to ignore his heart, which seemed about to burst through his chest. "Nothing. Just to talk to you."

Her face was open and friendly, the way she looked whenever the myriad people who sought her counsel came to visit. I'll just pretend we're not related, Langston decided, trying to ignore that their familial connection was literally written all over her face.

"I've...I'm...I got an apartment, Grandma."

Her brows came together, her lips pressed into a tight line, and all hints of welcome faded. "You've *got* an apartment? You mean, already?"

Langston's stomach felt like it was on fire. He swallowed hard. "Yes."

"When did you tell me about this?"

"I didn't," he mumbled.

"So you're grown enough to get an apartment, but not grown enough to tell me about it? What else have you been lying about?"

Her eyes, underneath her creased forehead and v-shaped brows, seemed to be glowing. *That's* why I'm afraid of a little old lady, thought Langston. But he still had no intention of telling her about Marietta.

"How was I lying?" he managed, willing himself to sound calm.

"Chuh!" Grandma Felicia kissed her teeth loudly. "Are you going to sit there and tell me you didn't deliberately deceive me?"

Langston looked down, but he could still feel her glare. "No."

After a terrible silence, she said, "When are you leaving?"

"This weekend."

Another silence. When Grandma Felicia spoke again, her voice was low and hard. "I thought I raised you children to have a backbone, but if you can't have that, at least show some common sense. Why would you waste your money on something so unnecessary when you can save it? I don't understand you."

Words of explanation eluded him, once again. Probably because it's pointless to explain, he thought. He stood, about to walk away. No, slink away, like the coward I am, he thought, and he couldn't stand it.

"I know you don't understand me, Grandma Felicia," he said quietly. "That's why I need to leave."

She looked up at him, her eyes wide with fear. "That's what your mother said."

"You know I'm not—"

"I knew you'd never lie to me. Marcus, yes, but not you. I knew that for years, and then you got that job behind my back, and now this. Lord Jesus..."

Langston stared at the ground. He could almost feel her praying for him, but he knew she couldn't match the intensity of his pleas to God for the right words, just this once, because he couldn't keep silent this time, or walk away.

"I love you, Grandma Felicia," he said, gazing at her. He'd referred to her as a little old lady, but for the first time, she actually seemed both small and ancient. When she met his gaze, he couldn't continue for a moment, because her eyes were glistening. He blew out a slow stream of air between his lips, and said, "I'm not trying to hurt you. I just need to...I need to take care of myself. You've done so much for me that I can't take anything more from you."

"Do you mean you need to take care of yourself," she replied, wringing her hands, "or you need to feel like you can do whatever you want without me telling you you're going wrong?

Satan is the father of lies, Langston. Once you give him even a piece of your heart, he can fool you."

Langston clamped his eyes shut, then opened them. "You think I'm in league with Satan?" he said impatiently.

Her hands became still. "I think you've opened the door to him, Langston. Be careful."

Langston decided not to argue. "Okay."

"I pray for you every day."

"I know you do."

"Do you pray?"

He smiled. "I prayed in the middle of this conversation."

She chuckled. "Good."

"Please don't worry about me."

His grandmother's face became serious again. "I buried your grandfather fifteen years ago. Your mother is alive, but I lost her too. I don't know if I can stand to lose..." She took a deep breath, straightening her posture as she exhaled. "Paul had a thorn in his side, and he prayed that God would remove it, and God told him His grace was sufficient. Worrying about you children is mine."

Tears sprang to Langston's eyes, but he blinked them back.

"I'm not on drugs, Grandma Felicia."

"Your mother said that, too." She turned away again, paused, and asked, "Are you leaving on Saturday or Sunday?"

"Saturday."

She nodded, then picked up the remote and brought the

TV back to life. Before he left the room, Langston considered hugging her, then decided against it. He'd absorbed the verbal reprimand, but he wasn't sure, if he put his arms around her, whether or not she would hug him back. And he wasn't sure he could survive if she didn't.

CHAPTER FIFTEEN

Teddy wanted Cecile to see NYU, so she met him at the Washington Square train station. She would have been happy to stay in the park watching the play of water in the fountain, reveling in the grandeur of the replica of the Arc de Triomphe, studying the trees, their summer green now replaced by paintbox shades of ochre, rust, and gold, or listening to the street musicians, especially the middle-aged Asian male guitarist who played and sang Autumn Leaves with so much soulful longing that Cecile felt like a voyeur. But when she asked if they could take in Washington Square just a bit longer, Teddy looked so disappointed that she smiled, took his hand, and let him lead her away.

As they walked through Greenwich Village, visiting multitudes of buildings flying dark purple NYU flags, Cecile tried to mirror Teddy's enthusiasm. He seemed to be acquainted with half of the university's population, and even though he kept the small talk to a minimum, even a few sentences exchanged with that many people became time-consuming. Cecile managed to smile every time he introduced her as his girlfriend, the Juilliard student, even forcing a grin for the females whose reaction was more competitive than friendly. After a while, though, she couldn't contain her boredom. She was trying to think of a polite way to end the ordeal when he put his arm around her shoulders and said, "Hungry?"

She nodded, gratefully.

He took her out for steaming hot dumplings and chow mein at a shabby little Chinese place on Canal Street, buzzing with waiters in faded, red brocade jackets that matched the walls. She had originally planned to practice the Duparc songs she was supposed to be rehearsing with Allen for his junior recital early in February, but she reasoned that it was barely November, so Allen would just have to understand if she postponed.

Usually, Teddy wanted to cut short the preliminaries, but this time he made no move to put on his coat after their dinner plates were cleared, requesting more tea when the waiter came with the check, then gazing out the window.

"Your place or mine?" Cecile said breezily, trying to hide her nervousness. He'd spoken very little during dinner, and for the first time since they'd met, she couldn't help wondering if they'd already run out of things to say.

Teddy glanced at her, his lips just upturned enough to qualify as a smile. "Definitely not mine," he said.

"What's wrong?"

He exhaled slowly. "Nothing."

"That can't be true, Teddy." Cecile reached for his hand, and squeezed.

He sat silently, opened his mouth to speak, then changed his mind. Finally, he focused on her. "My mom is really depressed every year on this day, because it's the anniversary of when my brother got shot."

Cecile felt instantly queasy. She took his other hand and

said, "Teddy, I'm so sorry."

"Thanks." The waiter returned with the tea. Teddy slipped his hands from Cecile's grasp and filled their cups, picking his up and blowing on the contents.

She hesitated, then said, "Do you want to tell me about him? Or would you rather not talk about it?"

He shrugged. "It was a long time ago, but Mom never seems to heal. At least, she always gets just as upset."

Cecile closed her eyes for a moment, her stomach still churning, and decided to trust him as much as he had just trusted her.

"My brother is dead, too," she said quietly. "He only died a year ago, but my parents seem better about it than they were. Then again, they're really religious."

Teddy exhaled sharply. "Man," he said, leaning back in his chair. "What happened?"

"Calvin was a drug addict. He overdosed. Or maybe he killed himself. We're not sure which." Cecile felt her cheeks flushing, cursing her pale skin's failure, yet again, to conceal her discomfort.

Teddy gazed out the window again. Dusk had fallen, and the street was full, as streets always seemed to be in Manhattan. Cecile was about to suggest that they go to Mimi's when he finally spoke.

"David was 13 years older than me—I was definitely an accident. Though my mom calls me an afterthought, or a gift. I think I only got that status after David died." Teddy chuckled, then began to speak softly, more to himself than Cecile. "He was good at everything he ever tried to do. Or maybe they made it seem that way after he died. Anyway, one day he went out to the store and never came back. Got caught in crossfire, they said. Wrong place at the wrong time. He was at Stanford trying to become a doctor. I was seven."

He wiped his eyes quickly with the side of his hand, then focused on the table. "Of course my parents couldn't get to him right away, so he died far from his family, and I know that's part of what haunts my mom so much. Mom and Dad did the best they could not to fall apart over it, which was hard because she didn't want David to go to California in the first place. Dad talked her into it. The thing is, David would have lived out there eventually anyway. He always believed the hype about the West coast."

Cecile reached for his hand again. This time, Teddy squeezed back. "I lost my parents when David died." He looked into her eyes. "They were always interested in black issues, but the only way they can handle losing their son to street violence is to try to prevent the same thing from happening in our neighborhood. That means addressing the root causes of poverty, not just lobbying for better gun laws. It's a 24 hour-a-day job. I think they're afraid they might lose me, too, if they don't change things. They definitely didn't want me going to school anywhere outside New York, for the same reason. So in one way, they want to control my life, but in the other, they always have something else to do. But I guess it's all for my good."

His voice became more conversational. "Having a common cause kept them together. So who knows, maybe the fact that they're preoccupied is a reasonable price to pay for having two parents at home."

"You miss David too, don't you?"

Teddy rubbed his thumb gently against Cecile's palm. "Sometimes. It feels like a long time ago, and we were always in very different phases of growing up, you know? He played with me and took me places, and I watched him play basketball, but I was only five when he went to California. So I can't say I knew him that well, in a way. I know he loved me."

This time, when their eyes met, and Cecile felt a warmth deep within that had nothing to do with their adventures on park benches or in hotel restrooms.

"I'm sorry about Calvin," said Teddy tenderly.

"And I'm so sorry about David."

"You say your parents are religious? Are you?"

Her pulse quickened. "In a way."

Teddy laughed, releasing her hand and picking up his tea. "What does that mean?"

Cecile could feel her ears burning, as usual. *You aren't supposed to be ashamed of the Lord, or He will be ashamed of you...*

"I believe God is watching everything we do, and that we'll be held accountable later on. But I don't always make it to church on Sunday."

"Wow. So you think God is going to zap you if you step

over the line? That's a lot of pressure, isn't it?"

"I think God is merciful, but I also think He has expectations. Which are hard to live up to, sometimes." She gazed at Teddy's face, took in every beautiful inch of it. Meeting him had to be a gift from God, and expressing her love for him fully couldn't be wrong. It couldn't. She smiled.

"Was it tough, growing up with so many rules?" he asked.

"I mean, if you don't have rules, there's chaos. I don't think any loving parent lets their kids grow up without rules."

Cecile took a deep breath, trying to relax the defensiveness out of her voice. "If you meet my parents, you'll see that they're not rigid people. They just want the best for their family, which means having standards. That's why Calvin's addiction was so hard for them. They focused most of their energy on trying to save him, and they failed. At least, that's how they felt about it at first. I think they've started to accept that he was the one who had to decide to change."

"Which proves that you can't control everything by following the rules," Teddy replied, "because things happen anyway. Like David. My parents didn't do anything wrong, and neither did David, but he still got shot. So you may as well live your life, and do what makes you happy. That's what I think, anyway."

Cecile sipped her tea. He didn't mean you should do drugs if it makes you happy. Even though Teddy had no idea of the collateral damage caused by living in a family run by a drug addict, she knew he couldn't mean that.

"Even if it hurts other people?" she said.

Teddy glanced at the check, then reached into his coat for his wallet. "I mean, you shouldn't murder or rape, or anything, but life's too short to worry about what hurts some people's feelings, because there are people who will use your caring to manipulate you."

He put some money in the folder with the bill, then motioned for the waiter. "I bet your parents don't always care what people think. I mean, there were probably some neighbors who had their feelings hurt, just knowing a black family was moving in next door." He grinned, and Cecile smiled back. "I can't believe people actually called you a nigger. That's...man. It blows my mind. No wonder you wanted to go to school so far away."

"I wanted to go to Juilliard." The defensive tone was back, but she didn't even try to fight it this time. "If Juilliard had been in Edmonton, I would have stayed there. Besides, there are racists everywhere, even in New York. Bensonhurst, for example. Well, all over. They just don't say what they're thinking. Alberta is really beautiful. The prairie isn't very interesting to look at, but there are the Rockies and the Badlands, and even the North Saskatchewan River Valley, right near where I grew up."

Teddy was still smiling at her. "Wow. I used to think Americans were way more patriotic than Canadians, but I guess I was wrong. I must visit your little farm house in this wonderful land of beauty someday." The waiter returned with the change, and Teddy selected a few bills for the tip, pocketing the change.

Then, he put on his coat and stood, waited for Cecile to do the same, and put his arm around her, guiding her out the door.

"Your place?" he said.

"Sure," she replied, grateful for Aunt Mimi's church choir, book club, volunteer work, and, most importantly, that Teddy was so charming that Aunt Mimi chose to look the other way when he followed Cecile into her room and closed the door.

Once they were outside, he pulled her close to him, leaning against the wall of the Chinese grocery store next door, just beyond the flow of pedestrian traffic, sheltering her against the biting November wind with the warmth of his body.

"Thank you," he said, his voice a caress that made Cecile shiver with anticipation.

"What did I do?"

"Nothing. You're just you, and that makes it okay to tell you anything. It's...it's hard for me to trust, sometimes, and..."

He glanced away. When his eyes found hers again, the intensity behind them made the queasiness she'd felt earlier come back.

"Cecile," he said, "I...can I—"

"It's okay," she urged him.

A smile flashed across his lips. "You're right. It's okay. Because you're you." He took a deep breath, and said, "If we're going to go further with this relationship, I need you to be...I really need to know that someone in this world is there for me. I know we've only been together a few weeks, but...the thing is, I know...well, there's shit I need to deal with, but you make me feel like I can get through it and be a better man. What I need from you is a promise that you'll hang in there. Maybe that isn't fair—"

Cecile squeezed him as tightly as she could, her eyes filling with tears. "I promise, Teddy," she said. "Thank you for trusting me."

She felt him inhale deeply, letting the air go in a rush. "Thank *you*, Cecile."

Cecile sighed, tilting her chin to receive a kiss, then another, the world falling away, so lost in him that she almost didn't hear him breathe the words, "I love you."

Teddy stopped, wide-eyed.

Cecile smiled. "I love you, too," she said.

His face relaxed. They kissed each other passionately, then he held her so close she could barely breathe, his arousal hard against her stomach.

"What are you doing to me?" he whispered. "I'm not sure I can wait." They looked at each other for a moment, and then he began to laugh. "I don't think the men's room in that restaurant is nearly as nice as the other one."

Cecile felt a familiar rush of adrenaline, ready to do whatever he asked. Again.

He kissed her, then released her, taking her hand and leading her away from the wall. "We'll wait," he said. "It'll kill me, but you're worth it."

"I love you," she said, barely restraining the urge to say it over and over, just to hear herself speak the words she'd never thought she'd be able to say, except in a dream, wishing for language that could adequately convey the explosion of emotion inside her.

"I love you too, Cecile. You're so damn special...God, I love you!" He looked up at the sky, then grabbed her and spun her around suddenly, nearly knocking over an unsuspecting man wearing a well-tailored coat and carrying a briefcase.

She couldn't stop laughing, even though the guy she'd almost hit didn't look amused. "I love this woman," Teddy explained, and the passerby shook his head, hurrying on his way.

"My place?" she said, regaining her composure, tucking her forehead just under his chin and giving him a quick kiss on the neck.

He pulled away from her just enough to gaze adoringly into her eyes, and said, "I can't wait."

CHAPTER SIXTEEN

By the beginning of November, Langston's apartment truly felt like home. He'd gotten used to his new furniture, which meant first getting used to the fact that he owned anything other than the clothes on his back and his textbooks. Everything was in shades of beige and brown, with an orange lamp, rugs and placemats for contrast, because Zora had insisted. He was glad he'd listened.

He was just as glad he hadn't listened when she tried to talk him out of taking the apartment. The night before the move, she'd called to inform him he was breaking his grandmother's heart, and besides, with Marcus planning to get married in the spring, there would soon be nobody to take care of things that required physical strength. Langston argued that his grandmother knew everyone in the entire neighborhood and beyond, and besides, he wasn't supposed to live there forever anyway. Was he?

Zora grew quiet. Then she offered to help him decorate. If you can't beat 'em, join 'em, thought Langston.

At first, he'd continued his old habit of studying in the library, eating at school, working, and heading home mainly to sleep, incorporating Marietta where their schedules allowed. But after about a week and a half, it dawned on him that he could go home a lot more now, because he lived midway between school and his job. And that he was free to do as he liked once he got there. Just as he'd planned.

Besides Marcus, the only person he told about Marietta was Glenda. As expected, she didn't raise any objections about the interracial dating, because of her parents, but she still didn't think dating his boss's daughter was a good idea.

"I know," said Langston.

"Unless you're planning to quit. Or take over the family business, of course."

"Well, I *am* working my way up. Mario likes the way I do the food prep enough that he sometimes tells me how he cooks things. Not that I couldn't figure it out by watching him."

"So you're watching him," said Glenda, "while you're chopping? Not very smart, Andrews."

Langston laughed. "You don't need ten fingers to be a teacher."

"True."

He didn't tell Marietta about the move until two weeks later. It was Friday night and the movie they'd just seen, *Less Than Zero,* had left Langston in a foul mood.

"It wasn't that bad," said Marietta, reaching for his hand as they left the theater. Neither of them was wearing gloves, despite the frost in the early November air, so the warmth of her fingers felt good.

"I hated it," he said.

"We could have seen *Cry Freedom*, you know. That wasn't a joke. I hear Denzel Washington is excellent."

Langston glanced at her. A drama about Stephen Biko's

death at the hands of racist white authorities in apartheid-era South Africa seemed like a bad choice, even if an interracial friendship was central to the plot.

"What's really bothering you?" she asked, and when she squeezed his hand, he squeezed back.

He no longer cared who saw them, now that his family was out of the picture. Besides, since they'd started spending time together, he'd noticed that they were hardly the only mixed couple in Toronto. As expected, black women glared at him, but he ignored their judgments more and more easily. After all, they didn't know him, he didn't know them, and they certainly didn't know Marietta.

Not that he knew her that well, either. Her concern seemed genuine, though.

"I was telling you the truth," he said. "I hated the movie."

"But why so much? I've never seen you like this."

He hesitated for a moment, then pulled her away from the constant stream of people heading to the Bloor and Yonge subway, and looked into her eyes, holding both of her hands. Everything between them had been superficial, to this point, including their physical contact, which was limited to warm hugs and affectionate, but not passionate, kisses. But maybe he could go deeper now. After all, he was gazing at her, on the verge of self-revelation, and he didn't feel anything more than friendly. He would miss her if she rejected him over this bit of truth, but he was sure he'd get over it, and rather quickly.

"I hated that movie," he said, straining to sound matter-of-fact, "because my parents are both addicted to cocaine. At least, I think they still are. I haven't heard anything about them in years, and I don't want to. So seeing all that shit on the screen...I just feel...I don't know."

Marietta put her arms around him, leaning in to hold him close. The warmth of her body made him let go. He inhaled the impossibly sweet floral scent of her hair, and as he closed his eyes, the noise of cars and people faded to a vague wash of sound, much softer than the pounding of his heart. For the first time, he needed her.

"I used to live with my Grandma Felicia, but I moved out," he whispered. "I told her I had to leave because she doesn't understand me, and she said my mother told her the same thing."

Marietta pulled away. "I'm so sorry," she said, looking into his eyes for a moment. Then she hugged him again, tighter this time, rubbing his back with her hand.

Finally, she released him. "Maybe we should have seen *The Princess Bride*," she said, smiling.

Langston laughed. "I saw it, actually, with my little sister, Maya. We both loved it."

Marietta wrinkled her nose. "Wow, seriously? You like fairy tales?"

"It's an excellent film," Langston replied defensively. "Very funny, in a clever way. Perfect cast, and I happen to like a well-choreographed sword fight."

"I was going to ask you to show me your new place," she said, "but I think you just killed the mood."

Langston bit his lip, frowning. "Really?"

She put her hands on her hips. "You don't know me very well, do you?"

He shook his head.

"Maybe it's time you got to know me better, then," she said with a sly grin, taking his hand and pulling him away from the wall, then stepping back and letting him lead her into the subway station.

#

I should do this more often, Langston thought, holding Marietta against his chest as they lay on his narrow, mildly uncomfortable bed. With someone besides myself, that is. But as he ran his fingers through her hair, he couldn't help imagining Zora and Maya, judging him. He wouldn't allow himself to conjure up his grandmother. Or worse, Mr. Zappatore.

Marietta turned on her side, very nearly falling over the edge of the mattress. Langston grabbed her, laughing, and turned on his side too, so that they were nose to nose, then kissed her.

"I'm going to have to leave soon," she said, her voice full of reluctance.

"I figured you would." He kissed her again, then pulled away, propping his head on his hand. "Can I ask you a question?"

"Of course."

"What do you tell your dad? I mean, when you're with me."

"Not much. I mean, he's at the restaurant a lot."

"What about your sisters?"

"I don't tell their business, and they don't tell mine. We have a deal." She smiled.

"Your priest?"

Her smiled faded, and she pushed him playfully. "You should know you don't get to hear my confession. Didn't you learn that in Catholic school? You are Catholic, aren't you?"

"Uh-oh."

"I'll convert you. Don't worry about it." She put her hands on his cheeks, pulled him towards her, and gave him a lingering kiss. Then, she sat up, reached around on the floor until she found her clothes, and started to get dressed.

Langston turned on his bedside lamp, making the room glow orange. Someone down the street was having a party, and he couldn't resist moving his head to the beat of the calypso that reminded him of what used to be home.

"Oh, I love this music," said Marietta. "Can you show me how to dance?"

Langston hesitated. "There isn't just one way," he said.

"I know that," she said with a grin, coming over to the bed and throwing back the covers. Langston quickly retrieved his underwear from the floor, suddenly self-conscious, pulling on his jeans moments later.

"I want to dance the way you like," she went on. "I mean, I showed you how to do something the way *I* like. It's only fair."

Langston smiled. She was obviously far more experienced than he was, but she couldn't bring herself to name what they'd just done. Maybe she's trying to convince herself she isn't in league with Satan, he thought, just like I am. What was that verse about the children of the light? Something about them doing what they did openly.

She was waiting expectantly, with the same wide-eyed, childlike expression on her face he'd seen the day they met. All at once, her skin looked extra pale.

"I'm not really a dance instructor," he said.

She rolled her eyes. "And I'm not a sex instructor."

"I disagree," he said, resolving to stop trying to figure her out, so he could stop being wrong.

She smiled. "Thanks. Hey, we're running out of time, here! I tell you what. You dance, I'll take notes."

"No."

"*Mama mia! Y*es, I said that on purpose." She grabbed his hands, and started moving her hips from side to side. "Is this it?"

Just then the music changed to dancehall.

"Well, if you must know," said Langston, "it's more like this."

He did the butterfly, bent knees touching then spreading apart as he worked his hips, then planted his feet and started winding his waist.

"Wow," she said, nodding approvingly. "I'm going to have sweet dreams tonight."

He laughed. "At your house, since you have to leave now. Right?"

"Right."

He found his shirt, which he'd thrown on the couch, and

pulled it over his head.

"I'll walk you to the subway," he said, retrieving his shoes and coat.

"Of course."

As they stepped into the hallway, Langston said, "Hey Marietta?" and she turned towards him.

"Are you ever going to tell your family?"

She ran her hand through her hair, her eyes hardening for a moment. "Are you?"

"Touche.

"Have I told you lately that you're the best accompanist ever?" said James, as he and Cecile stepped out of the room where he'd just sung his December jury exam in front of the likes of Ellen Faull, Oren Brown, Marlena Malas, and Edith Bers—some of the most famous voice instructors in the world.

"No," she said with a grin.

"Well, you are."

"Thanks."

They began to walk towards the stairs—James was always looking for ways to get more exercise, and rarely took the elevator.

"Sure you can't make it to Ollie's for dinner?" he said. "Everybody else is gonna be there."

Cecile sighed. "I know. I'm sorry, but I promised Teddy..."

"Do you know how many times you've said that?" said James, stopping. "What's up with Teddy, anyway? Is he allergic to musicians?"

"Well, obviously not, since he's dating me."

James pushed open the door to the stairwell, waiting for Cecile to go through it then walking beside her as they descended the steps.

"How many times have you seen Olivia?"

As Cecile started to consider, he spoke again.

"Exactly. A lot."

"He's got a busy schedule," Cecile protested, "and NYU isn't very close by."

"Number 1 train stops right by the door."

"What's the big deal, James?"

He pushed open the door to the lobby. "We miss you."

Cecile gazed at him as the door closed behind her. There was nothing flirtatious in his tone. "Really?"

"Really. I mean, we were all talking about it. We bump into you, sure, and yeah, we hang out when we're collaborating on music. But just because you've got a man doesn't mean you can't have friends."

Cecile frowned. "So you're not my friend anymore?"

James shook his head. "Come on, Cecile. You know what I'm saying."

"We'll all get together before Christmas, okay?"

"With Teddy, right? So we can meet him."

Cecile cocked her head. "And give him the seal of approval?" she asked sarcastically.

"He should pass, right?"

"Of course."

"Okay then." James smiled, and gave her a quick hug. "Thanks again for doing such a great job on my jury."

"Hey, you get what you pay for."

He laughed. "I hear you, baby. Okay, I owe you lunch, how's that?"

"It'll do until I get really expensive."

"You're right," he said, still grinning. "I'd better exploit you while I can. Okay, lunch it is. Are you going home?"

"I'm going back upstairs to practice."

"Okay, see ya."

She watched him for a moment, turned towards the elevator, then changed her mind, deciding to follow his good example and take the stairs.

Climbing alone in the semi-darkness, she knew why she'd never introduced Teddy to her Juilliard friends. Teddy was always friendly, but whenever they were around men who were even slightly attractive and close to their age, he'd suddenly get physically affectionate. Not that he wasn't affectionate anyway, but he ramped it up in front of "the competition."

 I'm going to bring him to a concert so he can finally meet them, she thought. That way, he can get more used to classical music, and I can stop missing so many performances to be with him. In the meantime, I'll tell him I don't like it when he grabs my ass in public.

Then again, he always said how much he loved her body whenever he did it, and she knew of other women who didn't seem to mind that kind of thing. Cecile was sure he wouldn't do it in front of her parents when he came with her to Alberta in June for Teresa's older sister Karen's wedding. So why would he do it in front of Allen and James?

Either way, she was going to get together with her Juilliard buddies before Christmas. Without Teddy.

Deep down, he knows I meant it when I promised to be there for him, thought Cecile as she reached the fourth floor, smiling at the memory of Teddy looking into her eyes the last time they'd made love and swearing she was the only one who could bring him such pleasure.

I'll introduce him to my friends in the New Year, she decided. But if I have to choose between them and Teddy, I know who wins.

A fragment of a song from her dad's Shirley Bassey album started playing in her head, insistently enough to supersede the snatches of classical melodies that came and went as she searched for a vacant practice room:

I dim the lights, I think about you,
Spend sleepless nights to think about you...
It's like I'm losing my mind.

CHAPTER EIGHTEEN

When Marietta stopped dropping by in mid-December, Langston wasn't surprised. Christmas was coming, and with it, family gatherings. Then again, as much as Mr. Zappatore seemed to like him, Langston wouldn't have been surprised to be invited to his house as a surrogate son, which might have unsettled the Langston who hadn't given a corner of his heart to Satan, the Father of Lies. The current version, however, would have been just fine with it; Marietta was such a willing, creative sex partner, the deception had become easier and easier.

Langston expected to miss her warm, eager body, for obvious reasons, but he didn't expect to miss talking to her so much. He liked hearing stories about her mother, who had died suddenly two years before they'd met, her three older sisters, and the many ways they'd gotten around her father's rules. To Langston's surprise, Marietta knew a lot about world history, not just European history, and while he had many opportunities to point out her ignorance of West Indian culture, she had just as many to point out his ignorance of the colonial slave trade, among other things.

She didn't ask him a lot of personal questions, so he ended up listening more than he talked, but he didn't mind. They were both busy, so if he had to choose between baring his soul and baring his body, the decision was easy.

He wasn't really lonely without her, because Glenda was back in town, now that the first semester was over. Hanging around with her would have cut into his time with Marietta anyway, and he was grateful not to have to choose. Or have to introduce them.

"I don't get that," said Glenda, sitting at the card table that was meant to imply a dining room. She'd stopped at Langston's apartment with a belated housewarming gift, in the form of a ficus plant. "I mean, your girlfriend has to meet your best friend sometime."

Langston turned on the kettle, then searched in his cupboard for two mugs and a canister of dried hot chocolate mix. "She's not my girlfriend."

"Whatever. I still want to meet her."

"What difference does it make?"

"No difference at all, Andrews." She smirked. "You are being extremely weird about this. I hope you know that. Are you ashamed of her, or something?"

Langston poured hot water over the chocolate powder, mixed, then added some milk, whipped cream, and a touch of cinnamon.

"Sorry this is instant," he said, bringing the cups to the table, "but I did get it in a gourmet shop."

Glenda's eyes narrowed. "Since when have I required gourmet anything?"

"Never."

"So, about that question you dodged—"

"The answer is, no. I'm not ashamed of her."

He sat at the table, warming his hands on his mug. "Why

do I have to explain this?"

Glenda stuck her finger in her whipped cream, then licked it pensively. "You don't. I mean, why have any idea what the hell you're doing with your life?"

"It's a riddle, wrapped in a mystery, inside an enigma," he replied, grinning.

"Who said that?"

"Churchill. About Russia. I learned it from Marietta."

"You're starting to annoy me."

"It's mutual."

"You're using her, is that it?"

Langston was beginning to get a headache.

"Not really. I mean, no more than she's using me." He stared at his hot chocolate. "I don't know why it doesn't feel like a real relationship. I don't think it's the secrecy. Well, it is the secrecy, but not from our families."

He met Glenda's eyes, saw that she wasn't judging him anymore, and sighed. "I don't let my guard down completely, and neither does she, except in bed. I think that's it. We're both holding back a lot unless we're having sex."

"Because you both know it can't last, because neither of you is willing to fight for it."

He chuckled. "You sound like such a romantic."

"Ha! Look who's talking!"

Langston leaned back, eyebrows raised. "Huh?"

"You can't fool me, Andrews," Glenda insisted, pointing at him. "It's why you couldn't be a jerk in high school, and it's why you loved *The Princess Bride*."

He took a sip of his hot chocolate. "Marietta laughed at me for that one."

"What? Dump her!"

Langston coughed. She'd commented just as he was swallowing another mouthful, making the drink go down the wrong tube.

When he recovered, he said, "Just because of one statement that wasn't even serious?"

"Because she doesn't get you. Do you have a picture of this person? Now I really have to see what she looks like."

Glenda's unflinching stare made him nervous.

"We went to a photo booth once," he said.

"Perfect." Glenda sampled her hot chocolate, and her face softened slightly. "This is really good."

"That's why it's gourmet."

Glenda stuck out her tongue at him as he passed her chair on the way to the kitchen. He kept the pictures on top of the cupboard, so no guests would accidentally find them. This is ridiculous, he thought, handing the strip to Glenda without glancing at them.

She studied the photos, which started with crossed eyes and ended with tongue kisses, then gave them back to him, with a serious expression. "You have fun together?"

"Yes."

She rested her chin on her hand. "You need to have fun."

"I agree."

"I just want you to remember that some people are for a season and a reason. You know that expression, right? Don't forget that this is seasonal."

"Of course not."

She took a long drink of hot chocolate. "What brand is this, again?"

#

Langston spent Christmas Eve with his family, as he always had, arriving with a small bag so he could stay the night in his old room, which still felt like home, but had somehow already achieved the distance of childhood memory.

He'd been to Scarborough for two brief visits since moving out. The first time, Grandma Felicia was noticeably cool, but by the second time, she seemed to have forgiven him, maybe because he was lucid whenever she called or saw him. Luckily, she went to sleep early, because if he'd picked up the phone after a session with Marietta and a bottle of wine, he might not have passed inspection.

The Andrews' Christmas Eve tradition meant decorating the tree in the afternoon, having a smaller version of the next day's feast, then eggnog and fruitcake (both made with the overproof rum reserved for the occasion), followed by going to a late church service.

Everyone got to sleep in on Christmas morning, since Maya no longer woke up at the crack of dawn. After breakfast, which usually included Grandma Felicia's famous bran and marmalade muffins, the protocol was to get dressed in fancy clothes, then wait for Zora, Bernie, and their children, Will and Claire, to come over so everyone could open presents. Since Danita was all but family, she joined Marcus when he came by, but if they arrived more than half an hour after Zora's family, the presents were to be opened without them. Grandma Felicia's rules, so she'd have ample time to cook the feast, for which Zora had supplied the side dishes since her marriage. After dinner, Maya played the piano—she could just manage the required Christmas carols—and everyone sang together, even Bernie, who couldn't carry a tune. Then the younger relatives cleaned up the kitchen, and then either cutthroat bridge, equally competitive dominoes, or conversation.

As his family chattered around him, Langston found himself wondering what the Zappatore's were doing, and imagining how Marietta would have fit in at his family gathering. He thought of calling her, but decided against it. He'd given her an off-white cable knit sweater as an early present the last time she'd come to his apartment, and she'd given him Armani, her favorite cologne, daring him to joke about the designer's nationality. After sex, they'd wished each other Merry Christmas, which made calling her redundant.

Only two weeks had gone by, but it felt longer, because he'd gotten spoiled. Was he allowed to get in touch as soon as Christmas Day was over, though? Or were they supposed to wait until school started again?

He had to work four times in the next week, including New Year's Eve. Maybe she'd come in to Gino's. He smiled, imagining how they'd pull off pretending they didn't know each other. Then again, now that he didn't bus the tables, he probably wouldn't see her unless she made a special effort.

The more he thought about it, the more he hoped she didn't come. Bob had started getting used to Langston's elevated status, but he still watched him warily, as if...well, Langston wasn't sure. Maybe only Italians were supposed to cook in an Italian restaurant. That must have been it. Then again, Langston had been watched warily by so many white people, by that time, that the anger he'd felt at noticing their distrust had become existential, and vague. He'd achieved the serenity to accept the things he could not change, perhaps. Nar-Anon, by osmosis.

Either way, Langston couldn't be sure nobody would sense his connection to Marietta if they were in the same room. Mr. Zappatore tended to be absorbed in running his business, and Mario would probably focus on his work, too, but Bob could be a problem. Langston hoped that even if she didn't have a backbone, Marietta had enough common sense not to tempt fate.

As it turned out, he didn't have to wait until he went back to work, because Marietta called him two days after Christmas, waking him up.

"Can I come over?" she said.

Langston blinked repeatedly, willing his eyes to focus. "What time is it?"

"Seven. I wanted to make sure I wouldn't miss you."

"Anymore."

"What?"

"You wouldn't miss me anymore."

"Right. When can I come over?"

"Any time before noon. I have to work later."

"Great."

Langston hung up the phone, then pulled the covers up to his ears. She'd sounded businesslike. Maybe someone was listening.

He debated getting out of bed, since he was pretty sure whatever clothes he put on would soon come off. I should at least take a shower and brush my teeth, though, he thought. Maybe put on some Armani cologne.

He smiled. The drought was about to be over.

#

Marietta rang his buzzer an hour later, just as he was making up his bed. When he opened the door, she allowed him a hug, but turned her head slightly when he tried to kiss her, so that his lips met her cheek.

As he stepped away and let her pass, he felt a mild burning sensation that started in his throat and ended in his gut.

"Can I take your coat?" he asked uncertainly.

"Oh wow, I almost forgot." She smiled slightly, handing him a bright red, woolen trench he'd never seen before. Underneath, she had put on his Christmas gift.

"The sweater looks good on you," he remarked.

"Thanks! I really like it. The Armani smells good on you, too."

"Did you eat breakfast?"

"No, but I'm not hungry."

Suddenly, neither am I, thought Langston. Her initial frostiness had thawed, but only a little.

He followed her over to the table, and sat down across from her. After less than a minute, he couldn't stand the silence, and said, "Can you please just tell me why you're here? I think I know, but I'd appreciate your saying it."

She ran her hand through her hair, a gesture that had become instantly irritating, then looked in his eyes. "Langston, you knew this wasn't going anywhere. Right?"

His eyes darted away, landing on his bed. Bad choice, he thought, gazing at his new ficus tree instead. "I guess so."

"No, you knew," she said firmly.

When he faced her again, her eyes weren't unkind, but he was nevertheless amazed at how comfortable she seemed to be with dumping him, in his own house, in person.

"You do this all the time?" he asked.

A small line formed in the center of her forehead. "What do you mean?"

"I mean ditching me doesn't seem to bother you at all."

"Of course it bothers me," she said angrily. "I like you."

"So why now, then? What happened?"

She drummed her fingers on the table. She always kept her nails short. He liked that. Not that he didn't like to look at women who spent a lot of time on grooming, but that detail had always seemed to him as proof that she was down-to-earth, unlike Anthea Tanner, the wannabe princess who had seduced and dumped him in high school. Yet here Marietta was, with her short, unpolished nails, dumping him anyway.

"It was just time, that's all," she said, with an edge.

"Why are you mad at me?"

"I'm not," she said, her face like a gathering storm.

"Marietta, you don't have to lie. I mean, why bother? We're never going to see each other again, except by accident. Or maybe not even that, since if you tell your dad about us, he'll probably fire me."

She laughed. "No, he'll kill you. But don't worry, I won't tell. Like I said, I like you."

"Thanks."

There was another silence, then she said, "Well, I'd better go..."

"No. No, you'd better not."

Her hand went through her hair again, her eyes wide. If she does that one more time, thought Langston, I think I'll break her arm. He blew air out, hard, between his lips, disappointed with himself.

"I'm sorry," he said. "I didn't mean that. Of course you can go. But I think the least you could do, before you leave, is tell me the truth. The whole truth, this time."

She bit her lip, considering. "Do you promise to do the same?"

"Sure."

"Okay." She folded her hands in front of her, tilted her chin up for a moment to look at the ceiling, then focused on him again. "The truth is...okay, I have a boyfriend. We've been together for years, ever since junior high school, on and off, though we got serious in eleventh grade. He went away to college, but he's home for the holidays. I'd never cheated on him before, but he's still talking about marriage, like he was last the summer, too. I got a little scared, because I'm only 21, and there are a lot of things I want to do, and I'm not sure I'll be able to do them if I get married so young. So..."

"Was fucking a black guy on your list? I guess you can check that one off, huh."

She laid her hands flat against the table, leaning forward. "I should smack you for that."

"Just answer the question. Honestly." His insides were burning again. *You knew nothing good would come of this...*

"I wasn't *fucking* you," she said evenly, "because you're black. I was *fucking* you because I like you. If you recall, it took a while before I *fucked* you. If I was only interested in *fucking* you, we could have done that right away. Correct?"

"No, because I wouldn't have *fucked* you right away, anyway. I had to decide I liked you first."

She leaned back, with the innocent expression he'd always found so disarming. "Wow, really?"

"Really." He took a deep breath, trying to dissipate his anger by slowing down his heart.

"No wonder you weren't very experienced."

"I think you fixed that."

She chuckled. "I'm going to miss you," she said, smiling

fondly. He couldn't help smiling back.

"So can I ask you anything, just this once?" she continued.

"You could have asked me lots of things before this."

"I kind of liked *fucking* you, though. We only had so much time."

He had to laugh. "I agree."

"Anyway," she said, "isn't there a curiosity with black men about white women? Because I'll admit, I wondered how you'd be different. Aside from the stereotype about your penis, which I was glad to find out to be true."

"Wow, you don't care, do you?" he replied, shaking his head in disbelief. "I think we expect all vaginas to feel pretty similar."

"Are you offended?"

"No. Do all white men have small penises?"

"No."

"And not all black men are big. Can we move on?"

"Sure."

He blinked a few times, then glanced at her and smiled. "Maybe some black men are curious about white women. I mean, if you're curious about anything, you're curious about a lot of things, I think. I was more afraid than curious."

"Seriously? Why?"

"Because of my Grandma Felicia, and the rest of my family. She always said that black men who date white women think they're getting some special prize, because historically white womanhood has been artificially elevated to the status of an ideal. And she always said white women only date black men out of curiosity, or to be rebellious. So there's no real caring, just using."

Marietta's face fell. "Interesting."

"Since we're asking all kinds of frank questions..."

"Too late to take that back?"

"Yup." He grinned. He'd never felt so comfortable around her, not even after sex. Well, maybe, but it was different. What would have happened if they'd started off this honestly? Mr. Zappatore would still have been her father, that's what.

"Why me?" he asked. "I mean, I get that you were looking to sow some wild oats, but I couldn't have been the only possible guy to do that with."

She shrugged. "It was sort of impulsive. I had a conversation with Carlo the night before that really freaked me out, talking about kids and stuff. So when I recognized you and remembered that my dad had said nice things about you, I ended up saying things I hadn't planned. Plus, you're really cute. Cuter than you seem to think. Great body, too."

He looked away, embarrassed.

"Back to your Grandma's views on black/white relationships. Do you agree with her?"

"Wow." He almost wished he had long hair, so he could run his fingers through it. "Um—"

"Honestly."

He exhaled, then looked up, studying her face. Thick

eyebrows, dark eyes, long straight nose, wide, relatively full lips, and that little beauty mark to the left of her mouth. She wasn't stunning, but she was attractive. Her skin didn't make her more so, in his book. He did like the feel of her hair. Black girls he'd met who used relaxers didn't seem to quite achieve the same texture. Then again, he also liked the soft wooliness of an afro. Mainly, he was happy to be close enough to any woman to be allowed to touch her hair in the first place.

"Honestly, I think it's true in some cases, and not in others. In your case, no, I didn't think I was getting something special, just because you're white. I had to get over the idea that I was doing something wrong, fooling around with you."

Marietta nodded. "So did I. And not just because of Carlo."

"Do you want some coffee?"

"Sure."

Langston went to the kitchen to plug in his coffeemaker. He usually liked to grind the beans each time, but he was glad he'd accidentally bought it already ground. When the machine had started to drip, he sat down again.

"Why would your father want to kill me if he found out?" he asked. "Other than the obvious."

She bit her lip. "I don't know. I mean, I know, but I can't explain it." She glanced away. "He likes you a lot. He even respects you. But it doesn't mean you're good enough for his daughter, even if you're way smarter than Carlo."

Langston tried not to grin. "I am?"

"He's a good guy, but he's not as...well, I won't say smart. It's just different. I do love him, you know."

"I'm glad. I mean, if you're thinking about marrying him, that's a good thing."

She sat silently for a moment, then searched his eyes. "Do you think...hmm."

"Go ahead," Langston said softly.

"Do you think I could have loved you? Or maybe you could have loved me?"

Langston caught his breath sharply. "I don't even know how to answer that," he replied. "Besides, what difference does it make? I'm not good enough for you, in your dad's eyes."

"But he really does like you, Langston!"

"I'm not even angry about it," Langston said, surprised at his own reaction. "Maybe I would be, if my Grandma didn't like so many white people she'd never want to call her in-laws." He shook his head. Their eyes met again. "When you say it out loud, it's kind of stupid, isn't it? I mean, culture is what it is, and I bet you're a lot different than a German girl would be, so it's not just about color. I'm different than most of the West Indians I know, to tell the truth. It's just the hating people for no reason that makes no sense, you know? Although I've looked at white people and assumed they thought negatively about me, until I found out differently. And even then, I expect there's something about me they're assuming based on my skin. I've also looked at interracial couples and wondered if they can possibly love each other, and why they couldn't just find one of their own, like most people do."

Marietta's hand went through her hair again.

"You do that a lot, have you noticed?" said Langston.

"What?"

He ran his hand over the top of his head.

She rolled her eyes. "Who cares?"

"Just an observation."

She was quiet for a moment, then she said, "Last bit of honesty?"

"Sure."

She looked at him, folding her hands on the table again. "It is a bit easier, in a way, when you have something deep in common that doesn't need a lot of explanation. I'm not saying all Italians are the same, or all Sicilians, or whatever, but...I don't know. People are complicated, and life is complicated, and having something already there that you can relate to—"

"I know what you mean," he said. "Then again, if you're going to spend your lives together, isn't there time to explain?"

"There should be. The thing is, sometimes you can't explain, because people just can't understand, no matter how hard they try."

"True, but by that argument, we should all be gay, because men and women can't understand each other, either, no matter how hard they try."

She laughed. "Maybe people need to listen to each other more, and judge each other less."

"Maybe." His eyes teared up, unexpectedly. "So no more

conversations like this?" he said. "Not even as friends?"

Her eyes started glistening, too. "I don't think so. I don't know. Maybe, down the road. If I run into you at the restaurant, we could pretend we were just meeting. That could happen, right?"

He nodded. It couldn't happen. There no way to pretend well enough, at this point. He was sure she knew that.

"Coffee?" he said. "Or maybe you want breakfast now. I make great omelets."

"That sounds amazing." She sniffled, then glanced over at his bed, and back into his eyes. "And if we hurry, I might have time for dessert."

"Is that a good idea?" he asked, his loins stirring at the thought of it.

She smiled. "Nope."

CHAPTER NINETEEN

Teddy and Cecile held hands during the entire trip from New York to Edmonton, releasing each other only long enough to hurriedly eat and drink. Hour after hour, they talked or sat silently, enveloped in the bliss of togetherness, each needing nothing more than the presence of the other.

The stated purpose of the trip was to attend Karen's June wedding. In Cecile's mind, however, the reason for bringing Teddy to her hometown had morphed from sharing her past with her beloved into letting her family and friends see that even though she had appeared to be an exception, there was indeed someone for everyone. Not just someone, in her case—a magnificently handsome, tall, muscular, intelligent man who wanted to help humanity, and needed her by his side to have the strength to do it.

She knew her family would like him as much as her friends had. He'd attended an opera scenes concert in February, and while he didn't love it, he'd appreciated the staging, costumes, and especially the singing. The highlights of the program were excerpts from *Rigoletto,* featuring Tonya and Allen singing a beautiful duet that Cecile instantly decided to include in her own wedding, and James nailing the famous low note at the end of the aria sung by Sparafucile. Afterward, Cecile's Juilliard crew, Olivia, and Teddy went to a diner for coffee and dessert. Despite the obvious playfulness between Cecile and her male friends, Teddy had put his arm around her, but that was it. In fact, he'd joked and laughed with them as much as she had.

And the reason he'll like my family just as much, she decided, watching him dozing beside her on the plane, five hours into the journey, is that our dysfunction died with Calvin.

As soon as she and Teddy came through the doors that separated travelers from those who had come to greet them, Cecile spotted her dad, straining the seams of a t-shirt that used to be the right size, before he'd padded his imposing physique with a layer of fat. He was a grown man, as her mother had said, but Cecile still didn't understand why her mom refused to insist on making him wear clothes that fit. Then again, Mary Alexander didn't seem to care about a lot of things. In a relationship where physical attractiveness had obviously been part of the foundation, her parents had achieved a level of acceptance that embraced both her father's growing paunch and her mother's eternally slender form with equanimity.

The Alexanders broke into broad grins as Teddy and Cecile came close. So did Cecile, because the approval on their faces meant Teddy had passed the first test.

"Teddy, I'm Norman," said her dad, shaking Teddy's hand firmly.

Teddy responded in kind, with a luminous smile. "A pleasure to meet you, sir."

"And I'm Mary," said Cecile's mom, the music of her Bermudian inflection a sharp contrast to the New York accents of Teddy and her husband.

Teddy shook her hand, too. "I can see where Cecile gets

her beauty."

Cecile barely restrained the urge to roll her eyes at all three of them—at her parents, for letting Teddy call them Norman and Mary when they'd always looked down on the disrespectful practice of calling people of an older generation by their given names, and at Teddy, for sucking up so shamelessly. And yet she couldn't help bubbling with joy, starting the visit so auspiciously.

Teddy met Betsy later, when she came in from a friend's house. She spoke to him when he spoke first, but otherwise acted as if he weren't there, gently making fun of Cecile's love-struck state when she and her sister were alone. Which didn't bother Cecile at all. It would have taken a lot more than a few bratty comments from a fifteen year-old to ruin her glow. Still, showing him off to Teresa, who could barely stop herself from drooling, even with Edwin sitting beside her, was a lot more fun.

Teddy and Cecile had arrived six days before the wedding, which allowed Mr. and Mrs. Alexander to take everyone to Banff for two nights—standard procedure for anyone visiting from a place without Rocky Mountains, but Cecile couldn't stop herself from seeing the gesture as further evidence of parental approval.

Half an hour into the trip, Mr. Alexander turned down the radio and said, "Cecile tells me you're the head of the African American Student Union."

"Yes, sir, I am."

Cecile's heart sped up a bit. She hoped her parents

wouldn't embarrass her by giving him the kind of interrogation she'd endured from his mother.

"What does that involve?"

"We organize informational events, invite speakers, do outreach to the community—"

"So it's all serious?" Mr. Alexander interjected. "No parties at all?"

Teddy chuckled, unfazed. "I'd be lying if I said we never do things just for fun."

"The West Indian Students Association had parties when I was in school," said Mrs. Alexander. "Nothing wrong with being social."

"Where did you study, Mary?" Teddy asked, his voice eager enough to betray his relief about the change of subject.

"Dalhousie, in Halifax, Nova Scotia. Have you been to Nova Scotia?"

"I can't say I have, although I've heard the Maritimes are beautiful."

"They are." Cecile's mother turned towards him, smiling warmly.

"What did you study? Oh wait...Cecile mentioned that you're an elementary school principal. I have so much respect for educators, especially the ones who deal with little kids. Then again, I suppose you have to love young children if you're going to go into elementary ed."

"I do."

"I didn't say there was anything wrong with being social,"

said Cecile's dad, his tone neutral, as if he needed more evidence that he should be impressed. "How long have you been running the group?"

"I'm not running it," said Teddy affably. "I'm just one person. I don't make all of the decisions, or anything, I'm just the name on file with the administration."

"You're too modest," said Mrs. Alexander.

Cecile slipped her hand in Teddy's, gazed into his eyes and smiled. She knew that he relished his role as a campus leader, but was tailoring his response to the audience, deciding to charm her father rather than to justify himself. She didn't know whether to be alarmed at his bullshit or to applaud it.

Teddy gave all the right answers to the rest of the Alexanders' friendly but probing questions, articulately talking about the need to address discrimination and his parents' dedication to the cause, asking about Edmonton and the life black people lived there, surprising Cecile with his knowledge of obscure Stevie Wonder songs, expressing the right amount of awe at the Rockies, and ample gratitude for being treated to the experience of seeing them.

Not that any sentient being could help being in awe of the Canadian Rocky Mountains, Cecile reflected as they neared Banff, especially the first time. Gazing out the window, she decided that words like "grandeur" and "magnificent" were useless to describe the height, heft,and splendor of those ancient peaks—the job required music. Something like "The Great Gate of Kiev" from Mussorgsky's *Pictures at an Exhibition.*

A few miles from their destination, Mr. Alexander slowed down when a pair of bighorn sheep wandered across the road, staring with disdain at the car full of humans. Cecile glanced at Teddy's open mouth and grinned. He sometimes joked that she'd missed out on a lot in life, growing up in the "country."

Bighorn sheep beat Central Park rats.

Mr. Alexander took the scenic route into Banff, a town built to match the towering, fragrant evergreens that surrounded it, with pseudo log cabins mixed with modern architecture, all against the ever-present backdrop of the mountains. When they finally arrived at the Rimrock, a hotel whose name was inspired by its precarious location on the edge of a cliff, Teddy carried the heaviest suitcases without being asked, continuing his quest for the Alexanders' blessing by keeping a respectable distance from Cecile until she knocked on the door of his adjoining room in the middle of night, leaving her parents snoring in one bed and her sister fast asleep in the other.

The terror on his face when she lifted her nightgown over her head made what happened next more exciting, at least for her. He looked twice as nervous when she pulled the same stunt the next night, which made her laugh—quietly, because she didn't really want to get caught. She'd lost her mind just enough to feel like she could do almost anything, with Teddy in her life, but not enough to be completely reckless.

Watching Karen's wedding, Cecile couldn't help wondering what she would wear when she married Teddy. As it turned out, though she'd never told anyone about her fantasy, she wasn't the only one thinking about their long-term union. The night before Teddy's flight back to New York, Norman Alexander took him out for a drink. One look at Teddy's face when they came through the door was enough to make the perfection of the previous days a distant memory.

Her parents never left them alone, and Cecile didn't have the guts to sneak into Teddy's room in her own house, so she had to wait until right before he boarded the plane back to New York to ask him what was wrong.

Teddy glanced at her mom and dad, smiling a few feet away, then turned so that they couldn't see his face and glared at her.

"So this whole thing was a set up?" he demanded.

Cecile's eyes narrowed. "What?"

"Your father asked me what my intentions were. Was that why you invited me here? So they could try to railroad me into marrying you?"

Cecile's stomach filled with acid. "I don't know what you're talking about."

"Yeah? My dad warned me that you were probably going to try to trap me, but I didn't believe him."

Cecile frowned. "Trap you? Seriously? Do you think I'm pathetic enough for that?"

"I come from a very prominent family."

"Who gives a fuck?"

Teddy's eyes widened in shock. Cecile hadn't intended to swear. She glanced at her parents. They didn't look mortified, so she assumed Teddy had blocked their view of her enough that they couldn't read her lips.

"Did you have fun in Banff?" she continued, more calmly.

He paused. "It was beautiful."

"Great. Hey, you'd better go through security." She needed him to either leave or hold her very close. The former seemed like a better bet.

He gazed at the line of travelers, waiting to be screened before boarding the plane. His jaw relaxed, and he faced Cecile again.

"You really just wanted me to see where you grew up?"

"Yes."

She cursed the part of her that still wanted him to say something about a long term plan. Too early, she reminded herself. Even if he seems to need you, a man who knows from the beginning that he must make you his wife is rare. At least, it could never happen to her.

He paused again. "Thanks."

"I'm sorry my dad interrogated you," she said sincerely. "I had no idea that was coming. Do you believe me?"

Teddy searched her eyes. "Yes." He kissed her cheek, then dropped his carry-on bag and hugged her. She melted into him, trying not to cry from relief.

"I'm not ready to be anyone's husband yet," he said, in her ear.

Cecile swallowed hard. "I understand."

"I'll call you when I get home." He kissed her cheek again, and walked towards the security screening area, waving to her parents before he disappeared from view.

Cecile climbed into the back seat of the car, waited until her mom and dad had closed their doors, and said, "I know you meant well, Dad, but please don't butt into my relationship with Teddy again. Okay?"

Her father looked at her mother, then started the car. He turned up the radio, filling the silence that followed with Barbara Frum on the CBC. Finally, he parked in front of the Alexanders' house, turned to Cecile and said,

"If talking to your father is too much for him, he's not much of a man."

Cecile flushed with anger. She opened her mouth to say something, then changed her mind, jumped out of the car, slammed the door, and ran into the house instead.

When Teddy finally called, she took the phone in her room.

"Did you have a good flight?"

"I slept most of the way. Listen, I'm really tired, and my parents insist on hearing about my trip. I'll talk to you tomorrow, okay?"

Cecile was glad that no one in her family could see the disappointment on her face. "Sure. I love you."

"Me too. Good-night, Cecile."

He hung up just as she was about to tell him she already missed him, leaving her even more grateful she'd taken the phone somewhere private, so no one could see her weeping.

CHAPTER TWENTY

By the end of September of his sophomore year, Langston had started to reconsider his apartment, and all the hours at Gino's it required. On one hand, he still valued his freedom. On the other, he was so busy, he rarely slept. This had seemed okay when Marietta was around to give him energy, but with her gone and no one, overt or covert, to take her place, he found himself constantly drained.

He settled into a routine of waking up by listening to the news, showering, then eating a quick breakfast before heading to school to either use the gym or go to class, followed by homework, Gino's, and more homework, depending on the day. He studied at his apartment less and less. Langston didn't mind being alone most of the time, but he couldn't predict when the bustling on the streets would create a painful reminder of his solitude.

One positive result of his split from Marietta was getting to know his neighbors, especially the young couple down the hall. He'd bonded with their four year-old son, Andy, one cold, January weekend. Andy and his parents happened to be in the same Jamaican meat patty shop as Langston, waiting in an extremely long line to place an order, then waiting just as long for their meal. The little boy had gazed so longingly at Langston's unopened can of Kola Champagne soda that Langston asked Ron and Wynette if Andy could have it. They agreed, and Langston got a friend for life.

If he wanted to, Langston could go to Scarborough for fried plantain, oxtail stew, peas and rice, or curry. He could also make them himself, having memorized his grandmother's techniques, but he'd never learned how to prepare escovitch fish, so he was very happy when Wynette served that particular dish the first time he was invited for dinner.

When he promised to return the favor, his neighbors refused, saying they couldn't have him go to that expense, since he was still in school. Instead, they let him teach their son French. Luckily, Andy was very bright, which made working with him relatively easy. The friendship lasted from a few weeks after Marietta's farewell until August, when Ron and Wynette moved into a "better" neighborhood just in time for Andy to start school.

With them gone, Eglinton West felt less and less like home. The novelty had worn off, and now Langston saw mainly the bills. He still appreciated watching *The Frugal Gourmet* and *Wok with Yan* without ridicule, though, and being able to rent artsy foreign films without worrying about anyone's tastes but his own.

Breaking up with Marietta had left him even more cautious about relationships. He knew he shouldn't judge his future prospects based on his past experiences, but he found himself wondering, whenever a woman smiled at him or tried to catch his eye, what she was up to.

"I hate to repeat myself," Marcus said when Langston told him of his reluctance, "but getting laid isn't that hard. If that's all you're looking for, you don't have to worry what women are up to. Makes everything simple. But use a condom, because if you don't, it can get really complicated very fast, trust me."

"Trust you?"

Marcus didn't elaborate, so Langston didn't ask, deciding instead to stop asking Marcus for advice.

Maybe it isn't *bad* advice, though, Langston thought, sitting alone in his apartment after work on the Saturday before Thanksgiving. If only I were a normal guy, I might actually be able to follow it.

He looked around. The furniture that had once seemed thrilling evidence of his independence now seemed a testament to his low income. Almost a year since I moved, he thought. Would the money saved be worth admitting Grandma Felicia was right, and crawling home?

I'll survive going back, he thought. And maybe she'll be gracious...

No. Because even if living on Eglinton Street hadn't turned out to be perfect, at least he could breathe.

CHAPTER TWENTY-ONE

When her phone rang, Cecile was working on the last page of Chopin's Fourth Ballade. She ignored the interruption, but when the ringing started again a few minutes later, she reluctantly abandoned the piano bench, racing up the stairs and lifting the receiver just as her answering machine began to tell the caller that she was unavailable.

"Hello?" she said, her heart pounding at the thought of the obvious emergency that had prompted two calls back to back.

"I knew you were home," said Teddy. "How's my beautiful piano diva?"

Cecile smiled, sitting on her bed. "She's working. Can I call you later?"

"Actually," he said, lowering his voice an octave, "I was hoping I could see you tonight."

Cecile glanced at the clock. 7 p.m. After her last bad lesson, two weeks prior, she'd promised herself that her time with Teddy wouldn't infringe on her time with the piano anymore.

"I'm sorry, babe, I can't," she said. "I have a lesson tomorrow. Got to keep Mr. Balog happy."

"I can make you so happy, you won't care about that."

Cecile laughed. "Save it for tomorrow night?"

Teddy paused. "I really need you," he said quietly. "I don't know why I feel so alone here, I just...you're the only one who makes it go away, baby. Are you sure you can't come over?"

Cecile felt her heart drop into her gut. "Can you come here?"

"Is your aunt home?"

"Yes."

There was a silence, then Teddy said, "I don't have the energy to be sociable tonight. I'm...I'm really sad."

Tears formed in Cecile's eyes. "What happened, babe?"

"I don't know. I was making my own dinner, and the house got really empty, all of a sudden. Please come over?"

Cecile closed her eyes for a moment. He sounded like a frightened child. Every other time, she'd dropped whatever she was doing to rush to his side, but the requests were getting more frequent, and leaving him once she got there had become more involved.

I promised. But...

She glanced at the clock again, then at her music, waiting impatiently on the piano. "Teddy, baby, I'm so sorry. Listen, I'll call you as soon as I'm done. I can only practice until 9, so—"

"You're turning me down?"

"I'll make it up to you," she purred. "I promise, I'll call you the moment I'm finished practicing."

"Wow. You're really turning me down."

"I have to practice, Teddy."

"So you're gonna hang up on me, too?"

"No—"

"Why are you being such a bitch?"

"What?"

"You heard me."

"Good-bye, Teddy."

Cecile slammed down the phone, blinking hard. Suck it up, she thought fiercely, trying to heal the ache in her gut by taking slow, deep breaths. She'd been sitting on her bed for five minutes when she realized that her practice time was slipping away, so she hurried back downstairs to the piano, where she sat for another five minutes before she could focus enough to play another note. She tried to lose herself in the fury of the last page of the Chopin, but her fingers refused to find the notes she'd just mastered, because a part of her brain couldn't stop listening for the phone to ring. Half an hour later, she gave up, running upstairs to apologize, then trying unsuccessfully not to cry when the phone continued to ring, over and over, because Teddy had turned off his answering machine.

That night, instead of sleeping she found herself thinking that if she and Teddy could be together—really together—it wouldn't matter so much that she was busy, because they'd see each other every night and wake up side by side every morning. If their daily contact was all but guaranteed, she wouldn't have to choose between her lifelong passion for the piano and her consuming passion for Teddy. He wouldn't have to question his importance to her, even if she couldn't be constantly available.

He can't deny that I'm there for him, she decided. I have the right to do what I love, and do it well. I wasn't being selfish. It's not my fault his parents don't pay him enough attention.

Cecile strung her affirmations together like beads on a rosary, touching them again and again until she fell asleep. But when she woke the next morning, the first thing on her mind was an overwhelming need to hear Teddy's voice, telling her he loved her.

As she got out of bed, her stomach began to ache. I should have seen him, she found herself thinking. After all, as it turned out, I hardly practiced last night.

Riding the train to school, she wondered if there was a way to free up more time to spend with him. If I get up earlier, she reasoned, maybe I can practice before I go to school. I'll be tired, but I can sleep in on the weekend. Or maybe—

A sound like two dying cats mating jolted her back to reality. She looked up to see a thin, dark-skinned man wearing a woolen coat that was much too heavy for the mid-October weather, oversized sunglasses, and a headband with antennas on it. When he threatened to keep playing his broken saxophone if he didn't collect money from the passengers, Cecile glanced across the subway car at a Latina in a dark gray business suit, and grinned. Cecile often gave money to panhandlers, but this time, she was determined not to reward the man's manipulations. The woman shook her head, also smiling, then resolutely ignored the panhandler as he came through the car soliciting cash.

After he moved on to the next car, Cecile thought about her mother's warning not to look New Yorkers in the eye. Wrong again, Mom, she thought, embarking on a mental journey past all of the scary assumptions she'd had about New York. How overblown her fears had been: no one had mugged her, she'd quickly understood the transit system, the air didn't seem too polluted to breathe, she'd never seen a crack addict. As she stepped out of the train at the 66th street station, it occurred to her that the only negative expectation that had come true was the rats she'd seen on her first date with Teddy.

And just like that, he invaded her mind again, to the point that, when she saw him waiting in front of Juilliard's front door, for a moment she thought she'd conjured a hallucination.

Before she could say anything, he embraced her, pulling away after a long moment to hand her an elaborate bouquet of pale pink lilies, wrapped in green tissue and tied with a white satin ribbon.

"I'm so sorry, Cecile," he said. "Can you forgive me?"

She swallowed the lump in her throat, blinked back tears, and said, "Of course. Can you forgive me?"

"Always." He hugged her again, rubbing her back. "I love you."

She felt herself dissolving, the same feeling of formlessness she'd felt kissing him for the first time. "I love you, too."

Three months later, Cecile found herself wondering what "I love you" meant to him. And to her. And to normal people.

She'd just finished talking to Teddy on the phone when tears started flowing uncontrollably down her cheeks, like rivulets washing into a gully, eroding the earth beneath. She lay on her bed and wanted to die, hating herself for being so weak. Why couldn't she adopt his calm approach to getting married? Everything would be so much easier if she could stop thinking about it.

She reminded herself that she'd only known him a year and a half, and that she shouldn't be fixated on a lifelong commitment when she was still too young to drink legally, at least in America. That marriage was a big step, nothing to rush into. And yet, all she could think about was that Teddy never raised the topic, and changed the subject if Cecile mentioned the idea.

He told you he isn't ready. Why can't you wait?

She knew the answer. Her student visa would run out in a couple of years, which would mean going back to Canada without Teddy or staying in the States illegally. Unless he married her, of course, but he'd made it clear that he wouldn't even think about a wedding until he had a Master's, which would take at least two more years. More importantly, despite her attempts to escape, God's relentless eye had bored through the drapes in her soul, so that every time she made love to Teddy, she felt the Almighty watching her, and disapproving.

She pulled a tissue from the box on her nightstand, wiped her eyes, then used another to blow her nose. He's only 22, she thought. He'd told her that nobody in New York thinks about marriage at 22—that was for small town girls, like her.

Cecile walked to her bedroom window, looking out at the

tiny, snow-covered big-city yard, so narrow that she could imagine lying down and touching one fence with her fingertips and the other with her toes. She'd learned to ride a bicycle in her back yard in Alberta.

If only I had something concrete to look forward to, she thought. Like knowing I'll get a decent job when I graduate. I don't know what I expected, majoring in piano performance. I think I'll audition for the Juilliard Master's program when I finish undergrad. I can get in. Right? There's nothing wrong with believing in yourself. I know that "pride goeth before destruction," but there is no glorification or exalting of depression and insecurity in the Bible, either.

I guess I need to pray, she thought, and try to accept God's guidance.

Her resolution lasted until the next time she and Teddy made love, which was when she became certain that her prayers were bouncing back unanswered, and would continue to do so until she stopped deliberately offending the Lord.

On Valentine's Day, she finally mustered the courage to tell Teddy how she felt. They'd just arrived at his house after having dinner out. He made sure nobody else was home, then smiled at Cecile conspiratorially and took her hand, leading her to his parents' bedroom, closing the door, and playfully throwing her on the bed.

He was climbing on top of her when she said, "I can't."

"Why not?" he replied, kissing her neck.

"In your parents' room? You have to ask?"

"C'mon," he whispered, unbuttoning her blouse.

"I feel like they're watching us."

He laughed. "Are you the same girl," he said, kissing between her breasts, "who came into my hotel room in Banff—" he kissed her stomach— "with her parents in the next room?"

"No."

He stopped, and rolled onto his side, and propped his head on his hand, gazing at her and frowning.

"What's going on with you lately, Cecile?"

She sat up, fastening her buttons as she did. "Can we go in your room? I feel weird here."

His face relaxed. "Sure. I just thought it would be fun, that's all. Change of scenery."

He stood, extending his hand and pulling her to her feet, then waited until she was in front of him, grabbed her ass and squeezed it.

Cecile flinched. It's Valentine's Day, she told herself. You can't hold out on Valentine's Day. But when he climbed on top of her again, this time completely naked, and began to kiss her and stroke between her legs, instead of feeling a release, she stiffened.

"I'm sorry," she said. "I need...can we talk?"

Teddy continued to fondle her. "Of course."

She pushed his hand away. " I'm sorry, Teddy. I need to talk to you now."

He sat on the edge of his bed, stared at the ceiling, then focused on her, frowning. "Sure. I mean, it's got to be important."

"It is." Cecile cleared her throat, wanting to maintain eye contact, and finding it impossible. "I feel...I feel guilty about making love to you," she mumbled.

"I'm sorry, Cecile, can you say that again? I didn't hear you."

She forced herself to look at him. "I feel guilty about making love to you," she said, louder. "I know you think it's stupid, but I was raised to believe it's wrong unless you're married. I've tried not to feel this way, but I can't help it."

Teddy stared at the wall for a long time. "So what do we do now?" he finally said.

Cecile cleared her throat again—her windpipe had suddenly squeezed shut. "I guess you break up with me."

Teddy faced her, his forehead creased, but this time in confusion. "Is that what you want?" he said, his voice tinged with hurt.

"No."

He was quiet for a long time. "Then what?"

She hesitated, then let the words come all at once: "I want to be with you, but not make love anymore until we're married."

Teddy stood, and turned his back. Cecile hesitated, then began to get dressed, unable to tolerate the silence. She was putting on her pantyhose when he turned again. She tried to focus on his face, but his body was too distracting—there had better be a good reason for this, God, she thought, forcing her eyes up above his waist.

"You really feel guilty?" he asked softly. "It's not just

some trick to get me to propose?"

Cecile sighed. "I should go," she said.

"It's a fair question, don't you think?"

She met his eyes. "I guess so."

"Why are you leaving?"

"Do you still want me to stay?"

"Why wouldn't I? Don't you believe I love you?"

She felt her cheeks flushing with shame as he held her close, felt his skin against her arms and hands as she squeezed him, and regretted everything, even her existence.

"I'm buying you a ring," Teddy said, his voice like the sound of a cello. "I haven't finished paying for it yet. I didn't want to tell you until—"

Cecile released him abruptly. "A...what kind of ring?"

Teddy laughed. "An engagement ring. Wow, this isn't how I planned it, but...will you marry me?"

For a moment, she was too stunned to answer, remembering all the times he'd angrily ended any discussions of long-term plans. But as she looked into his eyes, she saw nothing but love.

"Yes, Teddy." She threw her arms around him again. "Yes. Yes!"

When he undressed her again, this time as her fiance, she didn't resist.

#

Teddy gave her the ring in April. Two months later, she wrote him a letter. She had no intention of mailing it, but talking to herself in a diary wasn't enough, and she couldn't tell anyone else. Sitting at the desk beside her dresser, she opened the spiral-bound notebook that was her latest repository for thoughts too obsessive to be left only in her head, and wrote:

June 3, 1989

Are you bored, Teddy? You never suggest activities anymore. Forget about anything romantic. Plus, you make no effort to see me, and barely pay attention to me when we do get together.

It's summer! This is not the time to start pulling away! You always talk about how much fun you have with your friends, but you don't want me to spend time with them. I want a man who doesn't exclude me from gatherings with his friends. Are you ashamed of them? Or me?

I don't make you happy, no matter what you say. I give you headaches and I smother you. And you don't make me happy, either. You make me feel like it's a major favor to do anything for me, yet I'm a selfish bitch if I don't do whatever you ask. You don't have to call me a bitch to make me feel like one.

Maybe you don't ask much. I only know that I don't feel like I can call on you when I need you. Maybe for big things, but not little things, and they are more important, because they're more part of normal life. Maybe I should have asked more of you to begin with.

I don't enjoy sex. I look forward to it in fantasy, but it's not romantic. It's you getting your rocks off and begging me to tell you I love you while doing a few things for a short time even though it takes me at least as long as you, y'know, like a typical woman.

You're not being mean. It's just that you've been looking for someone to cater to you all your life—as much you talk about community activism, you complain just as much about how your parents are always focused on someone or something other than you. But you know what? I'm getting tired of hearing it. Maybe it's time to accept them, and move on. Or actually get some counseling, instead of just talking about it.

I can't tell you my specific complaints when you ask me what makes me unhappy, and sometimes I feel really close to you, but sometimes I feel like when I graduate I'll get a job somewhere and never see you again and that it might be for the best. Even if you need me. Even if I'd miss you.

CHAPTER TWENTY-TWO

In October of 1989, Langston moved back to Scarborough. When asked, he said he wanted to have something saved when he graduated, and that he felt guilty knowing Grandma Felicia had to ask neighbors and members of her church for help around the house after Marcus moved out. Maya should have been able to do more, but Grandma Felicia cut her youngest grandchild a surprising amount of slack. Walking in on his grandmother washing windows while Maya napped on the couch was the final straw. Deep down, though, Langston knew a big part of the reason he'd left Eglinton West was that he'd given up on finding a woman who would want to spend the night in his apartment. Admitting this to himself was too embarrassing, however, so he convinced himself that the main goal of his move was to whip Maya into shape.

At first, living in his childhood home grated on him even more than it had before he knew what freedom felt like. He solved part of the problem by having a TV and VCR in his room, and another part by kicking Maya out when her attempts to use them conflicted with Langston's tastes.

Cinema Paradiso was the turning point. Afterward, Maya willingly watched anything he wanted to see without protesting the occasional subtitles, or his selfishness in not sharing his VCR more democratically. Even better, she didn't tell anyone that Alfredo's bequest to Salvatore, a reel of passionate kisses that the priest in the movie had forced the projectionist to censor, made

Langston cry. Or that he bought her Ennio Morricone's score, arranged for piano, and got mad when she wouldn't practice enough to play it decently.

"Why don't you just get a recording?" was Maya's response to his badgering.

"Forget it," said Langston,choosing not to explain that while he wanted to relive the experience, he didn't think he could bear the longing a soundtrack recording would provoke.

The movie convinced him that he'd never loved Marietta. He'd wondered if the fondness he felt for her and his eagerness to have sex with her were love, but seeing Alfredo and Elena in the film, he decided against it. Or maybe his eagerness and affection were proof of a kind of love, but not the kind he hoped he still might find.

The reason for the shift in his attitude towards his grandmother was harder to nail down. She hadn't changed—still chased him out of the kitchen, and made harsh pronouncements. These days, she was pushing him to find a girlfriend.

"It's hard to meet people after you graduate from college," she said.

"I thought I was there to learn to be a teacher," he retorted when, after months of constant pressure, his strategy of keeping silent finally became too difficult.

"If you can hold a job and go to school, you can have a job, a girlfriend and go to school."

"The thing is," he replied, "I know I'll get rewarded for holding the job. I have no idea what I'll get from the girlfriend, though. Maybe a disease."

Grandma Felicia glared at him. "Not if you both live by the Word of God."

The Word was the reason Langston finally learned to drive, at the age of 21, so he could chauffeur his grandmother to church. Maya could drive, too—Marcus made sure she learned before he moved out to be with Danita—but Grandma Felicia felt more comfortable with a male behind the wheel, even one who had a lot less experience.

When Marcus had lived in the house, Langston often slept in on Sunday mornings. He wasn't hostile to the church, but given a choice, he preferred his bed to a pew. After a while, his grandmother gave up on him, insisting only that he say grace when they all ate together on Sundays. His debut was, "Good food, good meat, good God, let's eat," which earned snickers from everyone at the table except Grandma Felicia.

"Giving thanks to the Lord is not a joke," she'd said. "There are people all over the world who would be grateful for even a small crumb from this table. Now say it again."

So Langston wiped the smile off his 16 year-old face, and said, "Thank you for all of the wonderful food on this table, especially the delicious roasted chicken. You are truly good, Lord, and we are grateful that we may now consume this feast."

When he was finished, Zora cut her eyes at him and Marcus kicked him under the table, but if Grandma Felicia realized he was paraphrasing, she didn't let on.

Despite his recently checkered past, Langston actually

started to enjoy taking his grandmother to church. The sermons usually gave him something to think about, the hymns reminded him of his childhood, and he felt better about himself, on some level, for going. On top of all that, Grandma Felicia, who seemed to have aged ten years in the two years he'd lived downtown, was in her element in her church: dressed to the nines, usually with a hat, greeting everyone in sight and brimming with energy, even if she sometimes dozed off during the sermon.

He was driving her and Maya home from Grant AME's Mother's Day celebration, a few weeks after the exams that marked the end of his third year of college, when the reason he could put up with everything Grandma Felicia dished out became clear. For the first time, he realized she wouldn't live forever, except with Jesus.

Langston turned to her, as regal as a queen in a turquoise straw hat with peacock feathers that her dear departed husband had given her, and said, "I love you, Grandma."

She looked at him suspiciously. "What do you want, boy?"

"Nothing," he replied, smiling and shaking his head.

She smiled back. "I love you, too."

Then, she glanced at Maya, dozing in the back seat after partying till all hours of the morning.

"I love her, too, but Lord Jesus, she tries me sometimes."

"We all do, though."

"Amen to that."

CHAPTER TWENTY-THREE

The week after she broke up with Teddy, Cecile played the best piano jury of her life. She'd practiced six or seven hours each day leading up to it, turning the time she would have spent on Teddy into additional time with her piano. Concentration turned out to be a bit of a struggle at times, though, and she had to take breaks to wipe a constant stream of tears off her cheeks. Still, the extra preparation made a difference, allowing her to transcend technique and embody each piece. With her heart broken and her brain numb, the music came from a place where her conscious mind held no power to inject doubt, resulting in a catharsis that superseded grades or critiques.

Abbey Simon began Cecile's jury by requesting Chopin's Fourth Ballade, then interrupted her note-perfect, intensely expressive performance and asked her to jump to the famous coda—headlong, dramatic, and even more demanding than the ten minutes that precede it, set up by five pianissimo chords that always reminded Cecile of putting her head on the guillotine and waiting for the blade. She tossed it off as if it were a nursery rhyme.

The true test of her nerve, however, came when Oxana Yablonskaya chose the last two movements of "Les Adieux," one of the rare Beethoven sonatas named (in German) by its composer. The three sections are about saying goodbye, enduring an absence, and the joy of reunion. Though Cecile could occasionally rehearse the other pieces on her jury program without crying, she could never survive the Beethoven. Somehow, under pressure, she managed to convey the longing in the brief slow movement without feeling it, focusing her thoughts during the finale on executing brilliantly, instead of the future she and Teddy would never experience.

As she left the room, she heard the jurors murmuring. Yeah, that's right, she thought, the black girl can play. She would have felt some satisfaction two weeks earlier, but nothing mattered anymore.

She'd just greeted Nora and Joe, faithfully in place at the front desk, when she spotted Teddy just beyond them in the lobby, holding a bouquet of roses. Cliché, but she did love flowers.

"I've been waiting over an hour," he said.

Cecile glared at him, but didn't break her stride until he intercepted her, forcing her to either stop or run him over.

"I made an appointment with a therapist," he said, standing so close that she could smell the minty scent of his breath.

"That's great," she said, looking away. "I'm in a hurry right now."

"Don't you want your flowers?"

He extended them hopefully. Cecile glanced at the bouquet out of the corner of her eye. He might have actually gone to a florist for those, as opposed to getting them off the street. Not that it mattered, because nothing mattered anymore.

"Shouldn't you be giving those to your girlfriend?"

He lowered the roses, a pained expression on his face. "Cecile—"

"I don't want them." Half-true. They were beautiful, and he just might give them to that other girl, which made her feel suddenly cold. Too late. She had to stand her ground.

"Cecile, I love you! I don't want to give them to anybody else!"

Students were flowing in and out of the lobby with instruments and book bags in hand. Three dancers on a bench behind Teddy were having a spirited discussion until he declared his love loudly enough to make them rotate their heads on their swan-like necks.

Cecile's cheeks flushed. She pushed open the door, head down, and Teddy followed her. A discarded plastic bag swirled in the May breeze, clinging to her leg for the moment it took for her to brush it away.

"Don't do this," he begged as she picked up speed, heading towards the throngs of people on Broadway.

She stopped just short of the corner of 66th, turned slowly, and said, "I didn't do this, asshole, you did. Goodbye, Teddy."

The light changed. Cecile was halfway across the street when she realized she was heading in the wrong direction. She continued walking until she'd turned the corner, then stopped, exhaling slowly, her throat tight from resisting the urge to look at him.

Maybe he'd really go to counseling and figure

out…what? Would it take a counselor to show him that an engagement ring is supposed to be binding?

The week before, on Teddy's birthday, Cecile had planned a surprise party for two, complete with streamers, balloons, cake, a steak dinner, and afterward, her in the new blush pink satin teddy she'd hidden under her little black dress. She'd timed everything to be ready when Teddy got in from his job at a non-profit corporation run by one of his father's friends, the job that had allowed him to move out of his parents' house the previous August and take a small, one-bedroom apartment in a building on 96th Street. His apartment, for now. Their apartment, after the wedding.

With the steak marinating, greens cooking on the stove and cubes of seasoned potatoes roasting in the oven, Cecile had begun to decorate, hoping Teddy liked red. He didn't wear the color much, preferring more neutral shades or black, but she'd decided to be festive.

Standing on a chair, hanging a bunch of balloons above a bookcase, she'd noticed a card lying on top of it: "Happy Birthday, Darling." Which could have been from his mom if not for the couple embracing on the front.

Cecile remembered what happened next in slow motion—grasping the back of the chair, stepping down, opening the card as soon as her feet touched the ground. Her heart stopping when she saw the date: May 10, 1991. Which meant he'd just received it. From Angela. Who was so grateful that he'd made the last two years of her life so special. Whose 16 years before she met him were truly childhood. But now she was a woman, because of him. She loved him more and more, and would always be there for him. Because he was her "boo."

Cecile tore the card into tiny pieces, leaving them scattered on the hardwood floor, sat on the couch, and waited.

She remembered feeling nothing, at first. Then a spark of disgust at the thought of two years of lies and weak excuses. Then a flicker of anger when she considered her own stupidity, which grew to a bonfire, big enough to make her pace the floor to keep from exploding, as she reflected on all of the effort she'd put into giving Teddy a happy birthday.

When Teddy's key turned in the lock, Cecile became an inferno. As he appeared in the doorway, the engagement ring hit him squarely in the chest, bounced off, landed on the wooden floor with a clink and rolled across the room.

"What the hell..."

He noticed the pile of paper scraps on the floor, closed the door behind him, but came no closer, avoiding Cecile's eyes, gazing at nothing in particular.

After a long silence, Cecile said, "Were you going to tell me?"

Teddy sighed and leaned against the door, sinking slowly to the ground. He bent his knees, rested his arms against them, and lowered his head.

"I'm sorry," he said.

"Because I found out?"

He looked up, meeting her eyes. "Because I hurt you."

She turned away, fighting not to cry. As she did, her eyes found the cake. Carrot, with cream cheese icing, his favorite. She'd give it to him anyway, since she didn't like cakes with nuts in them.

"Who is she?" she said quietly.

Teddy stared at his hands.

"I mean Angela. Who is Angela?"

"Just some girl."

Cecile clamped her eyes shut, pushing the heels of her hands hard against her forehead. "You *know* that's not good enough, Teddy!" She glared at him. "Two fucking years? With a 16 year-old?"

"I'm sorry," he mumbled.

"What the fuck is wrong with you?" she shrieked, dropping her hands, which had clenched into fists, away from her face. She wanted to pummel him.

He shrugged. "I don't have an excuse."

"Where did you meet her?"

He gazed at the floor. "She's a student. She started college early. I didn't know she was so young until..."

He stopped.

Cecile rushed towards him, shoving him into the door with a thud. The primal scream that escaped her throat startled both of them. He grabbed her wrists before she could push him again.

"I know you want to beat the shit out of me," he said, looking her determinedly in the eye, "but I think you also know it won't change anything."

She twisted her arms violently free, and dropped to her knees. "Two years?"

All at once, she was spent. She sat back on her heels, tears flowing freely down her cheeks. When Teddy started wiping them away with his thumb, she had no energy to resist.

"I'm so sorry," he said, his voice barely audible. "I just...she just...she really looked up to me, and...you're always so busy." He sighed deeply. "You didn't deserve it. I don't deserve you. I'm really...I know I'm really fucked up, but we can work it out, can't we? Can we please try?"

Their eyes locked. Then, Cecile gently pushed his hand away from her, sniffling. "You don't want to marry me anyway, Teddy," she said.

"I do! I'm just...I was just scared."

"Whatever." She stood, slipped on her pumps, and collected her purse. She glanced at the steaks, still marinating on the counter. "There are potatoes in the oven, and greens on the stove," she said in a wobbly voice. "Don't worry, the wedding is off. Happy birthday."

"No," he said firmly, still sitting in front of the door.

"Get out of my way!"

"No, Cecile. We need to talk about this—"

"Will you get the fuck away from the door? My god, Teddy, stop torturing me!"

She was crying again. He rose to his feet and tried to take her in his arms, but she shook him off.

"Cecile—"

"Good-bye."

She heard him saying, "I'm sorry," one last time just as she slammed the door.

CHAPTER TWENTY-FOUR

To honor Langston's graduation, summa cum laude, the Andrews family did what came naturally, gathering at Zora's house for a celebration dinner. As soon as he sat down to eat, Langston's oldest sister did what also came naturally, deflating what joy he felt over finally getting his degree by asking if he'd applied for a job yet.

"Zora," he said, "I graduated a week ago."

"You should have started looking months ago."

Langston decided that silence was the way to go, lowering his head to dig into his jerked chicken, peas and rice, yams, and salad.

"Can you believe Diego Maradona?" said Marcus. "I mean, I'm not shocked about the drugs, but I never expected him to get convicted. His lawyer—"

"So you're still at Gino's then?" Zora interrupted.

Langston sighed. "Yes."

"Which makes sense until he gets another job," said Bernie.

"But he won't get another job, because he hasn't applied for one," said Grandma Felicia.

"Can someone please pass the yams?" said Maya.

"She's right, you know," said Zora, handing Maya a half-empty casserole dish.

"Oh, definitely," said Langston. "The yams are so good, we should all have seconds."

Zora frowned. "Why are you being so pigheaded?"

"I'm going to apply for a job, Zora," he snapped. "I didn't spend all those years in school not to get a job. But I'd appreciate it if you'd leave me alone at least for one evening. Can you do that?"

Their eyes met, then she looked away, her nose crinkled with disgust.

"Maradona has no excuse," said Bernie, and the subject was changed at last.

The next day, Langston got a newspaper to check the classifieds. The day after that, he went down to his school to check the listings there, halfheartedly making notes of possibilities.

He was lying on his bed, two days later, watching *The Cook, The Thief, His Wife and Her Lover* on video, when the phone rang. A few minutes later, Maya yelled for him to pick up. He paused the video gratefully, just as the cook brought the lover, a bookseller who had been gruesomely murdered by the thief for sleeping with the wife, out of the oven.

Good thing Maya didn't join me for this one, he thought, lifting the receiver.

"Hello, Langston."

"Aunt June?"

"Congratulations on your graduation, dear."

His mother's older sister was rarely in touch. He was surprised she even knew; Grandma Felicia maintained that Seventh Day Adventists were a cult, so June's membership in that denomination was a constant source of friction. Major events called for a truce, though. Besides, Langston had graduated summa cum laude, which was reason enough for a phone call, especially since Grandma Felicia had raised him and felt entitled to some of the credit.

"Thank you," he replied. "How are the twins?"

"Oh, they're fine. Linton is working on his Masters now, almost done. And Jeremiah will be interning soon."

"That's great. Please tell them I said hello."

"I will. So when will we see you next?"

"Are you coming to Toronto?"

"I wish I could, but you know how it is. Seems there's always some new obligation."

Like preserving your sanity, Langston couldn't help thinking.

"I don't think I've been to Edmonton since they opened the mall," he remarked.

"Then it's been ten years! That's a long time."

Out of the corner of his eye, Langston glimpsed the TV screen, where the browned, naked body of a man sat on a table, waiting for the next act of depravity the filmmaker had dreamed up. He turned away, queasy. He hadn't read the reviews, and had hoped for something like *Babette's Feast*. The Peter Greenaway film was undeniably well-made, but it definitely didn't inspire Langston to embark on a new culinary adventure, like the Danish picture had.

A new adventure. All at once, an idea formed in his head,

something much more appealing than polishing his resume, or looking for more leads for employment, or grossing himself out by watching the end of the movie, even though he knew he would do all of those things, too, and very soon.

"I'd like to come and visit you," said Langston impulsively. "Would that be okay?"

"Oh...oh, how lovely. When?"

She didn't sound enthusiastic, but he didn't care. He needed one last fling with freedom before he committed to the ball and chain of getting a teaching job. Just like Marietta did, he thought.

"I'll call the airline and let you know," said Langston. "I won't stay long. I have a friend out there I haven't seen in a long time, and it might be nice to catch up with her, too."

Haven't seen her, haven't talked to her, either, he thought. Still, after years of Christmas cards, birthday greetings, and very random additional phone calls, he was confident that Teresa would want to get together.

"Okay, then, let me know," said Aunt June. "Goodbye."

"Bye."

Langston knew this bid for freedom would end the way the last one did, with him right back at square one, and that in this case, the escape would only last a few days, and that it made a lot more sense to just save his money. Then again, did freedom, even if it was temporary, have a price tag? People went on retreat weekends all the time, trying to preserve their inner peace. Wasn't his trip to Edmonton close enough to a retreat to be worth the expense?

Definitely, he thought, opening his nightstand drawer and digging out the phone book.

CHAPTER TWENTY-FIVE

Less than two weeks before her aborted wedding, and Cecile was strapped in a narrow seat on an airplane to Edmonton, in the final stages of descent. She'd been in the process of writing another hate letter to Teddy, a follow-up to the one she'd written in the airport in New York, when a familiar fantasy formed in her mind: Teddy and his teenage slut dying in a hail of bullets, leaving Cecile standing over them with a thin smile on her face, the assault rifle still in her hands, a wisp of smoke trailing from its barrel.

She'd almost filled a notebook with hate letters, and the fantasy was a rerun too, drawn from a strangely pleasant dream. She got relief from neither. She still loved Teddy so much that she ached whenever she thought of him. She knew that part of him was difficult, dishonest, and wounded enough to inflict his pain on her, too, but now that it was over, she could only recall the hours on the phone, or in his arms, the warm caress of his voice, his brilliant mind and spontaneous spirit. The way he'd looked at her sometimes, as if he was amazed someone so perfect could even exist. The way he'd needed her, before everything came apart.

Then again, was what they had experienced love? There had to be better ways to describe the relationship—what was the word for a single-celled organism engulfing its prey?

The plane touched down, braked sharply, and began to taxi. Cecile shut her notebook and reached under the seat in front of her to stuff it in her carry-on, then slung the bag over her shoulder and reluctantly joined the line of deplaning passengers, hoping the grin she'd pasted on her lips looked more natural than it felt. When she opened the double doors into the waiting area, Betsy and her parents were in the front row, giving Cecile a clear view of their worried faces. As she watched their features relax at the sight of her fake smile, she couldn't help wondering if she should have auditioned for the Juilliard drama division, too.

"Hi, sweetheart," her mother said, holding Cecile very close and patting her back as if she were a baby. "Trust in the Lord, precious. *All* things work together for good to those who love the Lord."

Romans 8:28— *Please, not now…*

She knew her mother meant well and that only a complete loser would feel irritated by such a loving gesture, but the consolation was going to miss the mark until Cecile could convince herself that being unwanted for the rest of her life was a good thing.

"Did you have a good flight?" her father asked, putting his arms around her, then releasing her just as she started to relax.

"Yes," Cecile said, avoiding his eyes, afraid she'd tear up, unsure she could stand to see him hurting at the sight of her in pain.

"What did you bring me from New York?" asked Betsy.

Cecile smiled genuinely for a moment, and replied, "An ass-whuppin, extra large," in a mock American accent. She watched her parents find a position close to the conveyor belt, where her mother pointed out her suitcase so her dad could grab it. "Who's at the house?"

"Aunt Lucy and Uncle Amos, Uncle Arthur, Aunt Mimi, and Aunt Phoebe. Cousin Cece and Louis are staying in a hotel."

Cecile nodded. The only one she felt close to was Aunt Mimi. It was mortifying to have called off her wedding so late that her relatives had already bought plane tickets. Maybe they wouldn't ask any questions. *Yeah, right.*

"We haven't had this many people since Calvin died," said Betsy.

Cecile looked at her. "Wow. That bad?"

"All I'm saying is that we haven't gotten together for five years. We should start having family reunions. It's crazy that people only see each other at weddings and funerals."

As they left the airport, her mom put an arm around Cecile's shoulders and said, "Everything's going to be okay."

Bullshit.

Exposition

June, 1991

Since Langston had never been one for clubs, Teresa had to all but threaten his life to get him to agree to her plan for his last night in Edmonton. After an hour dancing and laughing, he started to think he'd been missing something. More the company than the location, he thought, marveling at how easily he and Teresa had fallen back in step.

Not surprisingly, Teresa had filled out since 8th grade, and no longer towered over him. She'd remained the same in a lot of ways, though, including her complete disinterest in flirting with him, which had amplified to the point that she seemed to have trouble focusing on his face, looking all over the room instead.

When a set of rock music all but cleared the dance floor, Teresa and Langston barely beat another couple to a pair of the red velour and aluminum chairs that nestled around the tiny, circular black tables in Darling's, the club at the Four Seasons in downtown Edmonton that happened to be popular at the time.

"Still good at track, I see," said Langston.

"Even in heels," said Teresa, grinning.

"Thirsty?"

"Sure."

When she glanced at her watch and scanned the room for the umpteenth time, Langston said, "Are you expecting somebody? Or am I just that boring?"

Teresa rolled her eyes. "You know how happy I am to see you, Langston. Just looking around, if that's okay. Or is there a law against it?"

"Nope, just an unwritten rule."

Teresa touched his cheek. "Terribly sorry, old chap. Now, can you get us some drinks? Rum and coke, please. Next round's on me, I promise."

Fifteen minutes later, Langston had just come back from the bar when Teresa jumped up and said, "Stay here. And don't let anybody sit in my seat."

A few minutes later, she returned with two tall, very attractive women, one with skin the color of milk chocolate and black, spiky hair, the other with skin the color of honey, her light-brown hair pulled into a bun.

"Langston Andrews," Teresa said, "Cecile and Betsy Alexander."

Langston stood, bumping the table as he did, grateful that his rum and coke didn't spill, because of both the embarrassment it spared him and the price of the drink. He shook the short-haired one's hand first—that was Betsy—then took Cecile's hand and became so mesmerized he almost forgot to let go.

"Nice to meet you," Langston said, when he finally released her.

"Langston lived down the street before I moved to Alberta," Teresa explained, a knowing expression on her face, "and Cecile and Betsy lived down the street after I got here."

Cecile nodded, with a forced smile.

I held her hand way too long, Langston thought. He was about to look away when he saw the sadness in her eyes.

"Do you still live in Alberta?" he asked.

"*I* do," Betsy replied. "Cecile lives in New York City."

"And Langston still lives in Toronto. We need to sit before we lose our place," said Teresa.

There were two seats and four people. Betsy took one of them and Teresa the other, grinning like Cheshire cats.

"I'll see if I can find some more chairs," said Langston.

When he returned empty-handed, Betsy said, "Maybe you two should go and dance."

Langston looked at Cecile hopefully.

"I'm sorry," she said, gazing at the empty dance floor, "but I don't really like this song."

"There are chairs in the lobby," Teresa said pointedly, shooting him a glance that said, do I have to do everything?

Langston noticed Cecile's long neck and couldn't stop himself from imagining what it would be like to kiss her just under her ear, and then maybe lower, on her throat…

In the years since Marietta, he'd gone out with a few assertive women who had seen him as a challenge, but being the pursuer still put him at a disadvantage. I'm leaving in a few hours, he remembered, so it's not like there'll be consequences to deal with if I screw this up completely.

"Brilliant as always, Terri," he said. He took a long drink of his rum and coke—liquid courage. "Cecile?"

She glanced at her sister, who gestured towards the door with her head, then looked back at Langston. "Sure," she responded, with a small smile.

Cecile followed him into the lobby, empty except for the night clerk, who didn't look up. Langston sat on one of the russet leather couches, and Cecile sat in a matching chair at a right angle to him. He watched her gaze intently at the coffee table, or maybe the Edmonton Journal someone had left on top of it, her graceful hands folded on her lap. He let his eyes travel up her slender arms and rest on her face, wishing they hadn't come out of the club, because wherever her mind had gone, he was clearly not invited.

Finally, Langston asked, "How long have you been in New York?"

She startled, then focused on him. "Four years."

"Do you like it?"

"Most of the time. The homeless people are kind of disturbing."

"You get tired of the begging?"

"Well…yes, but mainly I just feel bad. I mean, I can't give money to everybody, and some of them must really need it. I guess they all do, even if they're addicts, because even addicts need to eat."

Her response surprised him so much that he couldn't think of anything to say. After an awkward pause, something came to him: "I guess helping even one person makes a difference."

"Allegedly." She smiled with her lips again.

"Why are you so sad?" *Liquid courage.*

Cecile turned her head, her eyes darting away.

"Homelessness is depressing."

"It's more personal than that, isn't it?"

She bit the inside of her lip. "Maybe."

Langston cleared his throat. "Sorry," he said. "New topic."

"It's okay."

He groped for something innocuous. "So you're here to see the family?"

Cecile chuckled. "Sort of."

"What's so funny?"

She sighed, gazing into the distance for a while. Then her eyes found Langston's face, and stayed there. "I'm here because I was supposed to get married next weekend."

The couch squeaked as he fell back against it. "Wow."

"It's for the best," she said softly.

"What happened? You don't have to answer, of course."

She looked at her hands, then rested her eyes on him again. Her face relaxed. "It's okay."

She told him, speaking hesitantly at first and then more freely, about what had happened. When Langston offered his heartfelt condolences, she brightened a bit. Then they talked about her being a musician, life in New York and Toronto, and their mutual study of French, and the more they talked, the more natural her smiles became. By the time Teresa and Betsy emerged from Darling's, they were leaning towards each other, laughing like two old friends.

Betsy yawned. "You coming, Cecile?" she said.

Cecile glanced at Langston. "Is it closed already?"

"Yeah, it's closed already. And I'm not going anywhere else but home, so don't bother to suggest it."

"Yes, Queen Elizabeth," Cecile replied, remaining seated.

Teresa grabbed Langston's hands and leaned back.

"Okay, okay!" he protested, allowing himself to be pulled to his feet. He glanced at Cecile, who was looking at him and smiling. I'm leaving in a few hours, he thought, this time with dismay.

As the four of them ascended in the parking garage elevator, Langston became aware that his chest was touching Cecile's back. She turned in surprise, her mouth so irresistibly close to his that he couldn't stop himself from kissing her.

For a moment, he felt oxygen reaching places he hadn't known were there. Then she pulled away, blushing, and whispered, "Stop, okay?"

But when he followed her off the elevator, instead of getting off at the floor where Teresa had parked, she smiled and glanced at her sister, who rolled her eyes.

Cecile was leaving town in two days, and he in less than that—four and a half hours, not even enough time for a decent night's sleep.

"I really like your poems," she deadpanned, with a twinkle in her eye. "I hear American kids study your stuff in high school."

"Will you write a song for one of them?"

She laughed. "Maybe."

"Then I need your address."

No one had a pen.

"There's a pen in the car," Cecile remembered, and the three of them walked towards a decade-old red Corolla. There wasn't any paper, though, so she wrote her address and phone number very carefully on a tissue, and he did the same.

Betsy sang, "Goodbye, Langston," climbing into the driver's side.

He held up his hand and waved self-consciously. Had he really kissed a woman he barely knew in front of her younger sister, who looked like her attendance at the club could only have been due to a fake ID? Part of him didn't want to look at Cecile, still standing in front of him. He'd had a few drinks, but he wasn't drunk. Why had he done it?

He made himself meet her eyes, and he immediately understood why, not in a way that could be put into words, but in terms his body grasped perfectly.

"It was nice meeting you, Cecile."

"I'll write you a letter," she said, smiling at him again.

"I'd like that."

"Have a safe trip."

"You too."

He was turning away, a series of knots forming from the top of his throat to the nether regions of his intestines, when he remembered that his ride had undoubtedly left.

"Cecile!"

He waved his arms, realizing he looked like an idiot. Her

sister was about to pull out of her space. Thank God she'd checked behind her, as deserted as the garage was. Had he really sent his soon-to-be-former friend Teresa to her car alone in the middle of the night? I'm definitely losing my mind, he thought.

Cecile rolled down the window.

"I'm sorry—can I have a ride? I think Terri is gone."

Cecile laughed unabashedly. He wondered if men were generally so overwhelmed by her that they forgot where they were, or how they were getting home. Her little sister pushed the button to unlock the doors, rolling her eyes again.

"Thanks," said Langston, surprised to be more excited than embarrassed.

The back seat was too small for a man of his height.

"Are you okay?" Cecile asked him as he bundled his knees toward his chest.

"Yeah."

"Your legs are kind of long—here." She pulled her seat up a few inches, sacrificing some of the space her own long legs required.

"Thanks," he said, touched.

When the Corolla arrived at his Aunt June's house, Langston thanked Betsy for the ride and got out of the back seat, wanting to be bold enough to kiss Cecile's soft lips again but knowing he couldn't. He looked back as the car pulled away and saw her gazing at him.

He wondered what her ex-fiance looked like, and what kind of an asshole would cheat on a woman like that, especially so close to the wedding. He wondered how she could smile at all after such a devastating experience. Most of all, he wondered why Cecile had told him so many secrets when he had just met her. And hoped it was for the right reason.

CHAPTER TWENTY-SEVEN

June 27, 1991

I cant' believe that guy kissed me. Nice lips. Caught me completely off guard, though. I wasn't expecting anything except a lot of loud music and misery when Betsy forced me to go out with her.

So that was Langston. Teresa was right—he's really cute, in an unusual way. Asian-looking eyes, high cheekbones, and incredible teeth. I liked the way he smiled. There was something soft about it, instead of the usual looks you get from guys in clubs, as if you're a T-bone steak and they haven't eaten in days. I guess maybe he was worth buying a nice dress for. I should thank Betsy for forcing me to do that, too. Even if it had to be black, to suit my mood.

Somehow, Langston didn't seem to mind that I was unfriendly. And the look on his face when I told him what Teddy did to me...he was completely appalled, as if he'd never heard anything so heinous before. Doesn't he watch daytime TV?

Thinking of his face right then makes me cry, because he seemed to think I deserved better. But if I did, wouldn't Teddy have known?

It felt good to fool myself, for a while, into thinking Langston was looking at me that way because he cared. Then again, he's a man, so he probably has no feelings. Just urges. He did make good conversation, though. He's very smart, and I like that he's traveled to interesting places. He seems really artsy, too, or at least, he seems to appreciate the arts. Then again, it doesn't matter if he's an asshole underneath, because I'll never see him again.

Maybe remembering our conversation will help me deal with the rest of this trip. I doubt it, though. Being back in my old room in a twin bed reminds me I won't be sharing a bigger bed with Teddy, which reminds me I'm the same loser I was when I left here. One more pitying look from my relatives, one more meaningful hug from Mom and I think I'm going to kill myself. No, not really, although the idea of going away forever seems really peaceful, right about now. If only I could find a way of committing suicide I can live with! Ha, ha, very funny, Cecile.

I feel like someone's sawing me open with a knife, and cutting open my organs too, just to make sure. Of course, I wake up feeling that way every day, so it's not exactly new. Most humiliating, painful experience of my whole life, with tons of people watching me to see how I'm handling it, and I'm not going to end it all permanently? Wow. I'm stronger than I thought.

It was so easy, talking to Langston, that I almost forgot to hurt. Maybe all of that prayer earned me some mercy. I've begged for enough energy to get up by noon every day since I got here, so I guess that puts Langston in the getting more than you can ask or imagine category. Or proves God wasn't really listening to my request. Either way, I can't help believing Langston's truly a nice guy. That means they exist, and maybe there's one who might like me who I could like back. Of course, it's moot since I'll never see Langston again.

I was supposed to marry Teddy in less than a week. Why do I miss him so much? Why can't I hate him? It doesn't matter that he gave me roses and begged me to forgive him. He doesn't deserve another chance, no matter what, but if he was here right now, I'd probably make love to him. Maybe that's how Calvin felt about cocaine. Great, now I'm thinking about Calvin, too.

This is my punishment for having sex before marriage, right God? Doesn't matter that everybody else does it, I'm the one who gets punished. I should have been stronger. If I'd held out, maybe Teddy's fucking that teenager would have made sense. Maybe it wouldn't hurt so much. God, how long does it have to hurt this much? I'm not sure I can take much more.

You did send me Langston, though. And he kissed me. He'd been drinking, but I can't stop myself from believing he kissed me because he enjoyed our conversation.

Which doesn't matter, because I'll never see him again.

CHAPTER TWENTY-EIGHT

Langston glanced at his watch as Glenda pulled up in front of him. An hour late.

"Wow," she said, jumping out and popping the trunk. "What were you doing in Edmonton? You look like shit."

Langston half-smiled, with effort. He'd slept on the plane, but evidently not enough. "I went out last night. I'm fine, thank you, how are you?" He put his bag in the trunk and slammed it shut.

"Incomparable." A smile flashed across Glenda's face as she got back into the car. Once Langston had strapped in beside her, she pulled away from the curb.

He was glad she hadn't reiterated her criticism of his appearance because he was just tired enough to respond in kind. Glenda's long, thick, glistening black hair was pulled into three indistinct bunches held by elastics. She wasn't wearing makeup, which left the acne afflicting her cheeks bright red, instead of the quasi-skintone she usually achieved.

"No, really," Glenda said, glancing over her shoulder before she changed lanes on the way out of the airport. "I worry about you. Did you have a good trip?"

"I had fun."

"You went out last night? Where?"

"To a club."

Glenda laughed, drumming on the steering wheel. "I can't believe it."

"Because?"

"You need to ask?"

"I like dancing," Langston said, trying not to sound defensive.

"Oh, I know. You're just not a club person."

"Whatever."

She punched him on the arm. "Lighten up, Andrews. Damn, you're moody today."

"I'm tired."

"Well, that's obvious."

They were whizzing along the 409, heading for the 401, Toronto's major superhighway. Standing outside in the summer humidity for half an hour had made Langston's t-shirt stick to his back. It occurred to him that part of his irritation with Glenda had to do with the heat, and relaxed.

"I met someone," he said casually.

Glenda whipped her head towards him, her mouth open, then quickly focused back on the road. "Don't say things like that while I'm driving! I nearly crashed."

Langston smiled. "Okay, I admit, it's not an everyday thing."

"It could be. But that's another topic. So, is she cute?"

"More than cute."

"Cuter than I am?"

"Of course."

"Impossible. One-night stand?"

Langston frowned.

"Man, she got you good. That had to be a joke, Langston Andrews. You've got to lose your virginity to have a one-night stand."

"Well, if you'd stop turning me down…"

"Hey! I'm still driving here! You want me to throw up?"

He laughed.

"Tell me more."

"Like what?"

"Does she have a name?"

"Cecile. Are you watching the exits?"

"Okay, which one of us can drive?"

"I can drive. I just don't have a car yet."

"Bullshit!"

"So pull over, I'll prove it."

Glenda kissed her teeth, in an exaggerated West Indian display of disgust. "You think I'm stupid? I'm gonna give my brand new Audi to some neophyte crazy from the testosterone? Not likely."

"Whatever." Langston was still grinning.

"Don't change the subject."

"I beg your pardon, Your Majesty. Shouldn't you be in the other lane?"

The Audi suddenly edged between a tow truck and an eighteen-wheeler.

"Raatid, 'oman! Yuh mad?"

"I used my turn signal."

"Which proves how you feel about your brand new Audi,

right?"

She chuckled. "Whatever. Now focus, Andrews, we're practically there. What's so special about Cecile?"

Langston couldn't put it in words. "Just a feeling, I guess."

Glenda smiled. "Mysterious, aren't we? Listen, talk to me about her when you do lose your virginity. Then we'll see if she's special."

"Actually," he said, "I am still a virgin, in a way. I've never made love, because I've never been in love..."

He trailed off, barely managing to control an urge to add something ridiculous. A letter from Cecile would be the sign—until she wrote, he'd keep his fantasies to himself.

"Thanks for the ride," he said, as they pulled up in front of his house.

"Don't thank me until you get the bill."

"The check's already in the mail."

He kissed Glenda's cheek, jumped out of the car, then carried his bag up Grandma Felicia's walkway. If Cecile comes to visit, he thought, what will I cook for her? Maybe lamb curry—

Stop. Just...stop, okay?

CHAPTER TWENTY-NINE

Cecile changed her plane ticket, escaping from Alberta just before her wedding date. Even though none of her relatives regretted coming to Canada and the idea of getting together more often got mentioned every day, Cecile never lost sight of the reason she was there.

When her plane landed in the mid-afternoon on July 1— Canada Day, not that anyone in New York seemed to care—the temperature outside had reached 100 degrees. Since Aunt Mimi had bought a non-refundable ticket to Alberta for "the wedding" and the room Cecile rented from her was on the top floor of an uptown brownstone with no air conditioning, Cecile spent the cab ride from the airport dreading the inferno a week of closed windows guaranteed. A much more pleasant thing to consider, though, than "the wedding."

As expected, going inside felt like stepping into an oven, or through the front gates of Hell. The heat increased as Cecile ascended the stairs backwards, bumping her suitcase on every step and smiling, because there was something comical about achieving this level of misery.

She dropped her suitcase in her room and lay on the bed, covered by a heavy quilt of thick, stale, humid air. She wanted to stare at the ceiling for a while, but she wasn't interested in drowning in her own sweat, so she opened the window instead and inserted her box fan. Even on high, the relief was minimal. Should've paid the extra ten bucks for that oscillating one, she thought. "Penny wise, pound foolish" was one of her mother's favorite sayings, along with "The fool and his money are soon parted." Her mom never bothered to explain which applied when. Then again, it was undoubtedly a common-sense thing; since Cecile wasn't sure she had much of that, she'd resigned herself to a life of hit-and-miss financial decisions.

She had enough common sense, however, to know that a cool shower would help her situation. When she emerged from the bathroom, still damp, the air from the fan finally made a difference.

Cecile dug through her underwear drawer and extracted a slightly misshapen pair of panties and a gauzy nightgown that looked like something a great-grandmother would wear. She had no plans to do anything but stay in the house, basking in self-pity, and more attractive clothing would have spoiled her mood. I should unpack, she thought, sitting on her bed, but I can't.

At this point, the part of her that found weakness repulsive, at least in herself, began to rise up with every intention of kicking her in the ass, a fate Cecile avoided by opening her suitcase.

Thirty minutes later, everything clean was in its place and the rest was in the washer. Cecile felt better. Moving forward always helped—one foot in front of the other.

She sat on her bed again, trying to think of something else to do. After a very long minute, it came to her: Call home. She dialed the phone reluctantly.

"Hello?" said her mother.

"Hi, Mom. I just wanted you to know I'm back in New York."

"How are you, precious?" Her mom's voice had taken on the tone of deep concern that Cecile had been trying to avoid— her parents' worrying made her feel both pathetic and guilty.

"I'm fine. It's very hot here, though. This room must be at least 110 degrees."

"Really? It's lovely here. A little cloudy, but that makes it very pleasant."

"Great." *Maybe she isn't trying to make me feel bad for leaving early. Yeah, right...* "Mom, I'm kind of tired. I thought I'd take a nap, or something."

"Call me if you need to, okay?"

"I will. Tell everybody I said hello."

"Of course, sweetheart. I love you."

"I love you too. 'Bye."

"'Bye."

Cecile's gratitude about ending the conversation lasted a moment, which was how long it took for her to realize she was back at square one. A heaviness began to settle on her brain. *I'm not going to cry,* she asserted firmly. Which meant she had to come up with something to do. Immediately.

Dinner. Except she wasn't hungry, and besides, the choices were few, unless she spent some money, which she quickly ruled out.

So I get to be creative, she thought. She tried to feel excited about this, as she often did when challenged with making a meal out of next to nothing, but she couldn't do it—*Suck it up, dammit!*

Canned tuna, canned tomatoes, diced onion, spices and powdered Parmesan cheese over spaghetti turned out to be fairly flavorful. One foot in front of the other.

She cleaned up the kitchen, put her laundry into the dryer, and went back upstairs. The roaring fan nearly deafened her, but she couldn't turn it down since it was still barely cooling her room. Despite the noise, the house had become too quiet. Cecile thought of all the times she had been in that house by herself, glad to practice uninterrupted on Mimi's baby grand, or listen to music, or talk to Teddy on the phone…

Now she was thinking about not being alone in the house. Of lying in Teddy's arms, of the woodsy smell of his cologne, the feel of his lips...

No more crying, she reminded herself fiercely, wiping her eyes, as memories continued to assault her, their impact undiminished by familiarity and repetition.

She was disgusted that she still craved Teddy's affection, but she couldn't help it. Every time he crossed her mind, a list of positives crowded out his obvious faults: he was one of the most charismatic humans she had ever met, he could strike up a conversation with absolutely anybody, he knew his black history forwards and backwards, he was committed to community service, he could defuse even the most serious argument with a joke, and four years after they'd met, Cecile still found herself staring at him, drinking in his coffee-colored skin and the angles of his cheekbones, marveling at his lush eyelashes and full lips.

She thought of all of these things, even though she knew they were trivial. What mattered most, the saw-edged knife that still ripped her open relentlessly, was how special she'd felt when he told her he needed her in ways that nobody else could satisfy, ways that had nothing to do with sex, ways that even his infidelity couldn't erase.

She shut her eyes and opened them again, trying to clear her head, determinedly reminding herself about offstage Teddy, the Teddy given to dark moods, irritability and sarcasm. One Teddy marveled at Cecile's skill as a pianist and bragged that she studied at Juilliard; the other became petulant when her need to practice interfered with his plans. One Teddy bought expensive flowers and professed his love for Cecile to random strangers; the other mocked her for being from a small town, dismissively calling her a farm girl.

Onstage Teddy, who always apologized for what offstage Teddy had done, was the only Teddy Cecile had heard from lately. Onstage Teddy kept saying he couldn't survive without her, but she couldn't allow herself to listen to him anymore. At least, that was the plan.

She turned on the TV and flipped through the channels. On July 1, there should have been some Wimbledon tennis. She glanced at the clock. Probably too late in the day. *Teddy likes tennis...*

Cecile turned off the TV and tried to focus on the fan. White noise was supposed to be calming, right?

Help me, Lord. Please help me!

She remembered Langston. Where was his address? In her purse, on a Kleenex. She retrieved her bag from the closet and found the fragile tissue in an inner pocket. The writing on it was still legible, despite a small tear. Cecile sat beside her dresser, at the antique desk that had belonged to Mimi's daughter, Anne, and copied the address into a notebook. Then she turned to a fresh page and began to write:

07/01/91

Dear Langston,

Here's my letter. See? I'm a woman of my word, although I don't think you are. Well, obviously you're not a woman of your word. You know what I mean.

Or maybe you don't. I don't even know what I mean these days.

Okay, this is a few sentences long, and already, I'm confusing. Back to the point. There was one somewhere. I think.

Oh yeah. You're already telling me lies. Then again, you are a man, aren't you?

Actually, I'm kidding, but before I assume you don't write poetry—because I'm guessing you were saying that you did because your name is Langston—I'll ask. Do you write poetry?

Maybe Teddy had that girlfriend all this time because he just wanted to be able to understand what the hell a woman was talking about, for once. Then again, maybe he had a girlfriend because she's "the one," and he didn't have the guts to tell me, having bought a ring and all. Which is ironic, because the whole point of being engaged (correct me if I'm wrong) is that you've decided who you want to spend your life with. So why pretend the ring means something if it doesn't anymore?

Whatever. Tell me about you. I mean, some other things besides what you told me before. Like what you want to be when you grow up. Do you have brothers and sisters? Did you think I was ever going to shut up? Then again, maybe it's too late to answer these questions, since Teresa undoubtedly took out a contract on your life.

Nice meeting you, though.

Take care,

Cecile

P.S. By the way, I actually used to write songs. I know you were making a joke about that whole patron saint of music thing. I must say, I'm impressed. Not everybody knows about St. Cecilia. Anyway, I'm a really amateur songwriter, so you'll never hear them. No loss to you, though.

Cecile read the letter again, feeling better. Thank God for Langston.

As she was writing her address on the envelope, it occurred to her that he might not respond. Maybe she shouldn't send it. She wasn't sure she could stand it if he didn't respond.

She thought about their ride in the elevator the night they'd met, how sweetly he had kissed her, and the look in his eyes afterward.

He'll write back, she decided. He doesn't know me well

enough yet to realize I'm not worth it.

CHAPTER THIRTY

Langston opened Cecile's letter with a kitchen knife, then pulled it slowly from the envelope. He liked that she was down-to-earth enough to have written on a piece of notebook paper, not fancy stationery. He liked her handwriting, too: neat but not overly so, the work of a rational person, but with a heart. The same woman he'd met at Darling's.

He tried to savor the fact she'd written at all for as long as he could, in case the contents of Cecile's note turned out to be disappointing, but after about two minutes, he couldn't stand the suspense. He sat on his dark brown canvas couch and read her letter. Twice.

She was clearly still suffering, still thinking a lot about Teddy, but what would he expect? Mainly, he felt relieved to find her as engaging in writing as he remembered her having been in person. He couldn't wait to write back, which was unusual for him, but then again, the whole experience of meeting her seemed like a chapter from someone else's life.

He started composing the letter in his mind, trying to come up with the perfect opening. What if I just answer her letter? he thought. Let her know who I am?

He wasn't sure that was a good idea...*just a little bit, Stupid.*

7/11/91

Dear Cecile,

Am I really going to grow up? Do I have to? That's damned scary news, because I have no idea what I'm going to do. Lose my teeth and hair? I'll tell you what I won't do: what I'm doing now. Not that I mind what I'm doing, actually, but I think my family will disown me if I don't get another job. If you write me back, I'll tell you more.

Let's see—I have a brother and two sisters. Two of them are older—my brother and one sister, to be exact. *Ma soeur Zora a 32 ans, mon frere Marcus a 28 ans, et ma soeur Maya a 19 ans.* And I'm 23, so my dad got lucky at least every four years or so.

Did I think you would shut up? Well, I kind of hoped you wouldn't. I'm sorry to hear you're never going to sing for me, because you have a really nice speaking voice, and I bet you can sing. But what do I know? Not much about anything, and since I've gone into hiding to avoid Teresa's hit men, it's hard to pick up anything new.

Now, about your vicious attack on my character. You know the one: impugning my integrity simply because I have a Y chromosome and/or a penis. I never lie. But you should never believe me. I will, however, remind you that the name "Langston" only implies literary skill when combined with "Hughes." My last name is Andrews. Draw your own conclusions, realizing that if you won't share your songs, I won't share my poems.

But if you show me yours, I'll show you mine.

A bientot,

Langston

He read the letter again, wondering if she would still like

him after she got it. The last line in particular would either amuse her or turn her off completely. He wanted to make sure she saw him as having potential to be something other than a friend, but maybe it was too soon.

Take a chance, for once. He sealed the envelope, put a stamp on it, and went out to mail it before he changed his mind.

CHAPTER THIRTY-ONE

Langston's letter arrived the week Teddy called Cecile every day (instead of every other day) to apologize and swear up and down that he wasn't interested in anyone else and wasn't sure how he could live without her. That he'd made a terrible mistake, but if she'd just forgive him, he would never hurt her again.

She wanted desperately to stay strong, but she ended up wondering—with hope—if Teddy had changed. He was getting counseling, after all. Offstage Teddy might be dead. Besides, who else was there? Not that she was making an effort to find out.

There's Langston, she thought, smiling at the tone of his letter, and how much she liked the idea of flirting with him. With him so many miles away, the correspondence would be about nothing but fun, which she desperately needed. And as long as she let him know Teddy wasn't out of the picture completely, she wasn't doing anything unethical.

She picked up her pen:

7/19/91

My dear Langston,

You are a naughty boy, *n'est-ce pas*? Maybe you need to be spanked, but I don't do that kind of thing. At least, not for free.

Hey, thanks for forcing me to remember at least a bit of that French I said I knew. If I ever see you again and I have a glass of wine (one's my limit), we may actually be able to have a conversation.

This job must be intriguing. Or not, but either way, you didn't have to throw that mystery thing in. I was going to write back anyway.

So tell me—does the Y chromosome/penis thing (which one do you have?) give you any insight? I mean, why would a guy get engaged and then have a girlfriend anyway? And then, even after he gets busted, he calls and insists that he loves you? Does that make sense to the male brain? Because it doesn't make sense to me. But maybe I'm missing something.

So you're a middle child. Hmm...*tres interessant*. I don't remember what that's supposed to mean, but I'm sure it's significant. I used to be a middle child. You met my sister Elizabeth (suddenly Betsy isn't good enough for her). I had a brother, but he died. Kind of self-inflicted. He was the oldest; now I am. *La vie est imprevisible, n'est-ce* pas? Does that mean "unpredictable?" My French is pretty rusty.

Do you often come to Edmonton? Then again, if you did, I'd know. Any black man I haven't seen before stands out. We get fresh blood now and then—every year, the new crop of Americans trying to make it in Canadian football—but they're just tourists looking for some action before they go back South.

I'm acting like I still live there, or something. I'm thinking about it. If I leave New York and move back to Edmonton, at least I won't have to deal with Teddy trying to come over all the time. I don't think I can see him yet. Then again, maybe I should. Teresa might have some gun-toting connections in New York. Maybe I can arrange a meeting. When they give up on you, that is—okay, enough hit man humor.

I'm boring even myself now, so I think I'd better go.

Take care,

Cecile

She hadn't planned to mention Calvin. She debated rewriting the letter—no, it was okay. She remembered the kindness in Langston's eyes the night they'd met, and smiled, deeply peaceful for the first time in months, wishing Langston would call her. It would be nice to hear his voice. Of course, she could have called him herself, but she didn't want to seem forward. Too soon to drop her guard anyway; he could have an offstage side, too.

But he wasn't Teddy, and he liked her. For now that was enough, all by itself.

CHAPTER THIRTY-TWO

8/01/91

Salut Cecile,

I quit my job, so never mind. I'll tell you about the new one after I start ('cause I know I gotta have a J-O-B…not that the finance gets me much romance anyway. Maybe if I had more finance, there'd be more romance). By the way, that means I'm moving, but I'll write you when I get there. Honestly. Y-chromosome and/or penis be damned. (Which one? There are ways to find out, but not while you're in another country, since my new job doesn't involve starring in pornography).

Speaking of which, I have no idea why Teddy did what he did. I could guess, but anything I say would be pretty harsh, and it seems you still have strong feelings for him. So I'll just say it again: I don't know much about anything. Especially what makes some guys do some things.

I'm sorry to hear about your brother. I'd like to ask what happened, but if it's too painful, I understand your not answering that question. I can't imagine how I'd feel if one of my siblings had died.

Actually, I've been in Edmonton maybe twice. Well, thrice: There was the time my grandmother dragged me out there with the rest of the kids when the biggest mall in the world opened, but I'm trying to put that trauma behind me. My aunt is my mother's sister, but she's the only Adventist in the family, which may or may not be why they don't get together very much.

It could also be that the rest of us are in Ontario.

I think I mentioned that I lived next door to Teresa until eighth grade. She was one of my best friends. We didn't keep in touch like I'd thought we would, but we're still close. Meaning, she actually forgave me for ditching her the night I met you. Meaning, she knows I'm not always all there, and she's used to it.

By the way, you may bore yourself, but not me. To be honest, I hate writing letters, but I'm actually enjoying our little correspondence. On the off chance that I start disliking letters again, would it be okay to call? Assuming you gave me your actual phone number. I could start my new job by owing the phone company thousands of dollars in calls to the US of A. That is, if they have phones where I'm going.

Oh yeah, what island are you Alexanders from? Assuming you're like the rest of us.

Enough, already.

A bientot cherie,

Langston

CHAPTER THIRTY-THREE

8/29/91

Hi Langston,

Hope you get this. You've probably moved, given how long dear old Canada Post took to deliver your last letter. Let me guess—they're about to strike again, right?

Let's see. My mother is a Bermudian and my father is, believe it or not, an American, but his dad was born in Jamaica, so I guess that gives me island roots on both sides. He was stationed in Bermuda and one thing led to another, although not until after they were married, since Mom's an old-fashioned girl and all. At least, that's her story and she's sticking to it.

I did give you my real number. Yours, I assume, is out of service.

About your j-o-b...hey, the song never said you have to be a doctor. There are still some women who think there's more to a man than lots of money. Then again, that's why we probably end up getting treated like we don't deserve the best. Okay, that's my angry female remark for the day. There's one in every letter, isn't there? I admit it: I'm a teensy bit resentful.

So you really can't relate to cheating on a fiancée? I just figure any man who could get away with it would do it. (You're right, that's another angry female thing, so I guess I lie too sometimes, even without a penis.) I mean, Teddy and I were the couple that people actually stopped, stared, and smiled at (to quote Tony Terry—was "When I'm With You" a hit in Canada?).

How do you go from that to sneaking around with a sixteen-year-old? In my gut I knew Teddy was unfaithful, but I didn't want to believe it, so I talked myself out of acknowledging the obvious.

The sad thing is, I still love him. And in his own way, he still loves me. I just wish he hadn't proposed. I guess he felt he had to. Not an excuse, right? Right.

Which brings me to my brother, Calvin. I can talk about it, I just didn't want to if you don't want the details. My brother died five years ago, at the age of 20. He was a drug addict. He OD'd. It may have been an accident, or he may have done it on purpose. He was the most charismatic person you'd ever meet, but when he was high he was scary. This will sound awful, but I'm kind of relieved he's dead. His life was miserable by the end, and I didn't see it changing any time soon. And living with him was a nightmare.

The thing is, when I saw him at the funeral home, I couldn't stop crying, which felt strange because I hated him most of the time. It's hard to understand why I miss him at all. I guess that in the back of my mind I remember us being little, and somewhere else I imagine being middle-aged, like that would magically make him into a real big brother, or something. I used to dream about him all the time, but I don't anymore. Then again, it's been a while since I've had a dream I could remember.

Okay, enough seriousness. Call me sometime. Promise? Or write me a really dumb letter. Not dumb—you're too smart for dumb. But something trivial would be cool about now.

A bientot yourself, *cheri,*

Cecile

Langston's new job was a teaching position in Forestville, Quebec, a town with a population of about 3,000 on the north shore of the St. Lawrence River. Nothing about the position appealed to him, except the paycheck.

In spite of his grandmother's attempts at indoctrination, he missed working at Gino's. When he left, he'd been one step away from being on an equal plane with Mario, which was apparently the equivalent of shoveling manure for a living. Damn Zora and Grandma Felicia and the high family standards. And damn himself, for succumbing to the pressure to quit.

Seeing Cecile's handwriting on an envelope in the midst of his forwarded mail had raised his spirits temporarily, but as he finished her letter, he felt helpless. He re-read the part about her brother, walking in circles around his tiny living room, managing to avoid the boxes he'd left packed despite the miniscule amount of possessions he had brought with him, and wished he could have been there to protect her.

He tried to remember what his parents had been like on drugs and was glad that nothing came to mind. I lived with them until I was six, he thought, so I should remember something. Maybe Zora is right—I must be blocking it out. Just as well. Has to be.

Something else in the letter disturbed him even more. She still loved Teddy? He knew love was illogical, but shouldn't really smart people like Cecile be able to put two and two together?

Langston had avoided discussing Cecile with Glenda, because he didn't want to endure her ridicule unless he was completely at a loss.

Like now. Maybe he should call Glenda now. Maybe she could help him write a response that would make Cecile realize what a dead end a guy like Teddy was, without insulting her. No, what he *really* wanted was to find a way to make her forget about Teddy completely.

What for? he thought. Am I less of a dead end?

He'd started pacing again, still holding the letter, when the force of an inescapable truth, one he'd tried his best not to acknowledge, made him stop—*I can love her*.

He was going to call her without that revelation, but now he had a mission. He was sure he didn't have the skills needed to complete it, but he had to try.

CHAPTER THIRTY-FIVE

In a school full of great artists, some with the outsized personalities to match, David Dubal managed to stand out. With his piercing brown eyes, dark, flowing hair, olive skin, midnight blue velvet jackets, and neck scarves, Cecile suspected that even the actors had to notice him.

Even though her successful audition for the Juilliard Master's program gave her the freedom to choose most of her courses to suit her interests, piano literature, which was required, remained one of the highlights of Cecile's week. Mr. Dubal's love of grand pronouncements made his class entertaining and, with the necessary grains of salt, informative. His taste in recordings, however, needed no seasoning. The week he featured Solomon Cutner, Cecile begged him to make her a tape of some of Solomon's performances. He commissioned his assistant to do so, and now, a week later, she could finally listen to her current favorite pianist in the privacy of her room.

Cutner's "Appassionata" was thrilling—both virtuosic and profound, his touch the essence of refinement—but the late sonatas were even more astonishing; a whole different universe. Cecile wished she could live in the place where he had found his way to the very core of Beethoven's mature art.

The music defied accurate description. In Beethoven's late masterpieces there was sadness, perhaps, but the acceptance of the storms of life stood out much more prominently, undergirded with unshakeable serenity.

Lying on her bed inches from the wall, tears trickling from her eyes, she had given herself over to the healing quality of the sounds that filled the room, and her soul, when the phone rang.

Cecile's heart jumped into her throat. She dreaded another call from Teddy, because she wasn't sure how much longer she could stop herself from feeling that their reunion was inevitable, that there was a deep, irreplaceable, cosmic connection between them that couldn't be severed by mere logic and willpower. She still hated him sometimes, but she also missed having someone to go to movies or concerts or dinner with, especially since most of the people she'd gotten to know before Teddy began to dominate every spare moment had graduated. She minded going out by herself less and less, but she couldn't enjoy the places she and Teddy used to go anymore, and felt a twinge every time she saw a couple holding hands, never mind gazing into each other's eyes or kissing.

The phone rang for the third time. Answering it was unavoidable—despite her discomfort with Teddy, she still felt compelled to talk to him.

She reached her dresser in two steps, turned down the volume on her tape player, and picked up the receiver.

"Hello?"

"Hi. Is this Cecile?"

The voice was vaguely familiar. High baritone, slightly Canadian...

"Yes."

"So you were telling the truth. This is your number."

"Langston?" Cecile broke into a smile. As she sat on her bed, she caught her reflection in the mirror above the dresser, saw the light in her eyes, and smiled even wider.

"You did tell me to call you, right?"

"I seem to remember something like that. Have you moved?"

"I was already packed when I sent the last letter."

"So they have phones where you are."

"Nope. I drove two hundred miles, just to hear your voice."

Cecile laughed, feeling herself blush slightly. "I see you haven't overcome the effects of your Y chromosome. Or penis, whatever."

It was Langston's turn to laugh. "Oh ye of little faith."

"Begging your pardon. I meant to say, that was sweet of you."

"Apology accepted."

"Where are you anyway?"

"Two hundred miles from Hell."

Cecile laughed again. "At least it's warm."

"You'd think so, but not today."

"So Hell does freeze over? I should have known, since you called me." Cecile lay back against her pillow, crossing her ankles—she was missing the last movement of the Appassionata. She stood up, walked over to the dresser, and turned off the tape.

"So I should call every day this winter," Langston said,

"because I expect a whole lot of freezing around here. I think we're further north than Edmonton."

"Really?" Cecile resumed her reclining position on the bed. "So...I'll ask you again. Where are you?"

"Forestville, Quebec. I'm going to write you a letter with the details, though. Okay?"

"Okay." There was a short pause, and then Cecile said, "Langston Andrews. I'm glad you called."

"Really?"

"Why wouldn't I be? I like you."

"Thanks. I like you, too." His voice was quiet.

Cecile rolled onto her side, away from the wall (choosing to face something other than the light green paint wasn't a given for her, these days). "Thanks," she said.

"So anyway," he replied, his voice back to normal, "what's new? I know *you've* got something new to report."

"Meaning?"

"That your life is never dull."

"I wish it was, though. It would be a nice change."

"How are you?"

"Fine."

"I mean, really."

She pictured him with that look on his face, the one she had interpreted as demonstrating concern, and smiled. "I'm okay. Really. Teddy calls me all the time, but I'm trying not to talk to him too much."

"Any success?"

"Depends on the day."

"I can't imagine how hard it must be to let go of somebody you were going to marry."

Was she letting go of Teddy? She wasn't so sure. "I wouldn't wish it on anybody," she said. One innocent comment and she could feel her positive mood ebbing away. Maybe she needed to hang up and get back to Beethoven. She didn't want to inflict her depressed side on Langston again.

"Do you like classical music?" she asked.

"I don't dislike it. I don't listen very much, to be honest. Is that what you had on when I called?"

"Yes."

"Was that you playing?"

"I wish! A British pianist named Solomon Cutner. He was like Madonna in his day, I guess, because he was known as just plain Solomon."

"What day was that?"

"Mid-century. He had a massive stroke in the 1960's and died about three years ago, after twenty years of being incapacitated."

Langston was silent. "That's a terrible story."

"Isn't it? I should say that at least he got to play as well as he did and leave a bunch of fantastic recordings, but you know, what I really think is that it sucks. Then again, life is completely unfair sometimes, isn't it?"

"I wish I could argue with you."

Cecile tried to fight a familiar urge to turn over and stare at the paint on her bedroom wall from close range. She could feel depression creeping from her chest to her brain, wrapping her thoughts in a thick gray fog.

"Langston?"

"Cecile?"

"I'm so glad you called me. Listen, I have to go. I can't wait for your letter."

Another pause. "It's already in the mail."

"Even better. I'll talk to you soon. On my bill next time, okay?"

"Okay, but first I'd need a phone."

Cecile managed to smile. "So give me the number of the payphone you're calling from today, and I'll give you enough notice to drive the two hundred miles. Okay?"

"Sounds like a plan." He gave her his phone number, and added, "You take very good care of yourself, okay?"

For some reason, his simple request brought tears back to her eyes.

"Okay, you too."

She hung up quickly. Had Teddy ever suggested that she take very good care of herself? Or only of him? Why did she love him so much?

Her brain had always been both a friend and an enemy, making her academic career easy and everything else difficult. Thinking, overthinking, trying not to think...

But I do love him, she realized. And I can't think my way out of it. I've tried. Then again, the logical part of me has never been in control of our relationship—it was about me using parts of my brain I didn't know existed, and liking it. And now that I don't like it, I can't put things back the way they were.

The gray fog had become oppressive, wrapping itself tightly around her skull, making her chest feel heavy and her limbs leaden. She forced herself to walk over to the tape player, turning up the volume as Cutner resumed his conquest of the Appassionata. She stood for a moment, letting the music wash over and through her at close range, her eyes firmly shut. *Suck it up, Cecile!*

But she couldn't, just then. So she went back over to her bed, curled into a ball and waited for the fog to lift.

CHAPTER THIRTY-SIX

Langston's new apartment was in the basement of a large home. He was grateful for his lovely view of a stand of very old trees—for his measly rent, he'd have been lucky to have a view of a wall. Then again, he couldn't imagine anyone paying much to live in Forestville.

His room was spacious, with off-white Berber carpeting and a kitchenette. He'd divided the areas with furniture: his bed, nightstand and an old armoire on one side, closest to the bathroom, separated by his couch from the living room, which also contained a coffee table and the end table where his cordless phone usually rested, all facing his 19-inch television set and VCR, which sat side by side on a low bookcase. The kitchenette lay at the far end of the room, equipped with a small fridge, the narrowest four-burner stove he had ever seen, and a microwave on one end of the counter, which had two wooden bar stools. More than enough conveniences to accommodate his very simple lifestyle.

After he hung up the phone, Langston tried to watch the news, but his brain refused to stop contemplating his conversation with Cecile. Soon, he couldn't stand it anymore and called Glenda for advice.

"When she said she'd call me, does that mean I can't call her first?"

"How did she say it?"

"She didn't sound mean or anything, and she mentioned

paying for it, like she didn't want to run up my bill."

"Isn't she sweet!"

"Yes. Seriously, though."

"Okay, okay." There was a short pause. "I think you should wait for her to call."

"Really?" He'd hoped for the opposite advice. "Why?"

"Because you don't want to seem too eager. It's the kiss of death."

Langston sighed. He was sitting at the counter that doubled as a kitchen table, gazing out at the dense evergreens just beyond the back yard. "But Teddy is calling her all the time."

"Yeah, but if she isn't done with him, there's nothing you can do anyway."

"Really?"

"Really. Unfinished business always screws things up eventually, even if they could have worked out otherwise. You've got to give her enough space to figure out what she wants."

"But he lives there and I don't."

"Can you move?"

"No."

"You think she will?"

"Let's see. She's studying at one of the best music schools in the world, but she could give that up to live in the middle of nowhere so she can get to know me. Hmm."

Glenda chuckled, then said, in an uncharacteristically gentle voice, "Listen, Andrews. Are you listening?"

"Of course. I called to ask for input, didn't I?"

"She's not the last woman on earth."

"No, but..." He decided not to say he'd never felt this way before.

"I think you should look at this as a learning experience. If it works out, great, but if it doesn't, you've gained some skills for the next one."

"Sharpened my game."

"There's nothing wrong with that."

"Yes there is! Why does it have to be a game?"

"Because life is a game."

"And that means somebody's got to lose."

"That means," Glenda said, "that everybody's got to lose. At least sometimes, and then they have to decide to either give up or get back in the game."

"Uh-huh." Langston started drawing circles on the counter with his index finger.

"But since this game isn't exactly over yet," Glenda continued, "you don't have to make that kind of decision right now."

I know where the game is headed, though, he thought. But maybe I'm wrong. I could be wrong, couldn't I?

"So what I should do," he said, "is wait for her to call me. But in the meantime, she'll get my letter, so hopefully that will keep me on her mind."

"Exactly."

"Although it's such a ridiculous letter that it might just

help her decide to forget she ever met me."

"Chance you take."

"So when we do talk, do I say things to get her to think about what a piece of shit Teddy is or not?"

"I think that could backfire."

"So she has to choose me on her own? I'm not even supposed to try to compete?"

"If she still wants him, she is going to have unfinished business, and it will screw things up. Hmm—that sounds familiar because I said it two minutes ago."

She's been more patient than usual, Langston reminded himself. "You promise she'll call?"

"Nope. But if she doesn't, she's doing you a favor. Anybody that stupid doesn't deserve you anyway."

He paused. Stupidity wouldn't be the issue if Cecile didn't call, but he did appreciate the attempt to boost his spirits.

"Thanks, Glenda."

"As always, Langston."

As he hung up the phone, he thought of how he'd ended the letter and wished he had been bolder. Maybe it was okay. He hoped so.

Who am I kidding? he thought. As usual, I don't know what the hell I'm doing.

Langston looked out the window. The leaves were changing color, the sky was blue, and he realized there was beauty in the world, even in this tiny Quebecois town where everybody looked at him as if he were an alien, simply because he was black. There was beauty even if Cecile remained fixated on Teddy.

As usual, Glenda was right. Cecile wasn't the last woman on earth. And even if she was the only one Langston could imagine falling in love with, so what?

He closed his eyes for a moment to absorb the pain of his last thought. And felt a desperate urge to go outside for a walk.

CHAPTER THIRTY-SEVEN

Cecile always called home on Sunday. The weekend after she talked to Langston, she had a lot of practicing to do, so she kept the conversation shorter than usual—quite a feat, because her talks with her parents rarely lasted longer than fifteen minutes anyway.

She appreciated her family, but she had less and less of substance to say to them now that Teddy was working his way back into her life. She couldn't admit that she was still willing to give him a chance. Even to herself.

She'd called her parents more often right after her alleged wedding date, always putting on a happy voice, trying to prevent them from assuming she was too depressed pick up the phone. Besides, Teddy called her a lot, so she preferred to initiate contact with people as a way to be certain who would be on the other end of the line.

Her mother had already sent her three books about relationships, one of them written from the Christian perspective. Cecile had skimmed them. She didn't want to be seen as a project, which was why the books, which she knew were meant to convey loving concern, annoyed her. When the third one arrived, she asked herself why she felt angry and couldn't come up with a good answer. At least her mother was trying to be there. True, she was directing the healing, just like she took the lead in anything else she thought was important, but at least she was trying.

Besides, Cecile thought, I'm clearly in need of directing, since I'm still in love with Teddy. He's my story, and I'm sticking to him. Why? He's not even the first man I had sex with. First man I made love to, though. So what? Pathetic.

Her talks with Betsy were even more superficial than the ones with her parents, because Betsy never bothered to ask deep questions. Which was a relief. There were times when Cecile still felt a twinge of jealousy about Betsy's casual confidence in handling the opposite sex, but lately her sister's stories about meeting and disposing of men were more of a welcome diversion than a source for envy.

Cecile descended the stairs at Mimi's, intending to start practicing, and noticed the mail on the table in the hallway near the front door. She flipped through the envelopes hopefully and smiled when she saw a letter from Langston. She'd started mentioning him occasionally, especially to Betsy, since she already knew who he was. With her parents, Cecile would only allude to him, as an answer to the question of whether or not she had met anybody new. She always clarified that she wasn't ready to date, so her parents wouldn't get too excited. She didn't think it was fair to get their hopes up about her moving on until she had resolved her feelings for Teddy. If she ever actually did.

Cecile curled up in the off-white brocade armchair beside Mimi's grand piano, opened the envelope, and began to read.

9/15/91

Salut Cecile!

Oh great, Miss Neo-Yankee has decided to criticize her native land by dumping all over Canada Post. Have you no shame? Tell me that the postal system in Bangladesh is better than ours! And I've heard horror stories about the Lebanese system...

So you wanted me to write something dumb. How about something ridiculous? That about describes my job. I've been given the dubious honor of teaching *secondaire 3 (*14 and 15 year-olds) in Hell, Quebec. You have to understand that Hell (okay, that's unkind, but it's accurate) is a small, dying town high in unemployment—2/3 of the town is unemployed. The majority of kids don't know how to behave, never mind the fact that 14 and 15 year-olds are generally critical of everything. Needless to say, discipline is constantly a problem: "Don't touch that," "Stop talking," "Leave her alone," "Okay, sit here"...

The kids hate everything. It's incredible. They consider everyone and everything to be boring. The only exceptions to this would be sex, Metallica, and other head-banging, heavy-metal heroes.

Every day, I write two things on my blackboard. One is usually a question/statement pertaining to sports. You know, stuff like: "Is Patrick Roy a better goalie than Grant Fuhr?" The second thing allows me to wax philosophical. For example, the only French word that secondaire 3 has taught me is the word "s*late*" (boring). *"Je trouve cela slate!"* Well, the other day I wrote: "There's a world outside of Hell." (Okay, I called it Forestville). "Try to experience it, taste something different."

(Yeah, I know, pretty corny stuff).

LANGSTON: Okay, guys, I've got a little audio exercise for you today. We're going to listen to a few songs and try to fill in the blanks which represent missing words in the respective songs.

YOUR AVERAGE MEGADETH WANNABE/DEVIL WORSHIPPER: *"Si c'est pas du heavy-metal, c'est slate. Vois-tu?"*

LANGSTON: Well, get ready to be bored because I've got some reggae for you!

Y.A.M.W/D.W: *Mais non! C'est quoi, reggae?*
WAY TO READ THE BOARD, GUYS!

These kids come from an incredibly insulated town yet they think they know everything. They spouted off to me about the Quebecois being the "white niggers" of North America, yet none of them can speak a word of English, and only 3 out of 140 has ever been outside of Quebec…yeah, like they really know what it's like to be a minority.

Anyway, Cecile, I'd love to hear more of your life story. How much would you charge for piano lessons? Do you speak Thai? How tall is Teddy? How tall are you? What size shoe do you wear? Nice phone voice—where did you get it? How often do you frolic in the streets of NY? How would you like to visit Hell, Quebec? What about Bert and Ernie: were they lovers, roommates, or brothers? Do you like pasta with sundried tomatoes, smoked salmon, veggies, scallops and cashews in a four cheese (romano, parmesan…) cream sauce? Can you tap dance? Like me, do you believe that homosexual love is the true love while heterosexual love is merely for reproductive purposes? Do you really believe that 70% of black people in North America are in the middle class? Who was telling the truth, Anita or Clarence? Ever heard a gunshot? Have you lost all respect for me? When was the last time that you saw a "high-tech lynching for uppity blacks?" Have you ever killed a man?

Please excuse my little stand on the old soapbox earlier. It's just that the kids here are a bit different. All they think about is sex. Example: I told them that if they had an activity that they would like to try, all they had to do was ask me. Of course, little Annie Murray (who insists she doesn't have an English name) had to ask, "*Peut-on jouer aux fesses?*" (can we make love?). In order to get them to stop fixating on this subject, I told them that people from Ontario didn't believe in sex before marriage. They now refuse to go to Ontario on an exchange!!

Well, Cecile, I hope that you don't think I'm too psychopathic.

A bientot,

Love, (purely innocent in nature…like the "love" in the statement "I love my sister")

XOXOX (family tradition)

Langston Andrews

P.S. Send me a picture!

She read Langston's letter again. "Love, purely innocent in nature?" Does he really mean that, she thought, or is he trying to tell me something?

I wish he lived here. But he doesn't.

She put the letter in her pocket, sat at the piano, and started practicing scales.

CHAPTER THIRTY-EIGHT

Langston's trip to Forestville for his job interview had seemed long, but the radio, his tapes and the novelty of the landscape, especially the tall trees and glistening waters of the St. Lawrence River along the last leg of the journey, made the time pass relatively painlessly. Driving to Forestville to live had been an interminable ordeal even with the same distractions, because he knew exactly what lay in wait. When he drove home for Thanksgiving, however, he reached the border between Quebec and Ontario in what felt like a moment. Sometimes, the destination makes all the difference.

Or maybe his choice of music had shortened the trip. Cecile's story about Solomon Cutner had piqued Langston's interest so much that he decided to listen to the great pianist's Beethoven on his journey home. Grandma Felicia's tastes in classical music tended towards choral works and symphonies, leaving him with little background in what a classical pianist should sound like. Still, he didn't need a lot of education to know when something both thrilled and moved him.

Then again, maybe the time flew by because he was finally escaping from his job. He'd been counting down the days to his brief vacation for weeks. More accurately, months. Most accurately, ever since the first day of school.

Langston had tried to convince himself that the students would grow on him. Some of them had, but teaching them hadn't. He held onto his sanity by reminding himself that he was working in Quebec to get experience, even as something told him it wasn't teaching these particular students he could barely stand, but teaching in general. He did his best to ignore that voice in his head whenever it intruded, though, because listening left him dangerously close to depressed and, to quote Grandma Felicia, he "didn't have time for that kind of self-indulgent nonsense." He maintained just enough denial about his emotional state to get to the weekend, week after week, counting on letters and phone calls from his family and, especially, Cecile to lift his spirits.

Then again, Cecile was turning into a mixed blessing, with her constant references to Teddy. Langston knew that Glenda was always right, and yet he couldn't help trying to come up with an excuse to be more present in Cecile's life. He drove mile after mile, watching the scenery becoming increasingly less natural and more man-made, trying to allow the music to center him in a more spiritual place. Unfortunately, Beethoven can be tempestuous as well as serene, and either way, there was no power on Earth strong enough to keep Langston from getting more and more agitated as he got closer to home. He didn't want to spend all of his time away from Forestville obsessing over Cecile, but unless he could figure out either a way to forget about her or a brilliant plan to vault their interaction out of the friend zone, obsession seemed a distinct possibility.

The buildings had gotten much taller and closer together when the answer finally came to him. His students were very excited about visiting Toronto until he told them that nobody there believed in premarital sex. New York, however, was one of the sin capitals of the world. Times Square alone would satisfy even the horniest of those adolescent boys—they couldn't attend the triple-X rated shows, but just imagining the goings on would be enough to make the trip worth their while.

A field trip to Manhattan. He had no idea where the money would come from, but if he pulled it off, his stock would go up immensely at his next teaching job, which might help him to progress to a classroom full of kids who could at least pretend to be intellectually curious, which might make teaching something more than a way to please his family.

So the trip to New York was important for another reason, since even if Cecile still wanted Teddy after Langston saw her, having a springboard to a better job would save him from the loneliness he felt, being the only black person in Forestville.

Speeding along the 401, with all remnants of open country long gone, it occurred to him that maybe he was his own worst enemy, spending so much energy thinking about a girl he'd met only once. When Langston told his brother Marcus how difficult feeling like a Martian had become, the advice he got was, "You just need to go to a bar, pick up some French girl who wants to find out if black men really have big dicks, and get laid."

Of course, he'd have to change his personality to become the kind of guy who picks up a girl in a bar just to screw her. And since there was only one bar in Forestville, he'd also have to be immune to gossip, or willing to drive an hour to Baie-Comeau, the nearest "major" town. Still, he'd learned from Marietta, and even the Anthea incident, that sex with another person felt way better than doing it yourself. If he was holding out for Cecile, he was going to be in self-service mode for a long time. Langston hoped he could avoid the kind of desperation that kind of road trip would involve for a while, though.

As Langston turned onto his grandmother's street in Scarborough, he waved to Mr. Billups, a neighbor of his family's for as long as he could remember. He'd never thought it would matter to him so much to see another black face, but there it was, his delusion of color-blindness shattered.

By the time he rang the doorbell at Grandma Felicia's, Langston had committed to taking his students to New York. And when the door opened, he radiated enough optimism that Grandma Felicia, who was prone to greetings that would have drawn a retaliatory insult from most people if they'd come from someone less elderly, said, "Come in here, darling! Quebec can't be all bad, because you certainly look good."

The house shone with familiar faces, and smelled like turkey and pumpkin pie. Grandma Felicia looked resplendent as always in red velvet and pearls, her white hair pulled into a chignon. Even the worn furniture seemed beautiful. Langston smiled, at peace for the first time in ages. "I'm making the best of it," he replied.

He leaned down so his grandmother could hold him close, rubbing his back as she did.

"Amen to that."

CHAPTER THIRTY-NINE

For three years, Cecile had paid her expenses, including her nominal rent, by playing the organ at a small Episcopal church in Brooklyn (with a pastor so boring that her main challenge every week had to do with alertness, not music) and working for a voice teacher who lived five blocks away from Juilliard. Ingrid Rust was a plump, sixtyish, strawberry-blonde soprano with rosy cheeks and hazel eyes, whose performing career ended in her mid-twenties when she married a businessman and started a family. She'd opened a studio, after her three sons started school, as a way to keep in touch with her first love. Somehow, despite her many years in New York, she'd managed to maintain the accent of her native Oklahoma, which added just enough charm to her speaking voice to make her frequent boasts about her boys tolerable.

Cecile would wait in a back room while Ingrid warmed up the students, then emerge to play along, often to music she had never heard or seen before. The repertoire drew heavily on show tunes, since the clientele consisted mainly of dancers without the vocal skills to work on Broadway. Their voices sounded decent at best, but Cecile didn't mind. Ingrid and her students were pleasant, and Cecile enjoyed listening to them make progress. Most importantly, the job allowed her to get paid for doing something stress-free.

One afternoon in early October, a week after she'd received Langston's hugs and kisses through the mail, Cecile found herself sitting at Ingrid's piano during a canceled lesson trying to make conversation, but ending up revealing way more than she'd planned about what had gone wrong with Teddy.

"What makes it so pathetic," she said, "is that the minute he gave me a ring, I knew in my gut he'd started cheating. He wasn't even a good liar."

Ingrid nodded. "Don't be too hard on yourself," she said in her resonant twang. "I mean, he did propose. That's a very good reason to take somebody seriously."

"You'd think."

Ingrid gestured towards a floral-print rocking chair, separated by an end table from the matching chair in which she was seated. Cecile hesitated, then moved away from the piano and lowered herself into the rocker. She had never been invited to sit next to Ingrid before, and she felt weird moving from strictly business with a few superficial pleasantries towards actual friendship. Then again, with all the personal details she had been spewing, the shift in tone wasn't exactly Ingrid's doing.

The chair felt like a mother's arms to a toddler. Cecile began to rock herself gently.

"Have you spoken to him lately?" Ingrid asked.

"He calls me all the time to apologize. Says he can't live without me." Cecile tried, and failed, to sound sarcastic.

"Hmm. Do you believe him?"

Cecile stopped rocking. "I don't know. Well, I do know. I believe he's sorry, but I'm not sure why. I mean, he didn't tell me the truth until I caught him."

"Pretty standard, and it doesn't recommend him. Care for some tea?" Ingrid stood, her high heels clicking on tile as she reached her tiny kitchen.

"Uh…yes, thanks. Is there time?"

"I think so. Besides, Sam's my next student, and he's always late."

"True."

Cecile started rocking again while she waited. She regretted opening up, but it felt too late to turn back. A few minutes later, the kettle started whistling.

"Herbal or Earl Grey?" Ingrid called from the next room.

"Earl Grey, please."

Ingrid returned, placed a tray on the table between them, poured, and sat down.

"So," said Ingrid, dropping two sugar cubes in her cup and stirring, "are you dating yet?"

"No."

"Why not?" Ingrid took a sip.

"I'm not ready."

"You're probably never going to feel ready, you know."

"I don't think that's true."

"Maybe, but unless you try, you won't know where you are with your healing."

Cecile picked up her cup, blew a little, and brought it to her lips. The temperature was this side of scalding, but she swallowed anyway. "Is that fair to the guy?"

"Of course."

"I don't like the idea of using somebody."

"Oh please," Ingrid snorted. "It's just a date, Cecile."

"But shouldn't the guy have a chance? If you're not ready, he doesn't have a shot, does he?"

"There's nothing wrong with calling someone because you feel lonely and want to hear a friendly voice, or letting him cheer you up by buying you dinner," Ingrid said firmly. "Besides, you might find out you like the guy more than you expected."

Cecile thought about Isaac, who'd thought they were in love when she was 14. She felt bad enough about breaking his heart that she imposed a new rule of personal conduct: never give someone who didn't meet her standards a second date. Her rule guaranteed that she wouldn't date much, given her tiny compatibility pool, but at least she'd never have to feel guilty about giving a false impression of her feelings.

Take Langston. She suspected that he might be attracted to her, so she made sure he knew that things with Teddy weren't resolved. Then again, bad example, because Teddy was consistently on her mind, and she wasn't trying to avoid a misunderstanding when she talked about him with Langston. She just felt like she could tell Langston anything.

Still, part of the appeal of getting to know Langston, she had to admit, was that he was a friendly voice when she felt lonely.

The buzzer sounded. Ingrid glanced at her watch. "Wow, he's on time for once," she said, collecting the cups onto the tray. She balanced it on one hand, pressing the button that opened the door downstairs before placing the tray on the kitchen counter.

Cecile was walking to the back room when Ingrid said, "If you ever want me to set you up with somebody, let me know. There are lots of men who would be very happy to date a lovely young woman like you."

Cecile stopped and turned, tearing up.

"Thanks," she managed. Then she went into the back room and fell into a chair.

No, there aren't, she thought. At least, not for the right reasons.

CHAPTER FORTY

10/09/91

Salut cheri,

I like you, Langston Andrews! You're twisted.

So—regarding your questions: 1. I charge $25 per half hour, $45 an hour. That's for piano lessons. For other services, the fee varies depending on how much I like you. 2. Nope, I don't speak a word of Thai, although I love languages. 3. Teddy's 6 feet tall. 4. I'm 5'8. I wear a size 9 shoe. Why, are you buying? I could use a new pair of pumps. 5. Bought the phone voice. Cheap. Glad you like it! 6. I try not to frolic too much—could get one in trouble in a place like NY. 7. You make Forestville sound like such an appealing place to visit! Let's just say I'll think about it. 8. Ernie and Bert are room-mates. There's no sex on Sesame Street. Is there? 9. Wow, salmon and scallops in the same dish? Sounds yummy, but I've never tried it. Can you cook? 10. Not even close, but I should get with it, since all Negroes is sho'nuff supposed to tap dance. Or is it break dance now? 11. Homosexual love is the only real love? What a lot of crapola. 12. 70% of black people in the middle class sounds inflated, but what do I know? The media loves to make us look like a desperate bunch of underachievers. At least if it's wrong it's making us look good, for a change. 13. Clarence is lying and Anita is telling the truth, of course. She's the female. 14. I hear gunshots quite frequently, since I moved to Harlem, but I never see signs that someone was hurt. 15. Of course not! I respect you more, actually, for being so free to be yourself, despite your obvious eccentricities

(Eccentrics of the world, unite!). 16. Hmm—haven't yet, but I don't get out much lately. Plus witnessing a lynching, hi-tech or traditional, never struck me as a desirable experience. 17. I haven't killed anyone in reality, but I blew Teddy and his girlfriend away with a machine gun in a dream. Are you scared?

It's your turn. Tell me your deepest, darkest secrets. It's only fair, after all.

As for the story of my life, same old soap opera starring the usual character, I'm afraid, interspersed with a lot of time at the piano, the last part vaguely interesting, or at least goal-oriented for me, not worth mentioning to anybody else.

Okay, full disclosure: I have a piano lesson tomorrow and I have to practice some more, but I couldn't resist answering your letter because I can't wait to get another one from you, and I won't get one unless I respond.

Love, (we also share familial affection in my house)

Cecile

XOXO to you too!

CHAPTER FORTY-ONE

11/07/91

Salut Cecile,

Thanks for answering all of the questions posed. And no, I'm not scared. I spend every day in the company of a whole classroom full of teenaged delinquents. There's only one of you.

Oh, hold for a second.

Okay, sorry about that, one of the delinquents—I mean, fine upstanding kids—just pumped the volume to max on the ghetto blaster. The kids are forcing me to listen to the most edifying lyrics of Anthrax: "Ahhhh get the fuck out, get the fuck out!" These guys have nothing to say and 10,000 watts to say it with. It's payback time. You try to enrich the lives of these brats—I mean, children—by exposing them to a little Bob Marley, Black Uhuru et al and you have to promise to listen to head-bangin' devil-worshippin' noise.

It seems like the old pot is just a-boiling over with emotion for Teddy. I hope that you both see the light and get back together. True love is hard to find (or so they tell me), so you might as well latch onto it, even if it kills you. NEWSFLASH: Never listen to my advice!

Okay, you want the story of my life. What can I tell you that you don't already know? Did I mention my upcoming trip to Sweden for THE operation at the hands of Doctor Sven Johanneson—how dare you call my homosexual theory "crapola!" I'm still a virgin, and proud of it. I lie (what, like you don't) once in a while to give myself the illusion of grandeur. Not a male thing—just a Langston thing. I want to name my firstborn "Kweisi Kip Andrews" after my great-great-great-great (to the tenth power) grandfather, the King of Ghana. I am easily impressed by people like you who have achieved something. I am waiting for a sign from God telling me what my calling in life should be. Year after year, I wonder what I'll be doing next year. I often wonder if the words "underachiever" and "loser" can have an endearing connotation (just joking). I never joke—Jesus never laughed. I seldom compare myself to Jesus. I am often in touch with myself (especially since I'm still a virgin—ok, enough of the cheap shtick!!!)

Listen, I have to go, so I'll let you in on more of my deepest thoughts at a later time.

Ciao,

Langston

P.S. 1) Thanks for the 8 x 10 glossies. Holy cow! Pretty impressive.

2) Happy American Thanksgiving, Ms. Alexander. And Merry Christmas too!

3) I might be bringing some kids down to NY on Easter weekend.

See ya later…

CHAPTER FORTY-TWO

In theory, Langston's landlord—a seventy-three year-old woman, recently widowed—was responsible for snow removal. It soon became obvious, however, that she didn't have anybody to take care of the job, so he volunteered. His grandmother would have disturbed his dreams every night otherwise, and after a long day with a bunch of students from Hell, he needed the sleep.

He didn't mind, and not just because the lady made him breakfast on weekends. Mainly, he felt like he owed her for letting him live in her house. A number of the residents of that tiny town had never seen a black man in person, judging from their responses to him when he went to buy groceries or fill up his car. At first, he half expected someone to burn a cross on the lawn, but, as time went by, he realized that his neighbors weren't malicious. They just didn't know what to make of him. He couldn't blame them for that.

At least no one had said something racist about him in French, assuming he didn't speak the language. When he and Glenda had been on vacation in New Orleans the summer after their freshman year of college, he'd heard a man behind him in the line at a drugstore mutter, *"Singe!"* There were no other black people nearby, and although Langston could have chosen to remind the man that a white person was more of a monkey than any black person if you compared the lips, he figured that the point would be lost.

His first impulse was to sucker-punch the guy, but he

managed to control the rage roiling in his gut enough to ask the person in front of him for restaurant recommendations instead, very loudly and in French, before turning around and giving the offender such a murderous look that the man got out of line.

Glenda had been in the cosmetics section at the time. Having never seen Langston furious before, she demanded to know what was wrong, but he refused to tell her. He knew she'd cause a scene, and he was afraid they might get arrested. They were, after all, in the Deep South, and the freedom the man in the store felt to unleash a racial epithet made him very reluctant to fall into the hands of the police.

New Orleans had racists, but Forestville had biting cold and snow, and there were days when Langston would have much preferred to deal with idiots than flirt with frostbite. One of them was a Thursday in mid-November, a week before American Thanksgiving, when he came home from work and ended up shoveling snow for nearly an hour in minus 25 degree weather. When he finally came inside, his muscles ached, his nose was dripping and his fingertips were all but frozen, despite the allegedly advanced insulation material lining his gloves.

He had barely pulled off his boots, also inadequately warm, when the phone rang. Ordinarily he wouldn't have rushed to answer, but Cecile owed him a phone call, and he was hoping it was her. He rubbed his hands together for a moment, sat on his couch, and picked up the phone.

"Chateau Andrews, King Langston here."

Cecile laughed. "I'm so glad it's you, sire. I thought the

royal fool might have answered, like the last time."

All at once, his extremities didn't feel quite so painful.

"Oh, him?" he said, smiling. "I had to let him go. Well, actually, I had him guillotined. Prevents wrongful dismissal suits and all."

"That's a wee bit twisted, Your Majesty."

"You got a complaint?"

"I guess not."

"I do," Langston replied, gazing out the window at the snow-covered landscape. "It's too damn cold here!"

"So stay indoors."

"Yeah, I would, but this snow doesn't shovel itself."

"You could get a snowblower."

"They're for wimps."

"Then I don't know what to tell you."

"So don't tell me anything."

"Fair enough."

Langston wished someone would massage his aching muscles, but since that wasn't going to happen, he decided to content himself with a hot drink, forcing himself to rise from the couch, walk to the kitchenette, and turn on the burner under the kettle. He wondered if Cecile gave good massages...she's a pianist, he thought, she's got to have strong fingers. Then again, if she's going to massage anybody, it's going to be Teddy, at the moment.

Langston tried to focus on Glenda's suggestion that there was still a chance, because Teddy would undoubtedly shoot himself in the foot. Besides, weren't he and Cecile friends? Was that such a bad thing?

Yes, because he was a sidekick, just like in high school. Better than nothing? He wasn't sure.

"Is there a lot of snow there?" Cecile asked.

"That's relative. A lot for Edmonton, or a lot for New York?"

"Up to your ankles? Your knees?"

"My calves."

"That's a lot."

The water had already started to boil.

"I could go the rest of my life," Cecile said, "without another flake of snow. I had fun sledding and all that when I was little, but you know, the whole thing lost its charm when I started driving. Not that I drive in New York. Then again, the snow here is only white for about a minute before it becomes a brown, slushy mess. And forget about when there's a major storm. It's just horrible."

Langston extracted a canister of Rooibos tea from his cupboard, putting a spoonful in the infuser section of the glass teapot he'd found in a tiny shop in Little India. Then he searched a lower shelf for a mug, settling on the one with a caricature of Sigmund Freud smoking a cigar, a gift from Marcus. Langston was never sure if his brother had given it to him because of the amusing picture and the inscription, which made fun of Freud's tendency to sexualize anything long and cylindrical, or to make a point about Langston's distrust of psychology.

"I don't know," he responded. "I think the snow is pretty. Besides, you can't play hockey without ice."

"Do you play?"

"I used to."

"Man, you're all the way Canadian!"

"Hey, don't knock hockey. It's fun."

"Okay, I admit it's exciting to watch, but you can have ice indoors without the snow outdoors, if you must have your all-Canadian pastime."

"But what's winter without snow, Cecile?"

"Are your toes numb?"

"A little."

"I rest my case."

Langston smiled. "Aren't there any good music schools in Florida?" he asked, turning off the stove just as the kettle started to whistle, and pouring hot water over the tea leaves.

"Sacrilege! There's only one Juilliard."

"Oh, I know that."

"Actually, some of the teachers are on faculty at Mannes, Manhattan, Curtis, and Peabody. So maybe there's only one Juilliard, but you could get the same lessons other places."

"But you couldn't say you went to Juilliard."

"Well, that's true. To be honest, I don't buy the whole chauvinist thing about my school. It's fantastic, but you don't have to go here to play well."

"That's comforting."

"I can see this is really interesting to you."

Langston laughed, pouring fragrant Rooibos from his teapot to his Sigmund Freud mug, then adding a few drips of honey.

"Actually, it is. I know nothing about that world."

"Neither did Teddy."

Langston put his drink on the kitchen counter, seating himself on a stool.

"Ah, Teddy," he replied, trying to sound as neutral as possible. "How is Mr. White these days?"

"Better, I guess. I don't know."

"You haven't talked to him?"

"Um..."

Langston's smile faded. He sipped his tea. "Did he ask you out again?"

Cecile sighed. "You're going to think I'm really stupid."

"No, I won't."

"You should."

Langston swallowed more tea, too much this time, scalding the inside of his mouth in the process. "Did you sleep with him?" He didn't want to know the answer, but he couldn't stop himself from asking the question.

"Well…"

"I get it."

Langston wanted very much to be nonchalant. Why wouldn't he be? People do that kind of thing even after they've broken up, he reminded himself, trying very hard not to imagine her making love to somebody else. As if she hadn't already done it a million times with that guy. Besides, what difference did it make? He was in Quebec, she was in New York, they were just friends and they had no plans to get together, or at least, none that she seemed to remember.

"You do?" Cecile went on. "I'm surprised. I thought you were a virgin."

She'd caught him off guard enough that he laughed. "You accuse me of lying all the time, and that's the one thing you choose to believe?"

"Men don't say that unless it's true."

"Do you really believe I'm a virgin?"

"Would that be so terrible? There are times I wish I was still a virgin."

"The sex is that awful?"

She paused. "I didn't say that."

"What did you mean, then?"

"That we should change the subject."

"I'm sorry. I didn't mean to offend you."

"Don't worry about it." To Langston's great relief, Cecile didn't sound upset. "Hey, you wished me Merry Christmas way too early. Did you think we weren't going to communicate for a month, or something?"

"I wasn't sure when you'd get the letter. You know how bad it is sometimes."

"That's because you live in the middle of nowhere."

"Temporarily."

Langston blew on the contents of his cup and took another

sip, this time without injuring himself.

"Yeah? Where are you planning to go next?"

"I don't know. Maybe I'll like New York so much after my Easter visit, I'll decide to stay."

"I'm really looking forward to that, by the way."

He was disappointed he'd been the one to bring it up, but she sounded genuinely enthusiastic, which helped a bit. "Are you going to show us around?"

"Of course. I'm not sure I want to meet the brats—I mean, fine, upstanding kids."

"So I'll lose them. That would guarantee I never come back here."

"Good idea. Let me know when you have all the details."

"I will."

"We're going to have a lot of fun, Langston. I can't wait."

"Me neither." Good, he thought. He'd hesitated just long enough to keep all hints of longing out of his voice.

"Well, I'd better go."

"Talk to you soon, Cecile."

"*Au revoir, cheri.*"

Langston put down the phone slowly. Easter was a long way off, and she was sleeping with Teddy again. He'll fuck it up, Langston thought. Then again, she'll probably give him another chance even if he does.

CHAPTER FORTY-THREE

Cecile hadn't meant to sleep with Teddy. She had to admit, though, that she knew spending time alone with him in a private place would probably end with physical contact. No matter what he had done, being close to him still felt like coming home.

On that chilly Friday afternoon in early November, Teddy was waiting for her outside Ingrid's building, as he'd done many times when they were together. Cecile had her head down, trying to keep the frosty breeze from drying out her contact lenses, so she didn't see him slide in beside her as she headed for the Columbus Circle subway station. When she finally noticed him, she screamed.

"I'm sorry I scared you," he said, glancing around nervously. He needn't have bothered, since nobody reacted to her cry of alarm.

"What are you doing here?"

She could feel a spot in her core becoming warm, just looking into his eyes. She grasped for all the reasons she should hate him, or at least tell him to get lost, but they had become slippery: *He lied to you! He cheated on you...but he's apologized over and over for months. He must love you, because it's not like he couldn't find someone else...*

"I know I'm wrong for this," Teddy said, "but I had to see you, and I couldn't think of another way to do it."

She'd been hearing the honeyed warmth of his voice on the phone for months now, but seeing and hearing him at the same time was taking her back...

I should have dated other men, she thought. She couldn't imagine who they were, though, these men who would have blunted Teddy's appeal.

So lonely.

"What do you want?" she said softly, gazing into his eyes.

"I just want to talk to you face to face. Can I please, Cecile?"

She sighed deeply—it was the sound of all of her resistance being pushed out in one breath. She searched his face. The picture of sincerity, and yet she didn't feel a sense of peace. She didn't want to pray for guidance, as she'd started doing regularly, because she didn't want an answer she wouldn't like.

"Okay."

He bought her Chinese food, and when he suggested showing her his new apartment, she agreed. He had managed to get someone to take over the lease on the other one, because he didn't want to live there if Cecile wasn't going to be there, too.

One moment she was admiring the tasteful way he had arranged his furniture, and the next she was sitting on his couch. A moment after that, he took her hand and kissed it. Then he looked into her eyes and slowly leaned towards her. She couldn't catch her breath as he kissed her neck and throat and cheeks and forehead, because she had been starving for the smooth moistness of his lips against her skin. The rest was history, or déjà vu. It felt like the first time—urgent, passionate, overwhelming.

And afterward, regret, uncertainty, and weeping.

"I'm sorry," Teddy whispered, holding her tightly as they lay on his couch, which he'd pulled out into a bed when it became clear that she wouldn't resist him.

Cecile shook her head, unwilling to break the spell. Then again, her tears had literally dampened the mood. She walked to the bathroom, naked and self-conscious. As she blew her nose, she wanted to flee. He probably has an appointment with what's-her-name in a few hours, she couldn't help thinking.

When she left the bathroom, Teddy was still lying in bed, propped on his elbow. His arm and chest looked so muscular that Cecile stared at him for a moment, almost forgetting that she had just made a huge mistake. Almost. She collected her clothes from the floor and began to dress hurriedly.

"Don't go."

"I have to," she said, her eyes welling up again.

"Why, Cecile?"

He said it so tenderly she had to look at him.

"I'm not gonna hurt you anymore, baby. I'm so...I'm so sorry. I'll say it over and over and over, until you believe me. Cecile, I love you. I'm never gonna find another woman like you, and I don't want to try. Can you please believe me?"

She closed her eyes. Can't you just forgive him? Isn't that the Christian thing to do? She realized she was picking and choosing her Christianity, but forgiveness felt fundamental. How many times did Jesus say you were supposed to forgive? Seventy times seven?

"Okay," she heard herself tell him.

Teddy's face relaxed completely.

"Thank you, Cecile. I'm going to keep earning this," he said.

When she saw that his eyes were wet, Cecile let go completely. She lay beside him and held him close, immersing herself in him, fully alive for the first time in months.

The next morning, she woke up with a start, disoriented by her surroundings. And remembered that she was still in Teddy's new apartment, with her on-again lover sleeping beside her.

CHAPTER FORTY-FOUR

December 9, 1991

Bonjour Langston, mon cheri,

I hope this small token of my everlasting and extravagant affection reaches you in time.

I always read your letters over and over, because they're so original, but sometimes your sense of humor seems to be a thick defensive shield. What are you afraid of?

Then again, maybe you should be afraid. There are so many screwed up situations in this world. And people—I'm afraid I'll never get it together. Then again, does anybody really get it together? I hope so.

I'm going home for Christmas on Christmas Day, because of that church job I told you about. I don't regret the easy money (although getting up at the crack of dawn every Sunday has lost some of its charm), but missing Christmas Eve at home is something I'll have to get used to. I usually sing in the choir, which is a lot of fun because I get to make music doing something besides playing the piano. I don't claim to have a solo voice or anything, but it's great to blend with everybody, especially my old friends who have moved away and are visiting just for the occasion, too.

The other really cool thing about being home for Christmas break is the multigenerational parties. I'll go out with Betsy and my friends at least once, but what I'm really looking forward to is the good old family gatherings. All the ex-pat West

Indians we know get together to eat, drink, watch football, and argue—we're not West Indian, of course, but we're close enough to be included, since there aren't enough black people in the area to get technical. After dinner, the younger ones watch TV or play make-believe, and the older ones play dominoes, board games, and talk. Or pull rank on the TV room when they're bored.

The older teens usually hang out with the grownups, but don't say anything. That's still pretty entertaining, because the adults are usually drinking something rum-based, and the arguments get pretty loud. Nobody's serious, though, so no matter how heated they seem, the debates always end in laughter. I'm finally out of the transitional stage, which means I can speak in the grownups room and command respect, rather than indulgent smiles. I can't hang with them in the rum punch department, though. Then again, that's mainly a male sport.

New Year's Eve is all about dancing. One of the teenage boys is usually the D.J., but the old songs always get played— Bob Marley, the Mighty Sparrow, some of the hits from the 60's for the older folks. There's also whatever current songs we can get in Edmonton. They don't play much R&B on the radio, so you have to go to a small record store that gets imports or the university to find the latest music. All the kids who can stay up late, do, regardless of their ages, and even the wallflowers (like me, historically) get a kiss at midnight. At least on the cheek.

Anyway, since I've moved to NY that little town manages to inspire actual fondness, something I'd figured was impossible when I was getting called nigger in elementary school (before my friends and I starting beating up the perpetrators the minute they stepped off school property). Did you have to put up with that crap, too? When I think back on the ridiculous names they called us—like "chocolate bar" is a bad thing—they all sound so stupid that I wish I'd just laughed. That would have been the ultimate response, like calling them "fucking morons" without saying a word. Excuse my language…hey, maybe Anthrax *does* have something to say!!

Well, I wish you a Merry Christmas, I wish you a Merry Christmas, I wish you a Merry Christmas—you get the idea…

XOXO

Cecile

P.S. You're welcome. And now you owe me! Doesn't have to be 8 x 10, but I expect a picture, and pronto!

CHAPTER FORTY-FIVE

January 4, 1992

Ma chere Cecile,

What a sweetheart you are! Thank you very much for the book. Not only do I love Calvin and Hobbes, it'll come in handy in my classes. Here, have a big kiss!!!!

I wish you a very, very Happy New Year, full of joy, peace, and love.

Obviously my letters have become somewhat boorish: "Your sense of humor is a thick defensive shield." So tell me, how long have you had this unmitigated desire to nurture? You haven't exactly opened up completely yourself!!! *Dites-moi*, do you get along with your dad and your sister? Do you and your mother have a good relationship? How many guys did you toy with before Teddy? Okay, maybe my jokes are compensation for some physical shortcoming (could be, I have no point of reference).

Response to your question of the day: "What are you afraid of?"

To make a long story short, an experience in my graduating year of high school altered my personality. I have become somewhat of an anti-social loner (good thing I don't work for Canada Post). Fear doesn't enter into the equation. I'm just living, waiting for my soul to find a raison d'etre.

Hey, Cecile, please bear with me...I'm just a little different.

See ya soon.

Love (term of endearment, not a come-on),

Langston

P.S. I'm sorry, I don't have any pictures of me. Well, I do, but it's a nude shot, and I wouldn't want you to die laughing. By the way, the pictures you sent me must have cost a bundle! Why did you have them taken? What a handsome woman you are!

CHAPTER FORTY-SIX

Langston heard the phone ringing as he stepped out of the shower. The last call had been his grandmother asking, yet again, when he planned to get a Master's degree, but that was two days ago, and even though Grandma Felicia still insisted on sending him money every month, she was too frugal to call more than once a week.

He'd endured a particularly tough day, and he didn't feel like talking to anyone. After sending one student to the principal for smoking marijuana behind the school (despite a high temperature of minus 20 Celsius) and breaking up a fight between two girls, rivals for the affection of the class stud, a kid destined for prison or an early death or both, Langston had come home and spent what felt like years shoveling the snow that had been floating down steadily since before dawn.

His need to be left alone was about more than just that day, though. He was tired of living somewhere so far north that morning began after he left for work and evening had already begun to fall before he got home. Tired of the cold. Tired of the parade of moose heads strapped by proud hunters to the tops of their cars and trucks. Tired of being the lone black face everywhere he went. Tired of speaking French, a language he'd thought he adored. He didn't want to admit to being depressed, but he was tired of that, too.

The planned spring trip to New York gave him a shred of hope—there was still a possibility that when he and Cecile saw each other again, whatever had been kindled would be rekindled. Then again, he'd probably been imagining the spark in the first place.

No. She obviously liked him, even at his weirdest. They would have fun in New York. Anything could happen.

He wrapped a towel around his waist and stepped out of the moist warmth of the bathroom into the dry cold of the living room. The phone had rung at least a hundred times, it seemed. If he was going to answer it, he had to hurry—

"Hello?"

"Hi. Did I catch you in the middle of something?"

"It's okay. Can you hang on for two minutes, Cecile? Or maybe I should call you right back."

"Whichever."

"I just got out of the shower, so maybe I should call you."

"Or you could take another nude picture."

He laughed, remembering why he still bothered to keep in touch with her in spite of his all-but-dashed hopes for their relationship.

"Yeah, but I'm kind of cold, so I don't know if it would accurately reflect my virile masculinity."

Cecile laughed this time. "Oh, are you finally answering the Y chromosome/penis question?"

"Nope," Langston responded. "Damn it, woman, do you remember everything I ever write or say?"

"Of course. I hang on your every pearl of wisdom."

"So can you share that concept with the brats—I mean my

students? Please?"

"Next time I'm in town."

Somehow, he wasn't as lighthearted anymore. "Hey Cecile," he said, "I need to get dressed. I promise to call you back in a minute."

"Okay."

He pulled some underwear, a pair of sweatpants and a Montreal Canadiens jersey out of his chest of drawers, put on his slippers, sat on his couch, and punched in Cecile's phone number.

"Hello?"

"It's me."

"That was quick."

"Didn't want to keep you waiting for my next pearl of wisdom."

"You're too kind."

"So they say."

There was a short silence, and then Cecile said, "Well, I got your last letter."

"Oh, that. Look, I'm sorry." He'd been hoping she would respond in writing. "It had been a long day."

"No, *I'm* sorry. I was way out of line, psychoanalyzing you."

"It's okay."

"No, it isn't."

"Okay, it was horrible. Forty lashes!"

"Langston, I'm serious."

"Sorry. Must be my thick defensive shield."

"I hurt your feelings, didn't I?"

"No," he lied. Then again, what right did he have to be offended? He knew his last letter had been ridiculous, and he didn't need to be very self-reflective to figure out that sending Cecile any old shit that crossed his mind was a defensive reaction to the idea that she was going to fuck Teddy regardless of anything either of them did or said.

Langston gazed at her 8x10, which he'd framed and placed on his dresser. In the picture, her hair was slicked back and she had a hint of a smile on her perfect lips. The lips he'd kissed once, and would probably never get close to again.

"Well, even if I didn't hurt your feelings," said Cecile, "I'm going to answer your questions, because you're right. There are a lot of things I haven't opened up about, either."

"You're under no obligation."

"True, but you're my friend. There aren't a lot of people I can tell everything that's on my mind, like I can with you. I just need to remember that some of the things that cross my mind are better off unexpressed."

Can I please like her a little bit less? he thought, directing the request to God, or no one in particular. He stretched out on the couch. It wasn't quite long enough for him to be truly comfortable, but it was bearable if he angled his torso just right.

"I prefer to have you speak freely and then backtrack than censor yourself, if that's okay," Langston said.

"All right. Oh, before I forget, I'm so glad you liked the

book."

"It was perfect. How did you know?"

"I have ESP. No, actually, the letter before your last one was written on the back of a bunch of photocopied Calvin and Hobbes cartoons. I'm just glad you didn't have it already."

"I forgot about that. Hey, how was your vacation?"

He knew he was stalling, but a part of him didn't want an even deeper sense of who she was. It would just make things harder when she officially went back to Teddy for good.

"Great. Like I said, I've developed a fondness for my little hometown, so when I go home I enjoy the people and places, instead of counting the days until I can escape. I suppose my main problem with the place was that most of the black guys there were chasing after white girls. I hear they're easier—"

"Really?"

"C'mon, you've got to know that. They're easier to get in bed, easier to please. Or maybe that's just the excuse black guys tell black females. Anyway, I guess having somebody, even someone with issues, changes your perspective on things, because I don't care about that stuff nearly as much anymore."

"Uh-huh." Langston was about to debate her remark about the promiscuity of white girls, but the Teddy reference stopped him cold.

God—this time he was very specific—can you get me through this conversation? Maybe he could find a way to end it. He didn't want to, but he wasn't able, on this particular day, to deal with any more evidence of her pending or actual reconciliation with her ex-fiance.

"Stop me if I'm boring you," Cecile said.

"You never bore me." His voice was pained.

"Are you okay?"

"I was shoveling, and my back hurts a bit."

"You should stretch next time."

"I'll remember that. You were telling me about Christmas in Alberta."

"Right. Anyway, I went to the pool hall with some friends. I'd never played pool in my life, but it was fun. I could make shots in spurts, then I'd try too hard to perfect my form and start missing really badly. I mean make-the-cue-ball-jump-in-the-air badly."

Langston pictured her bent over a pool table, her lovely brow furrowed in concentration, launching balls onto the ground, and was amazed at how clear the image was, considering the fact that they had met only once. Then again, he did look at her picture a lot.

"One of Teresa's friends is an engineering major," Cecile continued, "so she was figuring out trick shots. Very impressive. I don't drink beer, so that wasn't part of the experience, but it was kind of cool to be in a dark place with a bunch of people hunched over tables, having a good time. But you know what the best part was? The '80s power ballads. It's scary to say this, but I knew all the words. Not something I could say about the '80s R&B songs. Although it seems they play more R&B on the radio in Edmonton now. Anyway, I must have been overwhelmed with nostalgia, because I enjoyed every one. Even sang along really loudly, some of the time, and I didn't care who heard me. Which isn't like me, but it felt great."

Langston imagined her singing power ballads in a dark, smoky room and wished he had been there.

"I like pool," he said.

"You do? Hey, when you come down, we'll have to find somewhere to play."

He felt warm in the center of his chest. "I'd like that."

"I'll reiterate that I'm really crappy at pool."

"I'm not that great myself."

"Perfect! Hey, tell me about your holiday. Did you go to Toronto?"

"First chance I got."

"Sounds great. Does your mom still cook the whole meal?"

"Nope."

"Did I say something wrong?"

He shifted position—the arm of the couch was digging into his shoulders. "Nope."

He debated the options: tell the whole truth, crouch in a defensive posture with no humor to shield him, or lie, making his accusation that Cecile wasn't open into hypocrisy.

"I haven't talked to my parents in years," he decided to reply. "They're both drug addicts. I was raised by my grandmother." And it's okay, Langston reminded himself. He wasn't about to add an emotional display, even a small one, to his deep, dark secret.

Cecile was silent for a while. "Then you know how things were with Calvin. Why didn't you tell me?"

"I hardly remember my parents. I went to live with Grandma Felicia when I was very young, and they didn't stay in touch. Honestly, I think they were relieved that somebody was finally taking us off their hands."

There was another silence, and then Cecile said, "How do you feel about that?"

Langston glanced around the room. His eyes landed on the plaque his grandmother had given him that said, "I can do all things through Christ who strengthens me."

"I don't know. I guess I'm grateful. She's a great woman, and they're drug addicts."

"But I mean, do you ever wonder where they are? Stop me if I'm asking too many questions."

"No, it's okay." He had never had this conversation with anyone outside his immediate family, not even with Glenda. "Actually, I know where they are. At least, Marcus and Zora do, so I could find out. They told me, but I didn't write down the address. My parents never left Toronto."

"Wow. So you're angry?"

"Actually, when I said I don't know, I was being honest, Cecile."

"I'm sorry, I didn't mean…"

"It's okay."

Could there be another reason he wouldn't bother to write

down an address for his own parents? Then something occurred
to him.

"You know what? I think it's more about what's best for
everyone than anything else. They could get in touch, but they
don't and they haven't, so what's the point in me tracking them
down? Some things are best left alone."

"You're probably right."

Langston sat up. Outside, the snow had started falling
again, and he suddenly felt like crying. He went to the fridge—
nothing appealing caught his eye. Cecile was still talking.

"I'm sorry if I ask questions that are a bit too personal,
Langston. I'm stupid like that sometimes."

"How else do you really know people, though?" He was
quoting Glenda. "You ask, and either they answer or they don't,
and vice versa."

He spotted a small piece of the blueberry pie his landlady
had baked a week ago and shared with him. It would do.

"Hey, Cecile, I'm kind of hungry. Can I call you back?"

"Or you can eat while we're talking. I don't mind. Unless
you'd rather call back."

He was miserable, but hanging up would only make it
worse. "Are you sure?"

"Yes."

"Okay." He found a fork, and sat at the counter with the
pie in front of him.

"You asked me some questions about my family," she
said. "Do you still want to know the answers?"

Langston swallowed. There was something healing about homemade pie. Maybe it was the fruit, or maybe it was the combination of sugar and lard—the woman had actually used lard! —but as soon as the first bite hit his tongue, he relaxed.

"If you don't mind," he said.

"No, not at all. Actually, I wrote you a letter in response, but it didn't seem right to respond in writing. That's weird for me, because normally writing's my favorite way to communicate."

Langston took another mouthful of pie. What was she trying to say?

"I'm glad you called," he said, when his mouth wasn't too full.

"I owed you a call anyway."

"I don't think of it as an obligation."

"Neither do I. Besides, it's really your turn, so the bill will be in the mail."

He wanted to ask her what calling him was, if not an obligation, but he stopped himself.

"Did you throw away the letter?" he asked instead.

"No. Do you want me to read that part?"

"Sure."

"Okay, just a second." While she was gone, he finished the pie, which was doing battle with his encroaching emptiness, just as he'd planned.

He heard Cecile picking up the phone. "Here's what I wrote." She paused for a moment, then said, "'I get along quite well with my family, although each person has things they do that annoy. My mom is overprotective and is always advising me in a way that suggests I'm an idiot and can't figure out things myself. That, or I might just make a mistake. Like she never makes mistakes! She's trying to protect me, but I find it really hard to make decisions. Ah, blame your mom. The All-American way."

"My dad is very quiet, and I think he lets my mom be the bad guy a lot, which isn't so cool. I learned a lot about sports from him, though. He watches everything! I've discovered this is good when you're dating. I'm a genuine fan, although I have less time to watch now that I'm actually practicing my instrument, instead of coasting on whatever God-given ability I was granted. I do wish I could talk to him more. I think sports are just a way to connect. But he means well. They both do, even if they let my brother run things until he died."

"My sister is cool. We have a good relationship, although we don't talk about a lot of deep stuff. She's quite a bit younger, so it feels like she's in a whole other stage. Maybe when we're older the differences won't matter. She's really upbeat, but she takes no shit from anyone, to the point of having a mean streak. I, of course, take all kinds of shit from all kinds of people, because I spend my energy trying to figure out why they do what they do, and once I have a reason, I make it into an excuse (I got that from the last self-help book I read)."

"You asked how many men I toyed with. How many toyed with me? I'm no man-killer. I've hardly even dated. I never pretend I'm more into someone than I am. Seems like "doing unto others," and it's about right, I think.

"Anyway, that's all for now. XOXO, Cecile.'"

There was a pause, and then Langston said, "Uh-huh."

"What does that mean?"

"You really didn't date much?"

"No. I'm a misfit. I don't even have many female friends."

"That's hard to imagine."

"Why? Haven't you noticed what a nerd I am? Besides, I'm defensive."

"I don't know what you mean. You're very smart, but that doesn't mean you're a nerd. And I've never found you unfriendly."

"Maybe I'm doing better. I was bullied in junior high, and that really messed me up for a while."

Langston frowned, putting the empty pie plate into the sink. "Who bullied you?"

"Ruth, this white girl who used to be one of my best friends in elementary school. She got new friends in eighth grade, Jennifer and Denise, and they started doing drugs. I was really worried about her. I told Calvin and he called her. Big mistake. I didn't confront him about it because he was trying to help, for once. I guess he didn't want to see her end up like him."

Langston sat on a stool, leaning his elbows on the counter. He wanted to tell her about Anthea, but it was too embarrassing, despite her revelations. "Did she beat you up?" he asked, surprised at his voice. He had never heard a sound so tender come out of his throat before, and it made him sad.

"Jennifer threatened me all the time, but no, they never did. They threw paper balls at me in class when the teacher's back was turned though. Which didn't hurt, in a way, but in a way hurt even more, because it was like—I don't know if this makes sense, but—well, it was like I was a slave, or something, and they were lashing me for no reason at all. I know there's no comparison, but it was really painful. It made me feel like less than nothing to have those three white girls throw things at me."

"What did you do?" Langston asked quietly, careful to avoid verbally caressing her again.

"I asked to be moved across the room. I never said anything back to them when they harassed me, but I also stood up very tall all the time, because I wasn't about to let those bitches break me. They got bored, after a while. Ruth apologized to me in high school, but it was too late, you know? Besides, the experience made me stronger, so in a strange way, I suppose I should have thanked her."

She sounded bitter. Langston imagined her as a young teenager, being assaulted and still choosing to walk with her head held high, and the urge to kiss her overwhelmed him so much that he was temporarily unable to speak. When he finally found his voice, he said, "I still find it hard to believe you didn't date."

"Why?" The bitterness was gone.

"Because you're very beautiful."

Langston closed his eyes. The blast of acid his stomach released with his last statement consumed what was left of his snack in an instant.

"Thank you, Langston. I think you're really attractive, too."

"Yeah, right."

"Why do you say that?"

"Look, you didn't have to say something nice just because I did."

"I know that."

"So why are you saying it now, when you've never said it before?"

Was the damned snow going to fall forever? His shoulders hurt just thinking about it. If he stayed in this godforsaken place another year, he was going to use some of his salary to buy a snowblower.

"I haven't?" Cecile replied. "I've thought it. I guess that wasn't the primary thing I liked about you, so I didn't mention it. I'm sorry."

He wanted to ask her what the primary thing was.

"I get it," he said, instead. "Thanks, Cecile. So…do you miss Calvin?"

Wow. Talk about overly personal questions.

"I'm not sure. Yes. I wouldn't want to live with him, but I wish he was alive. I mean, he could have stopped using drugs if he was alive."

There was an intensity in her voice that Langston had never heard before.

"He was so creative, Langston. Calvin drew gorgeous, lifelike pictures of anything and everything, from the time he was very young. He was an amazing guitarist, even though he quit taking lessons after two years, and he had a beautiful voice. Maybe if he could have gotten himself together…but it was unbearable to live with him. He was very handsome and he could be really charming, but when he was high, he was abusive. I mean, he'd scream anything at anyone, and he could be violent, so we learned to tiptoe around him."

She's been through so much, thought Langston. He didn't want to interrupt, but he wasn't sure how much longer he could endure the conversation. He took a deep breath, and focused on Cecile's words, which were coming in torrents.

"My father tried to handle it by putting his foot down. They got into physical fights a couple of times when Calvin was 16. It was terrifying. Calvin started running away soon after that. My parents were frantic, but whenever he didn't come home, I was relieved. I know that sounds horrible, but I couldn't help it. He was a thief and he lied so much you never knew when he was telling the truth. It made him a very interesting storyteller, because he would always spice things up, but it was exhausting trying to figure out what was real and what wasn't. Everything about him was exhausting. I tried not to invite people to my house if he was going to be there, because I wasn't sure what would happen. He started using drugs when he was about 13, I think, and he died when he was 20." Her voice broke, and he could hear her breathing change. She was crying when she added, "You're so blessed your grandmother took you when you were young."

Her sobs sounded distant for a moment, as if she'd pulled the phone away from her mouth. Langston cleared his throat, wishing he could take his question about Calvin back.

"I'm sorry I upset you," he said, after a while.

"It's truly okay," she managed, her voice getting stronger. "I guess I still haven't gotten over it. They say it happens in stages. I'm just emotional these days anyway. Can you excuse me?"

"Of course." He heard her blowing her nose, and wanted to hold her so badly that his heart hurt—there was an actual pain in his chest. He walked back over to the couch and sat down, wondering if it was okay to be funny yet.

"Sorry," Cecile said.

"No problem. I mean, you're paying for the call, so take as long as you want."

She chuckled. He was searching his mind for another subject, something impersonal, when Cecile continued.

"By the way, Langston, I'm surprised you think I'm capable of toying with people. That hurts me."

She didn't sound upset anymore, but she didn't seem to be joking either.

"It does?" he said, leaning forward. "Look, I'm sorry. Nothing personal. Everybody does it."

"Do you?"

He considered his past relationships. "No. But to toy with people, you need to have power over them. I don't tend to be in that position."

"But you also have to be manipulative. Do I strike you as manipulative?"

"No. Okay, that was unfair."

"I've been an oddball all my life, Langston. I'm glad you think I'm pretty—"

"Like I'm the only one!"

"No, you're not, but so what? I don't trust men who seem too interested in my looks. I have a lot of mixed-up shit beneath the surface that needs to be embraced, or at least accepted. I'm not interested in being valued as arm candy. Besides, there are a lot of women better-looking than I am, and even if that wasn't true, nobody is in their twenties forever. There has to be more."

"Like what you have with Teddy?" He couldn't stop himself. He tensed inside waiting for the answer.

"Teddy and I are very complicated. But yeah, I know he values me for things other than my looks. He needs me. He seems really strong on the outside, but he's a lonely little boy on the inside. I'm the only person who can make that feeling go away."

Langston exhaled deeply, leaning back. He didn't want to explore this topic any further, even though he was the one who had raised it, but he couldn't think of anything else to say. He knew Glenda was right about criticizing Teddy too much, but attacking Teddy was the only thing on his mind.

"Cecile, *cherie, il faut dormir.*"

"Already?"

"I have to get up early, and I'm really tired."

"Okay. I wouldn't want you to be unprepared for your

brats—I mean students."

"Exactly. Molding those eager young minds is so much more than a job for me."

Cecile chuckled. "Okay, Langston.   Well, *a bientot.* Lovely to talk to you, as always."

"You, too. Goodnight, Cecile."

"Goodnight, *cheri.*"

Langston stared at the phone for a long time. She really does like me, he thought.

So what?

CHAPTER FORTY-SEVEN

February 1, 1992

Salut, ma chere Cecile,

So picture this: You're minding your own business, trying to enjoy a night of dancing and debauchery at a club in the hotbed of excitement known as downtown Edmonton. Suddenly, you are accosted by an old friend who forces you to speak with a young black man she associates with because of a long-standing habit of kindness to idiots, a man who manages to dominate the rest of your evening, and even has the audacity to give you an unsolicited kiss.

You think_____? You say_____? Your sister thinks_____? She says_____?

You take his address. You think_____?

You are about to escape from this lunatic when he flags you down and jumps into your back seat. You say_____? Your sister says_____? ("Man, look out, he's got a gun!")

You offer to give him a ride. You drop him off. Your sister says_____? You say_____? You think_____?

Priere de remplir les vides! Please, Enquiring Minds want to know!

By the way, what do you think about Public Enema's video, which seems to advocate the assassination of Arizona politicians? This world is too scary. I saw a video by Sister Soldier (I think…no, I'm sure that I saw the video, it's her name that escapes me) which predicts that by 1995 blacks will be enslaved once again.

Why can't we divorce ourselves from the criminal element of our community, accept the fact that we are hated universally, embrace education, adopt a notion of right and wrong, stop making excuses about "the man" and 400 years of Hell and stop killing ourselves? Let's get on with it.

Sorry about the outburst, but I'm getting tired of only hearing from so-called black leaders of Montreal and Toronto when a cop blows away three black youths who are brandishing machetes (because "the man" doesn't teach black culture and they have low self-esteem?). Where are they on a day-to-day basis? Why aren't they trying to get rid of the "oreo" tag for the blacks who try to achieve? Why aren't they present in a positive mode?

Anyway, maybe I shouldn't talk. If I wasn't so lazy, I'd be furthering my own education and helping out.

So, how are things in the United States of Amnesia? I haven't heard from the Rev. Al for a long time. In fact, the only story that has filtered up here lately is the taunting of the U.S. by the Tokyo diet. Their superior attitude is quite amusing.

Look, I'm falling asleep all over the place. I've gotta go.

Hugs and kisses,

Love,

Langston

P.S. I'm usually too lazy to keep up prolonged correspondence. Can't believe that it's still going. I truly enjoy it!!! Hope your love life is in order!!!

CHAPTER FORTY-EIGHT

February 10, 1992

Dear Langston,

Okay, Mr. Enquiring Mind, I'll fill in the blanks, since apparently your favorite tabloid isn't covering the story (don't they know I'm famous?).

I met you and I thought, "Wow, a black guy in Edmonton I've never seen who isn't playing football in the CFL. And he's attractive—nice lips." Don't remember what I said. Hello, perhaps? My sister's thoughts, I don't know (see mention of limited grasp of ESP, previously discussed in response to your Christmas gift). She said she thought you were cute, and that you seemed nice. I don't think you asked this question, but after we started talking I thought, "Wow, he's smart too. What an interesting guy. He seems quirky. I like that."

When you kissed me, I was completely taken aback, but not in a bad way. My sister was completely taken aback too, but probably because she was jealous. And when you got in the car I thought, what a nice surprise—the interaction lasts a little longer than expected. I'll probably never see or hear from him again, but what a pleasant way to experiment with talking to men again.

Mainly, I was grateful to stop thinking about Teddy for a little while. For one evening, my trip was a vacation, instead of just time spent hanging with a bunch of people who feel sorry for me.

As for Arizona (and New Hampshire, lest you forget), hey, there's no excuse for them. The civil rights movement was a defining moment, not just in black history, but in the history of the U.S. of A. If you're going to recognize the important moments in this country's life with days off, you've got to honor Martin (since Malcolm X Day won't be happening any time soon). They honor Columbus; what did he do besides get lost and kill a bunch of Native Americans? I mean, Martin's got to be more worthy than he is. Besides, doesn't this country need another 50% off sale?

Regarding the videos, man, you're too serious. Do you really think blacks are so uncivilized that we're going to get guns and shoot people, just because a few rappers fantasized about it? Are you buying a gun? I imagined blowing Teddy and his little girlfriend away. Doesn't mean I was going to do it (although it was a very appealing thought for a while). By the way, it's Sister Souljah.

I think we should stop killing each other, too. I also think that abuse breeds rage, either at ourselves or the abuser, and the thought patterns get passed on from generation to generation. If individuals abuse their kids when they've been abused, what do you expect from a race that's been systematically belittled, called names, denied justice, and in some cases targeted for rape, torture, and/or murder?

I hate "oreo." It's ridiculous to make ignorance the standard for authentic blackness. But I do think that some of us who've been raised with a lot of privileges have so little respect for our less fortunate brethren that it's natural for them to strike back, even if the self-defense is terribly misguided.

FYI, I'm enjoying this correspondence, too.

Hope your love life is in more order than mine (my standards are, obviously, ridiculously low). Then again, do you have one? Enough about Teddy. I want to hear about YOU!

Take very good care, *cheri,*

XOXO

Cecile

CHAPTER FORTY-NINE

Langston read Cecile's letter with a mixture of fondness and sadness, certain she'd meant every word, and lacked the ability to sugarcoat her feelings in a way that would help him to swallow them.

He was "a pleasant experiment." She'd never felt irresistibly drawn to him, as he did to her—he was a just a convenient part of her healing process.

He wasn't just sad. He felt like a small, sharp wire had been wrapped under the skin inside his throat, and some unseen force was tightening it.

He had been wrong all along. There was no "knowing." There was no falling in love, not for him. There was only an incredible, fascinating, beautiful woman who didn't see him at all. He'd suspected the truth months ago: he was just someone to tell the intimate details of her relationship with that asshole. Not to mention a "pleasant experiment in talking to men again" in preparation for rekindling her passion for the true love of her soon-to-be miserable life.

Langston stared at the letter, thinking, why did you ask those questions, you fucking moron?

He read her words one more time, then crumpled up the letter and launched it across the room, in a perfect arc, into the trash. Something was dead, strangled by the wire in his neck.

R.I.P

When Langston suddenly stopped returning Cecile's calls, she decided he was busy with his job, but after two weeks and five messages, she knew something was wrong. What?

She knew that, too. She hadn't been aware of the possible impact of her last letter until after she'd mailed it. She'd told him she was using him, in a way. Who would want to hear that?

It was true, but only partially so. The night they'd met, she hadn't wanted to talk to him or anyone—her sister had almost literally dragged her out of the house—but once they'd started talking, she'd felt grateful. Admittedly, part of her appreciation was about ego massage, but not most of it. She'd genuinely liked him, right from the start.

I should have told him what he means to me now, she thought. That I get excited whenever I get a letter. That when I pick up the phone and hear his voice, I always smile. That I'm so glad he's my friend. Didn't I tell him?

Her stomach felt cold and clammy, as if she'd swallowed a lump of clay.

I'm such a loser, she thought dejectedly. I should know how to handle people better than this by now. But did he have to cut me off completely? Without a word?

She pulled out her notebook and reached into her nightstand for a pen.

February 24, 1992

Dear Langston,

I miss you SO much!!!!! Please call me!!!!

I'm so sorry for the way I answered your question about what I was thinking when we met. I wasn't lying, but I didn't say how much I liked you even from the start, and how much I care about you now. You are my best friend, even though we never see each other. I don't want to lose you!!!! I love you

What am I saying?

Every word felt true, but she couldn't tell him she loved him. Love was what she felt for Teddy—unsettling, all-consuming passion. The last thing she wanted to do was make things worse by misleading Langston. She cared about him way too much to hurt him more than she already had.

She tore the letter in half and started again:

February 24, 1992
Dear Langston,

I miss you!!! I'm so sorry if I offended you. Is there anything I can do? I don't want to lose your friendship!!!
Sincerely,
Cecile

She put the letter in an envelope, addressed it, and dug in her wallet for a stamp, knowing the whole exercise was futile.

I'll never speak to him again, she thought, tears spilling from her eyes. At least I said goodbye.

Codetta

October, 1993

Andrews family tradition dictated that holiday dinners were held alternately at Zora's house or Grandma Felicia's. Everything else about the meal was also prescribed: Grandma Felicia cooked the meats and baked the pies, Zora did the side dishes, Marcus brought the drinks, and Langston and Maya cleaned up.

One month after Langston moved back to Toronto to get a Masters in Education, Grandma Felicia died, and the mantle of family matriarch fell to Zora—a natural fit, since, at least in Langston's eyes, his older sister had been co-matriarch for years. What to do about the holiday dinners proved more problematic, though.

The matter of the alternating locations was solved when Marcus and Danita moved out of their rented townhome and into the old house Grandma Felicia had left them (with the directive that they stop making excuses about a lack of space and start a family). Zora did her best to convince Marcus he should sell the place, because the schools in their old neighborhood in Scarborough weren't the best, but Marcus was adamant, and his wife supported him.

The question of who would cook the main course and dessert, however, seemed insoluble. Zora didn't want to take on the whole meal, Maya could barely boil water, and Danita was a vegetarian who refused to cook meat for ethical reasons. The only other female in the family, Claire, was too young to step into the breach.

The issue had become urgent by the time the family gathered at Zora's house for Claire's ninth birthday party, three weeks before Thanksgiving and two months after Grandma Felicia's death. Claire, her little brother Will, and the invited guests were in the basement, where Maya had taken on the task of supervising old-fashioned party games—pin the tail on the donkey, musical chairs, and the like. Langston, Marcus, Danita, and Bernie sat around the kitchen table, while Zora stood behind the kitchen counter assembling a plate of vegetables to offer along with the hot dogs that were the kids' main course, an exercise in futility, in Langston's eyes. Every kid's first priority would be leaving room for chocolate cake and ice cream, but Zora insisted on giving the meal some sort of nutritional value, as if letting children eat nothing but junk food even once would be a crime against nature.

"I'll do the meats and desserts for Thanksgiving," said Langston. "Problem solved."

"I don't know about that," Zora replied, cutting celery.

"Why not? I can cook."

"He speaks the truth," said Bernie, leaning back in his chair. "That weekend you and Danita took the kids to the symphony? He outdid himself."

"Thanks," said Langston, and Bernie winked at him.

Zora arranged the celery sticks on a platter next to some carrots, broccoli, and tomatoes. "Pizza isn't an acceptable Thanksgiving dinner, you know," she said.

Marcus laughed.

"I make things besides pizza, Zora," Langston said. "I do a lot of cooking at the restaurant now."

"What was that you cooked for me?" Bernie said. "Artichoke ravioli, right? With cream sauce. He made the pasta from scratch. I practically licked my plate, and you know I'm not crazy about artichokes."

"Pasta isn't an acceptable Thanksgiving dinner either," said Zora, putting the vegetable plate in the middle of the table.

"So I guess Zora wants to cook the whole meal after all," said Marcus.

"I really don't see why we can't just do vegetarian," said Danita, who was seated beside Marcus and across from Bernie and Langston. "There are delicious meat substitutes...."

Bernie leaned forward. "I ain't eating no tofu turkey," he said, and everyone laughed.

"I know I'm an underachiever," Langston interrupted, "but that doesn't mean I can't roast a damn turkey. It's not like splitting atoms, Zora. Or maybe you think I can't do anything right."

The laughter subsided.

"Did I say that?" Zora replied, frowning.

"You didn't have to."

"When have I ever said anything like that, Langston?"

"Whenever you tell me what I'm doing wrong, which is all the time."

"Okay, this isn't going anywhere," said Marcus. "I say we

take a vote."

"I say I make the main course and the desserts," Langston said, standing. "If I screw it up, I'll never mention it again."

"I say we go out for dinner," said Marcus, looking around, then sinking back into his chair when nobody responded.

Langston's decision to stand left Zora more than a half-foot shorter than him, undercutting her air of authority. The height difference wouldn't have been an issue for Grandma Felicia, but despite her new official status as a matriarch, Zora lacked the intimidation factor that her grandmother had wielded so effortlessly.

"Look at my little brother, acting like a grown man," said Zora, and everyone laughed, including Langston. "Okay, Langston, show us how it's done."

"Thanksgiving is serious business," said Bernie, adding in a Jamaican accent, "Don't mess up, *bwai*."

Langston smiled. He wasn't worried.

Until a week later, that is. On the last day of September, it occurred to him that he'd never cooked a turkey, and that everyone expected two homemade pies, one apple and one pumpkin, and he'd never baked a pie, either. They'd have understood a store-bought dessert, but he'd raised the stakes by challenging Zora's assessment of his competence, so the pies had to be homemade, and failure was not an option. He'd read about making pastry in a previously unused cookbook that Grandma Felicia had given Maya. His grandmother's pie-making secrets had gone to the grave, so Langston hoped Betty Crocker could at least approximate Grandma Felicia's culinary mastery.

As he peeled and cored the apples for pie number one, he wondered what had come over him. He rarely argued with Zora anymore—paying lip service to agreeing with her was less trouble. Besides, what leg did he have to stand on? His sister had a loving marriage, and two unusually bright, well-adjusted children. He'd never even been engaged. Zora was solid financially: she was a school counselor, and Bernie was a dentist. Since he'd quit his job in Quebec, Langston was a teacher without a classroom, working as a garde manger (a fancy way of saying he made salads, appetizers, and terrines) at a restaurant; that Chez Jean-Louis—a French bistro whose sous chef was Mario's first cousin—was a step up from Gino's made no difference. Zora and Bernie were both active in their church and gave generously to charity. Langston had no community affiliations or money to spare. Langston had seen them argue, but unless Zora and Bernie were great actors on top of the rest, they actually "fought fair"— he'd never heard either one dredge up an old hurt or say something sarcastic just to wound. If Zora was occasionally self-righteous, she'd earned it by the near perfection with which she conducted her life.

So even though he found her advice annoying most of the time, Langston wasn't passive-aggressive enough to disregard Zora when she had a point. When he was in Quebec, Grandma Felicia's weekly letters always included a paragraph telling him he was wasting his brain stopping at a bachelor's degree. Still, the reason he'd left his job in Forestville after one year was Zora.

Although she never knew Cecile's part in his melancholy state, she got Langston to admit he was depressed, and suggested that he return to Toronto to work on a Master's in education, so he could get a better job and, more importantly, be near his family. She even encouraged him to work at Gino's until he graduated again, and remained relatively encouraging when he applied for another restaurant position after finding out his old job wasn't an option. There were many things Langston didn't want his family to know about him, but the idea of having them nearby again still managed to feel comforting.

His plan for a successful Thanksgiving involved assembling the pies at the apartment he was sharing with Maya, then cooking the turkey at Zora's. Maya had offered to help, but it was a holiday weekend, after all, so when her friends wanted to go dancing, of course she couldn't refuse. Which meant that when Langston needed to start working, Maya was asleep.

She was still in bed when Langston was ready to leave for Zora's, so he drove by himself, after getting Maya to agree to take the bus. He stuck a note to the bathroom mirror reminding her of the conversation, since it seemed likely she'd forget about it when she reached full consciousness. He felt a bit guilty stranding his baby sister, but he'd needed to drive because of the pies, which looked perfect. Not surprising, since his ability to prepare food seemed to be the only talent he could count on.

Claire and Will were cleaning the living room, under Zora's watchful eye, when Langston arrived. She gave him a quick hug, and then he followed her as she took the pies into the kitchen.

"These look nice," she said, setting them on the counter.

"I told you so."

Zora smiled. "You did. But if I were you, I'd save the gloating until after you've done the turkey."

"No problem."

Nobody had ever had jerked turkey with mango salsa before, but despite the initial raised eyebrows, the praise around the dinner table for Langston's creation was enthusiastic enough that even Danita had a small piece.

"Incredible," she said. "So you're smart, good-looking, and you cook? Why aren't you married?"

"He's determined to die alone," said Zora, smiling.

"Wow," Langston said. "That wasn't funny at all."

"Yeah, Zora," said Maya. "He's 25, and he's already in danger of dying alone?"

"I was kidding!"

"Ha, ha," said Langston.

"Are you dating?" Zora said.

"Not at the moment. But it's not like I never date."

"True, but how many serious relationships have you had?"

Langston glared at her.

"I'm just saying," she continued, "that at your age, it's time to start looking for someone you can be with long-term."

"Hey Zora," said Marcus, "if you wanted to carve, you should have asked Bernie."

Everyone laughed, and Langston forced a smile.

"Okay, ready for pie?" he said, standing up. "I'll clear the table."

Bernie stood too. "I'll do it," he said. "And Maya, I'll help you wash. We can't have the gourmet chef doing the dishes."

"Okay, you can wash," Langston said, "but I still want to help clear the table so we can get to the pies. Any objections?"

Mainly, he wanted to leave the room. He picked up a half-empty dish of macaroni and cheese, carrying it from the dining room into the kitchen, and found himself pausing midway to look at the pictures of Zora, Bernie, and their children that were hanging in the hallway. And when he did, Zora's words came back to him: "He wants to die alone."

He put the dish on the counter, trying to think of a comeback, because he knew that if Zora kept up this new plan of attack on his increasingly entrenched bachelorhood, she could seriously damage his defenses.

On his third trip from the dining room to the kitchen, it came to him. He thought of his grandmother, dying from heart failure, surrounded by family and friends. She had buried her husband nearly two decades earlier. Was Zora trying to say that none of the people in the room with Grandma Felicia mattered?

Besides, he thought, we all cross over to the other side by ourselves, don't we?

Langston had cut the first two slices of apple pie when Zora came into the kitchen.

"I'm sorry," she said.

He looked up. "Why are you always pressuring me?" He was more hurt than angry.

"I'll try to stop."

Langston put down the pie server. "You'll try?" He sighed. "Why is it so hard, Zora? I don't see you getting on Maya all the time."

"Because she doesn't hold things in all the time. I worry about you."

"Please don't."

"You have so much going for you, Langston. I don't always think you know that."

He cut another slice of pie and put it on a dessert plate. "If you think that," he said, "why are you always putting me down?"

"I don't mean to." Zora sat at the kitchen table, laden with the dishes cleared from the dining room. "I guess I'm Felicia's granddaughter, or something."

Langston grinned. "You don't have to be exactly like her, you know. There was room for improvement."

"Hush!" Zora said with mock alarm. "She'll hear you."

She stood, taking two of the dishes of pie in her hands. "Thanks for dinner, Langston. I'm proud of you, and Grandma Felicia would be, too."

He looked down, hoping she couldn't see that his eyes were moist. "Thanks, Zora."

CHAPTER FIFTY-TWO

October 10, 1993

    I can't sleep. I'm exhausted, but my brain won't be quiet, because I can't quite absorb the fact that Teddy is my husband, and I'm his wife. We actually got married! I had to write it down, because that's the only way to get my head around all my dreams coming true. Finally.

    He got so mad two weeks ago, I wasn't sure he'd go through with it. I probably should have asked him to help me decide who sat where at the reception, but he was so bored with the other stuff, like the color scheme and the flowers, that I didn't know he'd care. I didn't even recognize those people's names. How was I supposed to know they were old friends of his mother? I don't think I've ever cried that hard in my life. If he'd given me anything less than a bear hug even ten seconds later than he did, I would have thrown up. I was thinking about how I gave him another chance, even though Dad warned me not to, and how many times he put off setting a date, and how impossible it would be to tell Mom, and how everybody bought non-refundable plane tickets again...

    The thing is, I chose New York partially because I was too embarrassed to let Mom help with the preparations this time, partially so I wouldn't have to be trapped in my house with out of town relatives if Teddy backed out, and partially so my out of town friends and relatives would at least be stuck somewhere interesting. None of which would have helped me to survive calling off another wedding. Not even Langston could have cheered me up. I really wish we were still friends.

The pictures are going to be amazing. Mom's bronze evening gown was perfect, and I think I beat the odds with the bridesmaids, because Betsy would have told me if somebody hated their dresses. Then again, green satin looks fantastic on brown skin. And the bird of paradise bouquets were even more exotic than I thought they'd be. Loved the kente cummerbunds on the men, too.

The best part was the look on Teddy's beautiful face as he watched me coming down the aisle. He stared at me like he couldn't believe I was real, and he couldn't believe his luck. I don't think he's stopped smiling since after the argument.

None of that seemed to matter to Dad. I know it's hard to watch your daughter get married, especially the first one, but I also know that wasn't the reason Dad looked so sad.

We'll prove he was wrong. People can change, especially if they love you. The way Teddy and I made love last night was proof. It was the way it used to be—the only thing that mattered to him was pleasing me. When it was over, I was so happy, I started to cry, so he held me and told me he loved me, over and over. I couldn't believe how tender and sweet he was, and it just...I don't even know. I felt the tears coming, and I couldn't stop them.

The Hilton has been nice, but we're going to have an even better time in Bermuda. One day with the relatives, and then the rest on an empty beach, just like tourists would do. The weather's perfect this time of year, just like the music was today—I can still hear Tonya and Allen singing my favorite duet, and James singing "When I Fall in Love." Wasn't hard to tell where he got his inspiration, the way he looked at Olivia. I think she looks more like me than Betsy does. It's weird.

Teddy was right—we did need something that wasn't European. I'm really glad Nelson and Chelsea could help out, though, because I don't care if string quartets are a white thing, I've wanted one at my wedding as long as I can remember. Probably because I can't listen to keyboard players without critiquing them.

Teddy's still smiling, even in his sleep. I wonder what he's dreaming about? Maybe happily ever after. Corny crap, but that's what crossed my mind. Sort of—I'm so exhausted, I can barely form a thought, except about snuggling up against his naked body.

Which is perfectly okay. At last.

CHAPTER FIFTY-THREE

Despite Zora's assurances that Felicia would have been proud of his success with Thanksgiving dinner, Langston knew his grandmother would have been very disappointed by his decision to become a chef. He officially stopped caring what anyone thought about his career choices on January 11, 1995. That was the day he found out about his mother's fatal heart attack. At 28, Langston suddenly became aware that life can be extremely short—his mother was 62 when she died, just like her father—and decided to do the one thing he really enjoyed.

A viewing preceded the service, which was held at a funeral home because no one had the gall to involve the church except in the most limited way possible. Langston looked at the wax dummy in the coffin and tried to imagine a soul inside, breath in the lungs, and that this stranger had given him life. He'd seen pictures, but they were from years earlier, before his parents chose to re-imagine themselves as a childless couple and moved downtown, which was somehow so removed from Scarborough that visits and even phone calls were too much trouble.

Langston had hoped to catch a glimpse of his father that Saturday morning, but decades of cigarettes had given him emphysema and he was too sick to attend the funeral. Standing in front of the coffin, Langston considered finding out where his father lived and going to visit. Then again, what was there to say, given the diagnosis, other than goodbye? Best to leave his dad in the realm of shadow. His wax dummy would soon be available for viewing and burial, unless he got cremated, and since his father would be just as much use dead, what was the rush?

So there it was: the anger Zora and Marcus kept trying to draw out of him. He looked over at his siblings, sitting together on a padded bench against the light blue striped wallpaper in the back of the little room. Maya was sobbing hysterically. Zora, with her ever-devoted husband Bernie and her children at her side, looked serene. Marcus was unreadable. Langston wondered how he looked from the outside.

What could he look like? The hint of disgust he'd felt wasn't strong enough to compete with his emptiness, and his anger had dissipated. Which was good, because he felt more comfortable being in shock.

Marcus stood beside him. "You okay, Langston?"

He shrugged. "She doesn't seem real, does she?"

"Not anymore."

Langston glanced at him. "I still don't remember her very well."

"I do. She's a lot more peaceful now, believe me."

"At least Grandma Felicia died before she did. I know this would have been hard for her to take."

"She never gave up hoping Mom would stop using."

Langston smirked. "She always believed in miracles."

He'd grown tired of looking at the body. It gave no answers, except that his mother had dyed her hair an attractive shade of blonde. Langston decided he had to be the image of his father, with his grandmother's Asian-looking eyes thrown in;

there was nothing to connect him visually with the woman in the padded box. Her nose was aquiline, her lips relatively thin, her body almost frail, the opposite of his tall but stocky frame. Then again, her emaciated look could have come from the drugs. He turned away from the coffin.

"Zora wrote her a letter," Marcus remarked casually.

"She did?"

"About three years ago, when Grandma died."

"Did she get one back?"

"Yes."

"What did it say?"

"That we were better off without her. That she was sorry. Not to write her again."

For a moment, Langston didn't know how to respond.

"Am I the only one who didn't know?"

Marcus nodded, still facing the body.

"Why didn't you tell me?"

"Didn't think you'd be interested."

"In my own mother?"

"You don't usually like talking about that stuff."

Langston glanced around the room, counting the attendees. Ten people had bothered to show up: the four Andrews children, two spouses, three cousins, his Aunt June from Edmonton. Glenda would have come, but Langston wouldn't let her.

When his grandmother died, all of Scarborough must have been in the church. There were songs, testimonies, tears, laughter, black people, white people, Asian people—a bit of everything and everybody. Had he cried? He couldn't remember.

He turned back towards his mother. Marcus patted Langston's back and walked away. Marcus hadn't apologized for neglecting to tell him about Zora's letter. Langston knew neither of them would mention it again.

Langston studied the husk in front of him, and decided not to file this experience with all the other things he'd banished from his conscious mind. Instead, he would remember this face. Every wrinkle, the way her cheeks barely concealed the teeth beneath them, the slightly furrowed brow. Everything. If no one thought him worthy of hearing about, never mind reading, a letter from the woman who had brought him into the world, then at least he'd have a photograph, indelibly printed in his mind. A memento that could neither be lost nor destroyed.

The funeral director took him by the arm. It was time to start the service. Langston sat beside Maya and squeezed her hand. She glanced at him in surprise, using her free hand to wipe her eyes with a tissue. Grandma Felicia gave occasional hugs, but preferred to show love by being involved and giving money, and her grandchildren followed her example by always keeping in touch, but with words, not physical contact.

This is so fucked up, thought Langston. What the fuck is wrong with this family? Maybe it's me.

Two weeks later, he applied to the culinary program at George Brown. Four weeks after instruction began, he asked the prettiest student in his class out. A week later, they had sex, and three weeks after that he told her he loved her. Three months later he ended the relationship, realizing he'd lied.

Development

April, 2004

On a sunny day in late April, Cecile and her children, Malik and Elana, searched the park around the corner from their house for Shauna, a friend from church Elana was meeting for a play date—a challenge because, after a chilly week of rain, half the population seemed eager to experience the outdoors.

At eight, Elana considered herself a tween, that new marketing subcategory springing from media exposure to quasi-adulthood. Maybe eight year-olds had always yearned to be sixteen, but Cecile found them far more eager than she remembered being at that age, probably due to scantily dressed role models like the Bratz dolls. Were fourth graders really dating, as they did on Nickelodeon? And if not, who was writing that stuff, and why?

Cecile had told Elana repeatedly that all parents were different, and that since Elana was stuck with Cecile as a mother, she could forget about having a cell phone or a website any time soon, along with other things Cecile found ridiculous for kids Elana's age. Although Elana continued to raise these topics, there was no real hostility behind her whiny complaints. She was a very good girl, eager to please and extremely sensitive to any signs of maternal disapproval.

Elana's friend arrived at last. They hugged, then disappeared into the crowd of children who were climbing and running in the playground, which was built to look like a huge wooden fort. Cecile talked to Shauna's mother, who'd agreed to supervise the girls, then went after Malik, who had started running around in the nearby field.

At six, he was indefatigable—destined, Cecile imagined, for marathons. She caught up to him in the process of interrupting a loosely organized soccer game, played by a group of older kids. Adults congregated at two nearby picnic tables, eating barbecue and listening to Latin pop music. No one seemed to mind Malik's intrusion, but Cecile didn't think it was good manners to break into someone else's game, especially since Malik, a natural athlete, was hogging the ball.

"Malik!"

He kept running.

"Malik! Come here, Malik!"

He turned, and trotted towards her. The mischievous grin on his face made him look exactly like his father, something Cecile could never quite ignore, even though she knew they were two very different people, and treated them accordingly.

Malik wasn't nearly as willing to please as his sister; Cecile always had to call him at least twice. Elana would come the first time, but she did other, more passive-aggressive things, like conveniently forgetting to complete hated chores and developing selective deafness when homework conflicted with her favorite TV shows.

They are both very loving children, Cecile often reminded herself. When everything else feels like it's falling apart and despite my many failings, at least I can be proud of that.

She envied the many two-parent families she saw strolling

by. Since her children were too young to separate, when they chose two different activities she had to either drag one along and try to talk him or her into enduring the less appealing option, or find activities for each close enough together to allow Cecile to hover midway, praying that no one would snatch the one she wasn't watching while her back was turned.

She and Teddy no longer went on kid-related outings together. The first things to go were Elena's dance concerts, since Teddy hated ballet. Second was the children's string recitals, where Malik and Elana showed some promise on violin and cello, but in general the experience was long enough and standard low enough, due to multiple beginners, that Teddy sometimes fell asleep. Eventually, he was even excused from activities that were purely for fun. The last attempt had been a family trip to Chuck E. Cheese's, where Teddy sulked alone at the table while Cecile ran from child to child watching them play the games, trying to ignore the noise. Teddy's disinterest had been so obvious that Elana asked what was wrong with him and Cecile felt compelled to lie, telling her daughter that Teddy was ill.

After that, Cecile had decided that unless he volunteered to go with them, which only happened if the destination was a nice restaurant or occasionally one of Malik's soccer games, it was better to take the kids herself. Malik and Elana noticed that the things they enjoyed weren't important to Teddy. But if he didn't attend, at least he'd be in a better mood when they got home.

Malik kept running right into Cecile's arms, and she

picked him up and swung him around. Lifting him had become a challenge. She remembered the children as babies, falling asleep on Teddy's chest. When they were a bit older, he would throw Elana and Malik up in the air and catch them, or twirl them until they were dizzy, more roughly than Cecile would have liked, but the children always laughed, pressing him to do it again. She remembered how he used to blow raspberries on their fat little tummies, how he watched each one slumbering in the bassinet. He seemed endlessly interested until the children were old enough to sleep in a real bed.

Maybe his work got more demanding, Cecile thought, taking Malik's hand and walking over to the swings. Malik smiled at her, then broke free and launched himself in the other direction, scaling a small climbing wall in a moment, sliding down a pole, then repeating the process over and over.

Teddy excelled at his job—a natural, with effortless people skills, a master at diffusing tension with a well-placed joke or compliment. Both the kids at the community center and his co-workers loved him, some of them a bit too much. Cecile often marveled at how the patient, gentle, supportive person his colleagues always talked about vanished as soon as Teddy stepped in the house. Onstage Teddy, offstage Teddy. Not so surprising.

"Those kids have nothing," he sometimes said, explaining his willingness to go beyond the call of duty. He meant also to remind Cecile of her own selfishness in demanding that he be more available for Malik and Elana. Teddy's statement about what the kids at the center lacked always ended the conversation, because if Cecile pressed on, he inevitably reminded her of all the other great men who put the common good ahead of the needs of the few—namely, their families.

"They appreciate me so much" was the other thing he often said, beginning a different lecture, contrasting the lack of admiration Cecile showed him with the esteem he got elsewhere. She'd always admired his commitment to his work, but her appreciation for his accomplishments had been eroded by his overly close relationships with female co-workers and clients, two of which became full-blown affairs.

She'd read that men need to be looked up to, and tried hard to do it, but she couldn't respect Teddy's alleged wish to preserve their marriage, despite giving his best to everyone outside his home. That didn't stop her from wondering if she could be accused of the same thing, at least where Teddy was concerned, regardless of the reassurances of her therapist.

She missed those reassurances, having quit therapy six months ago. At the time, she'd been feeling more optimistic and peaceful, especially after adding daily yoga, aerobic exercise, and inspirational readings to her routine, changes Teddy protested, saying she'd become even more unavailable (though he was generally asleep early in the morning, when Cecile's focus on herself took place). She'd avoided raising her voice, most of the time, and done her best to accept Teddy as he was. Still, after the first two months away from therapy, some of the old doubts and fears began to resurface. At least she'd learned in Nar-Anon that "this, too, shall pass."

Malik moved on to the swings.

"Push me, Mommy!" he said, and Cecile obliged, even though he didn't need her help. Soon he was swinging high in the air, leaning back to stare at the blue sky, scattered with fluffy white clouds, and laughing with delight: "I'm flying!"

Cecile smiled, sitting nearby in the grass, which was not yet uniformly green, but soft enough to show the promise of the coming summer. Malik made her feel like swinging, too. Was that all it took to feel free? How wonderful to be a child!

My freedom, she thought, would require something much more dramatic. She often imagined leaving Teddy, these days. A terrifying thought, even though it seemed the only sane possibility.

They no longer had sex, not since she'd discovered he hadn't really given up his second girlfriend. She'd confirmed the existence of the first one, a co-worker, by accident, after praying that God would show her the truth in no uncertain terms. One day she answered the phone and it was Stacey, whom Cecile had met at an office party. Stacey started asking questions: Are you and Teddy really divorced? No. You mean you're married? Yes. And living together? Yes. I'm so sorry. He told me you were always having affairs, and that he finally filed for divorce. Oh, really?

Elana had been five at the time; Malik was three. Cecile had no family nearby, no close friends, and no real support system. She'd been warned not to marry Teddy in an impassioned letter from her dad that prompted a stinging rebuke, hinging on how much Teddy had changed. When it became obvious she should have listened to the wisdom of others over her own heart, she felt too embarrassed to confide in anyone.

At the time, her independent earnings were too little to venture out alone, and since Teddy refused to leave, moving half of their possessions seemed overwhelming. Besides, after she confronted him over the phone call from Stacey, he'd begged her to stay, promising that they would go to marriage counseling, and he would go to individual counseling again, so they could keep their family together for the kids.

Cecile had agreed to try again, with the hope—the wish, the dream, now on life support—that maybe things would finally be different. Teddy and Cecile didn't argue about going out anymore, because everything had been said so many times already. He used to tell her that he missed her, and she used to try to find time to spend with him, but with the children it had become increasingly difficult for her to juggle everything effectively. She used to ask him to help her, and he would do it for about a week, then fall back into the pattern of coming home tired and spending the evening doing things that would help him let go of his responsibilities, not acquire more. Besides, nights out were so expensive, with a babysitter. They could watch a movie together once the children were in bed, but that had been Teddy's time to play video games, surf the net, and talk on the phone for so many years that Cecile no longer even tried to intervene. The last few times she'd tried, they were so out of rhythm they had nothing much to say.

There was still some common ground in the marriage. Cecile and Teddy remained movie buffs, although their tastes were starting to diverge; he refused to see foreign films anymore, so Cecile went alone, usually during the day, sending him solo to the slasher films she'd never known he liked. They still tended towards liberal political views, although Cecile was starting to think that some of the people Teddy thought the government could save had been downtrodden so long that it would be hard for them to function in any other setting, sort of like the elderly felon in *The Shawshank Redemption* who committed suicide soon after he was finally released from jail, an attitude that made her sad, not just for the poor, but for herself in admitting it. They both enjoyed fine cuisine, although lately Teddy had started collecting gadgets, leaving little to no money for nice restaurants, especially with babysitters factored in.

Cecile stayed because of Malik, Elana, her shaky finances, her fear, and the vows she'd made before God, although (that word again) at least according to some books of the Bible, Teddy's adultery gave her a free pass on the latter. The idea of traumatizing her kids, who loved their daddy no matter what he did, held the most power. The fear was a close second, though.

Actually, what she felt was deeper than fear. It was the kind of dread that woke her up at night from dreams of homelessness, causing her to spend fruitless hours trying to figure out how she could possibly cover the expenses for her and her children by herself. Of course, Teddy would have to pay child support, but she knew that the woman always ended up in a far worse financial position than the man. In theory, she could remarry, but finding Teddy had been almost impossible, so she wasn't counting on it.

She watched Malik jump off the swing, landing effortlessly on his feet, and wished she had his courage. Or was it recklessness? The difference seemed so slight.

Maybe I've become difficult, she thought as Malik came towards her, walking rather than running for once. Ungrateful. Maybe I always look at the negative. Maybe I'm driving Teddy away. He makes good money. He spends a lot of it on himself, but at least one of us has a real job.

The wisdom from the gurus was always to do what you love, and Cecile had always loved making music. What the gurus left out was that following your heart isn't a guarantee of success, unless success is defined as doing what you love. Then again, unsuccessful people never wrote books about following your heart, because nobody would buy them. That crap should come with an asterisk, Cecile thought.

She was an adjunct at the local college, which gained her familiarity and respect in her department, but not much money. Even though she had soloed with a few orchestras and released a few recordings, mostly as a collaborator, nothing she did professionally was very lucrative. When she was in high school and college, Cecile had often breezed through the first rounds of competitions, the supposed instant connection to career success, but then the weight of expectation became too much. Suddenly, it wasn't just about music; she felt obligated to justify not being cut. The realization robbed the music of its power to engulf her, making her hyper-vigilant against errors, resulting in stupid mistakes, a lack of passion, and elimination.

Still, her playing, when not under such pressure, touched and inspired people, including herself. She was amazed at the beauty of a phrase, the joy of flying through a technically difficult passage, the power of being able to create a deafening *fortissimo*, the delicacy of triple *piano*. She felt blessed beyond compare to be allowed the gift of music, so she wouldn't give up on her talent. It would be an insult to the Giver of the gift, a surgical removal of a vital organ.

Malik lay on his back in the grass beside her, gazing up at the sky.

"Mommy," he said, "look at that cloud! It looks like a rabbit!"

Cecile squinted, trying to follow his line of vision. "I see it," she lied.

"Look at the clouds with me, Mommy," said Malik. He uses the imperative a lot, Cecile noted. Another budding male control freak. Not on my watch.

"Did you forget a word or two?"

"Please look at the clouds with me," he said, the first word drawn out and very loud.

"Okay."

Cecile leaned back on her elbows, and Malik snuggled against her. A slight breeze blew the alleged rabbit cloud in front of the sun. The weather wasn't warm yet, or at least not enough for Cecile to go without a jacket, making the heat from Malik's little body very welcome.

They gazed at the sky for a long time. Then Elana thundered into view at full gallop, her long, curly hair forming a nebula around her light brown, oval face.

"Mom, Shauna's going home now."

Cecile sat up all the way, gently guiding Malik into the same position, spotted Shauna and her mother, standing ten feet away, and waved.

"Did you have fun?"

"Uh-huh."

Cecile stood and gave Elana a hug. Time to go. She hoped Teddy was either out, or engrossed in a video game or cell-phone conversation when she got home.

How did it get this way, despite all the time she'd spent in therapy? Cecile had started her sessions knowing she didn't want to break up her family but certain that she'd lost herself because of the strain of trying to keep things together. She'd decided to get counseling after an argument with Teddy. They'd had the same argument before, but for some reason his refusal to help her more around the house nudged Cecile from frustration to despair. Wasn't marriage supposed to be about two people who were mutually supportive? Was she asking for more than she deserved?

Going to see Miranda for the first time had felt like both defeat and grasping a lifeline. Cecile's mind traveled back to her first time in that office, decorated in the usual pleasing pastels, with framed pictures of flowers—boringly generic, but at least there weren't any uplifting statements superimposed on rainbows or waterfalls. She couldn't have handled the sight of a lame affirmation of her inner resources. Which had made her realize her problem might have been bigger than she'd thought.

Miranda ran late that day, something Cecile later came to both accept and value, because it meant Miranda never hurried anyone out the door. Her first visit, though, the extra fifteen minutes felt like an eternity. She sat scowling, gazing out the window without seeing the brilliant reds and oranges of the trees, because nothing registered except her fury about her life.

"Cecile White?" Miranda had said, finally entering the waiting room.

Cecile glanced up to see a petite, middle-aged white woman with auburn hair cut in a bob and parted down the middle. She had a slightly upturned nose, thin lips painted a neutral shade of pink, and eyes of brilliant emerald green.

The eyes had drawn Cecile in, not only because of the disarming contrast they created with Miranda's hair, but because of the kindness that radiated from inside them.

"Yes," Cecile replied, not bothering to fake a smile.

"Sorry I'm late. Please come in."

Cecile followed her into an office with light green walls and dark green carpeting, decorated with pictures of and by what she guessed to be Miranda's children. Miranda sat at the wooden desk on the side of the room nearest to the door, and Cecile slumped into the chair next to it.

There was a short silence, then Miranda asked, "Are you okay?"

Cecile's eyes widened in surprise, then filled with tears. Nobody seemed to care enough to ask that simple question. Then again, she didn't generally allow people to see behind her mask enough for them to suspect her distress.

"No," she said, in a quivering voice, reaching for a tissue.

Miranda leaned forward, her notebook and pen in her hand. "Tell me about it," she said. "What brought you here today?"

Cecile dabbed her eyes, wiped her nose, and straightened her spine. "I guess...I think I need...I want to feel better about myself."

"How do you feel about yourself?"

Cecile gazed out the window. The question was too big, her emotions too elusive. She let her eyes travel back in Miranda's direction, settling on her notepad. "I don't know how I feel about anything these days, except that I love my children. I'm not sure I love anybody else, really. Then again, like I said, I don't know."

"So you'd like to know how you feel. Is that right?"

Cecile nodded. Her head suddenly felt too heavy for her neck.

"Do you have support here?" Miranda went on.

"I have no family, but the people at my church are nice."

"Do you have a best friend?"

Cecile considered. "No."

Even her sister didn't qualify. Betsy was so uncomfortable talking about feelings that it was usually easier for Cecile to say nothing, or very little, about her problems. Every once in a while, Betsy would send a package, usually containing bubble bath and candles or some other thing that seemed to suggest Cecile take time to pamper herself. Cecile would thank her sister profusely, then dutifully use the products, trying to gain lasting calm from the scent of peaches or mangoes, staying in the hot bath a minute or two longer so she could tell herself she was savoring the moment. Which didn't help her emotional state very much.

At first, all Cecile talked about in therapy was Teddy, or Teddy and whichever girl he was having inappropriate contact with. After a few months of constant grievances, she and Miranda started going deeper by examining Cecile's insecurities—her history of feeling like a misfit, her role as the "easy" child in the family, her related fear that she wasn't "good enough," her interactions with family members, especially Calvin—which provided the rich soil that nurtured the toxic roots of her relationship with Teddy. Then she found out she was a perfectionist, and that the mental gymnastics she went through to avoid making mistakes were crippling her ability to move forward.

Cecile had always figured Teddy was screwed up, but apparently she was just as bad, which gave her an excuse, at least, for staying with him so long. The perfectionism wasn't much of a revelation—most of the people at Juilliard had it to some degree. She was taken aback, however, to find her intellect, previously an asset, listed as a liability. Apparently, she was so ruled by her head that her emotions didn't stand a chance. When Cecile protested that trusting her emotions was the reason Cecile and Teddy got married in the first place, Miranda countered that while it wasn't wise to rely only on emotions for direction, any extreme was unwise. Including spending so much intellectual energy avoiding risks.

Cecile often left Miranda's office feeling lighter, just because she'd gotten something off her chest. That time, she felt dejected. She knew all about her emotions: too unruly to be allowed to roam loose, too incomprehensible to everybody, including herself, way too prone to lead her into a dark alley or over the edge of a cliff. It was her brain that allowed her to keep it together for her kids, no matter who Teddy was having mental or physical intercourse with that day. Her brain kept her from sinking into despair when life seemed both too full and too empty—stuffed with activity but lonely, productive but a waste of time. Like Samson's hair, her brain was her strength. What other compass did she have?

Wow, she thought, walking to her car. All these years of praying, and I don't even trust God yet. I don't trust God, I don't trust anyone else, and I can't be trusted, either, because look at the terrible mistake I've made, marrying Teddy.

She felt, all at once, like she'd be in therapy forever, and even then she wouldn't be able to get it right. At least I'm feeling something, she thought sarcastically, even if it's spiritual hyperinflation: like the currency of some developing nation, she had theoretical value, but was, in reality, completely worthless.

She fought the temptation to go back and explain to her therapist there was more than one perfectly good way to live. Miranda is probably really emotional, she thought, and that's why she's against people who are more cerebral. There's nothing wrong with the way I think.

Cecile opened the door of her car, climbed in, and slammed it just in time.

There is something horribly wrong with me...oh God....

She hadn't cried, except a few random tears, since her argument with Teddy before their wedding, but she found herself sobbing so intensely that she couldn't make a noise. When the sound finally escaped, it was a sustained wail she was powerless to control. So many mistakes. Irretrievable years wasted, and where was she? Stuck. Financially dependent, emotionally scarred, fully responsible for two innocent lives, not quite good enough at anything to do more than survive, despite all of her alleged promise.

It took a long time, but she finally got tired of weeping. She fumbled in her purse for another tissue and wiped her eyes, glancing in her rear view mirror to see if her eye makeup was smudged. Not that there was any left.

You're not supposed to beat yourself up. You did the best you could with what you knew. It was all done in good faith.

She sighed. To her surprise, Miranda's words brought some comfort. Besides, what was the point of regret? Since there was no going back, the only choice was to go forward. By the time she saw Miranda a week later, Cecile had decided to start praying every morning, maybe writing positive affirmations in a prayer journal instead of using her diary to complain about what was going wrong.

#

Malik and Elana reached for her hands, and she swung her arms a little as the three of them walked across the field, now deserted by the soccer players, and towards the car.

I don't write affirmations anymore, she thought.

Maybe they would help her get through this next growth spurt. Miranda always told her that with growth, there are growing pains.

As she reached her car, Cecile recalled that she used to write in a diary all the time, too. She decided to read some of the old entries when she and the kids got home from the park. Things had been bad for so long, she'd forgotten what made her take those impossible vows in the first place. She needed to know, before she decided to give up completely.

CHAPTER FIFTY-FIVE

In 2002, with help from his family, friends, and his family's friends, Langston raised enough money to sign a lease on a small to midsized restaurant. To prepare for this huge step, he'd taken three positions post-graduation, each more prestigious than the last, then researched the idea for months by talking to his instructors at culinary school, every small business owner he could find, and every chef or restauranteur he'd ever met, including the people who ran his favorite hole-in-the wall Jamaican places in Eglinton West.

His first two employers turned out to be the most willing to help. Jean-Louis gave suggestions about efficiently laying out the kitchen, constructing the menu with just the right number of choices, and figuring out how many employees he would need and how to hire them (by valuing personality over experience, at least in the front of the house). Mr. Zappatore claimed he'd known from Langston's first month at Gino's that it was only a matter of time, then talked at great length about everything that had to be considered if Langston wanted to turn a profit—competitor's prices, décor, and hours of operation; average food and beverage purchases; number of customers per meal period; calculations of fixed and variable costs; and preparing a budget. Afterward, Langston seriously considered changing his mind, but Mr. Zappatore promised to walk him through everything, starting with a formal introduction to Sam and Ivan, who supplied Gino's with fresh produce and meat. Ivan didn't seem to believe

Langston could have really been planning to run a restaurant—probably because if black people were rare in the kitchen, they were harder to find in the office— and treated Langston with enough condescension to lead him to get a different purveyor of meat. Which was okay, because the guy didn't carry goat anyway, and Langston was determined to include all of his favorite dishes on the menu.

Mr. Zappatore also arranged for Langston to talk to someone who held the lease on a recently vacant spot on King Street, near the Toronto Convention Center. Prime locations meant higher rent and lots of competition, but Cimarron would be the only West Indian restaurant in the area. Mr. Zappatore seemed confident enough in Langston's success that Langston started to feel that way, too. As he listened to yet another pep talk, Langston couldn't help imagining how his life would have been different if his mentor had found out about Marietta. Water under the bridge, he decided.

"Cimarron" was the Spanish word from which "Maroons" originated; Grandma Felicia had descended from those fierce runaway slaves who fled to the hills of Jamaica and were never recaptured. He'd never thought of himself as having that sort of strength, but the story, and the fact that a few drops of Maroon blood flowed in his veins, inspired him anyway.

Langston's decision to enlist Maya and Zora's help with decorating Cimarron could have led to World War III, but somehow ended up bringing out the best in both of his sisters instead. Then again, since each had invested in his restaurant, recouping their money trumped asserting dominance.

They'd taken Langston's minimalist tendencies and added upscale touches, teaming the unstained, wooden floors with glass-topped tables and upholstered chairs in a shade of blue meant to resemble the Caribbean Sea, walls the color of sand, and colorful paintings from Grandma Felicia's collection, many of them by artist friends of hers from the Islands. A gilt-framed self-portrait of Felicia herself hung behind the gleaming wooden bar, stained dark brown, with stools in the same color as the chairs in the dining room. Zora and Maya also helped to choose music to round out the experience, ranging from the obligatory West Indian to jazz, with classic singers like Ella Fitzgerald, Sarah Vaughan, Johnny Hartman and Billy Eckstine prominently featured along with Bob Marley and Jimmy Cliff.

Their most important contribution, however, was to sit in on interviews when Langston assembled his staff. Langston took the lead in hiring the bussers, dishwashers, and especially the cooks, contacting culinary schools and putting an ad in the paper, but mainly getting leads from his old Jamaican neighborhood. He cooked for his potential employees first, conducting informal interviews along with his sisters while they ate, then invited the applicants to prepare a meal. The motley crew he assembled included the usual rebels and misfits one tends to find in a restaurant kitchen, with Andre, a dreadlocked Guyanese former medical student, as Langston's sous-chef, second in command. Maya and Zora got the final say on servers, except the bartender—there, Maya was judged to be the expert. Zora introduced Langston to Bernie's accountant, and Maya introduced him to her friend Liza, who became his manager. The end result was a mix of experienced and inexperienced people, half of them female, and all of them friendly, with Langston's teaching background as a crucial factor in making sure everybody worked as a unit.

Two years after opening, Cimarron could be considered successful, which meant Langston was paying all the bills with a bit left over. Then again, surviving on his profits was easy, because he'd stayed single, had no children, and his tastes had remained Spartan.

At 38, he'd had two very serious relationships, meaning they'd lasted over a year, with talk of marriage. He'd told each woman he loved her, because it had seemed like the thing to do. He hadn't lied to them, but he knew each of his almost-fiancees meant something far more intense when she'd told him the same.

The last relationship had been over for about a year. She'd been good wife material: very smart, attractive and organized. Not what you'd call sweet, but neither were any of his other girlfriends.

When he'd told Glenda he was thinking about proposing, she shook her head.

"I would tell you to go ahead and marry your grandmother if you were in love with her," she said, "But you're not."

He was offended, but only for a moment."You're too damn honest."

"Not possible."

They were meandering through the glass and marble of the Eaton Centre, an upscale mall in the heart of Toronto, killing time. Tia, Langston's would-be fiancée, was out of town, and Glenda's latest boyfriend, Jason, refused to attend movies that conflicted with the NHL playoffs. Monday was Langston's day off, and since he and Glenda almost never got together anymore, she'd all but threatened his life when he explained that he was too tired to hang out with her.

"I want to have kids," he said.

"So what?" Glenda paused in front of Holt Renfrew, then went inside.

"You're not trying anything on, are you?"

Glenda grinned. "Hey, I can afford wildly overpriced designer clothing, in case you forgot."

"And I thought you went into dermatology just to help people."

"The Lord helps those who help themselves."

Langston shook his head. If so, the Lord was helping her a lot. Glenda's complexion had undergone a miraculous transformation, and with pictures to prove it and a TV commercial to publicize it, she'd become one of the best-known dermatologists in Toronto.

"I'm trying to share here," Langston said.

"So talk. I can listen to you and look at lingerie at the same time."

She started walking again, and Langston lagged behind.

For once, her offhandedness hurt.

"You were saying?" Glenda continued, considering a lavender negligee.

"Nothing."

She looked at him. "My goodness, Andrews! You really do want kids."

"Why else would I say that?"

She put the nightgown back, shrugging. "I didn't know it was that serious."

"How could wanting to be a father be less than serious?" he retorted, his voice brimming with so much venom and bitterness, he didn't recognize it.

"I'm sorry."

For a moment, Langston was speechless. Glenda always apologized in code, not words—she would treat him to dinner or perform some other unsolicited act of kindness.

"It's okay," he finally said.

Glenda took his hand, something else she never did, and led him back towards the mall, where they found an unoccupied bench, and sat down.

"You can have children for years yet," she said, looking into his eyes. "Do you think it's a good idea to make a lifelong commitment to a person—because she's a person, not a womb-for-hire—just to have kids? What are their lives going to be like with you two as parents? Will Tia be okay with her marriage being just a contract to create children for you? Is that fair?"

As he listened to her, Langston's throat started burning.

He cleared it unsuccessfully. "I'm not going to marry her," he said.

"Good."

"But I still want kids. And before you say, 'so what?'…"

"That's why I said I was sorry. I didn't mean to hurt your feelings, Andrews. I didn't think I could, at this point."

He looked down. He had never felt this way around her.

"Why do you want kids so badly?"

He stared at his hands. "I don't know. Maybe because I see my nieces and nephew, and they show me how much love I could give."

When he glanced at Glenda, she was gazing into space. After a while, she turned towards him.

"You could adopt."

"I could. I just think it's better to have two people raising the kids, if possible." He sighed. "I don't know why I'm even thinking about this. I don't have time for you, never mind a baby." He grinned. "My restaurant is my baby."

The smile faded when he looked at Glenda again. "Why can't I fall in love?"

"You won't allow it."

"I try to."

She turned away again. "I know the answers to all of life's mysteries," she said quietly, "but figuring out Langston Andrews? I must draw the line somewhere."

He managed to smile. "We're still going to a movie?"

She glanced at her watch. "Immediately! Don't you dare

make me late, or I'll make you watch it twice."

He couldn't quite chuckle, but as they walked to the theater, he did feel more relaxed.

When it's right, it will happen, he'd thought at the time.

Since that day, he'd never asked Glenda, or anyone else, for more insight into his difficulties with love. He'd also never told anyone, especially not his family, that he wanted children. As the months had passed since he'd ended his relationship with Tia, his assurance that love would find him in due time was replaced by the suspicion that Zora had been right.

I'll die alone.

CHAPTER FIFTY-SIX

The morning after her trip to the park, Cecile waited until Teddy and the kids were gone, then dug through the drawer that held her personal mementos. Her diaries, spiral-bound notebooks meant for schoolwork, were buried under birthday cards and letters. The books were only semi-chronological; entries from the same year or even the same month appeared in several of them, depending on what happened to be available. Folded between the pages, thick with writing both neat and practically illegible, were additional scraps of paper torn from other notebooks, and unmailed letters.

Cecile had allotted fifteen minutes. She should have been practicing for an upcoming recital with a singer friend, but she justified the time by deciding she'd gotten enough work done on the repertoire on Saturday. She sat on the floor beside her unmade bed and leaned back against the mattress, legs crossed. Opening the diary closest to the top of the drawer, she began to read:

April 29/88

Teddy is upset about something--he's been acting distant, and I don't know why. I'm progressing from depression to very intense anger.

I want to do everything for him. I want to support him emotionally. I honestly don't care what the problem is or how stupid, I just want to be there. He says he needs to work it out alone, but I have no idea what "it" is. Whatever happened to, "I can tell you anything?" Maybe I was right all those times; maybe there is absolutely no one in the world for me.

April 30, 1988

Sorry, Teddy. I really get uptight sometimes, darling, but it goes away. Oh, for the record, Teddy didn't like the way he thought I was looking at Allen. I can be friends with a man I have no intentions of dating—Teddy's got to understand that. I can't say I've never been very attracted to anyone else (James, anyone?), but even before Teddy, I knew I could never be Allen's girlfriend.

We will make this work, and we will tear down any temporary walls. Because I love Teddy, and it will last forever...

April, 1988, Cecile thought, and that asshole was already cheating on me. It was so obvious! Why else would Teddy be so jealous when I was clearly head over heels in love?

But he loved her, too. She knew he did, regardless of what had happened. Or maybe he just thought he was in love. Maybe he wasn't even capable of love. Maybe reading this shit was a mistake, she thought, because all I'm learning is how much of an idiot I was.

Cecile sat on her bed, about to put the diary back in her drawer, but changed her mind, deciding to read one more entry.

May 14/88

This may turn out to be the Theodore White chronicles. He is taking over my life. He says I'm taking over his. I love him so much it's truly scary. And I'm always afraid of offending him, so I try not to tell him feelings that will upset him. Sometimes I think I'm weak. I really don't think I could easily lose him. Still, I have no strong opinions about most things, or I just go along with his wishes. He notices this. I have to stand up for myself.

Some day, are we both going to just snap? He defines the boundaries of my world. I know that.

#

Four and a half hours later, Cecile opened her front door, locked it behind her, and threw her purse on the floor next to the couch in the living room. After an hour spent wading through her past, she'd decided to go to a movie. She'd needed to get out of the house and clear her head, since practicing the piano wasn't enough of a distraction from her overwhelming urge to grab the twenty-something version of Cecile and slap some sense into her.

She'd hoped to see *Spring, Summer, Fall, Winter...and Spring,* a Korean film about the life of a Buddhist monk. She'd known that Teddy would never be interested, resigning herself to catching it on video on one of her many nights alone at home, after her children were asleep. As it turned out, her first choice was only showing in at the art house theater on the weekend, so she ended up going to the film that was starting when she got to the multiplex: *13 Going On 30.*

What should have been an escapist romp about a 13 year-old girl's mysterious transformation from a geeky teenager to a beautiful, successful, but despised woman left Cecile in tears. Where's wishing dust, she thought, when you need it? Because if she could go back and change her mistakes, she would have done it, just like Jennifer Garner's character in the movie.

Maybe I would have fallen in love with Teddy anyway, Cecile conceded, but there was no excuse for marrying him. One phrase in particular kept playing over and over in her head: "Some day, are we both going to just snap? He defines the boundaries of my world." What the hell was that? Not love. Addiction, maybe. Cecile needed to learn more about the girl in the diary, if only to try to understand this person she barely remembered.

Weren't we in love, though, at least for a while? She tried to visualize making love to Teddy when she craved it enough to defy God to indulge in it...I'm trying to remember being in love, she reminded herself, not sex. Maybe if she could remember one, she would feel like indulging in the other.

Or maybe not. Her last attempt had felt like prostitution, and left her in tears. She'd read in a magazine about keeping the physical alive as a way to reignite the emotional, but Teddy's infidelities stayed too fresh in her mind, and the kindness he had once shown felt too distant, and the contrast between how he spoke to her and how he talked on the phone to his female "friends," the tender tone he took, was too present, and although she was able to allow him to finish, she couldn't.

Afterward, he tried to soothe her tears, but she had to walk away. Two days later, she found out he was still talking to a girl he had promised not to speak to anymore. When Teddy asked if Cecile would like him to sleep in the guest room, she gratefully agreed. That was three months ago.

The love. *The love…*

Cecile sank into the couch, imagining Teddy the day they met, standing on the platform and watching her subway train pull away, his face full of longing. The glow of pride before he hugged and kissed her, not caring who saw them, the first time he heard her perform. The luminous smile and twinkle of mischief he would get whenever he saw her in the lobby at Juilliard before the trip to his house, or Mimi's, to express their passion physically.

She tried to remember the last time he'd looked at her that way. And couldn't.

#

That night, Cecile lay in bed, closed her eyes, but couldn't quite shut off her brain.

Why can't I let him go?

She thought of one of the last times Teddy had come home with a spontaneous suggestion, about a week before they'd stopped sleeping together. He'd stepped in the door with a handful of red carnations, the first flowers of any kind she'd seen in at least two years.

"These are for you," he'd said with a smile, kissing her cheek.

"Thanks."

Cecile couldn't help herself—she'd always liked flowers.

Something inside her, a part that had been hardened towards him for years, softened.

She took the carnations to the kitchen to cut and arrange. Teddy followed her, watching her select a vase and fill it with water.

"Let's go to a movie," he said.

"When?" She turned on the tap, holding the stems beneath the flow of water and reaching for the shears she kept in a drawer near the sink, so pleasantly surprised by this idea that she softened even more.

"Tonight," said Teddy.

For a moment Cecile saw how handsome he still was. She didn't notice it anymore, and if she did, his looks usually reminded her of how easily he could attract other women.

"*Ray* just came out," he went on. "I hear Jamie Foxx is incredible."

Cecile cut the stems, her smile fading. "I'd love to see it," she said, "but I have a dress rehearsal for that horn recital I'm doing on Sunday afternoon."

The water was still running. Cecile turned it off.

"We can go next week," she suggested. "Next Friday."

"Forget it."

Teddy turned away. Cecile hastily put the flowers in the vase and followed him to the living room.

"Why?" she asked, unable to keep the edge out of her voice. "I don't want to forget it. I just can't go tonight. Besides, we don't have a sitter."

He had settled himself on the couch. "Okay, whatever." He turned on the television, clicking through the channels.

"Teddy, this is unfair."

"We can't go. I'm watching TV. What's the problem?"

She took a deep breath, trying to focus on the last time she'd spoken to Miranda about getting drawn into arguments. He's hurt, she thought, somewhere in the recesses of her mind, because he tried to do something nice and you can't do it.

She tried to measure her voice, to control the pitch and delivery. "I'm sorry I can't go tonight," she said. "It was nice of you to ask."

"No problem. You can never do anything unless you have a month or so of notice. My bad."

Fuck therapy.

"Why are you being such an asshole?"

Teddy turned to her, his eyes narrowed. "What?"

There were two choices: an extended, pointless argument that would provide some catharsis but deepen the tension, and the high road, which was looking a little too steep, all of a sudden. There was a crash upstairs.

"Mom!" Elana yelled.

I take that path for my kids, Cecile thought. She knew she didn't consider them until it was too late most of the time, so she was genuinely glad for the reminder.

"I'll make arrangements for next Friday," she said curtly, her heart pounding because of the adrenaline her anger had released, "if you still want to go."

"Suit yourself."

#

Looking back, Cecile could understand his frustration. Teddy had always been high maintenance, but when she'd managed to give him enough of herself that he felt loved, there were no other women in their relationship. I set him up, she thought. I was somebody else for so long, he got confused when I started acting more like myself.

Cecile rolled onto her side, bending her knees and gathering a pillow in her arms; there was ample room for every maneuver now that she was sleeping alone. The pillow was comforting, but not nearly as substantial as Teddy's body, so that Cecile's arms still felt empty, somehow. Sleeping in different rooms was supposed to be temporary, until he realized how wrong he'd been to keep in contact with a borderline mistress. It didn't look like he's figured that out, though. Teddy certainly knew how to win Cecile back, and this time he wasn't even trying.

Maybe she wasn't, either. She used to respond to his extramarital indiscretions with tearful threats of divorce, hoping he would see her pain and repent. This time, she couldn't be bothered, since her hysteria always turned out to be a waste of energy.

She blamed herself less and less for their problems. For a while, whenever he told her how much he needed her, she'd wonder if she was causing their issues by being selfish, but lately, the only thing she wondered was who the hell could have a life that continuously revolved around a man.

Cecile was sure there were women out there who could do it. She wasn't one of them, so what was she doing? Holding on and hoping for a miracle.

CHAPTER FIFTY-SEVEN

Langston checked his email three times a day, in the back room of his restaurant. He didn't have a home computer, preferring to leave email primarily in the domain of business while maintaining personal relationships on the phone or in the flesh.

The price for his high standards was an extremely small circle of acquaintances. Outside of his immediate family and Glenda, he knew the staff at his restaurant staff intimately— although they knew him on a relatively superficial basis, considering how much time they spent together—his purveyors, his accountant, Mr. Zappatore, and Teresa, the last two more and more because of longstanding association than ongoing contact.

He wasn't trying to be a hermit. Running a restaurant was all-consuming, and since Cimarron was truly his, he had to make sure everything conformed to his vision. Most of the staff members had been with him all along, so they knew what he expected, but since all along meant a couple of years, Langston didn't want to take the chance of pulling back and losing control.

The size of his universe didn't bother him. He barely had time for the people already in it, so it was easy to ignore the many suggestions that he get out more to meet women. Still, the fact that everyone he knew said the same thing about him was rather conspicuous. Zora meddled less and less, attributing her hands-off approach to her 12-step program. Which left Maya, who had never attended Nar-Anon, to pick up the slack.

On a Tuesday morning in early May, Langston's work at his computer in the office at his restaurant was interrupted by a knock at the door, followed immediately by his younger sister poking her head in the room.

"Hi, Langston," she said, coming inside and closing the door behind her.

"Uh...hi." She had never dropped in at Cimarron unannounced before.

"I have a surprise for you."

He leaned back in his chair, pushing it away from his desk slightly. "That would make two surprises. Don't you have to work?"

Maya was the office manager for a consulting firm, a career choice that came as a shock to the rest of her family, since she'd never shown a knack for organization growing up. Despite his sister's repeated attempts at explanation, Langston had no idea what Maya's company actually did other than pay her bills. Which was enough.

"I'm going in a bit late today." Maya perched on the corner of his desk.

"Evidently. What's the surprise?"

"I've signed you up for a class."

Langston laughed. "You're making a lot of money at that job, huh? What does Ed think about your wasting it like this?"

"It's my money," she responded defensively.

"Banking on the honeymoon not being over yet? Two years is pushing it, Maya."

"Whatever. Anyway, here's the brochure."

She handed him a brightly colored piece of paper, folded in three: Elite Dance Studio.

"Seriously?"

"I signed you up for Latin dance. They have classes on Mondays, so don't even say you can't make it, because I know you're off."

Langston placed the brochure on his desk. "Did you sign up a partner for me too?"

"Why? Do you want me to?"

"No."

"Are you going to take the class?"

"No. Maybe. Wow, you're bold...Zora."

Maya laughed, crossing her legs. "Someone's got to get you unstuck."

"Uh-huh." Langston swiveled his chair, turning away from the computer. He'd been amused at first, but now he was annoyed. "Do you have any idea how much work it is to run a restaurant?"

"No, but I bet there are restaurant owners who date."

"So the only way my life will be worthwhile is if I'm dating?"

"Don't you want someone to come home to at night?"

"Maybe, maybe not. Depends who it is." Langston glanced at the clock and decided to give her five more minutes, unless she changed the subject.

Maya stood. "What are you afraid of?" she demanded.

The question triggered a distant, uncomfortable memory. "So next you're gonna tell me I have a thick defensive shield," Langston said.

"What?"

"Never mind." He hadn't thought about Cecile in years, and he didn't want to think about her now, especially not in the context of this conversation. He stared at his sister intensely, using her presence to block the picture of Cecile that was trying to form in his mind. "Was there another reason you stopped by?"

Maya shook her head. "So are you going to take the class or not?" She didn't sound optimistic.

Langston swiveled back towards the computer. "I'll think about it. But if I don't, you and Ed should do it. I bet Latin dancing is fun."

He focused on his inbox, waiting for her to take her cue and say goodbye. When she didn't, he looked up again. "What?"

Maya was gazing at him sadly. "I really think you'd enjoy this, Langston," she said. "It isn't only about fixing you up with someone."

"Oh, I know that," he replied, managing to keep all but a hint of sarcasm out of his voice. He smiled. "Thanks for thinking of me."

She smiled back. "Of course I think about you." She took a step backwards. "I'd better go."

"See ya."

As soon as she closed the door behind her, Langston tossed the brochure in the garbage.

CHAPTER FIFTY-EIGHT

June 21, 1989

So where am I now? Not quite sure. I'm glad I have the ring, but I still feel more like a girlfriend than a fiancée. We did need to step back, slow down. You certainly can't maintain fireworks for years. To be honest, I've been genuinely happy for a while for reasons that have nothing to do with Teddy, and today I feel no particular anticipation or need to see him.

August 23, 1989

Dear Teddy,

What's the big deal about even planning a wedding? Why am I wearing this fucking ring? It means nothing. From now on, when someone asks, I'm telling the truth. "Oh this? This is a friendship ring."

There must be men out there who actually want me. How much do you want me? Not too much, obviously.

\#

Cecile put her notebook down for a moment, rubbing her eyes. Teddy was out for the evening, presumably at an event to benefit the community center. She'd declined her invitation, unable to bring herself to go through the motions. An intern at the center set off alarms—Cecile didn't think they were sleeping together yet, but she knew this girl was next in line, and she didn't feel like watching her husband trading meaningful glances with someone else, familiar as his infidelity had become.

She didn't enjoy reading her diaries, but she was determined to keep confronting her past, hoping the process would help to set her free from repeating the same mistakes. Sitting in the pink velour reclining rocker she and Teddy had bought just before they became parents for the first time, the chair in which she'd breastfed her children, the place she'd realized how intensely she could love another human without pathology, Cecile tried to remind herself of what she'd learned before she delved, once again, into who she was before this crucial discovery.

She picked up where she'd left off, her throat tightening gradually as she read. In the first entry, Teddy refused, yet again, to set a date for the wedding. In the next, she called it off, resolving to end their relationship. He reacted by begging her to marry him, saying that his only objection was that he wasn't being consulted enough, which made him feel manipulated. The Cecile in the journal was exhausted with Teddy's antics, so she walked away from him, finally sure that she didn't want to marry him, either. But she was still in love with him, for reasons Cecile the reader couldn't figure out, so when he said he was ready to give her the piece of his heart he'd been holding back, she caved. Wasn't sure he was for real, mind you, but she caved anyway.

The next entry, written in an airplane en route to the wedding that wasn't, was a hate letter that nevertheless managed, inexplicably, to end by leaving the door open for Teddy to come back.

Cecile the reader couldn't stand anymore. What the fuck was wrong with me? she asked herself. How could I say I'll never trust him again, maybe never trust anyone, then turn around and wonder what it would be like to have him groveling for another chance? Even though I knew he could be saying the same thing to someone else the next day? I felt like something in me died, and he'd killed it, but I listened to him tell me he was miserable without me?

My life with him is a tale told by an idiot, she thought, full of sound and fury, signifying nothing. When she'd studied *Macbeth* in high school, she'd never imagined that one day it would resonate so deeply.

Cecile put down her diary. Her head hurt—a vague aching, nothing acute. She leaned back, allowing the recliner to lift her feet off the ground. I give so much love to my babies, she thought. Why couldn't I love myself? Am I any better at it now?

A bookcase sat next to the recliner, stuffed with novels, photo albums, and home movies. Cecile's eyes traveled across the closest shelf, which was full of videos of the children, family vacations, and other events she'd decided were significant enough to document. Right in the middle, she noticed a tape she hadn't seen in years, and probably should never watch again. But she decided to anyway, because she was in a masochistic mood.

"The Wedding of Cecile Alexander and Theodore White. October 9, 1993." The title was a knife in the gut, but no sawing followed. Her inner steel protected her, as it always had, with the exception of the brief time she'd allowed Teddy to melt her defenses.

There he was, talking about how they'd met at a McDonald's and fallen in love. A cute story, and he told it beautifully. In the next shot, Cecile mentioned that they'd been engaged once before and broken it off (a detail Teddy failed to include), but had gotten back together, because their love was undeniable.

The next scene was the morning of the wedding, with Teddy, looking young, handsome, and very nervous, surrounded by the groomsmen, NYU colleagues he hadn't heard from in years. As far as Cecile knew, anyway.

Next came Cecile and her bridesmaids. In the first shot, the clothes were casual—jeans, t-shirts, cardigans—and the expressions relaxed. Their hair and faces undone, Cecile, Betsy, Teresa, and Teddy's cousin Francine looked unpolished, but their loose limbs and frequent laughter gave them a sparkle they couldn't quite match in their wedding finery. Still, looking at the female members of the wedding party in their matching green satin, Cecile smiled. Betsy looked so beautiful that day. They all did. Especially the bride, a stranger in a mermaid-shaped, bugle-beaded, champagne-colored gown, her hair piled high, made up to perfection, a fitting sacrifice for the altar of societal convention.

Am I still beautiful? Cecile glanced in her dresser mirror. She looked tired, and she had permanent lines on either side of her mouth. But as she gazed into her own eyes, the answer was yes.

There were times when her face looked foreign to her, or formless, somehow. But tonight, even though she'd spent what felt like years staring at the pages of a book, watching herself turn into a shadow of the person she'd hoped to be, even though the biggest mistake she'd ever made was unfolding in brilliant color a few feet away on her TV, Cecile knew she was beautiful. Which didn't change anything, and was, therefore, irrelevant.

She turned back to the screen. She and her father were entering the church. The camera cut away to Teddy's face. No trace of anything but awe showed in his eyes. Then he smiled, and lit up from within. She wasn't sure she could stand anymore, but Cecile kept watching as she advanced towards him, then her father stepped aside, kissing her, and retreated, looking worried, sitting beside her mother, who took his hand.

I'm sorry, Dad, she thought. I should have listened.

I couldn't listen, I did not know how.

Perhaps I'll listen now. Starry, starry night...

She grinned, focusing on the lovely couple, Cecile and Teddy, standing side by side. The minister went into his introductory spiel, invited people to object, but nobody did, even though some of them knew better. Then the vows—Teddy, in a strong, clear voice, telling the world he would be faithful till death. As Cecile watched herself smile at him like she believed his bullshit, the string quartet began to play "E il sol dell'anima," and the camera panned to show Tonya and Allen, gazing into each other's eyes. Despite her attempts to control him, his constant flirtation with other women, their explosive arguments and the temporary but deep animosity that accompanied their split, they smiled with what looked like genuine affection. And sang divinely.

I should get in touch with them, Cecile thought. Allen lived in Germany and sang all over Europe, while Tonya was based in Houston, performing with the Grand Opera and other houses mainly in the States. They were both married, he to a German pianist, she to a doctor.

They did well, she thought. I didn't. Maybe that song was an omen after all.

When Cecile had asked Allen to sing the duet from Rigoletto at her wedding, he laughed.

"Do you know what it's about?"

"Doesn't it mean love is the sunshine of the soul?" Cecile responded.

"Sure. But look up the rest, including the way things turn out for Gilda and the Duke. That said, if you still want us to sing it, I'm in."

When Cecile checked the words, she discovered that the duet was a seduction scene. The Duke used insincere words of love to trick Gilda into joining his list of conquests, even going so far as to lie about his name. But even after she learned of his deception, Gilda still loved the Duke so much that she sacrificed her life to save him from her father's planned revenge at the hands of Sparafucile, a paid assassin.

Cecile had remained undeterred. After all, it was still a beautiful love song, and besides, it was in Italian. Who'd know what it meant? So Tonya and Allen sang with exaggerated affection, as if the whole thing were a bit of a joke, and created a magical moment.

I still don't believe in omens, Cecile told herself, listening to the pastor speaking about the need for honest communication and, more importantly, forgiveness. The way to have a healthy marriage, according to Colossians, was to put on love, which meant acting as if on the days when you didn't feel loving. As the minister droned on, Cecile became increasingly amazed that words that had been inspirational the first time she heard them could sound so trite, even if they were true. At least, for most people.

She watched herself jump the broom, hand in hand with her new husband, saw Teddy kiss her cheek as they started down the aisle. Listening to the strings playing Mozart's "Spring" quartet as the recessional, she resolved to reconnect with Nelson and Chelsea, too. He was still in New York, playing in the Metropolitan Opera orchestra; she was with the Baltimore Symphony. Maybe they could get together and do a trio concert. Collaborating with them was never boring, even when the rehearsals became less prone to drama after Chelsea finally came out as a lesbian.

The reception came next, filling the screen with faces she recognized, and a bunch she didn't. Cecile smiled to see dear Aunt Mimi, who had passed on two years later, sitting with Louis, one of Cecile's Bermudian cousins. Everyone seemed to be having a good time. Why wouldn't they? Weddings were a party for the guests. Marriages were a whole different thing. She wished someone had made a bigger deal of the distinction, instead of going along with the farcical, misleading idea that a single, flawless day was a magical gateway to a perfect life.

Although she had watched most of the video with objective detachment, when James started singing "When I Fall in Love" at the reception, in a voice like Luther Vandross crossed with Nat King Cole, Cecile felt wistful. She knew he would have asked her out, if he'd been single, and that they could have lasted a long time. But he was a good man, loyal and committed to Olivia. Maybe I'll look him up too, she thought.

She listened to the words, and realized she'd chosen two omen songs, not one, because when she fell in love, she'd foolishly decided it would be forever. And whatever Teddy said he felt, at that moment, she felt that way, too.

When James finished singing, she turned off the tape and sat in the chair beside her bed a long time, not sure what she was feeling—tiny, as insignificant as a blade of grass. It didn't matter what the emotion was called. It hurt.

Cecile finally gathered enough energy to glance at the clock. One a.m. She went to the kitchen, ate a slice of wheat bread and a handful of mixed nuts, then poured a tall glass of orange juice.

She'd hurt before. She was resilient. She would bounce back. Again.

She finished her juice, put the glass in the sink, and went upstairs to brush her teeth and get in bed.

CHAPTER FIFTY-NINE

Langston loved coming up with new additions to his menu almost as much as he enjoyed demonstrating their preparation to his cooks, but his favorite part of being a chef came when he stood at the pass, legs spread wide to avoid hurting his back as he bent over to arrange the elements of a meal so artfully that a simple, white plate became a kind of canvas. He'd never known about his talent for composition, which he was sure had come from his grandmother. The pass was also the place he confirmed the quality of his meals. Though he now left a lot of the final tasting to Andre, Langston still made sure to do enough sampling to feel that Cimarron's food properly reflected its owner.

Things weren't always perfect, of course, and he had to fire a cook or two for coming in too hung over to keep up with the often punishing pace of the line. Still, being in the kitchen was as close to Nirvana as Langston could imagine. Unlike his former bosses, he never screamed at his employees when they got "in the weeds," preferring to address the situation with a disappointed look, a quick, sympathetic pep talk or an instant reassignment of duties. He found that the elaborate dance of a busy service went much more smoothly when all of the participants were both relatively relaxed and sharply focused. Besides, everyone knew that two of his original hires had been dismissed after their first infraction—one for failing to grasp that

Langston, unlike most chefs, had zero tolerance for sexual harassment of the female employees, and the other for failing to manage her alcoholism as well as the other heavy drinkers on the staff—so raising his voice was unnecessary. Langston didn't need to be a dictator; he welcomed input from his staff. Still, he was surprised how much he relished having the final say.

Even though Cimarron fulfilled every aspect of his fantasies, Langston started off dreading the idea of asking his patrons if they were enjoying themselves. After all, he'd spent his life being slightly out of step and, more importantly, he wasn't sure how to respond to a negative report.

That skill turned out to be unnecessary. Occasionally, someone felt the service had been slow, but the food never seemed to disappoint anyone, or at least, nobody would admit it. Soon, Cimarron had enough regular visitors that dinner reservations were hard to come by. Then the Toronto Star wrote a complimentary review, and Langston finally felt confident that he hadn't imagined Cimarron's exceptional qualities. High expectations required extra vigilance, but Langston soon looked forward to his trips to the dining room, seeing them as an opportunity to accept praise and make small talk, instead of a possible ordeal.

By mid-May of 2004, the weather was already warm enough to open the windows, letting in a welcome hint of a breeze. Langston started at the back of the restaurant, chatting with the people seated at the bar before getting to the interior diners, leaving the patrons by the window until the end, as a special treat. After spending much of the day in the back room or the kitchen, he liked to glance outside as he moved from table to table, especially with the sky painted mauve and gold.

"Mrs. Allen," he said, spotting an elderly lady with impossibly bright red hair who came in every Sunday for brunch. "I didn't even think you knew we were open on weekdays."

Mrs. Allen chuckled. "Langston," she said, gesturing to her middle-aged companion, a buxom brunette in a tight pink sweater, "this is my daughter, Elaine, who lives in Nebraska. She's visiting this week and I wanted her first night to be special. But don't worry, I'll be back on Sunday, too."

Langston bowed slightly. "I appreciate that, Mrs. Allen. How was your meal?"

She leaned forward, her eyes open wide with delight. "Amazing! I'd never tried the goat, but it's so delicious, I'm mad I denied myself this long."

Langston smiled. "And you, Elaine?"

"I didn't think it could live up to the hype, but I have to concede that my mother was right." She shot Mrs. Allen a glance that implied a messy back story.

"I'm glad," said Langston, happy he'd asked Elaine's opinion second, and could make an exit. "Enjoy the rest of your evening."

He allowed himself an eyeful of the fading daylight, then proceeded to the attractive, sixty-something black couple at the next table. The man was built like a lineman, and the woman was the opposite, elegantly slender. Her hair was silver, what remained of his was white. Langston wondered if the woman was famous. She looked strangely familiar.

"Good evening," he said. "Is everything to your liking?"

"It's wonderful," said the man, with a slight New York accent.

"Visiting from the States?" Langston asked.

"Actually, we live in Alberta," said the woman, in a melodious, not quite British inflection.

"I'm sorry for being presumptuous," Langston responded. "Your...husband?"

They both laughed. "For 45 years," said the man. "We're in town to celebrate our anniversary."

"Wow. Congratulations! That's very impressive."

"Hard work, commitment, love, and the grace of God, who is the third strand in our relationship," the woman said.

Langston nodded. He wasn't expecting a sermon. "You have such a beautiful accent. Where are you from, if you don't mind my asking?"

"Bermuda."

Langston felt a twinge in the pit of his stomach, realizing why the lady looked familiar. Couldn't be...

"I hear it's beautiful," he said.

"It is," said the man. "I met my wife when I was stationed there. Nothing like it. You should go. Wonderful seafood."

"And onions," his wife added, with a smile.

"I'd like that." Langston was dying to ask them inappropriate, personal questions, but continued instead, "Happy anniversary, Mr. and Mrs..."

"Alexander," the man responded, and Langston turned his head quickly, blocking the cough that came out of his instantly constricted throat with the back of his hand.

"Excuse me," he managed, with a weak smile. "Thank you for letting us share your special day."

Mrs. Alexander reached into her purse. "Actually, can you do us a favor and take our picture?"

"Certainly." Langston's hands were clammy. He waited for the Alexanders to arrange their chairs side by side in front of the window, with the last vestiges of daylight behind them, took three pictures, and handed her the camera. "A pleasure to meet you. Please come back and see us the next time you're in Toronto."

"We will," they said in unison.

Langston had one more couple to greet. He kept his comments brief, then retreated to his office, closed the door, and stared at the wall. The encounter felt like an unsettling dream. Cecile's face tried to rise into his memory, but he squeezed his eyes shut, shaking his head.

I can't still hurt, he resolved. I won't.

But he did. So he went into the kitchen, grateful that the thrum of activity soon forced him to forget.

CHAPTER SIXTY

A year after her first session with Miranda, Cecile started trying to listen to God every day. She was never sure if this worked or not. Sometimes she seemed to be getting clear messages, but they were repeated a lot: "Seek ye first the Kingdom of God, and all these things will be added unto thee" or "Wait on the Lord, and be of good courage" or "Trust in the Lord and lean not upon thine own understanding." God generally favored the King James translation, for some reason, at least when speaking to her.

"You're an "A" student even in therapy," Miranda had once remarked jokingly.

Cecile realized she approached counseling like a typical perfectionist, but her emotional health was too important to do it another way. Not that she'd done everything Miranda suggested. It had taken her ten months to go to Nar-Anon, despite talking about Calvin enough to be forced to admit her anger with her parents for allowing her brother so much free rein. How many times had they threatened dire consequences for his petty thefts and disregard for curfews without following through? Or caught him yelling at Cecile and defused the situation by having them apologize to each other, even when Cecile hadn't done anything except standing up to him? When Calvin was 17, they finally said they'd call the police if they found drugs in the house again. A week later, a bag of cocaine surfaced under his mattress. Cecile waited for the sirens, but they never came. Instead, her mother distracted her father in the middle of a loud, frightening confrontation, just long enough for Calvin to bolt for the door. When he finally came back, four days later, her parents did everything except killing the fatted calf.

By the time she finished telling her stories to Miranda, Cecile's hands were shaking.

"What are you feeling?" Miranda asked.

"I don't know. I guess...I guess I'm really angry."

"What should they have done?"

"Kicked his ass out. Changed the locks. Sent him to rehab. Said something besides, 'are you okay, Calvin?' He was a fucking coke addict. Of course he wasn't okay. I don't even believe that shit."

"Wow," Miranda responded, her green eyes wide. "I don't think I've ever heard you use that much profanity."

"Welcome to my interior monologue," said Cecile, with a sarcastic grin.

Miranda laughed. After a moment, she asked, "Would you do that to Malik?"

Cecile fell silent. "I don't know."

She ended up calling her parents to tell them how horrible living with Calvin had been. That she rarely invited her friends over because she feared the chaos her brother could create. That she understood why her parents hadn't thrown him out—they loved their baby and remembered him when—but they should have been more aware that allowing him to live in their home had damaged their girls. That enabling Calvin made her feel like he mattered more than she or Elizabeth did, a wound Cecile was still struggling to heal.

Her mother listened silently, then suggested that Cecile "let go of the things that are past," to paraphrase Philippians, "and press on to the prize of the higher calling of the Lord Jesus Christ," a statement Cecile found both annoying and painful. Her father listened silently, then apologized so profusely that Cecile felt uncomfortable. It had helped to hear him say how sorry he was, though. It had helped even more to tell the truth.

After she started going to Nar-Anon, Cecile discovered they were both right. Apparently, if she wanted to be "in recovery" she had to "let go and let God." That, plus following the twelve steps and saying the serenity prayer a lot, although the wisdom to know the difference between the things she could and could not change seemed very elusive.

The best part about Nar-Anon was speaking, uninterrupted, and being understood. Teddy constantly interrupted and never seemed to understand, but in Nar-Anon everyone was just like Cecile—a misfit with low self-esteem just trying to get by—and everyone got a turn to share, within reason, whatever was on his or her mind. Actually, many of the people in the group did far more than get by; they displayed real wisdom. So she added Twelve Step literature to her list of books. And was relieved to discover that she could be wise at times, too.

Her efforts eventually paid off. I'm never going to be perfect, am I? she mused periodically. But that's okay. I don't need to be perfect to be loved. The thought had started to reverberate in her heart for the first time.

She learned to accept her shortcomings just in time, because Teddy reacted to her efforts by calling her "Miss Perfect." Whenever Cecile didn't live up to the title, he called her a different name—hypocrite. Which stung even though she tried to detach, just as they taught in Nar-Anon, by assuming that much of what he said had nothing to do with her, and everything to do with his insecurities.

There was another part to detachment, though. It was supposed to be done with love. She prayed daily to be in love with Teddy again, but couldn't do it. She got by on the hope that, as she developed, the dynamics between them would change and she'd be able to feel something for him besides contempt.

After a few months of attending Nar-Anon, Cecile came to realize that Teddy was just like an addict. What was he addicted to, though?

"Attention," Miranda had said. "He needs his young girls because they don't ask anything, and they give him a sense of being admired."

"I tell him all the time what a great job he does at the center."

"That's not the kind of admiration he wants."

Cecile gazed out Miranda's window. The tree just beyond the glass was beginning to bud, sending out tiny shoots of pale green, which promised to become leaves later on.

"It's the best I can do," she replied.

One week, she decided to try another twelve step philosophy:"act as if." She'd thought that if she could pretend she was still in love with Teddy, he would be reminded of how they were at first. She made lasagna, his favorite meal. He wolfed it down, complimented her, then went into the living room to play video games, leaving Cecile to clean up the kitchen. She swallowed her rising irritation, then sat down next to him on the couch and asked about his day.

"Same old, same old," he responded without looking at her.

She tried to think of the name of one of the kids from the center he was particularly involved with helping, but she couldn't. She was about to go and wash the dishes when Teddy turned to her and said, "What's up?"

"Nothing."

"I mean, you never try to talk to me anymore."

"You never seem available."

He nodded. "Oh, I see. I'm the one who spends all my time on the piano or dealing with the kids."

Cecile took a deep breath, trying to detach.

"It must seem that way."

"Look out! Here comes Robot Cecile!"

Teddy picked up the video game control and started playing Madden football.

"Do you want me to argue? I really don't enjoy it."

"Fooled me."

It's too late, she thought. No, it's never too late. So many of those Nar-Anon people were in much worse relationships than this and stayed the course until things turned around...but she didn't have the will or the energy to continue the exchange.

"I'll just let you relax," she said

Cecile stood. She had intended to kiss him, but she couldn't make herself do it.

"Dinner was delicious," Teddy said softly. "Thanks."

She searched his eyes, saw a glimmer of warmth and wished there was a way to vault over the unseen wall between them. Then again, there was that alligator-infested moat to deal with. Never mind.

"You're welcome."

She went into the kitchen, thinking, if you're that grateful, you could wash the damn dishes. She could have asked, of course. Again. Not worth it.

With Malik and Elana upstairs and Teddy engaged, Cecile could be alone with her thoughts for a while. So washing dishes was a blessing. Attitude of gratitude. Another principle to practice.

All at once, she felt so weary she had to sit down. She pulled a chair away from the dining room table and dropped into it. Tears didn't always get from her eyes to her cheeks, but they had become random and frequent. Something on television, or a hug from her children, or an article in the newspaper would trigger emotions she never knew she had. Sometimes, the subject that inspired her tears was injustice, but sometimes it was an act of kindness, tale of courage or perseverance, or, most of all, a story of lasting love.

"That's excellent," Miranda had told her. "You're not only grieving your past, you're letting your emotions have a chance to speak every day."

"Hooray," Cecile said sarcastically.

She'd been grateful for the encouragement, though. She had been working very hard to be healthier, and having Miranda acknowledge her progress had given her hope. For herself, at least.

CHAPTER SIXTY-ONE

Since the Alexander's visit to Cimarron, Langston had been unable to get Cecile off his mind for more than short spurts. She had become like the hum of florescent lights—if he let himself get too quiet, the thought of her became inescapable. His self-defense was uncharacteristically ferocious concentration. He noticed his employees glancing at him furtively and whispering among themselves, but their discomfort was easier to stand than his obsession.

Finally, Naomi, a petite Trinidadian with long microbraids who was among the first servers hired, asked him, "Are you okay?" after he snapped at her for putting too little chocolate sauce on an ice cream sundae.

Langston took a deep breath. "I'm sorry," he said, resolving to stay out of everyone's way as much as possible. Making the rounds of his customers helped a bit, especially since the Alexanders were nowhere to be seen. Which was a relief and a disappointment.

Usually, his day off was a time to catch up on myriad chores and errands, but he needed to talk to someone, anyone, to get out of his own head. He called Glenda, but she wasn't free. He tried his siblings, but they were all busy, too. He was about to despair when he remembered his gym membership. He changed his clothes, and hurried out the door.

He hadn't been to the gym in months; it was easier to run outdoors or on his own treadmill and lift weights in his living room. Besides, being a chef was so grueling, with countless hours spent on his feet, six days a week, that what he usually craved during his time off was rest, not exercise. The membership was a New Year's resolution of the previous year, partially because Maya had gotten to him enough that he'd decided to increase the chances he might meet Miss Longterm Relationship. Or Mrs. Longterm Relationship.

He handed his membership card to the pretty brunette behind the desk, picked up a towel, and headed to the locker room. Halfway there, he decided that he needed to clear his mind more than he needed to meet anybody, choosing to send the ghost of Cecile back to where he'd buried her with the longest cardio session, ever. So he could still respect himself.

He ran on the treadmill until he was soaked with sweat, his shirt so damp that he had to go to the locker room to change into another one, toweling off vigorously in between. He was exhausted, but Cecile was still flitting resolutely around in his heart, so he headed to the weight room. He was doing bicep curls when a feminine voice said, "Hey."

He turned. The speaker was a woman about his age, with long hair, bleached dark blonde and pulled back in a bun, large light brown eyes, full lips, and cafe au lait skin. She was dressed in a pink spandex tank and shorts, which accentuated the extravagance of her curves, and wore white terry cloth sweatbands on her wrists.

She smiled and said, "Can you spot me?"

He smiled back. "Sure."

The guy next to him, a serious bodybuilder, glanced at Langston with a half-smile, the visual equivalent of a high-five. Langston nodded in response. Because this woman was undeniably hot.

She took her place on the bench, furrowed her brow, and lifted the barbell, which had ten pound weights on each side. Langston stood behind her head, trying to focus on something other than her breasts, which were large enough that a spotter seemed unnecessary—if she dropped the barbell, her bust would undoubtedly make it bounce back into place.

She did eight repetitions, then put the weight on the rack without assistance.

"That's good," says Langston.

"Thanks."

He watched her chest heaving up and down as she caught her breath.

She did another set, and then another, struggling a bit with the last two reps.

"It's all you," said Langston, his hands hovering near the bar in case she faltered.

"Barely," she managed.

They both laughed. She wiped her brow with her wrist. Her cleavage was moist now. He searched his mind, grasping for something he could say to at least open up a conversation, but he couldn't think of anything.

She saved him by saying, "I know you."

His eyebrows shot up. "You do?"

She nodded. "You don't remember me?"

He focused on her face more intently. Of course.

"Shit!" He frowned, speechless for another reason.

"You're doing very well for yourself," she said, undaunted.

"How do you know?" There was time Langston would have relished flaunting his success in front of Anthea Tanner, but seeing her now, he felt nothing but disdain.

"I read about you in the Star. I'm impressed."

He smirked. "Queen Anthea gives her blessing. Now I'll be able to sleep at night."

She grinned. "I deserved that." She studied her fingernails, perfectly manicured, pink with rhinestone accents. "You'll be happy to know that I married Tommy Hall, and he dumped me."

"I'm sorry."

She looked up, wide-eyed. "You are?"

"I used to hate you, but to be honest, I haven't thought about you in years. You have to be aware someone is alive to be interested in revenge."

Her face fell. "True."

"So, you're done? Nice spotting for ya."

He was walking away when she said, "Hey, Langston."

He turned, folding his arms. She stood, and came close. She smelled like citrus, vanilla and sweat. Her eyes were soft, and she looked vulnerable, like another person completely.

"Do you want a do over?"

"What?"

She looked down. "I was so wrong back then. You were always a nice guy, I knew that. I got caught up in trying to be the popular girl, you know, all that bullshit that goes with it, being cruel to people. But now..."

He scratched his chin. He didn't feel sorry for her, half expecting to be videotaped if he accepted her offer. Which he found hard to believe.

"Are you serious?"

He looked into her eyes, and saw defeat. She nodded.

"He just left you, right?"

She shifted her feet, gazing off to the side. "Look, forget it—"

"We're not going to your place," said Langston.

She smiled. "I'll meet you in the lobby."

"I'll give you 15 minutes, then I'm gone."

"Fifteen minutes? That's barely enough time to take a shower."

"So I guess you'll rush."

She shook her head. "I like you like this."

"Fifteen minutes."

So this was how power over women felt. He enjoyed it, in spite of himself.

She arrived just before his deadline, and they agreed to meet at a hotel ten minutes away. He expected her to stand him up, but she walked in moments after he did, which was when he realized he was about to pay for sex. Because paying for the hotel was paying for sex.

The hotel they had chosen charged by the night, not the hour. He debated going to his apartment, but decided against it, because he didn't want her to know where he lived.

If Cecile were standing in front of me, he thought, I would want her to know where I live. I would want to wake up with her the next morning, or I'd want to wake up before she did, so I could make breakfast and serve it to her in bed...

Anthea was supposed to make him forget. He studied her face, focusing on her beauty. Then he approached the front desk.

The sex was desperate, angry, and intense. Langston had never been so rough with a woman, but Anthea liked it. Despite her screams of ecstasy, in the end, it was about revenge. When he kissed her, he was claiming her lips, her breasts, her body as his; bringing her to orgasm was about proving something to himself, not her pleasure.

As she lay in his arms, he checked the clock. 11 a.m. Was he going to have to pay for the whole day? Probably, plus an additional fee for checking in so early. He wanted to go home. Could he leave yet, though? Then again, what did he owe her?

Her eyes were closed.

"Anthea," he said quietly.

She opened one eye. "That was *amazing*," she murmured.

He smiled involuntarily. "I'm glad. Hey, listen, I know you don't actually like me. You just needed something. I'm not mad—I needed something, too, and we got it. So...thanks, and you're welcome."

Anthea pulled away from him. "How do you know I don't like you?"

"Because you don't know me. You know I have a restaurant, and that people like the food. Not the same thing."

Her eyes met his. Then she sat up, pulling the sheet over her chest. "So you got me back, then."

He held her eyes unflinchingly. "It was your idea."

Langston watched her jump out of bed and hurry to the bathroom, pulling the sheet close and wrapping it around her, then dropping it on the floor just before she closed the door. He listened to the clink of the toilet seat being closed, the dull thud as she lowered herself onto it. And the sound of her crying.

He knocked. She ignored him.

"I'm sorry," he said quietly, through the door.

When she didn't respond, he retrieved his clothes from the floor, put them on, and grabbed his gym bag.

"I paid for the day. Stay as long as you like," he yelled. Then he left the hotel room, closing the door behind him, and made sure the people at the desk were clear that the woman in 416 should be leaving soon, he wasn't sure when, but any further charges to his credit card were unauthorized.

He got in his car, disgusted with himself, because no matter how much fucking Anthea's brains out erased his previous reputation, he felt ugly. Worse, the whole thing had been a waste of time.

Because he didn't feel vindicated by leaving her in tears. And he was still thinking about Cecile.

Sitting cross-legged on the floor in her bedroom with a notebook in front of her, Cecile knew that getting absorbed today was a very bad idea. She had difficult music to prepare, and the weeks she had been cheating herself of much-needed sleep by obsessively wading through her history were taking a toll—she couldn't concentrate as well as she needed to, not only because she was tired, but because she spent so much time thinking about what she'd written, when she should have been focused on the score.

I'll be very disciplined about stopping this time, she decided. This proved difficult, even though the exercise had become depressingly repetitive. There were times she wished she didn't have such high moral standards, that the Christianity that kept her going hadn't taken root so early, if only because with a longer list of sexual partners she'd have a wider variety of experiences to write about.

I've tried to be good all my life, she thought, and I'm still not happy, so was it worth it?

Whatever. I am where I am now. No point in speculating.

Cecile glanced at the clock. It was nearly 11:30 a.m. She should have started practicing an hour ago. She had a concert with college students in two weeks, no big deal, but one of the pieces was tricky, and she was supposed to rehearse it the next day.

She closed the notebook and put it in the nightstand

drawer, where it stayed along with the other old notebooks and the current one, waiting for whatever nonsense she chose to scribble, usually when she should have been sleeping or playing with her kids (thank God for DVDs). Stuffing old letters into the drawer to make it possible to close the thing completely, she spotted a photocopy of a Calvin and Hobbes cartoon, which turned out to be a letter. May as well wait and practice after lunch, at this point.

She read a few lines, smiled, and continued until the end, remembering why she'd liked Langston Andrews so much—he was smart, unconventional, and funny, unlike anyone she'd met before or since. She hunted through the drawer until she found another letter from Langston, then another. She could only find four, but each one fascinated her.

He was a good man, she thought. What would have happened if I hadn't been so obsessed? I wish I hadn't offended him.

She wondered what he was doing, wondered if he'd reply to a letter now, or if he'd expunged every desire to communicate with her when he decided not to write her back thirteen years ago.

She put all the letters except for one back into the drawer, closed it (just barely), and stood, reading the return address on the envelope she'd decided not to put away, wondering if he still lived there.

It would be really bizarre to get in touch now, she thought. He's probably married, and besides, our correspondence lasted only a few months. Then again, was it really weirder than getting back in touch with Allen, James, and Chelsea?

Mainly, what have I got to lose?

Recapitulation

June, 2004

CHAPTER SIXTY-THREE

On a Friday just after midnight, Langston had just come home. The restaurant closed at 10:00, but two stragglers had come in at 9:30 with a story that started with it being the guy's birthday and him having to work late, and ended with "please, we read about this place in the paper and it got such a great review I knew I had to take him here. Please!"

So Langston conferred with the servers. Naomi agreed to stay, and he cooked the meal himself. There was still some coconut-frosted rum cake, so he gave his customers free slices, for which they were effusively grateful. He didn't expect them to tip more than usual, because people often don't care if you've gone out of your way, but he was pleased when they did, saving him from using his own money to make staying late worth Naomi's while.

Now he was exhausted. A stack of mail sat on his kitchen table, waiting for him to at least glance at it; he hadn't bothered yesterday and was sorely tempted to leave it until morning. He picked up the letters and fell into the leather chair bequeathed by his grandmother, which was distressed, to use the fashion term, from years of use, brownish, slightly cracked in places. The chair sat in front of his ancient TV and VCR. He knew he should get a DVD player, but since he rarely watched anything except a few favorite video cassettes, he'd never gotten around to it. He dropped the mail on the side table next to his chair, then selected the first item, a bill. Junk. Junk. Bill. Junk. Junk. Letter.

A letter? From Marcus. *What the…?*

When he opened it, there was another envelope inside. Something was familiar about the handwriting. Good thing Marcus and his wife decided to live there, instead of selling, as Zora had advised:

6/01/04

Dear Langston,

You probably don't remember me. I was looking through some old letters, and I found several you wrote me about 15 years ago. You were so funny and quirky and delightful that I decided to get in touch and see what you're up to now.

I think I did something to really offend you all those years ago. I'm sorry about that. I hope you can forgive me.

In any case, I hope your life has been, and continues to be, full of joy.

Take care and God bless,

Cecile

p.s. My email address is Cecilewhite@yahoo.com

Langston read the letter again. Cecile. After all these years. So meeting her parents was a sign. So was Maya's visit.

This time, he didn't try to stop himself from picturing her face. He wondered how the years had changed her. She was tall and thin when they met. Was she heavy now? Or just the same, only with a wrinkle or two? A lot of black women aged very well. He imagined her skin, honey beige, her expressive eyes and perfect lips, and decided she was still gorgeous, and that, more importantly, she still said brilliant, unexpected things that made him laugh, think, or feel deeply. Then again, maybe that last part wasn't something to celebrate, given the way things had turned out.

Cecilewhite@yahoo.com. So she did marry Teddy after all. Did happily married women wait fifteen years to search out men they met once, corresponded with for a few months, and have never heard from again?

Probably not. He felt a strange excitement. She never forgot him. Or maybe she did, but somehow his letters—she'd saved them!— were enough to rekindle her interest.

In the first few months after he stopped communicating with Cecile, he'd restrained his constant urge to call her by telling himself he had no good reason. He'd had to disqualify a few things first: she was the most exciting woman he'd met, her voice was music, things like that. With those motives eliminated, calling became pointless, especially if he reminded himself she loved somebody else.

And now? He looked at the postmark. She was living in the States, so if her marriage was over, she hadn't moved home. She probably had a job, had put down roots there.

Just like I have in Toronto, he thought.

There was an email address, but no phone number. His computer was at the restaurant, to maintain his clean break between work and home, but he was tempted to go back. He glanced at the clock. No. Too late. He would write her tomorrow.

He'd include his phone number, and then he'd wait, and it would be excruciating.

Why? You're so damn stupid, he chastised himself. Making something out of nothing. All she wanted was a diversion, probably because her marriage was so fucked up.

He inhaled slowly, then let the breath go in a rush. There. Much better. He opened the rest of the envelopes, threw away the ones that didn't matter, and went to his bedroom to get ready to sleep.

The next morning, far too early, he arrived at Cimmaron, went into his office, and sat in front of his computer. No phone number, he decided. That would look too eager. Just his return email, because there was nothing to get all excited about. He'd done that before, and he wasn't about to set himself up again, not for Cecile. She was merely a standout member of his Unrequited Affection Club. He would remember that, no matter how she replied.

To: Cecilewhite@yahoo.com
From: landrews@cimmaron.com
Subject: Hello

Maybe I should make it, "Hello!" No, too eager. "Hi there"? No. Too friendly, not cool enough. "Greetings?" That sounds like I'm from outer space or something. "Greetings, earthling…"

It was 6:00 in the morning. The restaurant opened for

lunch at 11:30 a.m., so Langston's presence at this hour was unnecessary, if not for the need to write this email, which had kept him awake most of the night and would prevent him from focusing for the rest of the day unless he got it done. And now, having composed it in his mind while lying in bed, he couldn't even write the subject line.

"Got your letter."

There! A statement of fact, neutral in intent. He continued:

Dear Cecile,

What a nice surprise to hear from you. I hope you are well. How is Teddy? Do you have kids? I think your parents came to my restaurant on their anniversary, by the way.

My brother Marcus forwarded your letter. My grandmother's been dead for years, so it's fortunate that we didn't sell the house, or you'd probably never have found me.

By the way, you didn't offend me, so there's nothing to forgive.

Take care,

Langston

He read it over once or twice, hesitated, then clicked "send."

No point trying to explain how badly she'd hurt him, because then he'd have to say he'd thought he was in love with her, which would be beyond awkward.

He leaned back in his chair and stared at the pictures on his desk: Marcus, Danita, and their twin daughters, Christina and Gabrielle; Zora, Bernie, Will and Claire; his grandmother in her Sunday best; Maya and Ed; him and Glenda in Costa Rica the summer of his junior year in college. His family. His nearest and dearest. No wife. No kids.

"No worries," he said firmly, clamping down the loneliness that occasionally escaped a tiny, walled corner in his heart. He pulled up his inbox and began to delete the spam.

#

When Langston checked his email before going home for the evening, he saw Cecile's address, and couldn't resist reading her correspondence first:

Dear Langston,

I'm so glad you wrote back. I was afraid that what I did was insurmountable, since you stopped communicating with me. You really don't remember? Just as well, I suppose.

I'm sorry to hear about your grandmother. You must miss her terribly. My grandmother died just before the wedding. I didn't know my dad's mother at all (she died a year before I was born) but my mom's mother was a big part of our lives, even though she lived far away. She didn't fit the soft grandma mold, although she baked incredible cookies. She was wise, though, and had a sharp wit (a sharp tongue is more accurate, actually).

I have two kids. Elana is 8 and Malik just turned 6. I could go on and on about them, but that's probably boring to everyone outside my immediate family. Teddy is who he is, which is who he was. I suppose I expected him to grow up, finally, and be someone else. It never happened, so I grew up instead and realized people don't necessarily become who you had in mind. Some do, maybe, but no such luck in my case. Anyway, I'm married, and I take those vows very seriously.

I'd love to talk to you. I can call Canada for free on evenings and weekends. When are you available? I can't wait to catch up!

Take care and God bless,

Cecile

P.S. My parents RAVED about Cimarron.

Dear Cecile,

I'm kind of hard to reach. Running a restaurant takes a lot of my time, although I'm free in the morning before we open or late at night when we close. I don't go in at all on Mondays, but I do end up catching up on a lot of other things. I much prefer talking on the phone to email, though. Maybe you could try me Tuesday evening after 9. It's a slow night, usually. You'll probably have more luck catching me at work. The number is 416-282-3958.

A bientot,

Langston

Cecile was relatively calm as she dialed Langston's number. She told herself this was good, appropriate for a married woman contacting a long-lost male acquaintance. Who happened to be single.

Since she was calling him at work, she expected the conversation to be brief. Still, she felt enthusiastic about talking to him again, even for a little while. She knew there were very questionable aspects about her level of anticipation, but despite his single status, she was confident she'd been clear enough in her email about her view that married was married, despite the state of the union, to dispel any aura of wrongdoing.

That's my story, she thought, and I'm sticking to it.

The phone rang twice.

"Good evening, Cimarron."

"Langston?"

"Cecile?"

It was 9:15 p.m. And, by some miracle, they were both free. Their schedules were incompatible; he was freest when she was getting the kids off to school, while her scheduled cleared when he was in the midst of overseeing and/or preparing for the dinner crowd.

Cecile could hear Teddy's video game blaring below her. Madden Football, as usual. The most recent version, of course.

"*C'est moi,*" she said. "How are you?"

"Great. And it's slow now, so I can talk."

"You sound just the same."

"So do you."

Cecile had forgotten how much she loved the sound of his voice, but she doubted she would again. It was neither baritone nor tenor, and radiated comfort, not seduction. She'd been sitting on her bed—with Teddy still making nightly phone calls to females, there was no prospect of his leaving the guest room any time soon—but now she reclined, smiling.

"Did you even remember my voice?" she asked.

"Yes, actually. Did you remember mine?"

"Yes, but I'd forgotten how it feels to hear it. I think you should do commercials. You've got this—I don't know how to explain it. You sound like Mom's chicken soup."

"Chicken soup?" He laughed. "Wow, that's really sexy."

"There are things way more important than sexy, believe me."

"Such as?"

"Honest. Reliable. Kind. I could go on forever."

"My voice is honest, reliable, and kind?"

"Honest and kind. I don't know if a voice can be reliable."

"Honest and kind. Like chicken soup."

"Well, soothing like chicken soup. Okay, okay, that was lame. Forget it."

"Actually, I like soothing. I like honest, kind, and reliable too. Pretty ironic, since you used to always say I was lying about something."

"You weren't, though. I know that now."

Cecile heard the wistful tone in her voice, and sat up, crossing her legs beneath her. When she got too relaxed, she gave away too much information. How do you know he's so honest? she asked herself. But in her gut, she just knew. She wished she'd appreciated things like honesty and kindness when she was younger.

"Tell me more about your kids," Langston said, and Cecile was glad for the new topic. She tried not to go on too long, despite having unusually talented, attractive, intelligent children. She reiterated names, ages, and genders, adding that Elana liked chess, dance and cello, and Malik enjoyed art, soccer and violin, keeping it brief with effort.

Langston listened without interrupting, then responded, "I've always wanted kids."

"Maybe there are some you don't know about."

He laughed. "Have you heard something?"

Cecile grinned, happy that he seemed to still enjoy her sense of humor. "I haven't heard a thing about you in thirteen years, darling. But I'll let you know, okay?"

"Thanks."

Cecile decided to ask what, to her, was an obvious question: "So, did you ever get married?"

"Nope."

"Why not?"

"Well, I'm not gay, if that's what you're thinking. Not that there's anything wrong with it."

Cecile smiled at the reference to *Seinfeld*. "I wondered there, for a while."

"Really?"

"No, but I could have, because you wrote something in one of your letters about homosexual love being the only true love, or some other crap. I think that's what I called it back then, too. What did you mean by that?"

"I don't even remember. Probably something like the only reason gay people get together is to be together, but straight people have another agenda."

"Which doesn't prove that straight people can't be in love."

"I can't disagree." He grinned, grateful that the years hadn't changed her ability to play verbal tennis. "I can't believe you still have letters I wrote thirteen years ago."

"I have letters a lot of people wrote throughout the years. I keep anything personal."

"Why on earth would you do that?"

"It's fun to look back, sometimes, and see what people had to say. Or it's educational. Sort of like a history of my mind. I can see what the people are responding to in my letters, and remember the situation. It's even more interesting to read my diaries."

"I'll have to check them out when I get a chance."

"But then I'd have to kill you, and what would all those people desperate to eat at Cimarron do then?"

"You're right. For the good of mankind, your diaries are

yours."

"Thanks. Well, you've dodged that question, so maybe I'll ask another." When Langston laughed, Cecile leaned back against her pillows again, deciding not to fight the comfort talking to him created inside her, and continued. "How'd you end up running a restaurant?"

"I own it, actually."

"Well, excuse me! I'm impressed. Then again, you always liked to cook. At least, you wrote a letter describing some very tempting food."

"Damn. You really studied those things, didn't you?"

"Nah, I just happen to have a steel trap mind."

He chuckled.

"So, anyway, how did you end up *owning* a restaurant?" she continued, smiling. She couldn't remember the last time she'd smiled so much. I'm lighthearted, she thought—all heaviness gone, and radiant, like the mist from a waterfall, glistening in the sun.

"I couldn't think of anything else to do," said Langston, "and after a bunch of years as a teacher, I decided I might as well try something I like."

"Good idea. All your life is a long time to do something you don't enjoy."

"People do it every day, but you're right. The funny thing is, I end up teaching anyway, every time I hire somebody or put something new on the menu."

"Ironic. But let's get back to my original question. You

never married?"

"No."

"Why not? If that's not too personal."

There's no agenda with this line of questioning, she thought. I just want to know what he's been doing with his life. She wasn't sure she believed herself, though.

"No, it's okay."

"So what's the issue? Never met the right person? Commitment-phobic? Perfectionist? Too damn smart?"

"I've never fallen in love, so getting married didn't make much sense."

Cecile sat up straight. "Wow. All these years, and you've never been in love?"

"All these years."

She hugged her knees to her chest. "You know, I read something not too long ago about arranged marriages. Kind of made it sound nice to get rid of all the erotic/romantic stuff, which is completely unreliable anyway. I mean, deep down I believe it's possible to have a happy long-term relationship...I think. Barely. But enough of that. So you're hard to please?"

"I don't think so, but what do I know?"

"What are you looking for?"

There was a short pause, then Langston said, "I'm a really simple guy. I don't need a lot of stuff, so I guess I don't understand high-maintenance women. I like movies, music, and really good food. I'd love to travel more. But basically, I just want someone who's easy to talk to."

Cecile's heart started beating faster. "Doesn't sound unreasonable," she responded. "So no physical ideal?"

"Not really. I mean, I stay in shape, so I like a woman who cares at least a little about being fit."

"Tall or short?"

"Doesn't matter."

"But you must have a preference."

"Okay, tall."

"Race?"

"Doesn't matter."

"Meaning you date women of all races, or you don't date black women and you're trying to pretend it's because you're open minded?"

Langston laughed. "The former."

"Good answer, considering the audience. Education requirement?"

"Not really, but she's got to be able to discuss what's going on in the world intelligently."

"Pretty?"

"I'm not immune to physical attractiveness, but it's not the deciding factor."

"Hmm. You sound ridiculously easy to please. What are you leaving out?"

Pause. "Nothing."

"Oh, c'mon."

There was another short silence. When Langston spoke again, he sounded uncomfortable. "No, really. Nothing."

"Then why the hesitation?"

"I was thinking."

"Yeah, right. Okay, hide things from me. I won't pry."

It occurred to Cecile that she hadn't had such an easy conversation with a man in eons. She'd made a few male friends, the result of musical collaborations, and she still considered Allen, Nelson and James her friends, even though they rarely communicated. Then again, the majority of her connections with people were made via email, lately, so maybe it wasn't Langston, it was the fact she was actually speaking, instead of reading and typing.

"Are you still thin?" he asked.

"Does it matter?"

"Of course not. I just haven't seen you in a long time and I'm trying to imagine how you've changed."

"I wear the same size I did twenty years ago." Cecile felt proud of this fact, even though she knew the sizing has changed, which meant she was actually a size larger than before. Still, size 6 was pretty darn impressive for a thirty-eight-year-old mother of two, natural metabolic advantage or no.

"Wow. I'm impressed!"

"I've got a few gray hairs, but people still occasionally think I'm in my 20's. Not early 20's or anything."

This sounded boastful. It's all just packaging, anyway, she thought. Plus, I'm leaving out the stretch marks and the smile lines.

"What about you?" she continued, extending her legs.

"Are you bald?"

Langston laughed. "No."

"Receding?"

"Not yet."

"Lucky."

"That's about right. Nothing I did to deserve it."

"I'd like you anyway."

"Yeah? Hey, you never told me what you want in a man."

"Odd question for a married woman." Cecile couldn't help feeling glad he'd asked, though.

"Oh, you don't have an opinion about that anymore?"

Cecile thought about Teddy, and the many ways they were a mismatch.

"I do, I suppose. I used to be interested in men who had an aura of mischief, as in, I didn't want them too buttoned-down or straight-laced. But now..." She paused, listening to the football game repeating inanities. Teddy had fallen asleep, it seemed. "Now, I just want someone who's nice to me."

Langston's voice deepened. "Sounds like my kind of girl."

This time, the pause was awkward.

"Do you like living in the States?" Langston asked.

Cecile felt warm. She wondered about the juxtaposition of the comment with the question, but his voice had gone back to normal.

"It's fine. I could live other places. Toronto is a great city."

"I love it, too. Have you ever thought about moving back to Canada?"

"I'd have to have a job there."

Was he suggesting something? "Besides," she added, "my kids have a father who lives here. It would be a very big step to move them away."

"Especially since you're not divorced."

"Or separated, actually."

There was an opportune knock at Langston's office door. "Cecile?" he said.

"You have to go?"

"I think so."

"Okay. Well, it was nice talking to you."

"I'm glad you found me."

"I am, too. Hey, why did you stop writing?"

"I don't know."

"Really?"

"Really. Listen, I have to go now. I'll talk to you soon, okay?"

"I'd like that."

"Good-bye."

"Bye, Langston."

She felt happy. Happy that he liked her, happier that she liked him. Happy because he was smart and single, and if she finally left Teddy, there was a smart, single man she liked who liked her. She knew he couldn't leave Toronto, she knew she couldn't move to Toronto…or could she?

She wanted to sit down the current version of Cecile and slap some sense into her. One conversation with a man she barely knew in the first place, a man apparently so incapable of love that he hadn't managed it in nearly forty years on earth, and she was fantasizing. Just a little, but it counted.

She took a mental step back and decided to be more clinical. She'd had a pleasant talk with a man about something other than a musical program. So it was still possible. That was all she needed to take from this experience. She knew she would talk to Langston again, but she resolved to cut off their contact if she started liking him too much, praying for discernment about when that fine line was breached.

All friendship is based on personalities that attract, she reminded herself. This is no different. Okay, it's different, but I can handle it.

She turned out her bedside lamp, closed her eyes, and fell asleep smiling.

CHAPTER SIXTY-FIVE

Langston hung up, knowing he'd said too much. Did he really need to ask what she wanted in a man? She'd been right: not a question to ask a married woman, even if she'd asked him a version of the question first. And there had been that one sentence, the one that slipped out without warning: "Sounds like my kind of girl." Completely inappropriate. He wasn't sure how Cecile had taken that. She'd been silent for a moment, but she hadn't seemed upset.

At least he hadn't said some of the other things. She'd asked him if he had a physical ideal, and he hadn't told her she was it. She'd asked if he was hiding something about why he'd never fallen in love, and for the first time in their conversations, he'd lied. More than lied—he'd omitted a crucial truth by not telling her he'd been strangled years ago by the wire in his neck, just before he stopped writing her. Then again, that wound should have healed by now.

He regretted responding to her letter. What was the point? Then again, did there have to be a point?

A well-dressed woman came to the restaurant for lunch at least once a week and flirted with Langston shamelessly. He felt no real chemistry with her, but she had an easy smile. He resolved to ask her out, and to tell Cecile about it. That way, he wouldn't be a single guy calling and receiving calls from an unhappily married woman.

Much ado about nothing, he thought. Even if Cecile and

Teddy split up, she'll never move to Toronto, and I'll never move to the States. And they'd probably never break up, because she seemed to be in the same holding pattern with Teddy that she'd been in for years.

There! He could really enjoy her now. He would still ask the customer out, though, as a buffer against the part of his brain that didn't want to fully grasp the situation.

He realized he hadn't responded to the knocking, and shouted, "Come in!"

The door opened, and Belinda, one of the servers, poked her head inside.

"Langston," she said, "The Walkers are here, and they want to say hello."

"I'm coming."

CHAPTER SIXTY-SIX

For two months, Cecile called Langston every week. The second time, Langston told her he'd asked out Lois, the regular lunch customer from Cimarron. Cecile responded by showing interest and giving suggestions about winning Lois over, until Lois turned out to be unapologetically materialistic and demanding. None of Langston's friends or family members liked Lois either, which was good news, because Cecile had the uneasy feeling that her disapproval came from a jealousy she wasn't willing to admit.

Whenever she talked to Langston, her affection for him felt deeper. He wasn't the man from the letters, it seemed—gone was the disjointed, off-the-wall sense of humor. But he remained even-tempered, level-headed, and a wonderful listener, in a way that put Teddy into stark relief. He didn't attack her or her ideas. He didn't call her names or belittle her. He simply disagreed sometimes, explaining his dissent with clarity, even conceding the point if Cecile had the stronger argument. Cecile struggled not to think about what might have been, trying to focus instead on wishing him peace and joy. With Lois, both seemed like a long shot.

Even though Cecile was guilty of hanging on to an unhealthy relationship for much longer than Langston had, she didn't understand why he refused to cut this woman loose.

"We have fun together" was his explanation, spoken like a protest.

"I might be projecting my situation on yours," Cecile said, "but I really think she's abusive."

Lois had called Langston stupid because he'd missed her hints about wanting a particular designer dress for her birthday. He'd bought her something similar, but much less expensive, and received a barrage of criticism instead of thanks.

"I thought she liked the style," Langston told Cecile. "I didn't think she'd honestly expect me to spend five hundred dollars on a dress. I mean, I probably wouldn't do it even if I could afford it, but after knowing her four months? Don't you think that's a bit much?"

"I don't even understand that thinking," Cecile said. "I guess I wasn't raised that way. I mean, with so many people starving, I can't imagine blowing that kind of money on a single item of clothing. Then again, my wedding dress cost more than that, and I knew I'd only wear it once."

"But a wedding dress is different. This was just a regular dress for work. I guess she saw the money I didn't spend as a measure of how little I care about her, but if that's the case, no poor people love each other."

Cecile laughed. "Yeah, I don't get materialism either," she said. "There are so many things in a relationship that are more important than money and gifts. But I suppose it's about having someone treat you like you're valuable. When Teddy and I first started dating, he'd buy me flowers all the time, but after a while that pretty much stopped. It's cliché, but a single rose or even some daisies were nice. It showed me he was thinking about me, you know? And there's something to be said for having beauty in your life, just because. Wow, that was long-winded."

"I didn't think so. I like to know what you're thinking."

"And what are *you* thinking?"

Langston paused. "Honestly?"

"Yes."

"I'm wondering why you call me all the time, but I can never call you. Does Teddy know we're in touch?"

"Yes." She sounded defensive, but she was telling the truth. She'd mentioned it casually, determined to stay right with both God and herself. She knew she would probably talk less freely if Teddy were in the room, but she was careful not to discuss anything she wouldn't want him to hear, except her descriptions of their relationship, which would be the case even if she were talking to Betsy or Teresa. As many times as she'd confronted Teddy about his inappropriately close relationships with co-workers and clients of the community center, she wasn't prepared to justify his occasional accusations of hypocrisy.

When Teddy asked why he'd never heard of Langston before, Cecile told the truth: she came across the letters and wondered how he was doing. With Teddy's collection of cellphone concubines, it would have been an amazing display of gall for him to question her too much.

"You can call, if you like," Cecile told Langston, trying to assure herself it was okay, cursing the years when her shame about her toxic marriage had led her to cut off all but the most superficial contact with almost everyone, male or female, including her family. "I just figured that since it's free for me to call you, there's no point in spending money on it. But go ahead. You're a rich businessman, anyway."

"Hardly. Anyway, don't get me wrong. I don't mind your calling. I just don't want it to be one-sided. Does that make sense?"

"Sure."

But the first time he called her, she felt nervous. The second time, Teddy picked up the phone, waiting until just after she hung up to interrogate her, admitting he was jealous. *Serves you right,* Cecile couldn't help thinking.

One day, Langston called asking for advice on Lois's latest demand, and Cecile found herself telling him to dump her. It wasn't the first time, although she'd tried to stay out of it, limiting her comments to asking how he felt about things and steering clear of the name-calling she would occasionally like to indulge in at Lois's expense.

This time, though, Cecile realized she wanted Langston to be single again, not so he could meet somebody better, but because if he were unattached maybe he'd be there for her when she finally left Teddy, and they could build a life together, full of mutual respect, reasonable conversations, movies, travel, music, and great food. He could be a true father to her kids.

Maybe she'd even remember how it felt to be physically passionate with another person. Now all her passion was channeled into her music, which wasn't a bad thing, but she still wished she could stop watching romantic movies and have one of those lingering onscreen kisses for herself. From Langston.

When Cecile hung up the phone after doing her best to convince him to break up with Lois, she had an uncomfortable feeling that wouldn't go away. She'd often thought that she would have respected Teddy a lot more if he'd ended their marriage before he started having romantic relationships with other women. Now she understood how it happened. Still, she couldn't allow herself to be a hypocrite, or, even worse, invite the judgment of God.

The next morning, her alarm clock's unwelcome interruption left her desperate to fall back asleep quickly enough to recapture the vision in her mind, but Langston had vanished, and with him, his touch, so substantial that her body was still tingling. She replayed the scene over and over—his face, next to hers, kissing him, like he'd kissed her in the elevator, and then longer, deeper...

She knew what she had to do.

From: Cecilewhite@yahoo.com
To: LAndrews@cimarron.com

Hi Langston,

I'm sorry to do this by email, but I really think I need to stop being in touch with you, at least for a while. I know I'm kind of vulnerable right now, with things so bad with Teddy, and I realize I'm not the person to give you advice about Lois because my motives are mixed. I'm really glad I got to know you again. I think you're a fantastic person.

Take care and God bless,

Cecile

When she saw Langston's email address in her inbox the next morning, her heart stopped for a moment. She opened the message reluctantly:

Dear Cecile,

I'm confused. Are you telling me to go away?

Langston

I'm a bitch.

She didn't want to call him, because she was afraid she wouldn't be able to stand listening to his voice. She couldn't see him in person, though, so that was the best choice available. She took a deep breath and dialed his number.

He wasn't home, of course. He wasn't home later that night, either. With Lois, maybe, she imagined, barely able to stand it. She tried two more times the next day, and then her endurance ran out. The children were in bed, and Teddy was downstairs murmuring sweet nothings into his cell phone. When a recording of Langston's voice invited her to leave a message, she did, with tears in her eyes:

"Hi, Langston. I'm not sure I should put this on your voicemail, but I didn't want to say this to you at work and I never seem to catch you at home. I just wanted you to understand why I can't be in touch for a while. I know you've never said or done anything to make it seem like you wanted to be more than a friend, but I find myself imagining what it would be like if we were together, I mean, really together and committed to each other. I know that isn't very healthy, especially since I'm still married to Teddy. Anyway, I just wanted you to understand if I'm not in touch for a while. I'm sorry about the way I've handled this. Well, good-bye."

She wanted to tell him so many things, but she'd said too much already. She felt a pain in her stomach, because she was sure she had ended the friendship for good. At least there would be no aura of mystery attached this time. After all, how do you relate to someone who has confessed a fantasy that seems to include marriage when you've never even been on a date? Why would Langston want to continue a relationship with somebody so obviously insane? And even if she did leave Teddy, Langston already knew about her past inability to let go completely. Why would he trust that things would be different any time soon?

Maybe it's time to go back to therapy, she thought after she hung up.

I've made progress, she told herself. I know I have.

She didn't despair anymore, but she felt sad. Every step towards the elusive goal of being self-actualized, whatever that meant, was full of struggle and turmoil, and she didn't want to do it just then.

"The Lord is my Shepherd," she said to herself, sitting beside her bed in the pink recliner and gazing at the floor, her stomach awash in acid.

She didn't feel like she was in the valley of the shadow of death. Instead, she focused on an earlier verse: "He restoreth my soul." Then there was the part about being made to lie down in green pastures beside still waters. And the reminder about the rod and the staff. She always thought about a sermon she'd heard in which the preacher had defined what they were for—hooking, rapping on the head—and mentioned that being brought back on track required that sort of treatment. In the end, though, it was comforting to be where you were supposed to be, as opposed to wandering alone in places where wolves lay in wait.

She remembered the time when she'd felt safe wandering even the farthest corners of the garden of her mind, imagining that the freedom she'd felt exploring her passion for Teddy could somehow translate into the strength to defeat every hidden danger.

Wrong. As wrong as her new fixation on Langston.

She didn't want to let go of him. He's an illusion anyway, she reminded herself. A fantasy on which she was projecting her desires.

And he'd never been in love. That included her.

Lord, please help me to let go of Langston, she prayed half-heartedly. At least until I find the strength to leave Teddy.

CHAPTER SIXTY-SEVEN

The night Cecile left her message, Lois insisted on going out after closing. Langston was exhausted, but didn't want to seem selfish, so he complied. He could barely make conversation, which didn't matter, because she was more than willing to fill in the gaps.

He usually didn't mind, because he liked to listen to people, but this time all he could think about, as he watched her gesturing to punctuate the tale of her ne'er-do-well brother's latest fiasco, was the realization that he was going to follow Cecile's advice, and dump her.

Lois wanted to get married—that had been obvious almost from the start. He knew she would keep their house in order, and he could even accept the short leash that would be part of the bargain, but he couldn't imagine being with her ten years in the future. He couldn't even imagine being with her in a year.

Was this Cecile's doing? He couldn't blame her, or if he did, he had to also assign blame to Zora, Marcus, Maya, Glenda, Teresa, and all the lesser confidantes of his life, including his employees. Still, there were things about Lois he enjoyed. She had a confidence, a fire and a sparkle that made her a person to be reckoned with. He always knew exactly where she stood, because she was very clear. Well, mostly—sometimes, she was clearly manipulative.

Her hair was a rich shade of auburn, almost the color of

her skin. The effect was very attractive. She always had her fingernails and toenails done just so, and her makeup was impeccable. She didn't look nearly as good in the morning, but who did? Although if Cecile still looked anything like she did in her old picture, he was pretty certain she was stunning twenty-four hours a day. Or maybe not. He would never know, so why wonder?

What he never had to wonder about was what pleased Lois in bed, because she always gave him reviews, positive and negative. She had all the latest gadgets, and had even bought him a Blackberry, which he continued to leave in places that made him just as unavailable as before. When he did carry it, he conveniently left it off or forgot to charge the battery. She never gave up reminding him to take it with him, though. He knew his passive-aggressive response was cowardly, but it was less trouble than being direct.

Lois had reached the climax of her story. Langston tried to listen, but he was both too tired and too distracted by the thought of breaking up with her. He trained his slightly unfocused eyes on her face, sipping ginger ale through a straw, acutely aware that if he had anything alcoholic he'd fall asleep immediately. When Lois was finally done, he said, "Honey, I'm really, really worn out. Look, I'll call you tomorrow, okay?"

Lois looked offended for a moment. Then she said, "I'm sorry. I just wanted to see you. You've been so busy."

"I stay busy, don't I?"

"You do. To be honest, sometimes I think you're a

workaholic. But then again, I know it's hard to have a business."

"It really is. I promise I'll call you when I wake up."

He rose and kissed her, a peck on the cheek, then walked her to his car. She'd taken the train to Cimarron, insisting that he drive her home. He caught himself drifting into another lane halfway back to his apartment, but he made it. When he walked in he was tempted not to check his messages, but he couldn't resist.

The second voicemail he listened to was from Cecile. He replayed it three times, then sank into his old leather chair, still holding the receiver.

He wanted to tell her he'd never been in love because she'd killed him, or at least the part of him that was supposed to fall in love. He wanted to say that she was wrong: he hadn't been clear that he never wanted her to be more than a friend, because that was a lie. He wanted to tell her he had held her many times, kissed her, not fleetingly, as their only real kiss had been, but slowly, tenderly, deeply, in his imagination. That he hadn't known what to say when she'd revealed her fantasy of their life together, because her vision was excruciating. It awakened something he'd thought was long gone, and whatever it was felt like a shard of broken glass.

He wanted nothing more than to be where he was, once, when he thought his spirit was telling him he could rest secure in the knowledge that he'd found her, that elusive soul companion immortalized in countless songs and poems. But he knew he wasn't that person anymore. He wasn't willing to take the risk.

He couldn't stand the torture then, and he certainly wasn't going to seek it now.

He listened to the message again, a rush of words. She sounded nervous. And sincere.

She likes me, he thought.

It wasn't a revelation, but he was beginning to think she might like him for reasons that would last long after the pain of her failed marriage had faded.

He couldn't stop picturing her face. He used to stare at the 8 x 10 photo she'd sent all the time, until the image had imprinted in his mind so securely that he didn't need to refresh his memory, even after all these years. He didn't even know where it was anymore. He'd ask her for another one, maybe. Oh, right—they weren't going to be in contact anymore.

It was better this way.

He saved her message, and put down the phone. Would it be rude not to reply? She'd said she wasn't going to be in touch for a while, but such a personal message seemed to demand a reaction.

She'd said she needed a break. So he shouldn't respond. But he couldn't sleep.

He went to the restaurant the next day, half-expecting to see her name in his inbox. It wasn't. It wasn't there the day after that, either. After a week, he was used to the idea. He broke up with Lois anyway—the two things were unrelated. He resumed his routine: job, home. Home, job. Occasional rendezvous with a friend or family member.

Simple. Complete. Carved in stone. It was better that way.

CHAPTER SIXTY-EIGHT

The afternoon after leaving her farewell on Langston's voicemail, Cecile sat in the kitchen eating lunch during a break from practicing, waiting for Miranda's receptionist to answer the phone, finally ready to take another step towards the inevitable, if only her therapist could guide her to the place where the kind of courage required to leave your husband was stored.

Glancing at the calendar, she realized Elana had a dental appointment in an hour. She'd forgotten to alert the teacher; now she'd have to call the school and put off working on the Brahms F Minor clarinet sonata for another day. Her long experience of getting music together quickly gave her confidence, mixed with the well-founded fear that this time, she was pushing it too far.

My life is a treadmill, she thought. The house was never really clean, the bills were paid, but one or two were always late, and although she played with great emotion and skill, she was never as well-prepared as she wanted to be. The family ate, but only a very limited repertoire of dishes she could prepare very quickly, punctuated by the occasional pizza. She took Malik and Elana out to a restaurant, movie, or other activity at least once a month, most months anyway, but the rest of the time she was always rushing them here and there, pressuring them to do their homework, practice their instruments, or clean their rooms. And in the midst of her hurricane sat Teddy, parked on the couch playing a video game or talking on his cell phone...the eye of the storm.

Calm. Cool. *Self-centered asshole.*

Miranda once told her he was incapable of seeing her point of view and that narcissism was notoriously hard to treat because of the inherent focus on self.

I can't spend my time blaming him, Cecile decided for the millionth time. He warned me who he was long ago, told me not to marry him in so many ways. I refused to listen.

She prayed for an answer to the question that haunted her daily: is it okay to take my kids away from their dad? They love him, and they will miss him, regardless of how bad our situation is and how little he engages with them. Can I do that to them? It's not their fault our marriage is so crappy. Still, she'd given Teddy enough rope to hang himself, and he's done it over and over. How many times should a man hang himself before he was buried?

She wished she could see what he was doing right then. He was away for a conference—she'd grown so indifferent that she hadn't even bothered to find out where—and she couldn't imagine he would turn down a golden opportunity to cheat. Not that she needed more evidence of infidelity to hold against him.

I have time to do some scales and the slow movement of the Brahms, Cecile decided. Then she'd pick up Elana and go to the dentist. Maybe she'd bring along some of the more recent diaries, too. She'd just flip through randomly. It would give her something to do while she was waiting, since Elana had decided she is too old to have her mother beside her during her dental exam. Maybe the woman in these diaries would show some growth, for a change.

CHAPTER SIXTY-NINE

Convention crowds included those who talked business throughout lunch and dinner, and those who seemed most interested in Cimarron's Island-themed alcoholic drinks. Langston expected someone from the second category when Belinda, a young, curvy Filipina with multiple earrings and a toothy grin, knocked on his office door and informed him that a customer insisted on meeting him. Right now.

Langston sighed. The interruption would take him away from looking over the latest report from his accountant. Then again, he never enjoyed the accounting report, even though the numbers are favorable.

The customer is always right, he thought. Whatever.

Belinda directed him to a group of men—two African American, one white, one East Indian—seated near the bar.

"This is the Mr. Andrews, the owner," she said, then excused herself.

"Is there a problem?" Langston asked.

"No," said one of the black men, the handsomest in the group, in a resonant baritone. "I just wanted to meet you. I mean, any friend of my wife's is a friend of mine."

Langston narrowed his eyes. There was something confrontational about the man's tone. Langston knew Lois wasn't married. Was this a jealous ex-husband? She'd never mentioned one. Besides, he wasn't dating her anymore.

"I'm sorry," said Langston. "I think you might have me

confused with someone else."

"No, because Cecile told me you own a restaurant in Toronto, and this is it."

Langston instantly achieved the black equivalent of turning white as a sheet.

"So you do know my wife." Teddy locked eyes with Langston.

"I met her a long time ago." Langston ended the staring contest, glancing at the glass in front of Teddy. Looked like something from the bar. Great.

"And now you're back in touch." Teddy's tone was still not quite casual. His companions had started nervously exchanging glances.

"Yes," said Langston. With the initial shock gone, the encounter struck him as ridiculous. At least, it would be if Teddy continued with it, because there was definitely nothing going on now, and there never was anything going on before, not as long as Teddy had been anywhere nearby.

So this was Teddy. He was much better looking than Langston, at least in Langston's eyes. Still, he understood why Cecile had gotten tired of him. Dealing with that much swagger every day had to be annoying.

"What brings you to Toronto?" Langston asked.

"Conference of community service professionals." Teddy finally looked away, picking up his drink.

"How was your meal?"

"Don't know. I guess she'll have to bring it before I can

answer that."

Teddy turned toward his companions, and they all laughed.

Langston's ears felt hot. He wanted to punch the guy, but he took a deep breath instead, as quietly as he could. "I see. Well, enjoy your stay in Toronto."

"Oh, I intend to." Teddy's eyes met Langston's again. Belinda returned, carrying a tray, and started setting down the lunch orders in front of the group, saving Teddy's for last. Teddy gave her a sideways glance, surveying her head to toe in an instant. Then he sipped his drink. "Thank you, sweetheart," he said, smirking.

Langston felt his face forming into a frown. "Tell Cecile I said hello," he said, turning away.

"Nice meeting you," said Teddy dismissively.

Back in his office, Langston closed the door behind him, wanting to slam it. This was the piece of shit asshole she chose over him, all those years ago? What the fuck was wrong with her?

He slouched into his chair. *What was wrong with me? Why didn't she want me?*

He remembered being in New York with his Quebecois students and two other chaperones, insisting that they tour Lincoln Center, even though no one else showed any interest. The students were impressed with the fountain, though, along with the chandeliers at the Met, and took many pictures of each other outside Avery Fisher and Alice Tully. A few of them had heard of the Juilliard School, but there wasn't time to do everything, and even though Langston had brought them into the lobby, he lost his nerve about trying to arrange a tour, especially since, by that point, the group had wanted to go somewhere else.

He'd tried not to show up at Cecile's school, hoping to run into her, but he'd done it anyway. Of course, nobody else knew he was humiliating himself, just as they didn't know that the whole time they were in Harlem, he'd kept hoping that she'd emerge from Mimi's, and remember him, and...

Want him. But she wouldn't have done it, because she wanted Teddy.

She used to want Teddy. She didn't want him anymore. She's finally figured it out, Langston thought, but she still won't leave him.

Because it's too late.

He blew air out forcibly, then crossed the room in an instant, grabbed his personal set of knives, bought, or more accurately, earned after he graduated from culinary school near the top of his class, and headed for the kitchen, where he retrieved an order for escovitch fish wrapped in roti, the West Indian version of fish tacos.

He quickly found a red snapper in the box, then announced, "This one's mine."

"Yes, chef," said Nina, the tattooed, blonde Norwegian former model who was his best fish cook, moving aside, and Langston began to slice, removing the bones effortlessly, expertly, the many hours of repetition making every movement meaningful, elegant and economical, like James DePriest, the great African-American conductor whose guest appearance with the Toronto Symphony Grandma Felicia had forced him and his siblings to attend when they were young. His hands knew his knife, his knife knew the fish, and suddenly, his life made sense, no matter what anyone else was doing, or with whom.

When I cook, he thought, I create something that brings pleasure to others. I send a message, and it's accepted with joy. My intentions are understood, and welcomed. As long as I can do that, nothing else matters.

And at that moment, he was right.

CHAPTER SEVENTY

12/10/00

This week, the Spirit said, "Be still and know that I am God." So I sat on my couch (didn't have time, but did it) and He spoke these things.

Wednesday: Lean not on your own understanding.

Thursday: Peace I leave with you...not as the world giveth, give I unto you. Let not your heart be troubled, neither let it be afraid.

Friday: Psalm 23--The Lord is my Shepherd.

Saturday: Psalm 27--"The Lord is my Light," especially "Wait on the Lord, and be of good courage."

As I do therapy to deal with marriage, my childhood, and my own bad choices, I need His help. As I try to remember how to feel deeply in love, I will need to break down my protective walls. I pray that Teddy will come to church with me, and that he will surrender himself to Your will.

I look forward to moving ahead, leaning on Your strength.

#

As she sat in the dentist's office waiting for Elana, Cecile leafed through the rest of the notebook, a prayer and gratitude journal. There were prayers for peace, for a rekindling of love in her marriage, for her children, for financial resources. There were pleas for guidance in dealing with her loneliness. There were prayers for strength and wisdom. For Teddy, and even for his girlfriends, the latter not because Cecile was a saint, but because she'd been advised that this was the best way to alleviate the resentment that gnawed at her constantly.

She had reached the middle of the book when a door opened and Elana emerged, followed closely by her dentist, Dr. Shaw. Cecile closed her diary and tried to smile.

"How do things look?" she asked, rising.

"Very good," said the dentist, a woman around Cecile's age. Cecile couldn't help wondering if she'd fucked up her life, too.

Cecile had come to view internal outbursts of profanity as a sure sign she needed to change her attitude, if not something more concrete. Driving home, she took stock: October of 2005. Elana was 9, Malik was 7, and Teddy was still entangled with other women. Cecile still did most of the work at home. She still prayed for strength and guidance, and she still confessed resentments. And God was telling her...what? She wasn't sure. Till death do you part? The Lord hates divorce? Keep praying for Teddy, and when it all comes together, it will be wonderful?

When she arrived home and discovered that Langston had unexpectedly forwarded her an email ridiculing the Bush administration, she wasn't sure how to react. They hadn't been in contact for two months. What was he up to?

She couldn't quite leave it alone, though, so she sent back a forwarded joke. A week later, he sent her another item, this one serious and thought-provoking, about the war in Iraq. She decided it was okay to be in touch with him like this. The contact was just impersonal enough to be harmless. At least, she thought so. She decided to mention it to Miranda at their next session, to make sure.

"I think he values your friendship" was the assessment. "What do you think about it?"

Cecile considered for a while. "Well," she said slowly, "on one hand, I have to wonder why he's contacting me when I specifically said I needed a break. But on the other hand, I don't have any fantasies about him right now, so maybe it's okay."

They didn't talk about men nearly as much as in their early sessions. Now the topic was usually Cecile's concerns with her children and her career. She looked at life in a much more mature manner, and even took more time for herself. The therapy was going well. In fact, there was only one thing that continually dragged her down. Her marriage.

"Sometimes," Cecile went on, "I find myself imagining how much better off I'd be if I didn't have to think about relationships with men for the rest of my life. Including Langston. Then again, I'll probably find out how that feels if I leave Teddy."

Miranda's forehead creased. "Really?"

"I never learned to play the game," Cecile replied, recalling Teresa's diagnosis right before Cecile's first encounter with Teddy. Then again, I played it perfectly that day, she thought. Hooray.

"So you think that you'll never be in another relationship?" Miranda asked.

Cecile gazed out the window at her favorite tree, the one that always gave her a place to focus when she couldn't say something and look Miranda in the eye at the same time. "I doubt it."

"Why?"

"I just told you." Then, suddenly, Cecile turned her eyes back toward Miranda. "It doesn't matter, though, does it? I mean, why does it matter so fucking much? Why is everybody so concerned about whether or not I have a man who takes me out to dinner or fixes my plumbing or whatever the hell men are supposed to do? Will that make me a whole, legitimate person? All my life, I needed a man to tell me I was okay. The thing is, am I less important as a human because I don't have a man? After all these years of women's rights, and all the rest? I'm okay touching myself if I feel I need to release some stress. Honestly, I do a better job than Teddy has for years. What if a man is just another thing to do, more trouble, someone else to take care of when I barely have the energy to get through the day? Seriously, most marriages suck. Most relationships suck, too. Why..."

Cecile exhaled slowly, then smiled. "Yes, that helped me a lot. Okay, you can get a word in now."

Miranda laughed. "Sure?"

"Sure. I mean, part of what you get paid for is listening, but I'm sort of curious what you'll come up with next."

"Feisty, aren't we? I like that." Miranda leaned back, a smile still playing on her lips, then focused on Cecile, her eyes soft, almost pitying. "There is such a thing as a loving, fulfilling male/female relationship, Cecile. It does exist. Yes, it takes two healthy partners and a lot of work, and if you don't feel like it, of course, you won't have one. The thing is, being a concert pianist is work, too. It's all a matter of priorities. There's nothing wrong with deciding you're okay all by yourself. I just hope that you won't close yourself off completely, because that isn't healthy. I agree, a lot of marriages suck, but not all of them do."

Cecile stared at her hands. Betsy's marriage to Leon, a contractor she'd met at the gym, seemed like a good one, and even Teresa and Edwin, who had never married, seemed to be content living together. "Mine does," she said quietly.

"You can leave him, you know," said Miranda.

"It's not that easy. We have kids."

"True. I'm not going to pretend that the process of being shuttled back and forth between two parents is easy on them, or that they won't have a lot of unanswerable questions about why you can't get back together. They will probably blame themselves, and you will have to reassure them over and over that it isn't their fault. Ask yourself how you think they are better off, though—being in the middle of your marriage and seeing it as normal, or being away from the tension, perhaps seeing you happy with somebody else."

Cecile couldn't answer that. On the way home, she imagined Malik and Elana grown and married to mates as ill-suited to them as she and Teddy had proven to be. All through her practice that afternoon, she couldn't stop thinking about it. Was she hurting them more by staying?

God, why won't you tell me? She tried to be quiet, inside her head, but she couldn't.

The next morning, Cecile called Alberta.

"Hello?"

"Hi Mom. Do you have a minute?" Cecile cradled the phone on her shoulder, taking the clean dishes out of the dishwasher and putting them into the cupboards as she spoke.

"Of course."

"I have a really serious question."

"Okay."

"Do you think God would approve if I left Teddy?"

Her mother paused. "Have you left him?" She sounded relieved.

"Not yet."

Another pause. "I don't want to tell you what to do about something so important—"

Wow. That's a shock.

"—but I've been praying for a while that there will be a peaceful resolution to your situation with Teddy."

Cecile bobbled a coffee mug, then caught it, nearly dropping the phone in the process. She put it in the cupboard, closed the dishwasher, and sat at the kitchen table. She always multitasked during unplanned conversations, but decided to make an exception.

"What does *that* mean?"

"Just that I've been praying fervently for you and the kids...well, for all of you, including Teddy."

"And?"

"What do you mean?"

"Did God tell you anything?" Cecile tapped the fingers of her left hand against her thigh. Sitting still felt unnatural.

"If you want discernment about your situation, Cecile, *you* should pray for it."

"I do," Cecile snapped.

"Then wait on the Lord, and—"

"I've been waiting for years!"

I'm supposed to be healthier than this, she thought, taking a napkin from the holder in the center of the table and wiping her eyes.

"Mom, I'm so tired," she continued, her voice trembling. She couldn't control her tears, so she allowed herself to cry. "I've prayed for strength, and for healing for me and Teddy. I've asked for the will to keep loving him. I'm tired of praying, and I can't love him anymore. There are people who do, no matter what, just like they promised at the wedding, but I can't. I don't want to hurt the kids, Mom. I don't even know what we would do about moving all the stuff I'd need to start over."

"He should be the one moving!"

"He won't, not unless I fight him in court, and I don't have the money, the time or the energy for that."

Cecile blew her nose, trying to calm down by gazing at the print of a painting by Jacob Lawrence from his Great Migration series that hung in the dining room, just beyond where she was sitting. She'd bought it because of the two signs above the heads of the dark-skinned figures in bright coats streaming towards what she guessed to be train platforms: Chicago and New York. Looking at the print always reminded her of her father's parents, and, as a result, her dad.

"I have so much to be thankful for," Cecile said. "I shouldn't complain, right? I should just count my blessings, right?" She felt utterly defeated.

"You should always count your blessings," her mother said, "but that doesn't mean you should spend your life in misery. The Israelites were delivered from Egypt, you know."

Cecile smiled. "How many years did that take?"

"More than it would have if they hadn't been so disobedient."

"So I'm being punished."

"For what?"

Cecile couldn't tell her mother about her guilt over having sex with Teddy before they were married, even now. "I'd rather not say."

Her mother's voice softened. "Well, whatever you did, I think you've paid enough, don't you? We all fall short, sweetheart. God corrects His children, but He also shows them mercy."

"What about the wages of sin?" Cecile closed her eyes. She wanted to believe she deserved better—part of her believed it, but she couldn't convince the rest of her.

"But the rest of the verse says that the gift of God is eternal life in Christ Jesus our Lord. Is that why you've put up with Teddy all these years? You thought you were supposed to let him kill your spirit?"

Cecile didn't have an answer. More tears formed in her eyes and rolled silently down her cheeks. She wiped them with a fresh napkin. The concept sounded ridiculous.

"Cecile, my precious child, the fruit of the Spirit includes peace and joy. God is a heavenly Father. What kind of father wants his children to live in constant degradation? There are rules and consequences, but they aren't to keep you down. They're to set you free."

Cecile sighed. "How can I be sure that what I'm doing is what God wants, and not just what I want? Sometimes He has a purpose I don't understand."

"When your actions are approved by the Lord," said her mother, "you'll feel a peace that passes all understanding. Stop trying to figure out what you're supposed to do and let the Spirit guide you. I know you've tried, but I really believe that if you stop debating the pros and cons, you'll get a clear answer. Listen with your heart, sweetheart, not your brain."

Cecile wiped her eyes one more time, feeling stronger. "Thanks, Mom," she said. "I love you."

Two days later, going downstairs for a late-night snack, she overheard Teddy caressing someone with his voice and saying the unmistakable words, "I love you, too."

Cecile stopped on the steps, leaning against the wall, trying to recover enough from the oak tree that had fallen on her head to catch her breath. When she finally reached the living room, Teddy, who was stretched out on the couch, startled. She sat on the floor in front of him, waiting for him to hang up the phone.

"I think we need to separate," she said, and as soon as the words left her mouth, she felt lighter.

"Do you mean that?"

"I really do." She managed, with great effort, to maintain a straight face.

Every other time she'd threatened divorce, she'd been hysterical, so he'd never taken her any more seriously than she took herself. He sat up.

"What about Malik and Elana?"

"I'll take them with me. Don't fight me, Teddy. You know you'll lose."

"They'll miss their daddy."

"You can see them regularly. I'm not trying to stop that. I just don't want to pretend we're married anymore."

Teddy stared into space. "We can get counseling."

"Again? It's too late, Teddy. It's dead."

He looked at her now, intently. "So you don't love me anymore?"

Cecile didn't hesitate. "No." She felt compelled to soften the blow, adding, "I'll always care about you. But I don't love you anymore."

"Can you look me in the eye and say that?"

She allowed herself to grin. "Wow, you are amazing. You think you're so damn handsome that focusing on your face will change my mind?"

Her place on the floor in front of the couch put her at eye level with Teddy. She gazed directly at him, as she had so many times before, although this time it wasn't to drink in his beauty, or even to try to read his mind. She didn't care what he was thinking, and his looks were irrelevant.

"I'm not in love with you, Teddy. I tried, God knows I tried to keep loving you. I prayed on my *knees* to stay in love with you, but I couldn't do it. And considering the fact that you just told somebody else you loved her—that was a female on the phone, right? Anyway, I'd say it's a good thing I don't love you, wouldn't you?"

Teddy smirked. "Ha, ha, Cecile. That could have been my mother, bitch."

Cecile nodded, standing. "You're calling me a bitch? Wow. Yeah, let's stay married. There's so much to work with."

Teddy looked down. "I'm sorry," he said, as she turned to leave.

Cecile stopped. "Uh-huh." She struggled not to unleash a torrent of verbal abuse, the kind girls raised in the suburbs of Canada weren't supposed to be fluent in. Then she noticed that he was actually shedding tears. She felt no sympathy, just fascination. And awkwardness.

"I can't blame you for leaving," he said. "I've treated you like shit. You deserve a lot better." He looked up, wiping his eyes.

Crocodile tears. Somehow, his admission only made her

angrier. "You're right, I do," she said coldly. "I have a question, though. If you know you've been treating me like shit, why have you been doing it?"

Teddy gazed at his hands, then into Cecile's eyes. "Because I could, I guess. I don't know. Maybe I didn't think you'd leave. I know I don't want you to leave now, even though I understand it."

She rolled her eyes. "I don't care what you want."

Teddy's face hardened. "That's not surprising, since you've never cared about what I want. And forget about what I need."

Her anger rose again. "What the…" She paused, taking a deep breath. *Lord Jesus...*"What do you mean?"

Teddy sat up very straight. "You promised to be there for me, Cecile. I asked only one thing from you, but I still ended up being the last thing on your list."

"I could say the same thing."

"Yeah? All the hours I bust my ass providing for you and the kids, and you can say that? You've got balls, Cecile."

Nothing he said hurt her even slightly. It was truly over. She wanted to dance. "I appreciate that you provide for us, Teddy, but for me, showing love is more than just giving me money. Look, you may be right. Pleasing you used to be the first thing on my mind, and it isn't anymore. The problem is, the way you chose to handle it means I'll never trust you again. I'm lucky you didn't give me a disease." He opened his mouth, but before he could speak Cecile said, "There's nothing you can say to change my mind. We had almost twenty years to get it right, and we didn't. It's too late."

Teddy turned away, then looked at her imploringly. "What happened to us? We used to have something really special, Cecile. Do you remember?"

She frowned, but then her face softened a bit. "I do," she said. "But that was long ago, Teddy. Our relationship was sick before we even got married. You were right—we never should have done it. I'm sorry I pushed you."

Teddy sat silently for a long time. Finally, he cleared his throat. "I'm not moving out," he said.

"Then I will."

"When?"

"First of the year. That way the kids can have the holidays, and the next time we have holidays they'll have settled in."

Teddy's voice was quiet. "It's going to hurt them."

"We're already hurting them by exposing them to this."

She turned and walked into the kitchen, suddenly thirsty. Teddy came up behind her as she took a carton of orange juice out of a fridge, and leaned in close.

"Should we make love one more time?" he said in her ear. "For old time's sake?"

Cecile wrinkled her nose with disgust. "Absolutely not. Excuse me."

She took a glass from the cupboard and filled it with juice, her hands shaking, then returned the carton to the fridge, drank quickly, and put the glass in the dishwasher.

"Good night," she said.

Teddy paused. "Good night, Cecile," he replied softly. "I'm sorry."

She restrained an urge to say, 'whatever,' choosing, "Uh-huh," instead, then stepping around him and heading back to her bedroom. She heard his voice stroking his cellphone before she got to the top of the stairs.

CHAPTER SEVENTY-ONE

Two weeks before she moved, Cecile sat at the computer in her bedroom after her children were asleep and wrote Langston an intensely personal email. She asked him what he'd meant when he asked if she'd ever move back to Canada. Why he'd said she was his kind of girl when she told him all she wanted was a man who would be nice to her. Was he ever interested in her as more than a friend?

Then she began to doubt her mission.

He's not moving anywhere, and neither am I. I have to take care of myself and my kids, by myself. Nobody else will take care of me. He's no exception.

She re-read the email, thinking, maybe we can still be in touch sometimes, but Langston doesn't love me—he said he's never been in love with anyone. Why mess up the occasional pleasant interaction by asking all these desperate questions?

She hadn't heard from Langston in nearly three weeks, not even a forwarded joke. She knew he was very busy, but if he really cared, wouldn't he at least do that much? It didn't matter what the reasons were.

Cancel. The message disappeared.

CHAPTER SEVENTY-TWO

In late January of 2006, with the gap in Langston and Cecile's correspondence going on a month, he sent her a brief email, just checking in.

The weather outside was freezing, and he missed her. Glenda was getting married in April, but that wasn't the reason, he decided. Sitting at his desk at Cimarron on a snowy Tuesday morning, he read her response to his casual question about how she was doing, three times.

Dear Langston,

I'm doing very well. The kids are adjusting, but I think they'll be fine. I moved out about two weeks ago, and we're still getting things together, but I feel truly blessed because we're in the same school district, so the kids don't have to deal with changing schools on top of their parents separating.

Teddy made one last bid for us to stay together, but really, I don't know what he thinks our relationship could be like, after all this. Something out of *Pet Sematary*, maybe (yup, that's how it's spelled). Have you seen it? It's a pretty lousy film based on a Stephen King story about pet owners who can't bear to part with their dead cats and dogs, so they bury them in an old Indian burial ground (or something) and the pets come back to life, only distorted. Meaning they're alive, but they look like they did when they were dead, and they have issues as a result. You get the idea.

How are you and Lois doing? How are things at

Cimarron? I hope you're not working too hard.

If you're wondering, I feel so much better now. I'm really happy, for the first time in a long time. I know I needed to feel like I'd tried, that I'd given it all I had, but I didn't have anything left and God gave me peace about leaving. It's great to come home and not feel that tension anymore, you know? It's not going to be easy, and I know that the true test of my new-found joy will come in a few months, but for right now, I feel so free.

Gotta run.

Take care and God bless,

Cecile

Langston hadn't come in early, so he wouldn't have time to respond until much later. Should he try to call her? Offer his condolences in a letter? She didn't seem to need them.

He couldn't believe she'd actually moved out. Did this mean it was finally over with Teddy?

Maybe, maybe not, he thought. Remember, you met her when she'd called off her engagement to that jerk, and look where she ended up. In a 15 year marriage, with kids. And leaving him meant she'd be looking for someone to lean on. She was going to be needy, and in danger of rebounding.

As soon as the lunch rush ended, he wrote back:

Dear Cecile,

I'm glad you're happy with your decision. I know you guys have been through a lot, so I know it wasn't easy for you. I also know it's hard for Elana and Malik. You're a strong woman with faith in God, so I'm sure you'll be okay.

Cimarron is doing very well, actually. I think we might even be trendy, which is kind of funny since I'm the farthest thing from trendy myself.

I broke up with Lois a long time ago. I realized I wasn't in love with her and that it wasn't going to work. She really wanted to get married, so it didn't seem fair to waste her time.

All best wishes to you, Cecile. I'm sure you did the right thing.

Cheers,
Langston

If she's really done with Teddy, he thought, maybe we can finally find out…what? And how? She'd just moved. She wasn't going to uproot her kids again.

He could try to move to the States, but what would happen if they didn't work out? Could he even begin to recover from giving her that much of himself, being rejected and having to either live the rest of his life far away from his family or crawl home to Toronto looking like a fool?

He resolved to look into buying a house. That way, he wouldn't be tempted to try to duplicate Cimarron's success somewhere else.

CHAPTER SEVENTY-THREE

Four months after Cecile and Teddy's separation, Langston and Cecile remained in touch, but the contact was measured in weeks, rarely days. She'd hoped the news of Teddy's departure would change something, that Langston would confess to feeling something special when he spoke to her, at the very least. But he didn't.

Langston did ask, in every conversation, if Cecile had divorced Teddy yet. She hadn't. Too expensive, and trying to figure out their assets seemed too much, and she didn't have time, and it didn't seem as important as a lot of other things in her life.

She was the only parent taking the kids to their after-school activities, and when Malik started showing signs of having anger issues, she added to her schedule by rushing him into therapy. Then Elana started showing signs of depression, so she started therapy, too. Besides, Cecile was insured through Teddy's job; she couldn't afford to pay for health insurance on her own. So a holding pattern set in, her early euphoria about moving out waned, but no matter what, she knew she would never go back. Anything she was going through was better than what she'd left behind.

Besides, Langston had bought a house in Toronto. Since the kids constantly wanted more time with their increasingly elusive father, Cecile knew she couldn't make things even harder by leaving town permanently herself. She'd decided to promote herself more, so she could make more money and maybe be able to file for divorce. That meant more performances, which meant more babysitters, which had made her kids even clingier.

The weekend of her first out-of-town concert after the separation, Teddy told her he wasn't available, forcing her to ask people from her church to help. While she was away, Elana called in tears because she missed her mommy so much. Then Malik didn't speak to Cecile for the first few hours after she returned.

Her next engagement away from home was too lucrative to pass up, so she called Teddy, who wasn't free that weekend, either. This time she lined up a parade of babysitters, which cost her a bundle—she thanked God for the lady from her church who volunteered to stay overnight. Cecile prayed that Elana would make it through more emotionally intact than the last time, and that Malik, having been better prepared for her absence, wouldn't hurt her with his silence upon her return. She knew not to blame them, but she still felt stressed out as she left for the airport at 5:00 a.m., too early for a proper goodbye. She kissed her kids as they lay in bed, gave instructions to the sitter, and hurried out the door.

Cecile fell asleep the moment the plane took off and woke up almost at her destination. Through the window, she saw the turquoise ocean she'd remembered, water so clear the bottom was visible even from high in the air. She gazed out the window at seaweed beds, uninhabited rocks, and then the island of Bermuda itself, dotted with pastel houses with white roofs made of limestone, which purified the rainwater before it was collected in tanks. Rain was the only source of drinking water; the island had no freshwater streams or lakes.

The plane touched down. Soon, Cecile's cousin Dante would pick her up—she was there to do a concert to benefit his church, as she did every few years.

Cecile liked going to Bermuda to perform, even if there was never time for fun. This time, though, her body slumped of its own volition. She was on the island doing what she did best, but making her career lucrative would require more practice, more time away from the kids, and more money to invest in self-promotion. She needed to get a website, but she didn't know how to create one, making the idea either too expensive or too time consuming. This concert should help, but she'd had car trouble lately, which would cost at least $500 to repair. She should have made Teddy take the kids, but he was working all weekend, and she didn't feel like dropping her children off to bond even more with the latest girlfriend, Martha, who was all of twenty-two.

Teddy had met Martha—a petite blonde, cute, with an arrogant air—when she was volunteering at the center six months earlier, in the summer. The kids liked her, as they had liked Teddy's two covert girlfriends, whom they'd met when Teddy had taken the kids and the mistress on outings together. He'd explained by saying he'd invited a friend along, because Cecile was busy and he needed help with the kids.

The passengers were deplaning. Cecile gathered her

things and perched on the armrest of the seat next to the aisle, waiting for it to clear. A small boy of about two, with dark hair and blue eyes, stood ahead of her, staring back. She wanted to smile at him, because she felt she should smile at all innocent youngsters. Ugly churl, her brain kept saying, even as she forced the corners of her mouth to rise. She looked away, disgusted, knowing she couldn't pass harsh judgment on little kids unless something was rotting deep inside her.

She moved forward, awash in pessimism. Her mother had told her many times to visualize what she'd like, to ask her Heavenly Father, who was rich, for everything. She couldn't make herself believe it was so easy. Did the starving of Africa simply lack imagination? It was her contention that God did what He wanted with a higher purpose in mind, making no guarantee of individual happiness. Why would Paul need to mention being content in all circumstances, including great want, if the anointed were supposed to always live in comfort? Did the great Apostle simply neglect to ask the Universe to spare him his various floggings?

The entrance hall in the Bermuda airport smelled of the island's native cedar. Four middle-aged men in floral shirts and Bermuda shorts (of course)—a singer, a guitarist, a drummer, and an electric bass player—serenaded arriving travelers with the infectious rhythms of calypso. Cecile always found the musical greeting both funny and ironic, since Bermudians were very quick to mention that they weren't part of the Caribbean, a factual statement, but also a reminder of their longstanding self-perception as inherently superior to West Indian blacks, an attitude Cecile hoped was finally dead. Still, Bermudians knew where their bread was buttered, so if tourists seeking a warm-weather getaway expected black people playing tunes from Jamaica and Trinidad, that was what they'd get.

Cecile moved through customs quickly, collected her suitcase from the carousel, and joined the slow-moving line of travelers leaving the baggage-claim area. Her cousin Dante saw her and waved. He was short, fat, and balding, with light skin and green eyes. There were a lot of Bermudians with light skin and green eyes, particularly in St. David's, the part of the island closest to the airport. Every time she visited, Cecile imagined herself blending right in, if only she could bring herself to buy colored contact lenses.

The high incidence of light skin in St. David's was allegedly the result of intermarriage. With a population of approximately 65,000, many people in Bermuda were related in some way, although the St. David's Islanders apparently took it a step further than most, for a while.

"How are you?" said Dante, taking her bag.

"Fine," Cecile lied, and they started walking towards his car. She nearly got in on the driver's side but remembered, just in time, that Bermuda was still a British colony, and followed the same rules of the road.

They talked about her flight, his kids (now grown), her kids, the advertising for the concert. Dante took her to ZBM, the national TV station, to do an interview, and then to lunch at The

Pickled Onion. The name of the restaurant and bar was a joke; Bermudians sometimes called themselves "onions," after the Bermuda onion, and "pickled" meant inebriated. The Pickled Onion, one of the few places open between the traditional lunch and dinner times, overlooked the harbor on Front Street, a docking spot for cruise ships and a good place to buy expensive clothes, jewelry, and perfume.

Cecile gazed at the water and the hills behind it, dotted with palm trees and houses painted mango, cerulean and lime.

"Do you ever get used to all this beauty?" she asked.

"No," said Dante in his booming bass voice, "but whenever I leave the island and come back, I always appreciate it even more."

Four young white people, whom Cecile assumed to be tourists, sat at the next table. She felt a deep pang of longing. To have money to come here, eat delicious food in expensive restaurants (because everything in Bermuda was expensive, by Cecile's standards), stay in a fancy hotel…

But it wasn't the fancy hotels she envied. More than anything, Cecile wanted to spend time on a beach. She hated the sun, but she loved the sound of the ocean and the feel of the sand on her feet.

"Can I walk to the water from where you live?" she asked. Her cousin had recently been reassigned, so this house would be unfamiliar.

"Sure. St. John's Park is five minutes away."

"I think I'll go there tomorrow."

"Did you bring your suit?"

Cecile cringed in mock horror. "I'm no tourist," she said. The temperature was in the mid 70's, typical for April, but she knew the protocol. She wasn't sure which holiday marked the unspoken beginning of the swimming season, but she knew it had yet to arrive. Besides, the water wasn't particularly warm at this time of year.

"You can still swim," Dante said with a smile.

"I just want to sit by the ocean."

"I can show you how to get there when we get back to the house."

They talked about Teddy. Dante was old school, believing that once you make the vow, that's it, even if there's physical abuse, because the Lord will either give you strength to endure, change your spouse's heart, or give you eternal life if your husband kills you. Cecile politely refused to debate him, saying that she'd prayed about the situation every day, and only left when she felt a deep peace. Her explanation wasn't quite good enough for Dante, but he let it go.

After dessert, he paid the bill, and they walked back to his car. He stopped to pick up his wife on the way home— Bermudians are only allowed one car per household, due to the lack of space on the island, unless one person drives a taxi—and then made his way through the narrow labyrinth of streets until he reached their house. Dante showed Cecile to her room, where she deposited her bags.

She closed the French doors that separated Dante's living

room from the rest of his house and spent the next three hours practicing on his baby grand piano. The music refused to speak to her, but she went through the motions as best she could, her mind wandering, missing notes, having little memory lapses, trying her best not to cry. By the time dinner was ready, her right hand had started aching, because she'd practiced with tense shoulders. She ate Bermuda lobster, farine pie, and salad with Dante and his wife, took some ibuprofen, then asked to borrow the phone to call Malik and Elana, and the computer to check email.

She was very relieved to find no one in tears when she called home to say goodnight. Her inbox was full: forwarded messages from friends and her parents, a note from Betsy wishing her good luck, which touched Cecile deeply. Her sister didn't often make those sorts of gestures, but maybe their two-minutes-and-gone phone calls had conveyed how close to the edge Cecile was. She skimmed the names attached to the unopened mail. No note from Langston. She'd written him about her situation, but evidently he didn't care.

Never had, probably. Cecile had hoped that, once she left Teddy, there would be evidence that Langston was more than a "might-have-been" who never was, pressed into another role by her imagination because she couldn't stand admitting to herself that Teddy was all she'd ever had, with nobody waiting in the wings.

I've heard good things about eHarmony, she thought...nah, I'd screw it up. Langston liked me once, many years ago, when I couldn't see him because my eyes refused to focus on anybody but Teddy. And now Langston sees me too clearly—a damaged, bitter, needy woman.

She had reached the point in her pity party where some cold reality was able to intervene. The truth was, she didn't want just anybody. Most men didn't affect her much, these days, but Langston's voice was like Valium to her. Not just his voice, but the essence of the person behind it.

It didn't matter now. Cupid wasn't a good enough marksman to pierce both hearts at the same time. Who could have accomplished such an impossible task? Maybe William Tell, but he was long dead.

Cecile turned off the computer, went to bed and finally allowed herself to cry.

The next morning, she ate a quick breakfast of toast and fruit, then walked to the beach, which was small and wonderfully unpopulated. She sauntered across the sand, slipped off her shoes and waded just in reach of the surf. The sand was pink—up close she could see the rosy flecks of broken shells mixed in with the white. She wanted to take some home, but she hadn't brought a bottle, just a book. There was very little shade and no good places to sit, so she wandered to the far end of the beach, where the sun hadn't risen high enough to dispel the shadows, making do with a rock until her bottom started to feel numb.

The rumble and whoosh of the surf and the salty smell of the ocean soothed her. The sky was blue, the water, turquoise, the palm trees, green and brown. Everything was all right. She exhaled deeply, at rest for the first time in longer than she could remember.

Let go, the voice inside her said, so she did, with one finger, then another. She let go of the fantasy Langston and embraced the real one. He had never tried to visit her, or suggested that she visit him. He didn't care enough about her to call or write more than sporadically. But why? He seemed to like her, or something more than like her, at times. Why didn't he truly care about her?

Suddenly, it rose to her conscious mind, this truth she had tried to deny. Langston couldn't care. He and Teddy were flip sides of the same coin in this crucial regard: Teddy was eternally searching for a woman to heal his lostness, unable to commit because of the inevitable disappointment that each female's humanity provoked, and Langston was unwilling to investigate the full range of human emotion for fear of the same disappointment.

Just like me, she realized. I can't chase him, though. I shouldn't have to, and besides, he's too far away to chase. If we were really going to be together, we would have seen each other in person at least once by now. I can't afford a plane ticket, and I'm not going to beg him to buy one.

Cecile watched the waves advance and retreat, feeling her grasp let go completely. She hadn't brought a watch, but the sun had climbed higher, so she knew it had to be late. She had to practice at the hall before the concert, eat, nap, and change into her evening gown. The tide had come in somewhat, and although the rocks where she'd been sitting were still dry, little pools had formed below them. She splashed through the chilly water for as long as she could. The gentle waves felt much more pleasant than the sand would once it had stuck to her feet.

Should have brought a towel, she thought, trying to scrape the sand off her skin with the bottom of a sneaker. It was okay, though. Everything was okay, and the concert would be okay, too.

Strolling back to Dante's, she was struck again by the beauty around her—the sweetly intense fragrance of deep pink and white hibiscus, leaves of dark green peeking over the low stone walls that lined the narrow streets.

I'm here, she thought. And God is restoring my soul, even though the water I just walked beside is anything but still. He always provides. Like He provided this concert. She thought of all the times she'd received a call for extra work just when she needed money, and the other performances she hadn't really had time to prepare for that gotten canceled.

I've been blind, she realized. All these years of praying, and I haven't truly been grateful, or trusted God. And God looked after me anyway, despite my bad decisions, and He keeps trying to teach me things, even though I'm too hardheaded to learn them. And He has something in mind for me, if I just follow the path where He is trying to lead me.

She knew she had no more control over most things than she did over the ocean, but it didn't matter. She wasn't sure why, but she trusted the One who was in control. For real, now, not just in theory, and that made all the difference.

CHAPTER SEVENTY-FOUR

Glenda's wedding reception was held at Cimarron. She'd made Langston swear not to do anything but eat, but he got around her edict by leaving very specific instructions and supervising whenever she turned her back. Which was a lot, because Glenda and her new husband, Dillon, celebrated their union to the hilt, dancing with equal enthusiasm to Irish reels and reggae.

Dillon's presence in Glenda's life came as an unexpected, wonderful gift. Glenda and her previous serious boyfriend, Jason, had seemed inevitable until, after five years of living together, Jason fell in love with a man. Seeing his best friend with her heart torn out caused Langston almost as much pain as Glenda, so watching her sparkle again gave him the kind of joy he hadn't experienced in a long time.

Every morning for the first week after Jason moved out, Langston knocked on Glenda's door at 6:30 in the morning to make sure she got out of bed. He'd tried to get her to cancel her dermatology appointments, but she'd refused. She'd also refused his offer to come and stay with him, insisting that everything was okay despite being unable to put two coherent sentences back to back.

By the time they arrived at her office, Glenda had always

composed herself enough to get through the day, but Langston made her receptionist take her home, commissioning their mutual connections to drop in with food from his restaurant at night.

After ten days as Glenda's caregiver, Langston was about to leave his house to pick her up for work when the phone rang. He debated answering it, then decided the caller must have had urgent business to bother him at that hour of the morning.

"Yes?"

"Hey, Andrews," said Glenda drowsily.

He smiled with relief. She hadn't called him by his last name since the breakup. "I'm coming."

"No, you're not. Listen, I understand why you'd want to see me in my nightgown whenever you can, but you're like my brother. It's a bit creepy, you know?"

He laughed, surprised by the moisture in his eyes. "Hi, Glenda." he said. "I'm glad you're back."

"I love you, Langston. Thank you."

"You're welcome."

Glenda met Dillon three months later, at a Raptors game. She'd given tickets away as a promotion to new clients, saving a block for herself and her employees. Dillon and his brother, who were cheering for the Knicks, sat beside them. They talked trash until the intermission, when he bought her a hot dog and some beer. By the end of the game, he'd learned a lot about Jamaica, and she about Ireland, but neither was sure of the score until the final buzzer reminded them about basketball.

"I'm going to hook you up with somebody at this wedding," Glenda informed Langston, supervising the fitting of his tuxedo, "if it's the last thing I do."

"Because?"

"You should fall in love. It's great. It might not last forever, you could get hurt, yeah, I know. But so what, Langston? I mean, really, it's gotten ridiculous."

The tailor, a balding Asian man named Mr. Chin who was a friend of Glenda's parents, motioned for Langston to turn around, nodded approvingly, then turned to Glenda.

"What do you think?" he said.

Glenda looked at Langston's reflection in the three-way mirror, and grinned. "Amazing. Somehow, you've made him handsome."

Langston scrutinized himself. She was joking, of course. Then again, maybe not. He didn't enjoy being so formally dressed, but he had to admit, he looked suave. Or something.

"Okay, Glenda," he said. "Find me the perfect woman."

Her eyebrows shot up. "Seriously?"

"Why not? Although I still don't see why everybody thinks being single is a disease."

The tailor chuckled. "I've been divorced for years," he said. "I love the freedom. Nobody telling me what to do. It's a beautiful thing." He and Langston slapped palms.

Glenda glared. "Thanks, Mr. Chin."

"Don't get me wrong," Mr. Chin continued, helping Langston out of his jacket, "weddings are beautiful, too.

Marriages, not so much, most of the time. Yours will be different, of course."

"That's right," said Glenda firmly. "Besides, I'm not trying to get Langston married. Just to fall in love. Baby steps."

Watching Dillon and Glenda laughing together, Langston believed her assessment of her chances for a beautiful marriage. They hadn't grown up with each other, as he and Glenda had, but he knew he'd lost his status as her primary confidante, and she, most likely, as his.

Maybe not. Dillon was completely at ease in his own skin, which meant Langston didn't threaten him at all. In fact, Dillon was an unusually great guy in general. He loved teaching because he loved the students, finding their personality quirks interesting. He enjoyed explaining things in a way that inspired and entertained, and seemed undaunted when some in his class didn't understand the concepts; to Dillon, such things were a challenge, not an annoyance. Then again, he taught at a major university, not in a speck on the map with rampant unemployment, and the problems that go with it.

I'm not jealous, Langston told himself. He teaches, I run a restaurant. He's white, I'm black. He was meant to be Glenda's husband, I was meant to be her friend. We're just different.

He assumed the fact that he'd never fallen in love with Glenda to be the reason she'd chosen her polar opposite as his potential love interest. Jessica, the bridesmaid Langston paired up with as they left the church, seemed quiet, polite, and elegant, with chin-length dark brown hair and eyes the color of sapphires.

Dillon's cousin on his mother's side, Jessica owned a spa, which lead to talk about the ups and downs of entrepreneurship.

Her initial quietness wasn't the same as shyness, as it turned out. Jessica liked to dance, and she also liked to drink, although not in a way that caused her to embarrass herself. She was the kind of person who enjoyed both work and play, and knew when it was time for each.

"Did you notice we're the only two single people in the wedding party?" she said, standing beside Langston as they watched Dillon and Glenda serving each other wedding cake— Cimarron's signature rum cake in three layers, decorated with coconut butter cream icing and edible flowers.

Langston smiled. "Funny how we ended up sitting beside each other."

Jessica shook her head. "My family is all over me about being single. Yours?"

He glanced at her. "Like it's a crime."

She linked her arm in his. "So we're partners in crime already, even though I just met you?"

He held her eyes this time. She had a rosy complexion and a strong, square jaw, softened by the bottomless blue of her eyes and the dimple that decorated her left cheek whenever she smiled.

"Seems that way."

"What's your story?"

"I'm still writing it."

She rolled her eyes, grinning. "Good answer. I mean, why

you're single." She leaned against him for a moment as she said it, then away, her arm still entwined with his.

"Never found the right person. You?"

"Do you want the truth?"

"Unless you can make up a really interesting lie."

She laughed, turning towards him and pushing him gently away.

"Are you making a crack about my Irish heritage?"

Langston grinned. "Never crossed my mind. Are you?"

She leaned closer to him. "You're funny. And not because I'm a bit drunk."

"Thanks. So are you. But you didn't answer me. Which seems unfair, since you raised the topic."

"True." She was talking directly into his ear, so close to him that he could have kissed her, if he'd wanted to. He decided he would, but first, he wanted her to answer the question.

"I'm too much woman for most men," she said, pulling away. "It bothered me for a while, but now I just see it as a way of weeding out the weak."

Langston laughed. "I believe you."

His eyes followed her index finger as she traced a line from her chin to the top of her chest, frowning. "It's annoying as hell. Men are so easily intimidated. And that's before they know I get bored quickly." Her eyes twinkled with amusement. "Are you scared?"

He recalled reading similar words in a letter from Cecile, but the memory was objective, for once.

"Why, do I seem weak?" he said, enjoying the game.

"I'm not sure," she replied. The newlyweds were posing for pictures with the people at a table near the window. She glanced at them, then held his eyes resolutely. "Your restaurant has a back room, right?"

He hadn't seen that coming, and yet, he wasn't surprised. He liked Jessica's style. Lois was equally assertive, but Jessica was playful, too. His heart started racing as he imagined having sex with her against the wall behind his desk. He looked in the direction of his office, quickly realizing there was no way to get there without passing the kitchen. *Shit.*

"It does," he said. "Near a room full of people who need to respect their boss tomorrow."

"Ah." She grinned. "I didn't think of that."

"So am I weak?" He wasn't concerned, one way or the other. He liked her, knew she liked him, but he was also pretty sure she did this sort of thing a lot.

She shook her head, still smiling. "And to prove it, I'm going to give you my number."

"How do you know I want it?"

"Because I know."

She extracted a business card from her evening bag, putting it in the front pocket of his tuxedo pants. Then she turned, just at the moment that Glenda and Dillon arrived beside her, and threw her arms around her cousin's neck.

Glenda pulled Langston aside. "Well?" she asked eagerly.

"She's interesting."

"I knew it."

Glenda turned toward Jessica, who hugged her as Dillon smacked Langston on the back and said, "Having fun?"

"Definitely."

After the reception was over, Langston asked his staff to take care of the cleanup, following Jessica to her downtown highrise. As soon as the door closed behind her, she pinned him against the wall, not bothering to turn on the light. At first, he thought they were going to have sex right there, fulfilling his fantasy from the reception. Instead, she took his hand and lead him through the darkness, laughing at him when he nearly tripped over her cat.

He was only mildly surprised that she had handcuffs, which he declined, tying her to the bedpost with two silk scarves instead. The experience was intense, but never quite serious. He was glad she hadn't asked him to do anything more than restrain her. If she'd wanted to be hit, he would have been happily labeled boring and discarded.

He woke the next morning to the smell of coffee and bacon, and wandered into the kitchen in his tuxedo pants.

Jessica was at the stove, wearing shorts and a t-shirt, her braless state very obvious as she turned towards him.

"Good morning," she said. "Scrambled eggs?"

"Thank you." He kissed her cheek, then sat at the table, already set for two.

"Do you have to work today?"

"Afraid so."

"When?"

He glanced at the clock on the oven. "A couple of hours. But I should go home and change my clothes first."

She placed a plate of food in front of him. "Why? Too good for a walk of shame?"

He laughed. "Something like that."

She fixed a plate for herself and sat across from him.

"Who's Cecile?" she asked casually, picking up her fork.

He stared at her. "What?"

She chewed some bacon and sipped her coffee. "You talk in your sleep. Do you want to know what you said?"

He focused on his breakfast. All at once, he'd lost his appetite. "Not really. But you're going to tell me anyway, aren't you?"

She laughed so hard that she snorted. "I'm sorry," she said. "You're just too perfect for me, you know that? Men who'll give me a hard time are rare."

Is that who I am? Langston thought. Only with Jessica. And Anthea. And maybe Marietta. Hmm...

He wondered what Jessica would do if he treated her gently. Probably get bored. She intrigued him enough to want to find out.

"So anyway, who is Cecile?"

"Someone I know."

"That's pretty obvious." Jessica finished her bacon, watching him.

When it sank in that avoiding the question wasn't an

option, Langston said, "It's hard to explain."

"Try."

He emptied his plate as he thought of a response, then put his fork and knife in the center and leaned back. "Why do you need to know?"

Jessica's hair fell over her face as she lowered her head, chuckling. She stopped, and tucked a few strands behind her ears, her deep blue eyes looking through him.

"I don't," she said. "You're right, we all have secrets, and I met you yesterday. The thing is, I like you more than most men I meet. I don't mind competition, and I don't really care what I'm up against, because whoever she is, I'm pretty sure she can't hold a candle to me. It's just that you were talking about this woman in my bed after some pretty mind-blowing sex. Tad disrespectful, don't you think?"

Langston sighed. "I'm sorry. Look, I haven't seen her in fifteen years. And I probably never will again."

Jessica frowned. "Oh my God, really? You were that into her?"

Langston gazed at the table, studying the patterns of the wood. He was embarrassed. And then, he wasn't.

"Is that so terrible?" he said steadily, facing her.

For once, Jessica looked uncomfortable. "No."

"It doesn't mean I couldn't be that into someone else," said Langston, and his heart started beating faster, because he knew he was telling the truth. He hadn't decided, yet, if Jessica was that someone—he found her arrogance both a turn off and a turn on. But the realization gave him hope.

Jessica had recovered her cool. "You mean the kind of being into someone that makes a guy think about you all the time, and want you to bear his children?" she said disdainfully.

"Maybe."

"Ah." She took a last sip of coffee, then cleared the table, placing the dishes in the sink. "Sounds kind of boring."

He shrugged. "Should I lose your number?"

Their eyes met. She smiled slowly, and so did he.

"Not yet."

CHAPTER SEVENTY-FIVE

Six months after her concert in Bermuda, Cecile was very surprised to check her voicemail and hear Langston. She hadn't spoken to him in a long time, and at least two months had gone by since she'd emailed him a joke too funny to resist forwarding to everyone on her contact list.

"Hi, Cecile. I was wondering how you were doing, so I thought I'd call you, but you're not there. Sorry I missed you. I'll call back later. Hope you and the kids are doing well."

She replayed it, in spite of herself. His was still the most soothing human voice she had ever heard.

He probably won't call back, she decided, almost indifferent. The wall that defended her from the potential wounds involved in caring too much about his interest or lack thereof was well-fortified.

When he did call, Cecile was about to go to sleep.

"Hey, I caught you at home."

"I was just getting in bed."

"I'm sorry. Is it too late?"

"No, it's okay." She stifled a yawn.

"How are you?"

"Pleasantly surprised."

"At least you said pleasantly."

"Of course. How's the restaurant?"

"Really good. Did I tell you we got three stars?"

When would that have happened? she thought. We rarely

communicate.

"Wow," said Cecile, impressed. "That's amazing."

She wished, for the first time in a long time, that he had cooked for her. Once would have been enough, so that she could have a frame of reference, a memory of his skills.

"It's pretty cool," Langston said.

"It's more than that, Langston."

His understatement struck her as irritatingly dishonest. Then again, he'd always been self-deprecating. She decided her new-found vigilance against putting herself down was making her intolerant, and resolved to do better.

"How are the kids?" said Langston.

"They're okay. Malik was acting out for a while, but he seems to have settled down. Elana's started this passive-aggressive thing again. At least she waited until he was less of a pain first."

"Are they seeing any more of Teddy?"

"Once a week for a few hours. His young girlfriend needs him, after all."

Langston was silent for a while. "You should tell him to get involved with them now, before it's too late."

"He won't listen."

Another silence. "So…what's new?"

She always felt like she dominated their conversations, but she ended up telling him a long story anyway, all about her last performance, pulled off through the grace of God despite far too little allotted rehearsal time.

"I don't know how you do it," said Langston. "I'm in awe."

"I guess it must seem pretty amazing, but to me it's just what I do, at this point."

"But you create an experience that moves people. I don't understand how you can be so blasé."

"So do you."

"I'm a cook."

"You're a chef."

"Whatever."

"There's a difference, Langston. If God gives you a precious gift, it's rude to pretend it's worth less than it is."

"You mean like telling me playing the piano is just something you do?"

Cecile smiled. She'd always appreciated his intelligence. "Touche, Mr. Andrews."

She yawned, thought of a question, and debated asking it, until curiosity quickly overwhelmed her. "So…are you dating these days?"

"Not at the moment. Even if I was, I've given up on the idea of getting married. Maya keeps telling me there's nothing more pathetic than an aging bachelor, but you know, I don't really have time for relationships. Besides, people change all the time. How can you promise to be someone's mate when both of you are going to grow into somebody else down the road? It doesn't make sense."

Cecile settled herself under the covers. "People do it all

the time."

"Yes, but should they?"

"Some of them seem very happy, even into their old age."

"So you're not jaded yet. Good for you."

"I wouldn't say I'm not jaded. Look, I don't want anybody myself, at this point, or at least I'm not going to put any energy into looking for him. I just refuse to stop holding out the possibility that there could be somebody I could really enjoy who'd enjoy me back, and that we could be partners. Anything else strikes me as living out of fear, and I don't want my life to be defined by fear anymore, if I can help it. I've given my kids enough crappy examples already."

There was a long silence. "Interesting," Langston finally responded.

Cecile yawned again. She wondered if Langston had changed over time. She suspected he probably hadn't, not since he'd lost his youthful sense of humor, or if he had, the change was incidental.

He's stuck. Listening to his voice had been lovely, but she realized she couldn't stand to have a deep conversation with him. Apparently her defenses weren't quite as fortified as she'd thought.

"Hey, Langston," she said, "I'm kind of fading here."

"Sorry to call so late."

"No, I'm glad you did. Let's do this again, okay?"

"Okay. Sweet dreams."

"You too."

She realized that she knew very little about him, after all this time. She knew his occupation, but not how he felt about most things—with all of her focus on God, she had no idea if he was even a Christian or not. Then again, she might not have found out even if she'd asked. He dispensed personal information in tiny drips, these days, and she wasn't willing to expend the energy it would take to get him to trust her enough to open up more. She still liked him, but she was grown, middle-aged, actually. More than old enough to understand that liking someone wasn't enough all by itself. Better to accept that he would probably never leave the "friendly acquaintance" file, and that, as expected when she met him, she would never see him again.

Then a question hit her, like a thunderbolt. Why had she even thought of filing Langston somewhere in the first place? Or Teddy? Or anyone? How different might her life have been if she'd just let her relationships be, without trying so hard to categorize them? If she'd looked at men, all men, as merely people, to be held closer or more distant, letting the future unfold without trying to predict or force it? What might have happened if she'd simply stopped making love to Teddy early on—since she hadn't found a way to reconcile premarital sex with the things her parents had told her since childhood—and watched their relationship either deepen or wither? Instead, she had become fixated on an end game that shouldn't have happened in the first place. And created two children, who were now forever involved in her folly.

She wouldn't make the same mistake again. So Langston

could come and go, freely, and she would live freely, and stop struggling to fit together the pieces of her life that she didn't yet understand, or couldn't control.

She felt a deep sense of peace, and offered up a prayer of thanks. Let go, and let God. Maybe this was what it meant. And maybe, if she spent less time trying to analyze everything to death, she would have a moment to truly listen, so that God wouldn't have to squeeze in His guidance edgewise.

She would write these thoughts in her journal later, and one day, she thought, unable to stop herself from pondering the future just yet, she would look back at this time and see not the pain, but the growth. Or even better, one day she'd be done with looking back, choosing to look forward instead. Or simply around at where she was at the moment.

Maybe she would still be alone then. Or maybe there would be a few men she'd see for dinner and a movie. Perhaps one or two would kiss her goodbye until the next time, a few weeks or a month later. She'd hopefully be able to afford to travel, visiting family and friends, also by herself, but she would be greeted at her destination with outstretched arms and warm smiles. And she'd continue to make beautiful music with her friends, like the concert with Chelsea and Nelson two weeks ago, and the one coming up with James in six months.

She wasn't sure she'd seek out Langston anytime soon. Maybe she'd contact him after she performed with James, just to see how he was doing. With no ulterior motive, no agenda, just a desire to check up on someone she had always liked.

For now, she would hug her kids, call her parents and her sister, and have lunch with friends. Go to a concert occasionally, not caring that she had no constant male companion, content in the experiences nevertheless, doing her best to avoid being too exacting or too afraid to be open to every worthwhile possibility that came along.

She smiled. Because while she knew her life was far from most people's ideal, she knew a lot about the woman who would share it—herself. And she was very good company.

Coda

April, 2007

CHAPTER SEVENTY-SIX

"She died instantly," Marcus said.

"So she wasn't in pain. That's good."

Langston sat behind his desk at Cimarron, holding the phone in one hand and his forehead in the other. Mercifully, it was half past three in the afternoon, between lunch and dinner, so he could afford to spend some time in shock.

"Bernie wants to schedule the service for next Saturday."

"That's really soon, Marcus."

"You know Zora. She's had her funeral planned for years."

"I hope everyone in Jamaica and Edmonton can make it on such short notice."

Langston gazed at the picture on his desk of Zora and Bernie with their very grown-up kids. The shot was taken in Paris, in front of the Arc de Triomphe. The kids were 19 and 16, and Zora was 42. And now, at 48, she was dead. His sister, who never drank or smoked, who exercised all the time and prayed every day and did everything right. Dead.

What the fuck.

"Did she know she had an aneurysm?" Langston asked. The question was pointless. She was dead.

"Bernie doesn't think so. Are you okay?"

Langston chuckled. He was only asked this question, it seemed, when somebody in his immediate family expired.

"My big sister just died. Are you okay, Marcus?"

"No."

"Why would I be?"

"I'm just asking…"

"…a fucking lame-ass question. Am I okay. No, I'm not fucking okay."

"Don't shoot the messenger, Langston. What the hell is wrong with you?"

He wanted to put his fist through a wall, do something dramatic to release all of the energy that was building, but all he could think of, the only thing that wouldn't cause the kind of disturbance he couldn't afford to create, being owner of the restaurant and all, was to curse.

"Zora is dead. That's what's wrong." As he said the words, his eyes filled with tears.

"When did you see her last?" It was an accusation.

"So I hurt your feelings," Langston responded. "Sorry, Marcus, for not being together. Then again, Zora was the most together person I know, and look what it got her."

"A spot in heaven."

Langston blew air forcibly out of his mouth. "Maybe she can say hi to Grandma, and wave at Mom and Dad. I mean, if she can see down that far."

"That was unnecessary."

"Not for me. Listen, I've got to go. Thanks for telling me. I'm guessing you already told Maya?"

He'd read about a tribe in South America that would release the tension whenever a loved one died by killing a anger. Langston understood, and knew he needed to phone before he took anything else out on Marcus.

Yeah," his brother replied. "She's a mess. She's going to e at Zora's."

"You guys gonna be up late?"

"Yeah."

"I'll call you."

"Okay…or…."

"What?" Langston's tone was unintentionally obnoxious. "I'm sorry, Marcus," he added. "I'm not handling this well."

"Why don't you come over too? Andre can manage things. If you were sick, you'd let him do it."

No, if I were sick, I would need to be right here, he thought. For me, not the customers. Maybe Lois was right. Maybe I am a workaholic.

Langston leaned his elbow on the desk, still cradling one side of his face with his hand, and closed his eyes.

"Langston? Are you still there?"

"Yep."

"So are you coming?"

"Yep."

"Great. I'll see you soon."

"Bye."

The urge to cry had subsided, along with the urge to kill someone. He wanted to run, though. He wished he had the right shoes. Maybe he'd stop at home before he went to Zora's house. And once he was there, he'd sit with his two siblings and his brother-in-law...and do what?

He hoped there would be hugs. And tears, and laughter, and stories—the West Indian version of the Irish wakes he'd seen in movies.

Zora was dead. It couldn't real, but it was. Marcus had just said it. His sister was dead.

When his father had died, Langston barely felt it. A twinge, a day spent wondering how his life might have been different with a real dad, and then a few days of anger, which subsided without anything that felt like sorrow. Maybe it had been the timing—just before Christmas, and there was a lot to do, and besides, who was that guy anyway? But Zora...without her, who would hold the family together?

His family wasn't close. They didn't share their secrets. Or rather, they didn't share their secrets with him. His family *was* close. He wasn't close to them, but they were close to each other.

Because...because I don't share my secrets, he realized.

And then, a random thought. He remembered Darling's, many years ago in late June, and a beautiful woman sharing her secrets even though she barely knew him. The scene was still vivid.

He hadn't talked to Cecile in months. Then again, they were different now. The last time they'd spoken, she'd yawned a lot and sounded distant.

Then he remembered something else. In that conversation, he'd told her one of his secrets: that he had no faith in long-term relationships, because people change unpredictably, and what was the point of signing up for the ride if you don't know where you're going?

He thought of Bernie and Zora. He knew how devastated his brother-in-law must have been. He knew Zora would have handled it better than Bernie, but she would be torn up, too. After all those years together, they still loved each other.

As he stood, he wondered how they'd done it. It was something he'd taken for granted—just Zora and Bernie being righteous, as always. But was Zora self-righteous, or just righteous with herself? Did she tell him what he should be doing because she needed to mold him, or because she knew something he didn't, with her more than eight-year head start in life? Did she look down on him, or love him so much she couldn't bear to withhold her wisdom?

"I still don't want you to die alone," Zora had told him a few months ago, unable to resist despite her twelve-step training and Langston's reaction the first time she'd said it. It was her final attempt to move him forward, offered as a reaction to the series of very casual relationships that had followed his breaking up with Lois.

"When you're dead, you're dead," he'd answered. "You can't take anyone with you—at least, you shouldn't, should you? Isn't that murder?"

She shook her head at his smart aleck response. "I worry about you, Langston."

"Falling in love is hard, at least for me."

"You make it hard."

"That's what Glenda says. What does it mean?"

"You're too defensive. And you think too much."

"You're probably right. Hey, I've still got Lois's number. Maybe I should call her up."

Zora kissed her teeth. "You know she's married to some rich guy by now."

"My loss, huh."

Zora smiled and dropped the subject. He could still see her smiling at him, even though he'd acted like a stubborn jackass.

I'm too defensive, he said to himself, and I think too much. But what else is there? Can I be different? What would have happened with Jessica if she hadn't been so determined not to get too attached? Or was that part of her appeal? Then again, I was open to her. Isn't that all that's required? Not a happily ever after, just being open to other people, and willing to see where things go, even if it ends, even if the end hurts a bit? But if I'd been that open to Jessica, wouldn't I have had trouble ending the relationship? Or was knowing it wasn't going to last the reason I was available to her?

He opened the door, and walked into the kitchen.

"Andre," he said, and the sous-chef turned. "My big sister died. She had a brain aneurysm. Think you can handle things? I mean, I know you can...."

The tears were supposed to be gone, but he was in danger again. Nina came over and gave him a hug. She had never done anything vaguely similar before. Probably didn't feel she could.

"I'm so sorry, Langston," she said.

"Thanks. Listen, I'm going over to my brother's house. If you need me—"

"I won't need you," Andre said. "Go."

"I'll see you tomorrow."

"Let me know if you change your mind."

"Okay." Langston turned and walked out of the kitchen, through the dining room, and out the door. He climbed into his car and started the engine, chuckling when Sam Cooke's soulful voice filled the air.

"Change is gonna come, huh?" He put the car into reverse, gazing out the back window. As he pulled out of the parking lot, he knew it was true. Change was gonna come. Because he couldn't keep running forever. But how was he supposed to change?

He thought of Zora and Bernie again. He didn't know how they'd managed to find each other, or rather, keep finding each other. He wished he could ask Zora now. Could he ask Bernie? Maybe the question would bring back happy memories, and not add to his grief.

I should take a chance, Langston decided. I certainly can't ask anyone else.

Stopping at a light, he thought about his other siblings' marriages, neither of which inspired him. Marcus and Danita were hanging on, just barely—"going through a rough patch," as Marcus put it. They had always been very different, but the differences were no longer fascinating, just hard to understand.

The marriage counseling they'd just begun would help, hopefully. Maya and Ed had always fought a lot, but as loudly as they sometimes complained about each other, they were also very affectionate. Still, Langston couldn't imagine being in a relationship so fraught with struggle.

He'd always admired Bernie and Zora, while feeling that their union was something he could never achieve, because nobody would ever love him that much, or at least, nobody he loved back.

As he made his way through downtown Toronto, he found himself thinking about Cecile. He was reliving their conversations when the question came to him: "What are you afraid of?"

He had never allowed himself to answer, and even though Zora's death disturbed his equilibrium enough that he was willing to try, he couldn't think of a specific response. Love? Too vast. Yet, just admitting to himself that maybe Glenda and everyone else had been right for years felt like a revelation.

Zora's familiar home in Islington, the upscale suburb where she'd lived until this morning, was nearby. He didn't want to be focused on himself when he got there. It was unreasonable to attempt to resolve the deepest riddle of his existence in one car trip, but doing so felt urgent. He didn't want to go back into his cage, but he wasn't sure how to live outside it.

Then another question came to him: "What would I do if I weren't so afraid?"

He knew the answer instantly and was so surprised that he

laughed. Turning into Zora's street, he decided to call Cecile and tell her he wanted to see her. That he would come to her, or if she preferred, he would buy her a ticket to Toronto. He felt terrified, and it might be too late, but he had to follow through. Because he was finally more afraid of not taking the chance than of anything that could happen if he took it.

CHAPTER SEVENTY-SEVEN

June 22, 2007

I'm trying not to overthink this, but it's really hard. I don't want to feel too excited. I want to relax and be myself. Then again, why shouldn't I be excited?

Maybe scared is better. I mean, when was the last time I spent the weekend with a man? Even if he's not staying at my house, we're going to spend the weekend together. Wow, I can't believe I wrote that. Actually, I can't believe I'm taking the time to write anything, because he lands in about an hour, and I need to get my ass to the airport. I have to get all of this out of my head somehow, though.

I should just take a deep breath. There. After all, there's no agenda. Right? I'm not putting him in a category. Right? We're just two old friends who haven't seen each other in 16 years, getting together to have fun. Right?

Right. Okay, Langston, I'm ready.

Ready for your lips, that is. Bring it!

Oh wait—that's an agenda. Or is it putting him in a category? I'm thinking too much. Still Cecile, after all these years. And I'm completely okay with that. Glory, glory Hallelujah!!

So I'll just say, this is going to be a playful, joy-filled experience. And leave it at that.

:)

ACKNOWLEDGEMENTS

First, I'd like to thank you, dear reader! If you enjoyed my book, I would be eternally grateful for an online review, no matter how brief. If you'd like to know when my next book is coming out, or more about me in general, here's my information:

Website: www.mariacorley.com

Twitter: @MariaCorley

www.facebook.com/mariathompsoncorleywriter/

This book has gestated (mutated?) for long enough that leaving out someone who helped with its conception and birth is almost inevitable. That said, here goes.

Next, I'd like to thank people I've never met whose books gave me important information about the business of running a restaurant: Marcus Samuelsson and Veronica Chambers (*Yes, Chef: A Memoir*), Scott Haas (*Back of the House: The Secret Life of a Restaurant*), Michael Gibney (*Sous Chef*), Roger Fields, CPA (*Restaurant Success by the Numbers: A Money-Guy's Guide to Opening the Next New Hot Spot*), and the contributors to *Chef's Story: 27 Chefs Talk About What Got Them into the Kitchen*, edited by Dorothy Hamilton and Patric Kuh.

On to the people who know I exist. Thanks to Sheryl Roche, who instantly and cheerfully agreed to proofread my rather long manuscript. I am also grateful to Adrian Joseph for his insights into life in rural Quebec, and John J. Muller for helping me to remember some details about Juilliard. I greatly appreciate the valuable suggestions I received from Dionne Irving, Moruna Shepherd and Doug Hales, readers of my first few drafts, and for assistance, slightly later on, from Janet Benton, whose continued interest in my project is an act of great generosity.

Readers of subsequent versions, partial and full, include Priscilla Oppenheimer, Kevin Wood, Louise Caiola, Cheryl Crider (whose gift for research resulted in various wonderful suggestions, and whose gift for titles saved this book from my two choices, one dull and the other incomprehensible), Meg Zapata, Colleen Rowan Kosinski, Linda Robinson Brendle, Kathi Kilgour, Cara Sue Achterberg, Heather Davis, Barbara Kyle, Wyn Cooper, Sheila Trask, Jennylind James, and Aaron Breymer. Your time, encouragement, and critiques are greatly appreciated.

Lennox Randon, a fellow author, morphed from a twitter acquaintance to a full-blown friend. Thank you for taking time away from your bucket list to help me, and for always being willing to give me whatever answers I needed. Catherine Ripley, also an author, was my toughest critic, and the reason the book is so radically different from the way it began. I know I am a much better writer because of your candor. Juan Jackson called me Fridays at 8 a.m. from Denmark to discuss his impressions, asking gentle questions about things I needed to address. I will always cherish those conversations.

Thanks also to Kirstin Myers, Kate Umble, Haley Simons, Gary Davis, Chris Gees and Syreeta McCoy for their help in bringing attention to my book. Personal recommendations reflect on the person giving them, and your willingness to do so will never be forgotten.

The superstar in the support firmament has to be Caroline Garland, who has read my book so many times, I'm sure we've both lost count. Your assistance in this long journey went way beyond any imaginable call of duty implied by friendship. Thank you!

I feel lucky to have my sisters, Patricia, marketing genius, and Alicia, willing ear, in my corner. Between them, they read excerpts, commented on other aspects of trying to get into print, and, most importantly, told me not to give up. I feel the same sense of good fortune when I think about my children, Kiana and Malcolm, whose mere existence deepens me, and whose unconditional love inspires me to take risks.

My mom, Eva Thompson, was there from before the beginning—it was her idea that led me to write LETTING GO in the first place. She read my book more than once (even though she doesn't like the curse words), and has done everything she can to help my manuscript get off my computer and out into the world. Although I can't begin to approach her level of faith and positive thinking, I know I would have given up long ago without her model of belief and determination. My dad, Lloyd Thompson, had nothing but praise for my writing, and while criticism can be helpful, it was nice to know that my father, who read compulsively, enjoyed my work. I will always miss you, Dad. I don't take parental encouragement for granted, and feel particularly blessed to have been assigned to Lloyd and Eva Thompson.

Above all, I thank God for whatever talent I may have, and for surrounding me with people who support my attempts at self-expression. There are those who, through no fault of their own, are denied the education and assistance that would allow them to share their stories with the world. That this novel exists somewhere other than my imagination makes me one of the lucky ones.

Made in the USA
Middletown, DE
07 November 2016